MW01492136

Kate Stewart xc

the
BOOKWORM
box

Helping the community, one book at a time

METHOD

KATE STEWART

Method
Copyright © 2019 by Kate Stewart

All rights reserved. Without limiting the rights under copyright reserved above, no part of this publication may be reproduced, stored in or introduced into retrieval system, or transmitted, in any form, or by any means (electronic, mechanical, photocopying, recording, or otherwise) without the prior written permission of both the copyright owner and the above publisher of this book.

This is a work of fiction. Names, characters, places, brands, media, and incidents are either the products of the author's imagination or are used fictitiously. The author acknowledges the trademarked status and trademark owners of various products referenced in this work of fiction, which have been used without permission. The publication/use of these trademarks is not authorized, associated with, or sponsored by the trademark owners.

1st Line Editor: Donna Cooksley Sanderson
2nd Line Editor: Christine Estevez
Cover by Amy Queau of Qdesign
Formatting by Champagne Book Design

DEDICATION

For any creative who lives for their passion and bleeds some for their vision. And for those who endure it with them, this one is for you.

Method acting—a range of training and rehearsal techniques that seek to encourage sincere and emotionally expressive performances, as formulated by a number of different theater practitioners.

When taken to extremes, this type of acting can sometimes wreak havoc on health and personal relationships.

ACT I

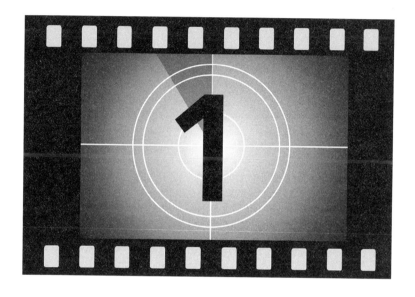

"All the world's a stage…"—William Shakespeare

PROLOGUE

MILA

ROLLING MY FOREHEAD ON THE DOOR, I TAKE DEEP BREATHS TO both calm and anchor myself.

"Mila, please." His tone is guttural, and I feel every ounce of reciprocal pain. We are thin hearts trying to break through thick walls. I peek through the hole and can't see him but hear the unmistakable clank of a bottle hitting the porch below. "Open the door, baby," his plea is a mournful whimper. "You promised."

I answer him with silence, a silence he deserves. The silence he punished me with when *I* didn't deserve it. Though his suffering is ripping me apart, I've been aching for him for months, desperate to break through the barricade he carefully constructed, the bricks he laid, that I allowed him to lay, between us. Those walls, they're still there. He's no longer my husband, he is the aftermath. What's left of the man on my porch is the evidence of a job well done and the cause of our demise.

"YOU FUCKING PROMISED ME," he rages, slapping the door with his palm, and I jump back stifling a yelp.

"You're my Dame. Or have you forgotten...have you forgotten?" His last word cracks as we collectively fall apart on opposite sides of our old universe.

Choking on tears, I shake my head, fighting the battle to remain idle. The cure to his ache isn't an open door, it's the closing of another. I can't make him see it, and he's too caught up in the charade to see it for himself.

I hear the faint unscrewing of the cap. "This makes you a liar, you know," he spouts sarcastically. "It makes you a fucking liar," he snaps. "You were the only one...the only one left that I trusted."

He smacks the door again. "Mila... Open. This. Fucking. Door!"

"Go home," I finally answer, my voice filled with lingering weakness. "Just go. You aren't wanted here."

"Not without you."

Gathering my resolve, I manage to steady my voice. "You need to leave. *Now*."

Glass shatters as he releases a string of curses. I hear shuffling and his weight falls against the door before he pounds against it. "You can't do this! You can't fucking do this, Mila! I won't let you do this! You're my wife," he cries out hoarsely, "and you love me."

Unable to take another second, I race through the cottage and lock myself in the bathroom. Cell phone in hand, I weigh the consequences of calling the police. I can't do it to him, no matter how angry I am. I shoot off a quick text and wait, sitting with my back to the door, rocking in indecision while humming softly, my arms wrapped around me. He doesn't let up, he doesn't stop, he just keeps pounding on the door—on my heart, on the ghost of us. Agonizing minutes later, I hear the crunch of tires on the gravel, doors open then close, and muffled words are spoken before a scuffle ensues.

"Get the fuck away from me! She's my wife!" The voices grow louder, but his is the only one I hear, and the hurt in it is enough to end me. "Goddammit Mila, don't do this! You promised me!"

Rocking back and forth, I do my best to self soothe as sobs pour out of me, tears fall endlessly, and my heart finally erupts. "I'm so sorry. I'm so sorry. I'm so sorry," I whisper as his cries pierce the air.

"MILA!"

FOUR MONTHS AGO

Casey and Bonnie Morning Radio Show

Casey: Oh, my God, Bon, not Blake West.

Bonnie: I can't believe it. I just can't believe it.

Casey: The world has lost one of our brightest stars today. Blake West was reported to have been found dead early this morning at his home in Venice Beach.

Bonnie: No, Casey, no! He was our boy!

Casey: Neighbors say music was blaring from his condo, and when police arrived due to the complaint, the door was unlocked. Speculation is that the cause of death was suicide.

Bonnie: Horrible. So horrible. I loved Blake. Why would he do that?

Casey: Blake has been in and out of headlines in the last few years. Between his divorce last year to former co-star Amanda George and his last two films tanking, he's had a rough go of it.

Bonnie: I knew things were tough for him, but damn, Casey, this is our man. I can't believe he's gone.

Casey: Me too, Bon. I'm at a loss, Hollywood. More details to come.

CHAPTER 1

LUCAS

Eulogies are bullshit. One should never be able to sum up a person's life with a few sentences. I make a mental note to tell my wife I don't want a single word uttered at my funeral. The people who mourn for me shouldn't be reminded of who I was or what I meant to them—they shouldn't have to be. Maybe that's cynical, but this whole funeral has been a shitshow since we arrived at the church this morning. It just goes to show how fucked up our world is. Lately, no one seems to know anything about anyone. A slew of recent scandals has rocked these hills into something unrecognizable. Mock shock and outrage have made everyone a hypocrite. The unearthing of these evil deeds has escalated into a landslide and perception is more skewed than ever. In Hollywood, transparency is an illusion. In our current world, pride is becoming scarce. Even with the notion that everyone is striving to be better, to perfect their craft, to be a part of something synonymous with legendary, it's only for the sake of the game.

Blake lost his ability to hide the minute he was found hanging in his office.

It strikes me that those gathering today are probably thinking much of the same and Blake isn't the only thing they're mourning. Cursing the sick parade, I'm barely able to keep my feet planted as rehearsed words are spoken at his graveside.

"...he was a believer in the good of humanity." Sentiments ring hollow around the large circle of people wearing their

Sunday best, designer sunglasses pressed firmly on their fixed noses to shield rolling eyes. It's an idiotic and mocking statement in comparison to the way Blake made his exit. It's far too apparent Blake didn't believe in *anything* when he left. He had no fear of an easy departure, of the Christian God who swears his last sin is unforgivable. Hollywood was his God, and before he took the step off his desk, Blake, like the rest of us, knew our God had forsaken us all. We've memorized the gospel much like those that surround us, and we've learned every verse. We've prayed to the shrines and offered up our souls. Blake concluded there was no point, no way but out, while the rest of us scrambled for some semblance of normal.

"This is a fucking circus," I grumble under my breath. Mila squeezes my palm in her hand in reply, pulling herself closer to me. Searching the crowd, I find Blake's ex-wife, Amanda, her head lowered as she tries to remain unseen amongst the elite. Like the rest of us, she doesn't want to be here, doesn't want to acknowledge what Blake's done. I gather this from her posture alone. I stood by Blake's side at their wedding six years ago as he wholly pledged himself to her. He'd believed in her. I'd never seen him so happy, and I never will again.

"Let's go," Mila whispers, tugging at my hand and ushering me through the crowd. My wife knows I can't listen to another word. In no way should his estranged mother have been the one to make the arrangements. I hadn't gotten my shit together in time to protest as much. It would be another on my list of regrets when it came to Blake. Though deep down, I knew. I've always known at some point I would lose him early. He was too volatile, too emotional, he needed too much validation, and he never grew out of it. He was far too weak against his pain. I hate that I think of him that way, but it's the truth. His exit strategy is a good slap in the face for all of us in the land of make-believe.

Mila's heels click on the sidewalk next to neon grass as she guides me toward our waiting car. I'm choking on a thousand words I want to scream back at those still huddled around the hole, the new home of my best friend, but I keep those words within and give Blake the last one.

CHAPTER 2

MILA

MY HUSBAND IS BRUISING IN HIS OWN SKIN, AND I CAN'T TAKE IT. He'll blame himself, he'll blame his best friend, and maybe he'll blame me a little too because our life was so far removed from Blake's before he took his own. And maybe Lucas's relationship with me is one of the reasons. I was always wary of Blake, of his personality. I was always fearful of the consequences of their entanglement as friends, and I'd spoken up on more than one occasion about my concerns. Studying Lucas, I realize that doesn't matter at the moment. He's still in shock. I want his pain because I'm not sure he knows how to sort through it. But I'm not sure what I feel either. This is my first funeral, I've never lost anyone close to me before Blake. I loved him for a lot of reasons. For who he was, and because he was the closest person to Lucas. I loved him for being for my husband what I couldn't be at certain times, for knowing when I was in over my head and getting Lucas out of his own. I'm pissed at Blake for sticking him in that place now, without his guidance, without his help. The limousine door is open and waiting, and I slide inside. Lucas shrugs off his suit jacket before climbing in next to me.

"Home, please," I instruct our driver, Paul, before I put the partition up. There's a party, a celebration of life we're all expected to attend, but I'm far too aware we're both teetering on the brink. Of what? I'm unsure. No one will suffer Blake's absence the way my husband will. Lucas just lost a soulmate. It's a tough pill to swallow, but it's the truth. And I'm a believer in having more than one kind of soulmate. I'm the lucky woman who gets to devour my husband's beauty, his brilliance, his depth. He chose me and even after five years of marriage his choice is still a bit surreal. Our courtship is a poor man's fairy tale and a little cliché but it's still my favorite. I was the nobody one of Hollywood's most eligible bachelors chose. The scrutiny cost me a little sanity, but he was worth it. At times, I'm still an ant beneath a magnifying glass. Except now, I know how to deflect.

But with this, today, I'm in unchartered territory.

For the last three days, I've been by his side, shoulders back and ready for whatever Lucas needs, but so far, he's been ominously quiet, a thousand miles away while remaining close. The morning after we got the call, I woke to an empty bed and found Lucas dressed on our porch, sitting eerily silent. He was searching himself for answers, answers only Blake could provide, answers he may never get, and I don't assume anything I have to say will heal him. He needs to hurt, he needs to experience the loss. I haven't always been confident in us, especially in the beginning. That took time. We reached a healthy stride years ago, and ever since, I haven't thought much about our ability to weather any shitstorm. For the first time since we got together, I'm at a loss, unsure if he can see me at all. Even when he's the most involved with his career, his roles, the silence has never lasted this long. The palpable ache emitting from him at first stifles some of my courage before I summon my nerve, pulling up the confines of my skirt around my thighs to straddle him.

He allows it as he stares out the window and I lean in and let him feel the weight of my body. His fingers absently stroke the bare skin on the top of my thighs as I work the silky material of his tie from around his neck and undo a few buttons of his shirt.

I need our connection. I am his life and he is mine, and that's the only way we've ever worked.

"I love you," I whisper, before pressing a soft kiss to the hollow of his throat. He's a wall of muscle, hurt, and frustration as I will my way back into his space, praying for any sign of life on his part.

"Baby," I croak out, frustrated for being unable to keep it together. Flailing, I clear my throat and press my lips to his chest once, twice, and then slide my fingers through his thick hair, my thumb running along his jaw back and forth as I admire him. His eyes, the color of a new leaf, are trained on the morbid sanctuary of Forest Lawn Cemetery. I can handle his silence, but his pain is like a gnawing heartbeat too loud to ignore. Each minute that passes in that white noise terrifies me. Briefly, I want relief for him, for us both. I slink down in front of him, spreading his legs and kneeling while I unfasten his slacks. Pulling out his ready cock, the throbbing muscle twitches in my palm right before I wrap my lips around it. I work my mouth, rolling my tongue back and forth over his flesh loving the feel of him, alive in this one act, allowing me to soak him in. Looking up, I see he's rapt on me, on my task. When we finally connect, his eyes glisten before a lone tear rolls down his cheek. Each pull of my lips, each stroke of my hand, every moan around his thick length is my assurance that I'll be whoever he wants me to be, whatever he needs. He takes a single finger and traces my stretched lips, spurring me on as I lick and suck, my desperation bouncing between us.

"I love you," he whispers as a tear spills from my own eye and he catches it with his finger before sucking it into his mouth. It's here on my knees, while he comes on my tongue that I know we're going to be okay. Not after when he pulls me into his lap and cradles me, not when he's kissing me so long and hard that I detect a small semblance of us again. It wasn't when he took me home and wordlessly fucked me all night. It was then, while I was at my most vulnerable, when he let me see him at his, that I knew we could make it through this.

CHAPTER 3

MILA

THE SLICE OF A TURNING PAGE ROUSES ME FROM SLEEP. I CAN sense his weight next to me and open my eyes to see him sitting up against the headboard, with a script in hand. He's nearly finished, and that lets me know how hard I've slept.

Noticing me stir, he palms my shoulder before trailing his fingers down my arm. I lay there basking in his touch as I study his stubbled jaw, one of the things that drives me craziest about him. But there are countless others. Soaking him in next to me, my fingers itch to run through dark locks so thick they give way in the direction of the slightest touch. His size is intimidating and the quiet strength he exudes beneath his muscular build is awe-inspiring. From his faded emerald eyes to the slant of his regal nose and generous full lips, it's clear his creator expected nothing less than worship for the gift bestowed.

The first time I fell in love with Lucas, I was sixteen years old sharing a box of Junior Mints with my mother. I, along with half the women in America, sat in a theater seat mesmerized while he outshined a majority of his co-stars. I can't say he was my first celebrity crush, but he hit me the hardest. Growing up in LA, I'd seen and met my fair share of celebrities, so I can't say I was starstruck, more awestruck by the way he delivered. Even my mother was impressed, and she's a tough sell. But we were both right in feeling wowed because that role thrust him into the spotlight, one so bright he's one of the reigning kings of Hollywood. I give myself a few seconds to admire him before I move to get out of bed. He stops me by pulling me back toward him. Resting my head on his chest, I begin to read some of the lines.

INT:
Richard pulls up in an old Camino where Sisco waits outside an abandoned warehouse.

> RICHARD
> (Rounds the car, flicking a cigarette at Sisco's chest and pulls his gun pointing it at Sisco)
> Where's the fucking money?

> SISCO
> (pats his pockets and shrugs with a smug smile)
> I don't seem to have it here.

> RICHARD
> (Leans in suspiciously and presses the gun to Sisco's temple)
> This is about her again? Fuck, Sisco, you were never going to see this through, were you? Leave it to you to make your one grand stand about pussy.

> SISCO
> (Presses his head against the gun to urge Richard to shoot)
> You can have the fucking girl, but you'll never see a dime of the money. Do it.

                    RICHARD
You have got to be shitting me. She came
onto me, man.

                     SISCO
Don't bother. It's all over.

                    RICHARD
It's not my fault your bride couldn't keep
her fucking hands to herself.

Two gunshots sound. Sisco falls to the ground.

                    RICHARD
          (looks   at   the   shooter   who   stands
          behind Sisco's lifeless body)
What the fuck did you do?

I'm unimpressed as I read on for a few more pages already
knowing Lucas is going to pass.

"What do you think?" he says, looking down to me.

"You know it's crap. I can't believe you entertained it this
long."

He gives me his first genuine smile in days and tosses the
script to the floor. "You shouldn't be so quick to judge. It has
decent bones. Somebody worked their ass off on that script."

He flips me so I'm pinned beneath him.

"I know you're looking to switch things up," I say breathlessly as he pulls one of my nipples into his mouth. "But *that's*
not the one."

"Find me a script then, Mrs. Walker," he orders, before
sinking between my thighs and pressing his cock an inch inside
me.

"I'm so sore," I plead as he eyes me, weighing my protest. I never deny him, I never want to, even when we're fighting.

Lucas dips his head, warm breath hits before eager lips trail over my skin. I grip his firm ass and drag him inside of me letting out a whimper. He stills, pulling back to peer down at me.

"I missed you," I say because that's all I can voice. It's the worst possible time to ask him how he's feeling. I know he's avoiding it, but I don't know how much longer I'll let him. I'm not the type to skirt around anything important and he knows that about me. He rears back and presses in hard, rolling his hips and lighting me up. My body pimples with gooseflesh and I hook my ankles around his back.

"No matter how many times I fuck you," he grits out, building his pace, "I need more."

Moaning in response, I meet his thrusts knowing full well I'll be in pain for the next few days. He's got the cock to match his smirk, but it's never been a problem for us. Before I met Lucas, I'd always been a fan of men who knew what they wanted, and because of that, I'm definitely a fan of my husband. Tracing his etched chest with my fingernails, I stare up at him as he gazes down at me with lust-filled eyes. It's always the particular way he looks at me that gets me, like he's constantly conveying possession. It's as if I'm the thing he's wanted most in the world and he's found it. My answering stare relays the same greed. I'm just short of being obsessed with my own husband.

He works me thoroughly, biting the shell of my ear as I come around him. Convulsing with pleasure I loosen my grip, my thighs falling open, and he dives, thrusting like a madman, skin on skin the only sound in the room. Lucas doesn't stop until he's covered in effort, his skin glistening when he pulls out and covers my stomach with his release, fisting himself until sated. I watch enthralled while his body draws tight and then relaxes before he falls to my side on his stomach.

Tracing lazy circles on his shoulder, I lean over and press a kiss to his bicep.

"Talk to me. Tell me."

He's already shaking his head buried in a pillow. "Tell you what? It hurts? That I'm pissed off? That I'm trying not to think about it right now?"

Leaning over, I nod into his shoulder.

"It hurts. I'm pissed off. I'm trying not to think about it right now."

"I don't want to fight."

"Good," he replies, still catching his breath, "then let's not fight."

He moves to get up, and I pin him down with my bare sex on his back straddling his waist.

"No."

"This is oddly arousing," he jokes, while I remain tight-lipped.

He exhales a weary breath. "Dame, don't. I just can't put words to it yet."

Seconds tick past before I concede. "Okay," I say moving off him to stand next to the bed.

Still on his stomach, he tosses a confused look over his shoulder and reads my posture.

"Don't treat me differently," he warns.

I guffaw while crossing my arms. "You want me to push you about something you don't want to talk about?"

"No, I don't want you to walk around on eggshells, you've been doing it since we got the call."

"So now you're going to tell me how to handle you?" I ask incredulously. "You must *want* to fight."

"You have cum running down your stomach," he says, nodding toward my body. "I can't take you seriously."

My nostrils flare a little at the demeaning remark, and his lips upturn when he sees my aggravation. He pushes to his knees and steps off the bed.

"Yep, you do, you want to fight. So, let's fight," I say, following him into the bathroom. He sighs when he realizes he's not getting out of the conversation, so I start. "He left because he was in pain."

"He *killed himself* because he was a narcissistic asshole."

"No, that's you being an asshole. You calling him a narcissistic asshole makes *you* selfish."

"He was selfish."

"It was a selfish decision," I argue as he twists the nozzle to start our shower.

Lucas gives me a look of warning I ignore.

"Babe, I'm no authority on Blake but—"

"You're right, you're not," he snaps, his cold stare chilling me as he pulls me into the shower and the heads spray out in all directions soaking us in seconds. His eyes roam my body, and it shudders in appreciation despite the rising tension. His next words stun me. "I should have come inside you, it's time for a baby."

"That's a mutual decision, one you can't make on impulse because your friend dies."

"Fuck," he slaps the tile next to my head. His eyes fix on the drain between us, and all I see etched all over his beautiful face is pain.

"I love you, but you can't disappear on me. That's not how we work."

"I know."

"You started it this way," I remind him.

"I know, baby, I know," he replies, already a world away.

"You're putting distance between us now," I point out.

Accusation dances in his eyes as they snap to mine. "Maybe because I want to think the way I want to, not the way you think I should."

Swallowing, I take a step back. "That's why you went quiet on me?"

Guilt mars his features, but his words slice. "Some of it. I don't need you to police me on what to think or how to feel."

Armoring up, I try to reason with my anger. "I don't—" I stop myself mid-sentence because he's right. I'm twisting his feelings into some sort of quest to make him see what happened was Blake's choice. It's all wrong. Still, I'm cut. His words hurt.

"I'm sorry," I offer with a sigh. "You're right. Say what you want to say."

He shakes his head. "I don't need any more guilt right now."

"Tough shit, you don't get to take that back," I reply with a little bite as I pour soap on a soft loofah and begin to scrub myself. I have no doubt this shower is going to be cut short by one of our tempers, so I do what I can to stop it.

"Be honest with me, or we've got nothing." He stares down at me wordless, and I can see so much of what he's not saying. He blames himself, and I've cornered him into discussing something he's not ready to talk about. I have to give him the space to sort it out, but I'm not letting it go.

"Maybe we shouldn't fight," I murmur. "I don't know how to help."

His low whisper twists the knife. "You can't help. Blake's dead."

It's final. That's the hardest part for him, maybe for us both. There's no solution, only finality.

"My dad told me, 'It takes fifteen years to be an overnight success,' and it took me seventeen and a half years."
—Adrien Brody

CHAPTER 4

LUCAS

"I CAN'T DO THIS SHIT ANYMORE," BLAKE SAYS, HAULING IN A BUS tray full of dirty glasses. "I'm done

"It could be worse," I say, wiping the sweat off my chest with a bar towel, "we could be passing out flyers in a chicken suit."

He frowns. "Who did that?"

"Brad Pitt." I pull bottles for yet another specialty cocktail. "I read it in an autobiography, I think."

He glances around the club full of drugged up and flamboyantly dressed men. "That sounds more appealing at the moment. I'll take the fucking chicken suit."

"The tips are better here, and you know it," I say, lining up martini glasses.

He tosses the soiled dishes into the waiting soap-sink beneath the counter and raises a sarcastic brow in my direction. "Tell you what, why don't you deliver Enrique's 'special' order next time." The regulars have a hard-on for Blake. He's the light to my dark with curly blond hair cropped close to his head and deceptive doe eyes.

I shrug with a grin. "Hey, it's the price you pay for real estate, pretty boy. We have to be close for auditions. You can't afford to quit." We've already been kicked out of two apartments in the last six months, always short on rent due to skipping work for last-minute auditions. It was how we met. I'd come home blitzed one night and decided to sleep it off outside my sealed front door brandished with an eviction notice. Blake had woken me when he came in from his own party and offered me his couch to crash on. Before that night, we'd been friendly in passing, but the next morning we'd gotten to know each other better through a nasty hangover. He even helped sweet-talk the landlord into letting me get my shit out of my apartment which now consisted of a duffle bag ready to move on a moment's notice. We had little in common aside from acting aspirations, but even in his state, he was steps ahead of me.

Blake was a child star for fifteen minutes. He's been typecast and unable to get many acting gigs since. I had yet to get my first real break, only scoring a few commercials with no lines in the last year. We were at the age where we were just young enough to land heart-throb teen or troubled son roles, but those were often passed out to those with a better portfolio. Our looks only gave us so much of an edge. And our headshots were shit. We'd let one of our regulars rip us off for a couple hundred dollars each only to get back underdeveloped photos on sandpaper to pass out to casting directors. Neither of us could afford to do better. We were both living hand-to-mouth and most of the time counted on the hospitality of the girls we bedded to get our next meal. We were literally fucking for food at this point, but just assholes enough to not let commitment deter our singular focus. I'd practically been a virgin when I got to Los Angeles and had spent the last couple of months making up for lost time.

In an act of desperation, Blake and I applied for and got hired to bartend at a dive aptly called Queens just off the strip even though we had no experience and were just on the other side of eighteen. Not that we had to fill out anything other than our jeans to get the job. The nights were long, but the work was easy and the tips we got in exchange for a shirtless few hours of objectification were worth it. Blake was uncomfortable with the attention, as hetero as they come, while I played nicer due to higher tolerance.

Blake glares openly as a few guys saunter up to the bar with up-turned lips. Anyone with gaydar could see Blake was straight as an arrow, but it seems to be the new pastime of the patrons to flirt with the *unavailable bartender. Blake is tested daily when our boss's boyfriend, Enrique, orders his cocktails up to VIP with a special request that he be the one to deliver them. Blake is fire though, in mind-set and temperament, and I know it's only a matter of time before he costs us the job.*

It's a little sad how formulaic we are in our circumstances. I'm the 'runaway fresh off the bus' to join the Hollywood circus, and Blake is already considered 'washed up' due to his role as a little brother in a sitcom, Buzzed, that ran one season. I had read far too many autobiographies to know that nothing happens overnight. Not even the overnight successes. Blake has very few connections since his falling out with his agent mother who took every dime of his momentary childhood wealth. He didn't even have to get emancipation to free himself. When Blake turned into nothing more than a temporary cash-cow, his mother left him to his own devices. In his words, he thinks she's still unaware he left her a year ago to hole up with his then-girlfriend. Blake's still pissed off about it and determined to prove her wrong. At least that's what he tells me when he's drunk enough to shed some story.

For me, the grass is always going to be greener when you grow up in a trailer in Shitville, West Virginia, where my parents will die fucking, fighting, and festering in the filthy life they've made. As far as our relationship is concerned, I have no plans to ever visit for the holidays. I don't play the victim. Their ignorance is incurable. As much as they lacked in work ethic, I make up for. I refuse the life I was born into. It won't be mine. So if I have to cash in on the looks I was given and serve a few guys who are vying for a peek at my cock to pay the bills, so be it. My tolerance stems from survival instinct. I've been taking care of myself my whole life. Blake fled from a far more opulent lifestyle. I sometimes think he regrets leaving home though he would never admit it. His hate for his mother stems deep.

As if he's reading my thoughts, he twists his lips up and nods. "We're going to land something, man."

"Damn right we are. We just have to get the dues part over with. This job is a joke, it isn't reality. Just a test. Don't take it so seriously."

"Right," he says, nodding repeatedly. "But it gets better." I can't tell if it's a question or a statement, so I stay mute. The fact that he has a taste of the business but needs so much reassurance should scare me, but I've been in far worse situations than prancing around half naked for tips.

My only consolation for my shitty childhood circumstances was that a few trailers over, an old starlet by the name of Maddie—Madelyn Rosera Darling—used to babysit for my mother and taught me the art of cinema through the retelling of her heyday as an A-lister. Maddie is the one who set my future in motion. I didn't know it then, but I'm appreciative now. She was the reason for my obsession. The one who planted the seed the first time she sat me down on her ancient sofa surrounded by a stack of reels and showed me her first movie.

"It gets better," Blake repeated more for himself than to me as I loaded Enrique's cocktail on his tray.

It only truly got better for one of us, for me.

I just didn't realize the same path we traveled together, we got to from different directions. I was too busy burning takes while he was fighting the demons he created to keep up. I should have known. I should have seen him fading, but I was blazing too bright. I, like everyone else who mattered to Blake, left him behind in a trail of stardust.

Staring out at the turbulent ocean, I row in my machine for the second time that day. I've been overdoing it since Blake's funeral. Speculation is front and center on every news station as to "why." They've dug deep, highlighting his worst behavior, his patterns with the women in his life with a heavy concentration on ancient addictions. When we were younger, his favorite drug was whatever brought a good time or numbed him from defeat, but my fear is that there won't be a trace of anything in his system once the autopsy report comes out. And with that, there will be no way to justify he wasn't thinking clearly. Everything in my chest constricts at the conviction he was sober. And the idea that he was agonizingly present in his final minutes makes it that much harder. I could be asking the typical questions, but I know the answers.

Why didn't he reach out to me?

Because I was unreachable.

Why didn't I know he was depressed?

Because I didn't ask.

The ugly truth is, we'd been on a different playing field for the last couple of years. Blake claimed he was doing no-budget independent films to help his creative flow—which is the standard excuse when no one wants to hire you—while I made blockbusters and cashed in. He was no longer invited to the parties, a self-made social pariah. More often than not, when Blake walked into the room, people fled from his conversation often wary and afraid of his temperament or what socializing with him could imply. People were cleaning their noses up, while Blake kept his full of debris. He'd been in the headlines more and more in the last few years for his behavior—possession of marijuana over the legal amount, public intoxication, and petty theft—which had to be bullshit.

The media hadn't been very creative, it was almost as if the press was gunning for him, like someone was keeping tabs for any minor slip-up and then calling him out on every misstep to keep him in check. But I didn't have to worry about distancing myself. I've been busy, so busy I left him to fend for himself.

Covered in sweat, I revel in the burn of my biceps and calves as I wade to nowhere, while memories of hidden hill houses and foggy nights behind the gates trap me with more questions. I'm not such an open book anymore because I don't fully know my own story, not the parts that include missing chapters with Blake. I have my suspicions that he was a rag doll for the business, maybe more of a puppet than the rest of us. And I wasn't there to protect him. He was the one who needed it, who always needed it.

My cell rings as a welcome distraction, and I tap my headphones to answer.

"Lucas," my agent, Shannon, coos over the line. "I've got something. Wes wants you for this part, and I think it's what you've been waiting for."

"Wes?" Wes Nolan is one of the most respected directors in the business but is heavily into big-budget trilogies.

"I'm done with franchise for the moment. I've made that clear."

"This is a departure for him, Lucas, and for you. *Silver Ghost.*"

I stop my movements. "Nikki Rayo's story?"

"That's the one," she pipes enthusiastically.

Rumors have been circulating that Wes was going to write a script. He must have been keeping it under wraps because no one has been talking about it as of late.

"Who picked it up?"

"Paramount. The offer is your standard *with* incentive. I'll courier the script over."

"Sounds good, thanks, Shannon."

"You doing okay?"

"I'm living." Which is more than I can say for Blake.

"Look, I know this isn't the right time, but I've gotten in touch with Leann just as a precaution." Leann Shear is my publicist who is hell-bent on making sure Blake's "incident" doesn't harm my career. Having an entanglement with a Hollywood has-been who just committed suicide is apparently bad press. I couldn't give a shit. Anyone who knows me knows my brand and also knows that Blake West was my best friend. It's not news. People can speculate all they want about his demons. My reasons for being silent about what he did aren't because I'm some asshole who can't admit we were close, it's because I have no fucking idea what to say.

"No comment, that's our stance. I mean it. No matter what surfaces. I'll make the call on this."

"Lucas—"

"Shannon," I bark, "this isn't negotiable."

She pauses over the line. "Understood. Look, I hate to pressure you at a time like this, but Wes is anxious to get started."

"How long?"

"As soon as they find the lead. Everyone else has been cast."

"Who's signed on?"

I hear the clutter of paperwork in front of her. "Looks like he went with a few up-and-coming for younger parts, Adriana Long as the wife and Matt Roth signed up too."

I'm impressed. Both have grabbed gold in the last few ceremonies.

"Send the contract so I can take a look."

I hear the click of her keyboard. "Done. Wes wants to set up a meeting for the day after tomorrow."

My cynical brain wins. "Who dropped out?"

Her silence confirms it.

"Shannon, if they're already pre-production, who the hell do you think you're fooling?"

I'm not pissed at being second choice, I'm pissed at the way my agent thinks I'm still too fucking naïve to figure it out. Years ago, I wouldn't have blamed her. It's a different story now.

"Shannon? Who dropped out?"

"Will Hart. Schedule issues or something."

"I've told you a thousand times this shit makes you look shady," I snap.

"Sorry, Lucas, I just…you know how it is."

I shake my head in frustration though she can't see it. "I don't need my ego stroked, I need honesty. You think you're capable of that? I don't want to have this conversation again."

"Jesus, Lucas," Mila whispers from behind me. I don't know how long she's been there, but her tone tells me it's been long enough.

Shannon's silence confirms she's just as shocked by my bite. "Sorry, Lucas, it won't happen again."

"Make sure it doesn't, or I'll find someone else to take a percentage to fucking translate." I end the call and continue rowing. I can't bring myself to look at my wife. I'm pissed, and I just want to stay that way. Somewhere between answering my phone five days ago and this moment, my confidence has been shaken in a way I can't grasp, and I don't want her to see.

"You're not ready," Mila whispers behind me.

"I'm not going to just sit in the house and wait for the egg to crack."

"Then let's go somewhere," she pleads. "Anywhere."

"I want to work."

She circles me to stand in my line of vision. Every time I see this woman, the epiphany strikes much like the first time I saw her. For me, she is the very look and definition of love. There's nothing I should be afraid to tell her, she's fully aware of my insecurities because she worked hard to unveil them and embrace them. I knew she was the one mere hours after I laid eyes on her.

My anger is overshadowing all of these facts as I gaze up at her astoundingly beautiful form. From her polished toes, her lithe frame, to bee-stung lips and almond-shaped gray eyes, she's unbelievable. My anger doesn't change my desire for her. I know I'm hurting her with my silence. We've never felt this far apart when I wasn't on the job. Not for a single day in the last five years we've been married, and I can't bring myself to try and fix it. I stop my rowing, exhausted as she kneels next to me, her chalk-white sundress flaring around her knees. She looks over at me through rain-cloud-colored eyes and thick black lashes, her lips still a bit swollen from all the unearned punishment I've been doling out. Most would consider our relationship a bit co-dependent, and they would be exactly fucking right. We don't do much of anything without the other. We don't need space to be individuals, because we're the better version of ourselves when we're together, at least I am. But when I got that call, something I didn't know was thinning in me snapped, and I can't figure out where it came from or how to tie it back together. I'm exhausted on a level I'm unfamiliar with, and I just want to get past it.

"Tell me what you need," she says, running fingers through my sweat-soaked hair. "You're pushing too hard."

"So are you," I let out gruffly, while contradictorily sinking into her touch.

She ignores my snark. "You're restless."

I pull her to me, dousing her clean cotton dress with the filthy aftermath of my workout.

Her eyes widen when she detects the evidence of my growing erection. I've been fucking her every few hours for the last couple of days. Maybe it's a way of coping, but it's also invigorating. Every time I'm inside my wife, I feel better, stronger, and worshipped, even if it's short-lived. I am loved by her in a way no other woman could ever master. Mila is the answer, my answer. I'm lucky. Blake never found his. But this problem she can't solve. This sin she can't absolve me of. I'm guilty in a way I can't be redeemed, and there's no coming back. There's no way to make it up to him.

I get to be happy. I get the career, I get to live. And the man I loved as a brother will never meet my future son or daughter because his instincts failed him. Life had disappointed him to the point he severed ties with it.

"What are you thinking?" she asks, looking down at me with a soft gaze.

"Baby. I want one."

She shakes her head allowing me to soil her before pulling me closer. "We can talk about this in a few months."

I kiss the skin of her throat as she wraps her long legs around me.

"You aren't well, my love."

"I'm fine. Stop it. He'll still be dead in a few months."

"Maybe so, but I want you to remember all of it."

I jerk my head back and look up at her. "What?"

She pauses, eyeing me cautiously. "Thanksgiving, last year. How did we spend it?"

I wrack my brain but can't come up with anything.

"I don't remember."

"Exactly." She pulls away and stands to linger above me.

"We weren't home?" Confused, I look up at her for an answer.

She slowly shakes her head. "You were working on *Erosion*."

"Oh," I say. *"Yeah."*

"Yeah, you couldn't repeat a word I said that whole damned two months you were shooting. This is a prime example of why I want to wait. You don't even remember where we were. You barely came home at Christmas."

"That I remember." South of France. It was a good one. Immersion isn't necessarily a bad thing; in fact, it's what's propelled me into the kind of actor I want to be, but my memory gets foggy in the weeks and months that I spend behaving as someone else. I find I have a selective sort of memory in those days. I'm not exactly somewhere else, but I'm most definitely *not* present. Mila's never been a fan of my routine, but she understands, I made sure of it. She supports me and is the best imaginable partner, even though she sometimes feels neglected while I shoot. It's easy to forget where you were and where you've been when you travel nine months out of the year.

Though we aren't separated while I film, I often have to isolate to get into character, and 'coming home' is Mila's way of letting me know when I was and wasn't in a brain fog.

"What's this script?" she asks, a trickle of accent kicking in. I love it when her mother's French tongue thickens her voice. It's one of the sexiest things about her.

"It's a movie about Nikki Rayo."

Her eyes widen. "The mafia guy?"

"Yeah. They're already in pre-production. It's going to move quick."

"You just wrapped."

"Mila," I say on a sigh. "That was a month ago. And I know I freed up a few months for us, but I can't pass on this, baby. It's a golden ticket." I've been waiting for years for an opportunity like this. I'd played the spy, the rock star, the superhero. I'd done some variation of it all. I'd just wrapped on a romantic comedy that left a bad taste in my mouth. I needed something to get my hunger back.

It was getting too humdrum, too comfortable and I hated it. Mila was right, I was restless, and this part could be just the one I needed to hit reset. The death of an actor's passion has everything to do with getting comfortable. It's one of the first things Maddie taught me. I was no longer testing my capabilities, and that was dangerous.

The look of disappointment on my wife's face exhausts me as I wipe off with a towel. I'm sure my expression matches hers for the fact she won't even entertain the idea of a baby, which we both agreed we wanted before we got married. We're in the perfect position to start. Where I go, my family can go as well. I'm trying to understand her holdup, but it's grating on me. I never planned on marrying, not really against it and never really thought much about kids. My end goal was always to be a working actor, but once I met Mila, and I started getting steady jobs, my dreams changed for the better. They got bigger because of her. Never did I think myself capable, but I have more to give. And I want to share it with a piece of the both of us. She thinks it's grief talking and maybe that's a part of it, but not all of it, and I can't seem to convince her otherwise due to the timing.

She matches my stare, the perfect picture of innocence. "Why are you looking at me like that?"

My arguing tongue gets silenced by the heavy chime of our doorbell, and I get to my feet. "That's the courier with the script."

I'm already halfway toward the stairs when she stops me. "Lucas …"

Hanging my head, I take a breath and glance back at her. "I don't like this."

"I need *something*. I can't just sit around here."

"This isn't it," she pleads with me.

The bell rings again, and I avert my gaze and take the steps to the front door.

CHAPTER 5

MILA

DREAD FILLS ME AS LUCAS PRACTICALLY LEAPS THE STAIRS FOR the front door. Something about the timing of this script has my nerves fraying. Something about Lucas's desperation, and the needs I'm unable to meet, instill a sort of fear. I'm beyond sore, my sex constantly pulsing with the ache of being overfilled and the unbearable emptiness of wanting more. He's fucking me constantly, but we aren't connecting the way I'm used to, and I'm questioning what it could mean because his silence has returned. Maybe he thinks I need the closeness for reassurance, or perhaps he does.

Everything is off, and it's to be expected, but the unease has me reeling. Blake is gone. Lucas is searching, and I'm unsure of what direction to step in. I'm not really a doting wife. Not in the sense that I wait on my husband's emotions hand and foot. He's self-made and doesn't need constant reassurance. But we're a team. Things seemed to fall into place for us when we met, and we've always gotten what we needed from the other. Now I'm unsure if he would ask for it if he knew. I'm terrified what he's looking for is in a place I can't reach him, but it's the place he wants to be. I'm not a superstitious or religious woman, but I find myself praying a little as the front door opens and closes while I pour him a glass of carrot juice. He stalks back into the kitchen where I wait and tosses the script on the counter. Eyeing the bound front of it, I read the title *"Silver Ghost."*

"That's a cool name."

"Yeah, it is. It's the name of the 1920 Rolls Royce that his body was discovered in, which is ironic because it was his first big purchase when he started making real money. Rayo reigned in the seventies and eighties but was obsessed with his predecessors."

My curiosity is piqued. "So, you're familiar with Rayo?"

"He's fascinating as a character." He takes the juice from me across our large kitchen island before taking a healthy sip. "I heard it from someone on the set of *Erosion* that Wes was working on a script and refused to show it to anyone."

I'm restless where I stand because I know if the script is decent, Lucas has already made his decision.

"Can I read it?"

He eyes me over the glass as sweat trickles down his forehead. His V-neck is drenched and clings to every pronounced indentation of his chest.

He shakes his head. "After me, okay?"

I nod and move to leave when I hear him sigh.

"Will you send her something?" he asks, before swallowing down the last of his juice and washing out his glass.

"To Shannon?"

He pauses at the sink, nodding. It's only fitting he would feel like shit after talking to her like that. Lucas rarely ever talks down to his team. It's his own rule.

When I don't respond, he flashes me bloodshot eyes.

It's just a glimpse of him, but it offers some relief. "Of course, I know what she likes."

"Thanks, baby," he murmurs.

I leave the kitchen as he turns the first page.

"You are not marrying a goddamned movie star." My mother's words echo as I sit on our deck overlooking the ocean with wine in hand. *"I raised you to make smart decisions, Mila, and this is not a smart decision. Marriage is hard enough without an inflated male ego playing a part in it. I promise you, actors are the weakest kind of men. They need way too much to be happy. They don't know how to be satisfied."*

The day Lucas and I got married she was the only one crying in the front row because she *wasn't* happy which I found hysterical. I still catch myself giggling when I recall how she was unable to control her snot-nosed protest when we exchanged rings. As a jaded ex-member of the Hollywood Foreign Press, my mother has never thought much of actors. When I was younger, she'd idolized old Hollywood but was very careful to keep me away from anything pertaining to it. I still remember her look of relief when I declared my major, and it had nothing to do with the movies. Still, every time she sees Lucas and me together, I see a sort of gleam in her eyes, a type of longing, as if I'm living out some fantasy for her. Though you would never know it with the way she shares a passion for my father. Their relationship was wild to witness growing up. They were openly affectionate. Most of my friends thought my parents were hippies. The truth was my father was a misplaced—as in a liberal state—right-wing conservative due to my mother's overt involvement in the industry. He bent for her, compromising the most and often, which is the way they worked. Often times, they would openly kiss and heavy pet in front of God and everyone, and I envied that. I secretly loved the way my father lost his sensibilities when he was with her. I wanted it for myself. And I declared it so when Lucas and I got together. I never shied away from our connection in public which took some getting used to on his part. He didn't want me to be a target. Now, there are probably thousands of pictures on the web of us exchanging affection. I've never paid much attention to the media where we as a couple are concerned. I'm a firm believer people interpret what's convenient for them and their mood.

Hours have passed since I left Lucas to his script. I've spent several of those hours trying to lose myself in a novel I can't get into on our wooden deck, just a stone's throw away from the surf. When he's home, we end our days on our sundeck sharing a glass of wine. It's a ritual to keep us connected. As I sit in wait, I feel like I'm expecting a verdict of sorts when his voice rouses me from my thoughts. "What you up to, Dame?"

I pour a second glass of wine and set it on the mosaic-tiled table next to his chair. "You know, the same old philanthropy. Supporting local wineries."

He chuckles, taking the offered wine. "Good?"

"Yeah, but you won't like it."

"I love wine." We share a smile as he takes a sip and I watch his reaction, which is typical. We drink in the setting sun peeking through a small patch of cotton clouds in silence, admiring the day's end.

I take another sip, letting the grapes ferment on my tongue before I swallow it down and break the silence. "It's good, isn't it?"

We both know I'm not asking about the wine.

"It's fucking incredible," he says, taking his seat in the chair next to mine. "I'm almost certain he's shooting in sequence."

Wes is one of a few Hollywood directors that shoots the scenes in order from beginning to end. It's the perfect setup for a Method actor like my husband because it helps his evolvement. Inside, I'm screaming, but I don't let on I'm terrified of what he may evolve into. The argument will be futile anyway. He's only taken on a few roles that require this much dedication and those had been taxing on our relationship. But we'd made it through, and the results were phenomenal, earning him his first Golden Globe, which Mother made sure to be present for as a former press member.

The hypocrite.

Still, it means I'll lose him for the time it takes to prep and shoot, and he's quiet because he can't assure me of anything. I signed up for it. I decide to hold any objections until I've read the script myself, but I already know it's too late.

"So, I can read it?" I say, standing, all too eager to see what we're up against.

"Not yet," he says, pulling me to sit between his legs on the comfortable deck chair. I lie back with my head resting on his collarbone. We sink into each other, relaxing as the tide pulls sand away from the shore. To our right, the Santa Monica pier bursts to life in violet and blue in contrast with the darkening sky.

"Tell me," I whisper.

"This is the one. It's what I've been waiting for and feels original. I mean it's a bit cliché in the rags to riches aspect, but you know I can identify with that and use it. But there's a lot I can't. You'll see when you read."

I nod. "How bad was he?"

His momentary silence speaks volumes. "Pretty fucking bad. Unpredictable, volatile, he had an insatiable taste for blood and vengeance. He was a closet heroin addict and a womanizer."

Sarcasm coats my voice. "Sounds awesome, honey."

We share a laugh as my chest sinks. Lucas takes the glass from my hand and sets it on the table before wrapping soothing arms around me. "It's the role of a lifetime," he murmurs as his hands cover me in a gentle caress. "The *Scarface* of the twenty-first century. I've got to go all in. And with the timeframe and the amount of prep I have to do, it's going to be grueling. I'll have to isolate a lot, and I don't want you to take it personally."

"Are you sure you want to do this?" I ask, knowing the answer.

"If the meeting with Wes goes like I think it will, it's going to go fast."

"Okay." He tenses behind me, and I know he heard my hesitation.

"Please, Mila, let me have this. I need you with me. You don't pass on something like this. And I managed to fall in second place, so I have a lot to prove." He moves my hair out of the way and presses a soft kiss against my neck while dread settles in my belly. "I'll make this up to you."

I squeeze his thigh. "I know."

CHAPTER 6

MILA
Present

Lucas: You called a fucking lawyer? We have to talk, Mila. Now. Please talk to me.

Mila: I can't trust you anymore. What am I supposed to do with that? You threw six years of marriage in the trash. Hope it was worth it.

Lucas: It wasn't me who hurt you.

Mila: I don't accept that. I refuse to accept that. I hate you for saying it.

Lucas: Tell me what you want me to say. Tell me what to do.

Mila: I can't look at you. I can't trust you. I don't even know who I'm talking to anymore.

Lucas: It's me. I'm here, Dame.

Mila: I'm sorry, I don't believe you. Not anymore.

Setting my phone down, I give myself time to reason with my anger and fail. The longer I'm away from him, the more I remember, the madder I become. I'm too upset, too furious to be a reasonable adult. I'm bloodthirsty, and no good can come of that. I need space to sort through the wreckage of the past month. I called a lawyer yesterday morning out of anger, and I have no idea how Lucas got wind of it. It was just a quick phone consult and wasn't anything I was fully considering. Hurt can cause anger to make decisions, that's the one I made before battling a thousand other emotions. I can't face this yet, and I deserve the space to figure it out. But when I retrieve my phone and read his text, I panic.

Lucas: Please, baby, please don't file. I'm coming over. I'm on my way.

Mila: I won't be here.

Scrambling to the car, I manage to make it to the end of the driveway when he pulls up in his Land Rover, the large SUV blocking my escape. I lock my doors and keep my window cracked while continually shaking my head as he approaches my window. Keeping my eyes fixed on the steering wheel, unease snakes around me while he lingers at my door. It's fear that tightens in my chest, and he reads my posture easily.

"Mila, I would *never* hurt you."

"Now who's the liar?"

"Please talk to me."

"Don't do this, Lucas, I'm not ready to talk. I'm too angry."

"Just tell me what to say."

I turn accusing eyes in his direction. "Don't have a script for this? How unfortunate."

Devastation twists his features. He's wrecked, his eyes red-rimmed and beneath lay dark circles. He looks just as tormented as I feel, his jaw covered in stubble, his clothes wrinkled, hair disheveled. Even in this state, he's beautiful, hauntingly so. He lays his hands on the glass, and I jerk my chin. "I swear to God, Lucas, if you don't let me out right now, I'll be done. *We* will be done." I crumble in my seat begging for a reprieve from the hurt his proximity causes, but it's not my wedge to remove, and it's his debris I can't see through.

"This isn't healthy. Can't you see what you're doing to me!?" Gentle eyes rove over me before they helplessly flash back up to meet mine.

"Dame," he murmurs apologetically, studying my face, a face ravaged with the same hurt, and the added bonus of betrayal. Recognition crosses his features as he realizes the true extent of the damage he's done. There's no way in. Not now, not today, anyway. Taking a step back, he covers his mouth with his palm before pulling it away. "Please, please, just talk to me."

"I can't," I say, "Please, just leave me alone."

Seconds tick by and I sense his probing gaze on me as I furiously wipe at my tears. Lifting my chin, I toss a glare his way. "I hate you for what you've done to us," He flinches as if I've just struck him. "I hate you for what you did," I declare vehemently. "You can't take it back. You made a fool out of me."

His eyes water as he palms his forehead in frustration. "That's not what it was about."

"No?" I tilt my head. "Well, that's all I can see, feel, taste, and it's bitter. It's not going anywhere. You need to give me space."

"Okay, just, please…don't do anything. Don't…" He can't even say the words and we both break at the thought, our faces collectively crumbling. He hangs his head for an excruciating heartbeat, then looks over at me with remorse. "*I'll* do anything."

"You should have done anything *then*. But I wasn't important enough, even after all we've built you couldn't trust me." Wiping my nose with my sleeve, burning tears escape as I glare over at him. "I've *never* made you feel that way. I would never hurt you that way…God, Lucas…just leave."

"I'm drowning without you." His voice rips, jagged and cutting, penetrating my aching chest. But it's the anger that wins.

"No, you threw yourself in the deep end," I reply lifelessly, "and you took me with you."

A shuddered breath leaves him, but I don't acknowledge the hurt I'm causing. Resentment is navigating my every move and I'm letting it drive.

Reluctant resignation coats his tone. "Okay, okay. Just… please remember, Dame, remember."

Agonizing heartbeats later, he starts his SUV and leaves, and I do too, determined to put some space between us I know he won't allow. He's conceded for now, but it's only a matter of time before he comes back. In minutes, I'm on the highway, mind racing. He wants forgiveness, but I can't find it sorting through his actions of the past few months. He wants mercy where he gave none. It's hypocritical, and it infuriates me. We've become the sum of all my fears when going into this relationship and as much as I want to take some blame, anger keeps winning.

But this? I never saw this, I never thought him capable of hurting me to this degree. But it just goes to show what an amazing performer he is. I can't even tell truth from fiction anymore. I'm not even sure how much of our story was a lie and that's the thing that angers me most.

My husband is an expert chameleon. He slips into a newly colored skin with such ease, you're blindsided by the completion of it and are only able to admire his new color briefly before he slips into another.

The first time he showed me one of his colors was the night we met. I'd been hired to steward at a star-studded dinner at a director's house. It was a dinner & movie tribute to Francis Ford Coppola, and I'd been hired to pair his wines with the dishes served. Earlier that week I'd toured the legendary director's winery, and by the time I left Geyserville, I had a vast knowledge of his selection. There would be a screening of his film *Apocalypse Now* in a large courtyard adjacent to the dining room after a six-course dinner.

Despite my mother's best attempts to keep me away from the business, it was only a matter of time before my line of work intermixed with the industry. No average, blue-collar Joe can afford to throw these types of parties. Sommeliers weren't in high demand, and I anxiously took almost every job offered.

I spent most of the night pouring wine while telling anecdotes and history about each selection. The first time I get an up-close view of Lucas, Marlon Brando is mid-tirade on the large screen spanning a good width of the courtyard as Lucas is spitting out a mouthful of pinot noir from Coppola's Diamond collection into some shrubbery. While the majority of the party is rapt on the movie, sitting in the comfortable lounge chairs provided, Lucas is isolated in the back, leaning against a wall across from a small, free-standing bar, looking bored and mildly uncomfortable.

I have to fight laughter when I see him dispose of his wine and damn near go into hysterics when he cocks his head left and right before tossing the rest of the contents of his glass in the same direction. It takes everything I have to keep a straight face when I approach him, presenting him with a bottle of the wine he'd just tossed out like garbage. *We're covered in shadows, the flickering movie the only thing shedding light across our faces.*

"You know, pinot grapes are really hard to grow," I whisper as he eyes the wine in my hand, apprehension flitting a split-second over his features before it disappears, and he reluctantly holds his empty glass out to me. *I'd been watching him for the better part of the night. He'd played it cool as new Hollywood, often stealing the room with his presence. I'm not the only woman having an impossible time taking my eyes off him dressed in a well-fitted Armani tuxedo and silky black tie. "They have thin skin and are disease prone."*

"I'm sorry, what?" he asks distractedly as he sloshes it around in his glass before taking a whiff, his eyes finally drifting up to meet mine.

"Not a fan of the pinot?" I ask, biting back a smile. *It's when our eyes hold that the air starts to thicken.*

"I love wine," he says, fixed in our stare a beat longer before his lips lift at the corners.

"Do you?" I ask, my insides coming to life. In our locked gaze, I notice he loses himself a little as well. Explorative eyes rake me, undressing me, and robbing my throat of any moisture. Utterly dazed, I hold my breath until he speaks.

"Have you been here all night?"

My smile widens as his grows and we drink in each other in the greenery-filled courtyard. The night breeze whispers over us and goose bumps erupt over my skin while our silent stare-off ensues. I'm in a black halter dress that hugs my curves and flows over my hips. It's elegant and understated and the perfect dress for a night like this. My lips are colored merlot, just as fitting, but underneath his penetrating gaze, I feel naked and worshipped.

"Yes, I've been here all night."

"Bullshit," he counters, leaning in conspiratorially. *"I would have noticed you."*

He sloshes his wine again, and I frown. "Do you know why you're doing that?"

"Doing what?" he asks, gracing me with another breathtaking smile. I find myself stunned by the sight of it but manage to find words.

"Sloshing the wine around and murdering the bouquet?"

"I'm not sloshing."

"You're sloshing. Now," I say, taking his glass and gently demonstrating. "Swirling the glass draws oxygen into the wine to offset the tannic acids which make it taste dry." I hand the glass back to him. "Now take a sip and let it briefly rest on your tongue before swallowing."

Never taking his eyes off me, he does just that. "Delicious."

"Is it?"

He narrows his eyes. "You saw me toss it." It's not a question.

"Yes, and as a representative tonight of Mr. Coppola, I'm appalled."

"And you are?"

"Mila."

"Mila," he repeats, "Lucas."

"Nice to meet you, Lucas. I'm a fan."

He wrinkles his nose. "Are you a fan of my movies, like I'm a fan of wine?"

"No." I laugh. "I'm being honest."

"Yeah, well, now I'm embarrassed."

I lean in because I can't help myself. "You shouldn't be embarrassed about that."

"No?" he whispers as the air crackles between us, he inches forward, and we get close to indecent in what little space we have left.

"No, you should be embarrassed that you're pouring it on my shoes."

"Oh, shit, sorry," he says with a chuckle before setting the glass *down on a nearby oak barrel before looking back to me. I can't help it then, I burst out laughing.*

He shakes his head. "You know you're partly to blame, you're distracting."

"Oh? I'm to blame for the abuse?"

"Absolutely."

"You really hate wine?"

He shrugs. "Honestly? No offense to Mr. Coppola but I'm only here because I've been strong-armed into coming. So, no, I'm not a wine enthusiast." He juts his chin toward the party, sliding his hands in his pockets. "My friend is somewhere around here trying to schmooze. You want honesty? I'd rather be home drinking a Yoohoo."

This time, I crinkle my nose. "Now that's disgusting."

"Chocolate wine of the south," he says, adding a little accent for emphasis.

"Impressive."

"Only if it's ice-cold and you hold your nose," he says matter of fact.

I laugh again and am hesitant to pull away from our exchange. "Well, it was nice to meet you, Lucas, and shame on you for not noticing me."

"Yes, I admit that was really stupid," he says in a tone that has chills racing up my spine.

"Forgiven," I say with a wink, "but be nice to the wine, okay?"

"Sure thing, Mila," he whispers, with a lopsided grin.

He's still got his hands in his pockets, and I'm utterly lost as I stand there ogling him with a bottle full of wine, empty glasses calling, and a job to do. I want to freeze time and just be able to look at him, but the moment has long passed, so I turn and walk back toward the crowd perched in front of the screen. Adrenaline peaks as I spend the night recounting the way it felt to be in his presence, to be admired by him. As the night goes on, I slowly deflate when I spot him talking to others amongst the party, particularly a handsy woman who can't seem to stop touching his chest. I decide that inkling I felt was probably a product of my starry-eyed imagination. Actors are well-known for having consuming presences, it's what makes them stars.

It's only when I'm grabbing my things to leave that I see him again. I'm halfway to the front door when he emerges from one of the parlor rooms next to it. A slew of voices still carries from the courtyard, but my job is done, and I'm too exhausted to cater to any lingerers.

"Mila."

I grin at the sound of his voice behind me. "Did you finally discover wine is your friend?" Turning his way, I'm struck with the same overpowering inkling.

"No, actually, I was hoping for a private tasting," he whispers seductively.

"Ew," I say, scrunching my nose as I slide my purse over my shoulder.

"Ew?" he repeats with a frown.

"Yeah, ew. Really, Lucas?"

"Shit," he says, palming his forehead. "I didn't mean it the way it came out." I can't help but laugh. I can tell he's buzzed. He looks over at me helplessly, and I give into the pull, folding my jacket over my arm and taking a step back toward him. "Want to try again?"

"I was hoping you would teach me about wine privately."

"Better, but it lacks romance. Is this a date you're asking me on?"

"Wow." He stalks forward, pinning me in the short space between him and the door. "First," he says roughly, "you shouldn't cut a man's balls off and dangle them in front of him when he's doing his best to ask you out. It's not nice."

"Sorry, French mother, we've been oppressing men since...forever. Then again, it may not have anything to do with being French, it may just be my mother."

He grins, inching closer and everything inside draws tight. It's been a long time since I've felt this type of pull. I can't decipher if it's because he's Lucas Walker or due to how incredibly handsome he is, but I assume it's probably a mix of both.

"Did you get your manners from your mother as well?"

"Absolutely," I answer unapologetically.

His eyes narrow a fraction. "I want to take you out, yes, but I would like an education about wine."

"It would never work, Lucas." I sigh dramatically. "You clearly hate wine."

"I could learn to love it," he says with a lift to his voice.

I snort sarcastically. "And will this be your very first date?"

He scowls. "Just the tasting then, no date. Something tells me you are trouble."

"That's fine because I'm not allowed to date actors anyway. Mom's rules."

He quirks a perfect dark brow. "Aren't you old enough to avoid obeying Mom?"

"You haven't met my mother." Renewed energy races through me when he takes the hand wrapped around my purse. It's as if he couldn't wait to know what it might be like to touch me. His warm hand encases mine. We both feel it, the jolt, I can see it in his eyes. His satisfied smirk lets me know I'm unable to hide my own reaction and he weighs it, scrutinizing the part of my lips. We stand there, simply staring until he finally speaks, his voice full of surety when it cuts through the silence.

"I'll get your info from the host."

I nod. "That's fine. It's a date."

"It's not a date," he says assuredly, before brushing his thumb across my wrist and then letting go.

"Right." We linger, both reluctant to leave but unsure of what to say. The connection makes me ache in the best imaginable way.

I'm in a daydream, standing in front of one of the rising kings of Hollywood. It's a memory I'll relive over and over even if he doesn't call. Without thinking it through, I push up on my toes and kiss his cheek, inhaling his scent, enjoying the sensation of my lips against the light stubble on his jaw. "It was nice meeting you. Goodnight, Lucas."

He leans in to reciprocate, pressing his full lips to my cheek, and my senses explode. My entire body shudders in awareness when he pulls away, his long lashes flit over his cheeks as his hooded eyes rise to meet mine. "I'll bring the Yoohoo."

"Ew."

We share a laugh before he opens the door for me. Descending the grand steps, I resist the urge to look back, but I can sense his eyes on me.

An hour later, I'm still in my car when I get a notification on my phone.

Yazoo Alert: Lucas Walker and his girlfriend Laura Lee have decided to call it quits, stating the break was amicable and they remain friends.

The gravity of the alert's timing keeps me staring at the screen in shock. Surely it had nothing to do with me. Still high from our exchange, nervous laughter bursts out of me as his first text comes through.

Unknown: Are you free tomorrow?

CHAPTER 7

LUCAS
Four Months Ago

I PULL INTO THE BEVERLY HILLS HOTEL AND TOSS MY KEYS TO THE valet with a quick thanks before making my way toward Bar Nineteen. I'm early for my meeting with Wes, and I just want to have a cocktail to take the edge off before we go through the details. I take a seat in a wicker chair on the patio that overlooks a little greenery, the pool, and the parking lot. The ancient hotel is still a stomping ground for the elite, and while I've only had one other meeting here, I detect the echo of Maddie's presence every time I walk through the doors.

"Again."

"I'm tired." I know I'm whining, which Maddie says isn't a desired trait of a good actor, but we've been doing it for hours.

"Doesn't matter. Your feelings don't matter. It's the feelings of your character you need to focus on," she says, rolling her eyes. "You need more stamina. You'll be on set day and night. You want stamina, don't you?" She looks down at me with wide eyes, the mole she colors above her eyebrow smeared due to the heat in her tin trailer. I'm burning up and feel like I'm going to fall asleep.

"Do you have any more of those burritos?" I ask, hopeful as she stares down at me with the look my mom gives when she says she's had enough of my shit. Maddie's been watching me after school so Mom can work her shift at the gas station. She's been keeping me fed ever since I saw her first movie and agreed to run lines with her. I can't believe the same lady on the screen is the same woman who

babysits me. But I can tell if I look really hard.

I told Maddie I never had a grandma before, and she told me I never will. She said she had no children for a reason and that reason is because she never wants the word grandma associated with her. I don't know what that means, but she didn't think it was funny when I joked and called her my grandma. She says someone from the studio is going to call her in someday, and she wants to stay sharp and focused, and that's where I come in. She says I'm her godsend. I sure wish she would feed her godsend. My stomach has been rumbling since I got home from school and I know I'll be lucky if there's some bread ends to stuff my face with when I get back. I always eat the ends, so Mom doesn't get mad. But Maddie usually heats up a frozen burrito in the microwave before we rehearse. Today she didn't, and my stomach feels like it's eating me from the inside out. All I can think about is that burrito.

"I'm out of burritos," she barks. "Again, Lucas."

"Sure you don't have one?" I ask. I hate begging, but I'm hungry all the time. Mom feeds me breakfast sometimes, and dinner, but I can't get enough to eat lately.

Maddie smiles as if she's not mad anymore and walks over to her fridge before taking out a container of bright orange juice and setting it on the counter. She pulls a glass from the sink with faded yellow flowers painted on it and fills it up.

I wrinkle my nose at the glass as she thrusts it in my face. "What is this?"

"The essence of life, boy, carrot juice. It will keep you trim if you're going to land the lead. It keeps you young too."

I can't help but think it's not working well for her as I down the juice while trying not to throw up at the taste. She tosses a pack of peanut butter crackers on the counter and I dig in, inhaling them with a mumbled, "thank you." Maddie said I have charisma and that's something you're born with. She says stars aren't born, they're shaped, and that's what she's going to do for me. I'm going to be a big star. Sometimes I still can't believe she was in four movies before she married 'that bastard Reginald' and he ruined her life.

"Don't ever compromise your dreams for anyone or anything, Lucas. Life won't cooperate with you if you do."

"Lucas," I hear Wes call as he approaches the table. I lift the carrot juice to my mouth and take a drink knowing damn well my wandering thoughts screwed me out of my cocktail. I must have ordered while I was somewhere in the past. It's a curse and a gift how I get so easily involved in my thoughts.

"Wes," I greet, offering my hand. We shake as he takes the seat in front of me.

"This is supposed to be a real drink," I say, tilting my empty glass before nodding toward the waitress. "Is this good or do you want somewhere more private?"

He glances around the sparsely-filled bar. "This is good. How have you been?"

I shrug. "Shit week."

Wes is a hundred years old. I don't think anyone but Wikipedia knows how old he is at this point. They seem to be the only ones who pay attention, but he doesn't look a day over sixty. Directors with budgets and an extensive list of hits like Wes don't ever age out of Hollywood. It's a supreme edge. Not to mention his wife dresses him in a wardrobe that keeps him looking sharp. I like his wife better than I like him, but we have a mutual respect for each other after our last film together. Two more hits to add to his long ass reel, pun intended.

"I was sorry to hear about Blake."

I nod because words don't mean shit. Wes's certainly don't. My silence intimates the subject isn't up for discussion and it's dropped.

He orders us both a beer and turns back to me with the twelve million-dollar question. "What did you think of the script?"

I lean forward. "I fucking loved it."

He gives me a sincere smile. "You up for it?"

"Definitely. I'm good with the terms, but I'm more interested in how you want to film it."

For the next two hours, we shoot ideas back and forth, both visibly becoming more enthusiastic as the minutes pass, recognizing what he's envisioned is the same as the picture I drew while reading the script.

It only takes another few minutes of details to seal it.

The part is mine. It will be my sixteenth movie, my tenth lead, and it's going to be the most grueling role of my career.

As I walk back to the valet, I can't help but smile at the memory of my mentor and hope she'd be proud.

"I've hit my stride, Maddie." Somewhere in the back of my mind, I can hear her distant voice.

"Good job, boy."

CHAPTER 8

MILA

I FLIP BETWEEN STATIONS AS ANOTHER NEWS ANCHOR DISCLOSES more grim details of the scene at Blake's apartment the day he took his life. The autopsy report was released earlier this morning revealing Blake didn't have a trace of drugs or alcohol in his system and speculation has run rampant.

"Police say there was no note and his wedding ring was found sitting on the edge of his desk. Blake is survived by his estranged mother, Jennifer Helms, who was present at the funeral along with his ex-wife Amanda George, a former co-star who played Katrina Dobbs in the sitcom, *Buzzed*. The two former child actors rekindled their friendship at West's movie premiere seven years ago, and they were married just three months later at a small ceremony in Carmel. Lucas Walker had been in attendance with his girlfriend at the time, Laura Lee."

Though they paint Lucas and me as a glorious picture, Entertainment News is always quick to remind me that I'm not the high-profile actress that Lucas was supposed to marry. The longer the report goes on, the more I know they're reaching for reasoning.

"Lucas Walker has yet to make a statement on the death of his longtime friend."

Clicking off the TV with the remote, I find myself thankful Lucas is preoccupied. At the same time, I dread his reaction to the news. I can only imagine how Amanda must be feeling. We spent a lot of time with them when Lucas and I first got together. They'd been married for a little over a year and seemed smitten. I didn't get a chance to talk to Amanda during his funeral. Picking up my cell, I make my way to our bedroom terrace. The call goes to voice mail, and as I start to leave a message, I see her name light up on the screen returning my call and accept it.

I forgo a typical greeting. "Amanda, I'm so sorry."

"We were happy, weren't we? When we were together? We were happy?" she asks tearfully.

"Yes, you were."

"I thought so. And then he just…"

"What?" I prompt out of curiosity. When they divorced a year ago, I'd never gotten the real story from either of them, and I hadn't pressed for it. I'd tried on several occasions to reach Amanda, but she'd withdrawn, completely heartbroken. She and Blake had that in common.

"What happened?"

"He just…changed. I think he got depressed. He was so busy worrying about keeping up…" she cuts herself off.

"Keeping up with Lucas?"

"I think so. He never said it, but I know he was embarrassed about the way things turned out. Eventually, it got to the point where he had to stop making excuses. I could never say that out loud, until now."

"I'm so sorry."

"I just don't understand why he would do this. We were in the midst of working things out."

This shocks me. "You were thinking about getting back together?"

"Yes, no, I don't know, maybe," she sobs. "Things were turning around for him, I think. He was up for this part, and he was so excited. I don't understand."

Her cries echo over the phone and my eyes well up and spill over. I can physically feel her pain over the line. "I wish I knew what to say."

"Nothing to say. I'm just glad you called." She sniffs. "You know, his bitch mother was fine with arranging the funeral, but she's refusing to help with anything else. His landlord called me. Tomorrow I have to go clean out his apartment and box up his things. How am I going to do this, Mila?"

"I'll help," I offer. "I'll be there, okay? Just text me, and I'll meet you."

"Okay," she replies quickly, gratitude in her tone. "Do you think Lucas will come?" she asks hopefully. "I want to talk to him."

I bite my lip looking over my shoulder to make sure he's still not home from his meeting with Wes. "He's not in a good place right now, Amanda," I say thoughtfully. "I don't think it's a good idea. I know that seems selfish, but is it okay if I don't tell him I'm coming?"

"It's fine. I get it, I do. Blake really loved him, you know?"

"I know. Lucas felt the same."

"What happened to our guys? They were so close. We all were. What happened to us?"

I didn't know how to answer that, so I tell her the truth. "I don't know."

"This is so fucked up."

An image of Blake flashes through my head and the guilt begins to feed. "I know."

"I just want to get this over with, leave LA for a while. I need to get out of here." Her tearful voice lifts. "Okay, so I'll see you tomorrow?"

"Yes," I assure her. "I'll be there. I swear it."

"Thank you, Mila, for calling, for everything because I

know you mean it. I'm so disgusted with these assholes acting like family with their words of comfort *after* the fact. Like where the fuck were they when Blake *needed* a friend?" Realization dawns tangling my gut in knots, and it occurs to me then that we hadn't seen Blake in several months before he died, maybe longer. Lucas probably doesn't feel like he's allowed to grieve. He'll feel like a hypocrite calling himself a friend.

I can't help but think my husband might be the very person Amanda's just described and that's why he refuses to release a statement.

"Shit," I whisper.

"What?" Amanda asks anxiously. "What's wrong?"

"I'm just worried."

"About Lucas?"

"Yes, and you. Text me when you get to Blake's, and I'll head over, okay?"

"I will."

CHAPTER 9

MILA

"**B**ABY, WHERE ARE YOU?"

He doesn't know about the results of Blake's autopsy.

I can tell by his tone. He's optimistic which means he had a good meeting, which also means things are about to change for us.

I don't know why I'm so wary, but I'm sure it's largely in part to the fact that it's too soon. We'd just buried Blake. I needed to have more faith and trust his judgment.

"In the kitchen," I call out, folding egg whites into my mixture. He walks in and sees the evidence of my labor as I drink him in. A thin cream V-neck sweater outlines his muscular frame and hangs over a pair of dark jeans. His thick, black hair is swept away from his face and styled carelessly, his sunglasses perched on top. Tiny laugh lines crease around amused eyes that roam me. My hair is loosely tied up and I know I'm covered in powdered sugar. I'm a messy baker, but I've run out of carpet to pace in our expansive beach house, and I needed something to do to keep busy. The whole situation is exhausting, and I hate that I'm a slave to indecisiveness when it comes to Lucas for the time being and even more so, I hate feeling useless.

So, you bake a fucking cake, Mila?

Inwardly, I roll my eyes at my own efforts. He doesn't miss it.

"What's that look for?" he asks, dipping his finger into the dark chocolate batter before sucking it into his mouth.

"How did your meeting go?"

"Don't change the subject," he scorns. "Tell me."

I wipe my hands on a towel. "This is no occasion for cake," I say, defeated.

He circles the island and puts his chin on my shoulder. "Did you do it to make me happy?"

I nod.

"Then it's an occasion for cake."

"I'm selfish. I just want you to be okay. A cake won't help that."

"You're appreciated, Dame." He slides his arms around me and squeezes before stepping away to grab some water from the fridge. The oven sounds letting me know it's pre-heated just as I pour the batter into the waiting pan. "How did it go?"

"Good, we're on the same page. I see what he sees." He pokes his head out from behind the stainless-steel door. "Did you read it?"

I tense because I haven't. A part of me doesn't want to and thinks I'm better off not knowing. In the past, I'd been intrigued as he got into character. Slowly and subtly while he immersed himself, I began to pick up on the tics, the new habits, the character change, and was fascinated by his brilliance.

"Not yet." Pulling the oven open, I slide the cake in.

When we first got together, I had no idea what to expect daily. I assumed we'd live our lives jet-setting, and some of the time, we did. I didn't care much for it because I'd already been to most of the places on my bucket list. But our life as of late has been a lot of the opposite. Lucas said one of his biggest turn-ons about me was that I cooked and that I was a homebody. He enjoyed the routine of having a dinnertime when he wasn't filming and loved eating on our patio overlooking the ocean. And I know I'm right to assume it's because he never had that kind of family atmosphere growing up. We do attend the necessary parties—the Oscars, the Globes, and the film festivals. For the most part, we have a pretty mundane home life that I'm more comfortable with and that he seems to thrive in. Often, his work can be grueling, his schedule exasperating which at times made us threadbare. I stopped working three years after we got married only taking local odd jobs to be at his side, knowing I could resume it at any point when I got bored, and I was getting there. My sense of self could never come second to his career and I've made that clear, but I can't say I haven't enjoyed the extended vacation.

He gestures toward the bottle on the counter as I take a sip of the wine.

"It's Domaine de la Romanée-Conti Grand Cru," I say, swirling it around, "1990, and it's also an invitation. I got a call from a man who's opening a new bistro near the promenade and wants to use me for the pairing. He's a Michelin star chef. It's quite an offer."

This gets his attention.

"You're going back to work?"

I shrug. "It's local, so why not?" I worked for years to get my reputation as a sommelier. The longer I stay absent, the less credible I am.

He pauses at the counter before he takes a sip of the wine and nods. "Good."

"$16,000 a bottle, good?"

His eyes bulge and then narrow. "What asshole sends a $16,000 bottle of wine to a married woman?" He's a little jealous which I find adorable. Even as one of the highest paid actors in Hollywood, Lucas would never pay that much for anything that isn't an investment. It's one of the reasons I love him. For a millionaire, he's as cheap as they come. "I'm sure that's not what he paid for it, you don't just give a bottle like this away."

Tension fills the silence.

"When do you start?"

He studies me, his expression unreadable. "We have the read through in three weeks."

"You're kidding." He gazes at me, and I swallow *hard*. "How heavy is this?" Depending on schedule, Lucas usually has at least a month or more to prep. He reads my mind. "I won it by default. Will Hart had to drop out."

I nod. "I know, I know. Okay. I'm with you. I'll read it tonight." He gives me a smile that for the first time in a week reaches his eyes. "Thanks, baby."

Attempting to stay upbeat, I put a voice to it. "I think it will be good for both of us to be working, but I'll be here for you for whatever you need."

I'm not sure either of us believes it.

"Yeah, sure," he says with a nod. "If that's what you want."

He reads the surprise on my face and frowns. "I'm not a fucking Neanderthal, babe. It's been two years, and it's been incredible having you with me, but I thought..." He shrugs. "Doesn't matter."

This time I'm frowning. "You thought what?"

"I thought you quit working so we could have a baby."

"Wow," I say, widening my eyes. "Now *that's* caveman."

"Is it?" he says, closing in on me. "Can't exactly drink daily with a baby coming." He towers above me at six foot two to my five-five. Looking up, I see the contempt I was looking for when I announced I wanted to go back to work.

"I quit working because I missed my husband. I wanted to be able to travel with you when you were filming. You know that. What is it with having a baby lately? We never even discussed it when I quit, and that's all you've been talking about since Blake died. We'll get there. What's the rush?" The idea of a baby with Lucas is a dream, but something about his urgency to have one taints the thought. A baby is not a solution for *anything*.

"People die," he speaks so casually it's terrifying, "that's the rush. If you died, I'd have a piece of you, and vice versa."

"I can't believe you just said that." I trail him into the living room as he sips on the beer that I thought was water, that he'd retrieved from the fridge.

"Well, it's true. I don't want to be left, period, but if you do, I want that piece of you. I want to know that what we have is going to live on, at least through our kid. I don't want to be left without anything."

Stunned, I watch him. "Is that what you think? He left you without anything?"

He shakes his head with evident irritation. "This isn't about Blake."

I ball my fists. "It sure as hell is. You weren't talking this way a week ago."

"And life happened, and that's how we evolve around it. We see things as they are, and we change things…adapt."

"Adapting isn't having a baby!" I've lost my patience, and my husband has lost his mind. I pace in front of him as he calmly sits on the couch and narrows his eyes on me.

"What's your holdup? Even if you think I'm asking because of Blake, the baby isn't coming overnight, it takes time," he gestures toward me.

"So, you think there's a time limit on grief?" I laugh sarcastically. "Are you hearing yourself? Okay, well I damn sure hope you're *over* sixteen years with Blake in nine months because anything you say or do can mess our child up for life. And honestly, I'm not sure *I* want to take on that responsibility yet. I like being able to do and say what I want. Behaviors have to change or there are consequences. You know that firsthand."

His retort cuts me in two. "Why? Because I came from white trash?"

Covering my mouth, I shake my head, my breaths coming fast. "I'm sorry. I'm so sorry. That's not what I meant."

He shakes his head dismissively. "It's the truth, Mila."

"It's not. That's not who you are."

I walk toward him slowly, a plea on my lips. "Please help me," I ask. "Tell me what you need."

I'm over the guessing, the analyzing. I need words to say, actions to take. I need a way to get to him, to be able to touch him without feeling like he's going to crack, explode, or both. His silence confirms my suspicions. He doesn't know himself, and he thinks work, a baby, and avoidance is the solution. To be someone else, to escape the gnawing questions. He can't evade this, and he needs to know it.

"You aren't ready," I say finally. "You know you aren't."

"I *need* to get back to work," he declares through the heavy air between us. His abrupt tone cuts our connection as he palms the edge of the couch, fingering the brass studs on the end of it. "And apparently you do too if we're…if we're not going to try for a family." He's hurt by my refusal to entertain it. For the sake of peace, I'm inclined to give in and agree, but that would make me a hypocrite. I want us both on more stable ground before we take on the task of parenting. He's just been delivered the blow of his life. He needs time, whether he thinks so or not. Taking on another movie is just a way of prolonging it.

"He was sober," I say softly. "There were no traces of any-thing in his system."

He pauses with the beer halfway to his lips and then nods, avoiding my watchful gaze. "I know."

CHAPTER 10

LUCAS

SITTING AT THE KITCHEN TABLE AS THE SUN CREEPS UP OVER the horizon, I scroll through the latest story full of accusation. Two more women have come forward naming Blake as being present the night they were assaulted, yet no charges have been filed against him or anyone else. Reports of an investigation are underway, but so far, it's just hearsay. The story is selling in the media in a major way especially since Blake died.

One of the women talking, a former co-star of us both, states it was the night of our very first wrap party and a sick foreboding washes over me. His name is there, in black and white, but it's just a mention he attended the party. What's unclear is why they would name Blake if he's not being accused and not the other hundred or more other people that were present? The hardest part to take is that if they're using Blake to garner attention, they're tarnishing whatever reputation he has left in the process and he's not here to defend himself. Wracking my brain, I stare at the brightening sky trying to remember the details of the *Misfits* wrap party.

Blake slides a line my way as he coats his teeth with the residue from the edge of his credit card. I'm not much of a fan of coke, but it's been a grueling couple of weeks on set and tonight I've decided to partake. I need the pick-me-up to make it through the party. None of this seems real. Two years ago, we were slinging drinks at Queens and trying to believe in our collective dream, hoping for more. This was the more. And it was nothing to sneeze at. The product of our labor led to a global theater release. This flick had cult classic written all over it. Because Blake had some formal training, he'd spent some of his spare time trying to school me on techniques he'd picked up along the way, and I'd paid attention. By the time they snapped the first marker, I felt prepared. And from the feedback, it seemed like I delivered. Blake had brought his A game playing the lead vigilante to the group of delinquents, and he'd pulled it off in spades. I'd played one of his recruits. We'd auditioned for every gig, big and small, but our break came when we were spotted at the Skybar sipping overpriced drinks by a petite brunette, a casting director with a no-bullshit attitude, who was looking for two guys who fit the mold to piece together a new movie. We fit. After a few minutes of conversation, she produced her card and asked us to come in to read for her. The next day we'd made it our first phone call, and the rest was history. We gave everything we had to the movie in hopes it was the beginning of more. I was optimistic, but Blake had been burnt one too many times and had a healthy dose of hesitance in declaring anything. Though even he was having a hard time getting past the fact that it wasn't a low budget film and the director had an extensive list of hits under his belt.

Leaning down on the porcelain counter, I sniff the line and wave my hand when Blake ushers more powder my way.

"I'm good," I say, wiping the residue off the bathroom counter. We're at one of the producer's houses and I'm a bit creeped out with how at home some of these people are making themselves in a house so grand. "And this never happened."

Blake eyes me curiously. "This your first time?"

"No, I did some with you last summer on the roof, remember? But it's probably my last time. I'm good with coffee."

He gives me his signature smirk. "Not really the same type of kick, bro." Blake never has been one to miss an invite or a party, and I'm his opposing personality. Somehow, no matter how different we are, as friends we work. I'd never tell him this, but he's like the big brother I never had. He'd been there to help me through the endless rejections and has taught me how to dust myself off. He plays off my drive while I soak in his experience. "You ever fucked on coke?"

Checking my reflection, I see a ring of white on my nostrils and the sight disgusts me. I decide this is definitely my last time. "No."

He wipes the rest of the residue off the counter before checking his nose in the mirror. "Do yourself a favor and get it done."

My lips turn up. "That good, huh?"

"See for yourself," he says with a wink.

"We need to go. I don't want to get spotted."

He shakes his head as if I was the village idiot. "Relax, man. Half the people outside this door have a bag of something fun in their pocket."

"I've just earned my first paycheck with more than two zeros on the end. I'm not wasting it on shit like this."

"I get it, but this came specially from Steve, at no cost to us," he assures me. Steve owns the bathroom we're standing in along with the mansion attached to it.

"Steve bought this?"

Another chuckle from Blake lets me know just how naïve I still am when it comes to matters like these. It's like the zip code itself gives you permission to do your worst. There have been so many times he's saved my ass in the last few years. He's kept me from being totally humiliated on several occasions, especially on set. No matter how well Maddie thought she'd prepared me, I had no clue how the process went. The first day of filming, I was lost. I knew so little about the production crew and their roles. I was sure back in Maddie's day the process was a lot different, but I hadn't done my homework when it came to filming, and I had Blake to thank for the Cliff Notes.

"Listen, I get that you don't want to get your hands dirty. There's nothing wrong with that, trust me. The more professional you are, the *less likely you are to fall in the fuck-up category like me."*

I go to object, and he shakes his head. "I'm not judging, just as long as you do me the same solid. Let me play my way. And do yourself a favor," he says, running a hand through his hair, "enjoy the dark side tonight."

"No problem there," I say as the rush hits me and my pulse starts to kick at superhuman speed.

Blake gazes at us in the mirror and claps my back. "We did it, man."

The buzz helps elevate my shit-eating grin. "Yeah, we did."

He opens the door and we head out into the party. Halfway down the gold carpeted hall, Blake's name is called. I recognize the guy summoning him as one of the key grips. Blake lifts his chin up toward him and turns to me with dilated pupils. "Oh, man, this is some good shit. Enjoy your high. I'll meet you downstairs."

"You sure? I can wait."

"Yeah, have fun, I'll catch up with you later."

I nod, embracing the flow of temporary adrenaline as he saunters down the hall toward one of the bedrooms. When it opens, I can hear several people inside, mainly women, laughing. Blake has been blunt about his sex life, and I've been on the receiving end of many sleepless nights in our apartment when he brings more than one woman home, always offering to share, but it never felt natural to me. I've been making up for lost time, doing what I can to learn about the craft.

Though a little less than an hour later, I'm getting sucked off in a butler's pantry by one of my co-stars. I know it's not a good idea, but she assures me it's all in good fun. And I have to agree with Blake, sex on coke is bliss.

"Fuck," I damn near scream as she licks me from root to tip, pumping me in her hand. I'm painfully hard, and her giggle around my cock has me damn near jumping out of my skin. Shortly after she swallows two minutes of hard work, I leave with her and spend the

whole night letting my powder-induced imagination take over.

The next morning, I meet Blake at our front door. He's lost his keys and is sitting outside of it with his legs crossed and his head tilted back. He's ghastly pale, and I can tell he's coming down. "Blake," I say softly as his eyes open, and he looks up to see me standing in front of him. He looks seconds away from death. "Jesus, man, are you okay?"

"Coming down with something." He moves to get up and falls flat back on his ass, a strangled cry coming out of his throat. I move to lift him, and he shakes his head. "I got it."

"Please tell me you didn't drive."

"Locked the keys in the car back at the mansion. I'll need help with that...later." I lift him to stand by throwing one of his arms around my neck, and he doesn't try to fight me.

"Seriously man, you look like hell. Want me to take you somewhere?"

"No," he says sharply before his eyes meet mine. He's got a blown pupil.

"Does that hurt?"

"What?" he asks, confused.

"Your eye is fucked up."

"Oh, yeah, it happens when I blow too hard." His chuckle does everything but ease my worry.

"Look, if there's somewhere—"

"Don't judge," he snaps, "'lest ye be judged,' or some shit like that."

"All right, man, all right."

"Lighten up and be a fucking teenager," he says, running his knuckles over my scalp. "You've still got a few days left."

"I'll try."

Eyes glazed he grins over at me as I drag him through our living room. "I'm going to take you to TCL and then we're going to get piss drunk."

"What's TCL?"

"God, you're clueless. It's like having a kid brother," he says, hugging my neck tighter while his head wobbles as if he's lost control of his motor function. "We're going to pick out our star plots, my man, have a five-star dinner on me, and then we're going to call Gina Juice over to service your birthday needs."

"Gina Juice?"

"You won't be questioning that name the minute her lips land on your cock, bro."

"I'll pass," I say, tossing him into his bed. "All right, man, need anything?"

"I'm good." He nods repeatedly, and I decide to leave his door open to keep an eye on him. I'm halfway out when he speaks again. "I have it on good authority that good things are coming our way."

"Yeah?"

He swallows, keeping his head forward. "Yeah. Night, man."

"Morning, Blake," I say with a chuckle, slapping my palm on the frame of his door before I leave him.

I spent my twentieth birthday alone at a bar down the street from our apartment while Blake holed up in his bedroom for the next week. He claimed he had the flu. Thinking back, I didn't hear him cough or sneeze once. We hadn't bothered buying another TV since we pawned our last one, so the apartment was eerily quiet. I spent a lot of my time reading then, and I can still remember the tick of the black plastic clock above our kitchen sink. The minute he emerged from his bedroom freshly showered, he'd made good on his promise, and we dined like kings before strolling down the walk of fame and picking out a spot for our stars. I'd passed a second time on Gina Juice. That name alone had my balls shriveling. At the premieres and after parties, everything seemed fine. No one had issues. Smiles were wide. None of it made any sense.

I suppose I should be grateful I haven't been mentioned in

any of the tabloids other than the norm, but I can't even bring myself to care. Tossing my tablet on the table, I lean back in my chair wracking my brain for any hint in past conversations, any clue as to what happened as Mila walks into the kitchen to start some coffee. I have industry relationships with two of the women who've come forward and mentioned his name, and I shoot off a text to my assistant, Nova, to set up meetings with either if they'll see me. I'm resigned to figure out what in the hell Blake has to do with any of it before the press does.

Minutes of silence pass as Mila busies herself with her morning routine. It's only when she sets some juice in front of me and runs her fingers through my hair that I relax a little. Catching my gaze, she gives me a hesitant look.

"What is it?"

It's pointless to tell her the media lies because she knows they do. It's pointless to reveal that I knew he was guilty, but I wasn't sure of what. How could I have been so fucking passive? The more I think back, the more I realize just how much got swept under the rug. I was just as guilty of playing blind to his demons and only reacting to his outbursts. It was all suspect, the late-night calls that had him bounding out the door when we roomed together, the whispers in the hallways of the parties we attended. And the fighting. Blake was a ticking time bomb during those early days. *What in the hell was he doing at all those parties? And why hadn't I ever come out and asked?*

Mila slides a chair back and sits directly in front of me, in wait. She's just as eager for answers.

"I don't know what he's buried with. I don't know, Mila."

She eyes my tablet with the latest article. "You mean those women?"

"None of them have implicated him. They just keep saying he was there."

She wraps her hands around her coffee cup. "Maybe they blame him for not putting a stop to it?"

"I don't believe it."

"Amanda doesn't either and she's just as confused." Her voice has a chilled edge to it. She sees my guilt and gives me a pointed look. "You don't think he…" She widens her eyes, so I catch her meaning.

"No way, no fucking way." I shake my head. "He didn't have to take, Mila. He didn't. He was way too capable. Trust me. The truth is, I don't know. I can't tell you what I don't know, beauty. I don't have answers for them, for you, or for Amanda."

"She's falling apart. She's leaving as soon as she can."

"You talked to her?"

"Yeah, I called her," she says, darting her eyes away, "yesterday."

"Where is she going?"

"She didn't say, but she's done with LA."

I nod. "She should be. This will follow her everywhere."

Silence stretches a little while she studies me cautiously. I hate that I've put her so on edge, but I don't know how to fake this.

"Before I forget, Mom wants to have dinner soon."

"You should do that," I say, passing on the invite. I can't tolerate her mother for the moment. She's always got my balls in a vice, and I'm afraid I won't be able to play nice this round. Leaving my juice untouched, I stand. "I'll be in my office."

"Lucas, stop. Stop avoiding me." She stands and walks over to me, placing her hands on my chest, her eyes imploring. "Where are you?"

I lean down and place a kiss on her perfect lips. Perfect wife, perfect life, but I'm totally fucking lost. "I'm here, Dame."

Unable to handle the distress in her eyes, I make my way

toward my office. I barely hear her admission as I turn the corner.

"I miss you."

Even with the sting of her words, I leave her there unsatisfied. I haven't touched her in the last few days, and it's unnatural for us. I can't get my days or my head right, and I'm not about to fake normalcy. It's not a part I'm willing to play. I'm not supposed to lie to my wife. Good, bad, or ugly, that's what we vowed. Even if it hurts her, I'll do everything in my power to keep them because aside from Blake, she's the only real thing I've ever had in my world of make-believe. When I get to my office my phone lights up with a text from my assistant.

Nova: Gabriela Parker will meet with you the first of next week.

She's willing to give me answers as to why she keeps bringing Blake's name up and I'm not sure I want to know them, but I don't have much of a choice.

What the hell did you do, brother?

Set it up.

CHAPTER 11

MILA

CRADLING THE PHONE TO MY EAR, I GLANCE INTO LUCAS'S office. He's focused on his script, a large stack of books he's ordered for research sit next to him as he scans the pages. Since his meeting with Wes, he's spent most of his time in his office and thrown himself into preparations. He's consumed already, and it's just a matter of time before he flips the switch and starts to isolate more and more. I quietly pad down the hall and close our bedroom door behind me.

"Mila, so good to hear from you."

"Yanni, thank you so much for the gift. It was much too generous."

"You're most welcome. I was eager to get your attention," he says with a hopeful rise to his voice. "I'm hoping we could have lunch at my Bistro, if you are interested."

"I'm very interested, I told Lucas last night that I was wanting to take on a project closer to home."

"This is good news. I'm so very happy to hear it. How about I email you the details and we can set up a date?"

"Sounds perfect, Yanni. Thank you for thinking of me. Talk soon."

"Au revoir."

Working with a Michelin star chef to open a world-class bistro comes close to a dream for me. Whatever his reasons are for using my services, I'm grateful. Yanni is a concept chef, and instead of a traditional menu, he uses poems or haikus. It's all very deliberate and carefully crafted for an experience. For the first time in years, I feel like I'll be a part of something productive. The text from Amanda comes through just as I'm stepping into the shower and I message her back telling her I'll be there as soon as I'm dressed. Submerged under the flowing water, I dread the hours to come. I can't imagine losing Lucas twice, once to divorce, and then to death and then having to sort through the remains of the life he lived without me. Rushing my shower, I step out to see my husband waiting by the counter with the towel.

"Hey, you," I say, wringing out my hair before I take it from him. "I have to run out for a little while. I didn't want to bother you."

He pulls me to stand in front of him, his eyes roaming appreciatively down my dripping form. "You never bother me, Dame."

Warmth washes over me with the way his eyes glitter. We spent last night polite enough to each other but avoiding conversation. He read his script on the opposite end of the couch until the late hours of the night. I woke in his arms as he carried me to bed. He lay me down gently, kissing me softly before drawing the covers over me. Our eyes met and held until he pulled away. It was as if he was trying to tell me something.

He turns me now to face the mirror and slides his hands around my abdomen. He doesn't have to say a word with the longing in his eyes.

"I really need to go." It's the truth, but I avert my gaze so I can't see the disappointment in his face. It comes across in his tone instead. "Where are you going?"

I have to lie. Have to.

"I just want to pick up a few bottles and test them out before my meeting with Yanni."

That part was truthful. I hadn't kept current with the new

labels, and I had a lot of catching up to do.

"Yanni?"

"Yanni Renaut, he's the one who sent the bottle. I don't know why he wants to use me instead of trusting his palate, but I'm excited."

"It's because you're good at what you do," he says, a pensive look on his face.

"Yeah, well if my success is based on my husband's taste in wine..." We share a short-lived inside grin.

"So, why is Amanda texting you that she's on her way?"

Dammit.

I look to see my phone flash with the incoming message I didn't acknowledge when she answered me back.

Busted and ashamed, I lower my gaze. "I'm going to help her clean out Blake's apartment."

His eyes flare. "You weren't going to tell me?"

I lift my head, looking directly at him. He's so beautiful, especially when he's pissed. There's something so supremely sexy about a man when he's at his worst temperament, his standoff demeanor makes me want to get closer to the fire. It's a bad habit being attracted to him this way, but Lucas is the master of angry fucking.

Was I going to tell him? "No, I wasn't."

"Well, that's just fucking fantastic, *wife.* You know there will be cameras there. Did you really think you would be able to keep this from me?"

"I hoped I would," I admit honestly.

His jaw sets, and I can't help but take a step forward for some of that heat. He angles his head away from my touch and then steps away from me completely.

"Lucas, I didn't know how you would feel about it, and Amanda needs the help."

"Do you care how I feel about it now?" he asks, peeling off his clothes.

"Yes."

"I'm fine with it," he says with a sigh, surprising me.

"And?"

"And nothing." He shrugs. "Help her. She needs it. She needs...someone."

"Is there anything you want?" I ask. "You know...of his things?"

He slowly shakes his head.

"I'm sorry. I just didn't think you would want me to go."

"We're not supposed to lie to each other, Mila," he says absently, starting the water as if lost in thought.

"Everyone tells white lies with a good enough motive. You included, Mr. 'I love wine.'" I smile, and this time he doesn't return it.

"I guess that's true."

"I'll text you on my way home. I'll cook tonight."

He merely nods and steps into the shower.

CHAPTER 12

MILA

STUCK IN TRAFFIC ON THE PACIFIC HIGHWAY DUE TO AN accident, I shoot a quick text to Amanda letting her know I'm en route. It's only a twenty-five-minute drive from our house in Santa Monica to Blake's apartment in Venice Beach, but with the line in front of me, it will take at least twice as long.

My cell rings and I half expect it to be Lucas with an apology of sorts, though I'm not sure why I would expect one. We're in a strange place, but I'll be patient. You don't snap back from something like this and move on as if your life hasn't been altered.

Though I wasn't that close with Blake, my husband loved him like family, relied on him and his opinion despite their life choices. Blake was always a variable. We never knew what condition we would see him in. I vow to myself that I'll try harder to give him the space he's indirectly asking for, support his project, help him get out of his head, and resurrect the career I started before I became a Hollywood wife.

My phone buzzes again on the seat next to me and I see my mother's name on the screen before letting the call go to voice mail. I'm not in the mood to give her a weekly report. Her idea of conversation is an interrogation. She means well, but she's the type that offers advice whether it's asked for or not. I'd learned over the years to just humor her, let her have her say and nod in agreement. It's not the most constructive way to have a relationship, but it's better than arguing. She's eased up on her aggression as of late, and though it saddens me, I can't help to think it's because she's aging. I'm still not in the mood. I'm already on edge. It's going to take all I have in me to go into Blake's apartment and keep Amanda calm.

A car horn sounds behind me, the driver impatient for me to take the five feet of space that's become available in front of me. I'm helpless in this gridlock. Amanda is probably losing her mind, and I'm stuck in at least a half an hour more of bumper-to-bumper traffic. Lana Del Ray sings "Young and Beautiful" as I pull my hair into a knot and open the sunroof on my Range Rover to soak up some sunshine. In an act of good faith, I shoot off a text to my husband.

It's beautiful out. Wine date later?

It takes the better part of ten minutes for a text to come through.

Oscar-Winning actor Lucas Walker: Sure.

I laugh hysterically at the new handle he's put for himself on my phone.

Oscar winner, huh?

Oscar-Winning actor Lucas Walker: You know the rules. 😉

I did. Lucas was a firm believer of manifestation. His philosophy was to put his dreams and aspirations out there and speak them aloud and frequently, not only to hope but to expect the universe to answer. He said that's how he indirectly became a success. He often tells me it was decided when he was young and there was no wiggle room, it was expected, so that's how it happened. The work he did in between the dream and realization was a part of it, and he doesn't deny it was necessary. He insists it was the road between vision and completion.

I know for a fact that the handle on my phone is a joke because Lucas cares more about the work than winning an award. He'd left his Actor statue from the SAG awards at an after party the first time he won anything.

Then again, what actor genuinely doesn't care about an Oscar?

When he first told me about his theories, I was a little hesitant to buy into it. Some people just need to see to believe, and I guess I was one of them. The truth is, I've seen the manifestation of so much since we met, I've traded in my cynicism and become a believer. Lucas made me one.

———————

After a somber greeting, Amanda hugs me tightly to her before letting me into the apartment. Seconds into our embrace, I hear the familiar click of the cameras. I hadn't seen any paparazzi when I pulled up. Lucas was right, I would have been busted by morning. Stepping inside, I survey the space. I'd never been to Blake's apartment, he'd never invited us over when he moved to Venice Beach after the divorce, and the minute I walked in, I knew why. It was a far cry from the house he'd shared with Amanda in the hills. His fall had hit him harder financially than Lucas and I realized. He had upscale furnishings in between mutely stained walls. He made good use of the space but, it was obvious that his once posh life had gone awry. Lucas always said

Blake was the comeback kid and that he would land on his feet, but before he passed, it seemed no one would touch him. His reputation had already been tainted.

It's a shame because Blake was insanely handsome, extremely talented, and I always got the feeling he didn't know his worth. Staring into his office, my eyes water when I recall the last time I saw him.

Blake was ushering a grimacing Lucas into our house when I spotted them at our door.

"Oh my God, what happened?"

Blake grins at me like he just found a million-dollar bill as they brush past me toward the living room. "You married yourself a real cowboy, Mila."

"Fuck you," Lucas growls as Blake deposits him on the couch and he lands with a groan.

Blake belts out the standard western showdown whistle before bursting into laughter and turning to me. "Your husband decided to take an unusual route to infertility. Looks pretty serious," he says before snapping his fingers and pointing at me. "You know," his eyes trail down my body. "I've been divorced a hot minute. Need someone to keep the home fires burning? Or maybe I should make a deposit just in case he no longer has any swimmers."

I shake my head unamused. "Be serious, Blake, he's hurt."

Blake raises a perfectly arched brow. "Oh, I can assure you I'm quite serious. I'm your huckleberry," he drawls out before pointing a thumb over his shoulder. "And it's a good thing because I think they might be changing his script name to Engorged Nuts Ignacio."

"Dame," Lucas whispers hoarsely, ignoring Blake's rants as if he's dying. I race to his side. "I need ice."

Scrambling to the kitchen, I grab a ready pack I keep for after our workouts and start scrounging for a towel to wrap it in while Blake grabs a beer from the fridge. Lucas groans. "Shut up, you pansy!" Blake taunts from the kitchen. "Pansy, can you believe that was actually an insult back in the day that constituted fighting words? My, my, how humanity has depreciated. We've gotten so much uglier over the years."

"Come on back in here, I'll be happy to show you just what ugly is," Lucas sounds from the couch.

"Cut the shit, Blake, what happened?"

Blake grins, and when he does, I can't help but note just how good-looking he is—rugged, blond with golden brown eyes and full lips. He holds a finger up to me indicating he needs another infuriating minute while downing his beer before grabbing another. Satisfied with my growing annoyance, he exaggerates his exhale. "He got fresh with his horse."

"The hell I did! That horse had it in for me the minute he saw me. Get the hell out, West," Lucas shouts from the couch.

Blake pulls out some prescription pills from his pocket, pops the top and swallows two of them down with his beer before handing them to me. I raise a brow. "It's Oxy and this buzz is my severance for playing nurse. He gets one every four hours, and he's all yours."

"Why didn't anyone call me?"

"He was trying to tough it out," Blake says with another throaty chuckle. "That lasted all of ten minutes. You know," he says, jutting his chin toward the living room, "I've never seen him cry before. At least not unless it was on cue."

"As soon as I'm able, I'm going to feed your nuts to you, asshole!" Lucas yells from where he struggles, exasperated. "Baby! Please! Ice!"

Rushing back into the living room I see my man has his pants and underwear at his ankles, cupping his dick, his hand outstretched for ice.

Blake rounds the corner, and once he sees Lucas, he bursts into fresh laughter. I hand Lucas the ice and he thanks me when I turn my attention back to Blake.

"What were you doing there?"

He sets his beer down next to the coaster on our coffee table and knuckles the top of Lucas's head. Lucas slaps his hands away attempting to get comfortable. "I came to see our boy."

"That's enough," I snap as Lucas looks at me with helpless, pain-filled eyes.

Blake holds his hands up. "You two are highly unappreciative. I might just not get you the fondue set I've been eyeing for you both for Christmas."

Lucas rolls his eyes. "It was great seeing you, bro," he snaps. "Really, if it weren't for you, I would probably have some dignity left."

"Anything to help," Blake retorts without missing a beat. "And you know damn well you missed me," he coos. They share a smile, Lucas's more of a grimace and it's obvious the statement is true. Blake slides his hands in the back pockets of his jeans. "Get that nut iced. Mila, my offer stands. Happy to donate to the growth of the family."

I can't help but smile because Blake's is infectious. Over the years I'd learned he's just the type of man you begrudgingly love. Where his charm is just enough to offset the asshole. "I'll keep that in mind."

"The hell you will," Lucas grunts out. "Thanks, asshole. I'll call you."

"I'll hold my breath, later bro," Lucas taunts as he makes his way toward the front door.

"You're the devil," Lucas yells, wincing before he eases himself down on the pack.

"Heaven for the weather," he grins back between us both, "hell for the company."

I speak up then. "Did you seriously just misquote Mark Twain? It's 'Go to heaven for the climate, and hell for the company.'"

"Clever girl. I adapted it to suit me."

I cross my arms, trying not to smile. "You ripped it off."

He shrugs. "Everything under the sun has been done. But I can duel with you all day."

I roll my eyes and respond with an annoyed, "Out, Grasshopper."

"Later, Ants."

I hadn't exactly been kind to him the last time I saw him, I'd dismissed him. Guilt gnaws at me as I stare into Blake's vacant office and imagine the horror of finding him lifeless, all the light and playful mischievousness in his beautiful brown eyes gone…forever.

Stifling a sob, I cup my hand over my mouth with grief for Blake, for the life he cut short, and for my husband who's suffering this very stab a thousand times worse.

"You okay?" Amanda asks.

Wiping the tears away from my eyes, I do my best to tamp down my own pain. I'm here for Amanda, to get her through this. I nod. "Memories. Just thinking of the last time I saw him. It wasn't here."

"Good, because I hate this place," she says, and I follow her past the office, through the living room into Blake's bedroom.

"I think maintenance has been in. Everything looks picked through. I wouldn't be surprised if half his shit were on eBay already," she sniffed. "His Emmy is at my house, thank God."

"Do you want to place a complaint?"

"I don't have the energy." She stands idle, too thin for her tall frame and ghastly pale. When I met Amanda, she'd been full of life, her tactless jokes terrible but her laughter contagious. We were on a high when we met. Lucas had just earned his first SAG award nomination, and Blake had guest-starred on a season of a crime series and won an Emmy. We were all on one edge or the other of thirty. Champagne and money were both flowing, and the red carpet was stretched out as far as the eye could see for both Blake and Lucas. We all looked the part, in both health and heart, we were unimaginably happy. And somewhere in the last few years, we'd lost sight of why. Looking at Amanda now, it feels like it had been a decade ago, but it was as close as yesterday. Her once vibrant auburn hair lay lifeless, piled on top of her head underneath two inches of new growth. Dark circles drown out the shimmer in her light blue eyes, and it's easy to see she's been doing the kind of crying that weakens the body but doesn't heal the soul.

"I can say something to management," I offer, surveying the ransacked apartment. "Do you have a list of things that are missing?"

She shakes her head. "It's not worth it. Let's just get this over with, okay?"

I nod because I can physically identify with her ache and I'm already on the verge of more tears. Amanda pushes past her emotion, pulling a box from a stack next to the wall. I feel like I'm circling in place as I try to muster up the courage to go through a dead man's possessions.

Amanda reads my thoughts. "It's okay to dig around. I know it might make you uncomfortable and I can't thank you enough for helping me. Just pack what you think I might want to look through. I trust your judgment. I'm donating his clothes, and I have someone picking up the furniture. A cleaning service will come after that. We're mostly here to make sure there's nothing that could hurt him further, you know?"

"I know."

Her chin trembles as she speaks. "They've already decided he hurt that woman who keeps bringing up his name. They think that's why he did it. His death being an admission of guilt."

My mouth goes dry. "What do you think?"

"I think he was too busy sabotaging himself. And I don't think he would hurt anyone else, not like that."

I'm at a loss for what to say. Silences with Blake were never comfortable. As far as my perception went, he seemed like a man with a thousand secrets, his personality split between the man he wanted to be and the side of himself he couldn't fight. He was both tyrant and sweetheart, and you never knew where you stood with him. I'm not sure the man liked me, but I truly believed he loved his ex-wife with his whole tortured heart. I'd witnessed that love firsthand. Adoration clear in his features every time he looked at her or spoke of her.

"Whatever you're thinking, you can tell me. If his death doesn't provoke anything else, the least it should do is provoke some honesty. I want so much to say I knew him better than anyone, but I didn't see this coming. I wonder now if I ever knew him at all."

"What you knew you loved, and he knew it, Amanda. He knew it. I don't think I tried to know him enough, but I do know he loved you. That I'm sure of."

"Thank you," she whispers.

I don't have to, but I speak the truth because she deserves to know I don't think ill of Blake, not in that way. "I don't think he took part in whatever happened to those women, and I agree he was too hard on himself."

She opens his nightstand drawer and begins to trash the contents. "You know one of the reasons he asked me for a divorce is because he didn't want me to suffer *for* him anymore. He told me when we got married that he felt calm for the first time in his life."

The words are eerily familiar. "Lucas said something similar to me when we got together."

"How is he?" She grabs another box and begins to tape it up.

"I wish I knew. He's just taken on a significant role. I think he's hiding."

Amanda pauses with a new box in hand and looks over to me with concern. "That's not good."

"I agree, and he won't listen to me. He's not ready, but he seems to think it's the answer."

"The job is what made him sick. It made him so sick," she whimpers. "There is no answer. I've looked everywhere, his laptop, his emails and at every fucking piece of paper in this apartment. There's nothing. There's no reason, no answers. And I still can't believe he did it *sober*."

Curiosity wins my idle tongue.

"When was the last time you talked to him?"

"The night before they found him. We were supposed to head down to my mother's in Santa Barbara and spend a few days together. I just knew it wasn't over between us, ya know? At least I was hoping he was thinking along the same lines as me. I was so excited. I was going to spend the morning getting pampered, and then I was supposed to pick him up. The landlord said he was blaring music and he had left the door unlocked. Every part of it was intentional. And I can't stop picturing him going through the motions." She cringes as tears glide down her face as if it's now second nature to talk through her anguish. It probably is. "I was leaving for the salon when I got the call," she says, her voice weakening as she drifts off in thought. "Maybe he was never planning on coming. Maybe he just used it as an excuse to talk to me one last time. He told me he loved me. Those were his last words to me. At least he gave me that. But nothing in his tone said goodbye. Nothing."

She visibly swallows. "All I kept thinking on the way to the funeral home was the biggest problem I was supposed to have that day was picking out what shade of nail polish I would wear. I was nervous but in that good way. I know it might not seem like it, but we had a decent marriage, Mila, for the most part. It was just so hard to love fire and ice. I never knew where we stood one month to the next. But his ambition, his need to be absolutely everything got in the way of us, our happiness, our life together. He lived for everyone but himself. He lived for them, and they turned on him. They ruined him. God," she wipes her hand down her face, "why, why did he do it now? It doesn't make any sense. If he needed me, I would've come running. I was already there. I was still so in love with him. I still am." She lets out a guttural sob and sinks where she stands as I go to her, throwing my arms around her and erasing the distance of the last few years of our friendship. "I'm so sorry," I whisper as she collapses on me. "I'm so, so, sorry, Amanda." I do the only thing that feels right in this fucked-up situation, I cry with her.

Numb and thoroughly exhausted from consoling Amanda, I drive home determined to keep my vows to my husband. If he's sick in grief, then I'll help him figure out a cure. As selfish as the thought is, I don't ever want to end up in Amanda's shoes. I know my husband. I don't doubt that. But he's just as susceptible of falling victim to his career. The thought has me speeding to our driveway, running up the pavers and through our front door.

"Lucas?" I'm brought to a halt when I hear the screech of his guitar.

Right after we were married, Lucas had played a rock star and had spent months prepping for the part, mastering the instrument. It was one of the roles he'd lost himself in, and that amazing effort got him his first real taste of stardom. His picture was everywhere. There was even some Oscar buzz though he wasn't nominated. He regularly played, more so when he was prepping for a role. He said it put him in a sort of meditative state. He is better now than he was when he filmed the movie. If the man weren't one of the best contributors to cinema, he would make an awesome rock star. Blake played as well, and they used to jam regularly when they worked together.

Following the sound of the strings, I find him on our balcony bathed in the half-light of the moon with his amp attached, his guitar howling out Smashing Pumpkin's "Bullet with Butterfly Wings." I can't help the light laughter that bubbles out of me as he serenades the beach and the surrounding houses with no shits given. But it's the sight of him shirtless, in well-fitting jeans and bare feet that has my tongue going dry. Head bent, his dark hair naturally falls across his forehead while he bites his lip, running in his own perfect time along with the bass and drums. It's chaotic but sounds incredible. I stand in awe of him and just watch. As he mouths the words, I see something take shape, something that looks like anger.

It takes the better half of the song for him to see me standing there and when he does, I'm slapped breathless with the intensity of his gaze. As if on cue, I get a flash of brilliant white teeth. He'd had them capped just after we met because according to the powers that be, they were too small. They weren't "movie star" teeth. It was the only unnatural thing about him, but you could never tell. I still hated it. I hated everything the industry tried to change about my husband. I didn't want them having any more than the time they paid him handsomely for. I was becoming resentful of how much they took from us, and it was apparent he was beginning to feel the same way. And now with Blake's passing, and the state of Amanda and her words,

I was more fearful than ever that one day they may take too much of him.

Lucas's smile fades marginally as he reads the sadness in my posture and observes me carefully for a few seconds before he turns his back to me, facing the ocean while never missing a note.

Tamping down my hurt to his indifference, I realize I have a decision to make. Fight or fuck. I choose neither, drawing a hot bath before going to sleep alone.

"There's a fine line between the Method actor and the schizophrenic."—Nicolas Cage

CHAPTER 13

MILA
Present

PULLING UP TO THE INN, I MOVE TO GATHER MY THINGS BUT SIT idle in my Range Rover when I hear Lucas's name mentioned on the morning show.

Casey: Bon! What in the world is going on with Lucas Walker?

Bonnie: Oh no, do we have another Britney meltdown on our hands?

Casey: Seems like it. Apparently, Lucas Walker was nearly arrested last night for attacking paparazzi. Sources said when the pap asked Walker about his wife's whereabouts, Lucas lost it. One of Walker's bodyguards broke up the altercation but not before he got a few punches in. When police arrived, no arrests were made, but those close-by said Lucas was slurring and still spewing threats.

Bonnie: That pap is going to get a great settlement.

Casey: Don't they always? But this isn't like Lucas. I wonder what in the world has gotten into that man. And where *is* Mila? We haven't seen them publicly together in months?

Bonnie: This is bad. So bad. If they split up, I'm literally going to cry.

Casey: Me too. Between the reports from the set of the film he just wrapped and this latest incident, it seems like our good boy has gone very bad.

Bonnie: He can still eat crackers in my bed.

Casey: Bon!

Bonnie: Just saying, if you need a place to stay, Lucas, I've got room. I'm all about the damaged goods.

Casey: You're so bad.

Bonnie: You know it. That boy is fine.

Casey: Truth. But let's put our hands together and say a prayer for our beloved Lucas Walker, Hollywood. It seems he could sure use them.

"What are you *doing*, Lucas?" I whisper before turning off the radio. He's throwing everything away because of my silence while publicly imploding. A part of me wants to go back and try to save him from himself, but the other part of me knows he has to see this side of things in order to hit rock bottom. Funnily enough, neither one of us had any idea bottom was coming. Blake's death had taken more of a toll than either of us could have anticipated, but Lucas was always stronger than his demons. He's been battling them for years without giving them any power. When I met him, he was focused, alert, aware of his limitations, and working hard to break through them. He was a force of nature, purely determined to make a name for himself with his unbelievable presence. I'll never forget the way I felt the first time he picked me up.

When I answer the door, he could knock me down with a feather. While he looked edible in the tux he'd worn the night before, the man could sport a sweater and jeans like no one's business. The material hangs on him showcasing his incredible build, and it's the sexiest thing I've ever seen in my life. I've spent my entire day polishing, waxing, and buffing, but I'm still unprepared for what greets me. His Wayfarers dangle from his fingers, his palms on the frame of the door, hip cocked as if he were peering through the peephole before I answered it. His thick, black hair is loosely styled and pushed away from his forehead. The sheer size of him is intimidating. A fucking movie star and last year's sexiest man alive is at my doorstep to take me on a date. I give myself some grace to be a little awestruck. Breath knocked out of me, I stand stupefied by him briefly before I get my shit together.

"Hi," he says, thoughtfully surveying my dress with an appreciative gaze as his words come out in a rush. "You look beautiful...so is your mom around?"

I realize he is just as nervous as I am. "Mom?" I ask with a laugh.

He looks past my shoulder apprehensively. More laughter bubbles out of me, and I let out a snort as he cuts his eyes my way. "You came prepared to win my mother over, Lucas, so this can be a real date?"

"You are unbelievable, lady," he mutters, taking a step back, thoroughly embarrassed.

"You thought I still lived with my mother?"

"It seems expensive to live here," he says solemnly, which sobers me.

What an odd thing for a millionaire to say. "That's...thoughtful."

"Thoughtful, huh? Great, because you already have a knack for making me feel like a jackass. Ready to go?"

This isn't starting well. There's an embarrassed edge to his voice, and guilt begins to gnaw at me. It makes sense why he would question why I'm living in a spacious cottage in the Cahuenga Pass in the hills that's worth well over a million dollars.

"Well, you're partially right. My parents do own the house. They bought it in the seventies and refuse to part with it. I grew up here."

He surveys the property, my cottage nestled in the hills with a private drive and spectacular view. "It really is beautiful."

"Thank you." *I reach behind me and grab the large picnic basket full of wines and other goodies I spent half my day preparing and thrust it toward him, hearing the bottles clank.*

"Peace offering?"

He raises a brow. "We'll see."

He moves to reach for the basket, and I hold it with hesitance as he looks down at me quizzically. "I've done nothing but look forward to our date all day."

It's honest, and it's all I've got to try to smooth down the feathers I've inadvertently ruffled.

His lips twitch with amusement at my ploy to make nice, and he flips open the lid of the basket and wrinkles his nose. "It's not a date," *he deadpans.* "And this looks…nice. I guess."

I lean down toward the bottles. "Don't listen to him. He'll love you, I promise." *He grins, taking the basket before walking to his Land Rover and opening the door for me.*

"Thank you," *I say, stepping up into the spotless SUV as he places the basket in the back behind me before shutting my door.*

Nervously I watch as he crosses the hood. The blinding afternoon sun gives me only a partial view of him.

My chest is already constricting with the recollection of just how much I loved our exchange last night and the anticipation of more. The chemistry is intoxicating, he is intoxicating which has the makings for an easy new addiction. Butterflies swarm my insides as he climbs into the driver's seat and eyes me before starting up the car.

"I've got a place in mind."

"Oh?"

He nods. "Huntington Library. Have you been?"

"No, but I've always wanted to go."

"I've never been, either."

"A day of firsts."

"Sounds good to me," *he says.*

"Me too."

We make small talk on the drive over as he navigates the hills. It's a warm day with just enough breeze to make it perfect. "Step" *by Vampire Weekend plays in a lulling melody in the background.*

"So, what exactly is it you do?"

"I'm a sommelier, which is just a fancy name for wine steward. I don't like to call myself an expert, but I'm hoping to get there. My dream is to have my own label one day, my own vineyard. Nothing too fancy, just a place to grow my own grapes."

He nods. "That's admirable. What does one have to do to become a wine expert?"

"I studied viticulture and enology in school. I was practically raised on a vineyard during spring and most of the summer months. My parents rented the same house for years, so it felt like a second home. My mother said she loved the peace, but I think she loved it more because it was hard for me to get into trouble there."

"You, trouble? That's surprising."

"I'll have you know I appreciate good sarcasm." *He twists his lips to hide a smug grin and I have to rip my eyes away to keep in conversation.* "Anyway, her ploy to keep me from becoming a pregnant teen paid off for both of us. I got interested in crafting wine, albeit it made me a little bit of an alcoholic at fifteen, but that's how it came to be. But what she never discovered was I wasn't the only kid isolated out near the grapevines."

My confession wins me his suppressed grin. He glances over at me, his eyes drifting from the exposed cleavage of my sundress to my lips before darting back to the road.

"You are trouble."

"I disagree. For the most part, I followed the rules and hid my rebellion well amongst the vines. Mostly in an old cellar."

"We don't have to go into the details," he assures me with a pointed look. I love the little hint of jealousy that leaks from his words. It's cute, if not a little premature.

"For now, I'm just taking odd jobs. I got back from France a year ago. I was there as an understudy to a world-class sommelier. I even got to test my own label."

"How did it turn out?"

"I wasted a few vines," I say with a laugh. "No one was impressed."

"Sorry," he says, catching my eyes briefly.

"You never know unless you try. It takes years to perfect a recipe and a fortune to execute. I'll try again. For now, I'm just taking odd jobs, like last night."

"Nothing to sneeze at."

"I agree. Making a living in this profession has been a dream in itself. At the moment, I'm networking, and it's paying off. I'm getting more and more offers. And there's just so much more I could be doing if I wasn't getting these gigs."

"Such as?"

"I could get a job at a vineyard, get my hands in the dirt, run tours, or present in the tasting room."

"Sounds nice."

I roll my eyes. "You're bored already."

"And you're here to change my mind and palate, right?"

"Right," I say, feeling strangely turned on at the idea of winning him over. With easy traffic, the drive doesn't take too long. When we

*pull up to the parking lot, there are only a few cars there. "Well crap,"
I say, nodding toward a sign posted next to the entrance. It's just after
closing time. I glance over at him. "What now?"*

*He puts the SUV in park and lifts a finger. A man appears out
of nowhere approaching us, and Lucas rolls down his window. "Mr.
Walker, sir, happy to have you with us today." The man eyes me.
"Both of you."*

*"Thank you," Lucas replies genuinely. "I really appreciate this."
The man motions for us to park.*

*"Of course, the perks," I mutter with a grin. He gives me the
side-eye, and I raise my hands in defense. "I'm not complaining."*

*It's still a few hours before sunset, and we have all the time in the
world to frolic...privately. I'm having a hard time concealing my elation. Huntington isn't just a library. Attached are extensive grounds
full of botanical gardens, a conservatory, and museums full of priceless art. We park close to the entrance and Lucas takes my hand to help
me out of the SUV. His grip is warm, and when he slides his thumb
over the delicate skin of my wrist, heat stirs in my belly before he lets
go. Gathering the basket from the back, he again grabs my hand as we
approach. At the entrance, an older woman stands in wait at the door
without a hair out of place, a friendly smile on her face.*

"Mr. Walker, welcome."

"Thank you, this is Mila."

*"Hello, Mila, I'm Sylvia, the operations manager here at the
library."*

"Nice to meet you. Thank you for having us."

*"It's my pleasure. I'm a huge fan." She does a quick sweep of
Lucas, and honestly, I can't blame her, he's magnetic.*

*"So you met Tim at the entrance, he'll be chauffeuring you
around as much of the grounds as possible."*

*"Sounds perfect," I whisper, a little entranced and Lucas squeezes
my hand in response.*

More pleasantries are exchanged as I stand in wait studying Lucas next to me. I haven't had a chance to talk to a soul about my date with Mr. Hollywood, and I'm not sure that I will. So far, it's still very new and a bit surreal. Tim takes our basket from Lucas and puts it on the seat of the golf cart, and we both hop on. Lucas insists I take the front seat and in seconds we take off past the conservatory. Tim acts like a tour guide about the property, asking us for the specifics of where we might want to go. I speak up, possibly out of turn in my excitement. "I'm more interested in touring the gardens…if that's okay?"

I look back to Lucas whose eyes are already on me, and he nods. "Sure."

"The Rose Garden, please, Tim," I say, clapping my hands together like a kid at Christmas.

After giving us a few details about the library, Tim stops on the pavement at the edge of the garden, and we both hop off.

"Take your time," he says. "I'll be here when you're ready to move on." We thank him, and as soon as we step into the expansive grounds, out of earshot, I'm exhilarated.

"It's all ours!?" Lucas nods, seemingly pleased to see my reaction as he takes my hand. "Let's go."

We follow the signs down the paver-laced walkway, and I gasp when the entirety of it comes into view. Most of the roses are in bloom, and the smell of them hits my olfactory senses, sending me into a cloudy haze of intoxication.

"Oh, my God." I'm stunned as I take in the number of blooms.

"Are you a fan of roses?"

"I am now," I say softly, squeezing his hand before letting go and walking ahead of him, eager to get lost. I approach a statue surrounded by sprays of delicate bushes and admire it.

"It's the temple of love," I say softly. Hands on my hips, I look back at Lucas still standing where I left him and see he's watching me with a mix of amusement and heat. "You have no idea just how good you did. How did you know this would be my jam?"

He shrugs. "Maybe I asked a few questions or maybe...I got lucky."

I stalk back toward him alight with possibility as I soak him in, in the best imaginable surroundings. "This is incredible, Mr. Walker."

"Glad you're happy," he says, again taking my hand. We spend endless minutes walking the grounds before we head back to Tim and our picnic basket. After a few more stops, we end up in the Japanese Garden on a patch of grass overlooking a curved wooden bridge covering a small pond.

"Even by California standards this is stunning," I say. "I'm a sucker for scenery."

"Me too," he whispers, and I can feel the heat of his stare.

"Did you grow up here?" he asks, setting down the basket.

"Yeah. California born and raised."

"Private school?"

I draw my brows at his question. "I think you might have the wrong idea about me."

"How so?"

"I went to regular high school," I say, spreading out the thin blanket I packed in the basket. "I wasn't chauffeured around, and I damned sure didn't use my daddy's credit card for my weekly allowance. My parents worked really hard for what they have and acquired their wealth along the way, but I wasn't given a Barbie pink Porsche with a bow on it for my sixteenth birthday. If I wanted something, I had to ask for it, and they would figure out a way for me to earn it. If I seem privileged to you, it's only because I really can appreciate the finer things. I have a taste for them, but by no means am I entitled to them or expect them. I work for them. Living in that house is my perk of being Maïwenn and Alan Badri's kid. And it's a big one.

But if I weren't working the way I do, they would take notice, and I'd be out on my ass, trust me."

He watches me from where he stands next to the blanket. And his silence wears on me.

"What?" I ask, gesturing for him to take a seat.

"You seem to know a lot about a lot."

"An education and good manners don't always equal rich and entitled. I don't know why I'm justifying it to you when you drive a car that could pay for a semester at Harvard."

We'd been sharing smiles and stealing glances at each other through easy conversation, but things seem to have turned serious. It's been months since I've been on a date, and I'm being defensive. I brave a look in his direction and can't tell if I've offended him with my blunt tongue. "I just…I don't want you to think that way of me. I'm no princess."

He takes a seat next to me as I carefully unpack the basket.

"Okay, then I won't."

I look to see his eyes scouring my face.

We share a slow building smile before he eyes the contents which consist of mixed cheeses, spiced pears, chocolate, and three bottles of wine.

His velvety voice surrounds me in a caress. "So, sommelier, you're on."

"And what do I get if you like one of the wines?" I'm blushing, I know I am, and it's rare.

He gives me a million-dollar flash of teeth. "I may know a few people who could use a sommelier."

"Oh, it's like that, is it?"

"Reputation is everything around these parts," he mutters dryly. "Or didn't you know?"

"I forgot to care," I say, uncorking a bottle and pulling out two plastic wine glasses.

His voice rumbles low. "Then we have that in common."

"Good," I say smartly. "I was beginning to think we wouldn't find much."

He pushes some hair off my shoulder, and I visibly shudder from the contact. It doesn't go unnoticed. "It's not necessarily a bad thing, Mila. I'm not the type of guy you want to have much in common with."

He's not apologetic about it, nor is he asking for sympathy. I frown anyway.

"What do you mean?"

"I didn't grow up in a beautiful place that inspired me."

"But something inspired you," I reply.

"Someone."

"Ah," I say, pouring the wine and handing it to him. "Tell me about her."

"Why does it have to be a her?"

"Isn't it?" I ask, sitting back with a glass in hand.

"Yes, but she was much older."

"Like Mrs. Robinson older?"

"Who?"

I lower my glass. "The movie. The Graduate? Dustin Hoffman and Anne Bancroft?"

He shakes his head. "Haven't seen that one."

"Wow. I assumed it was a prerequisite to memorize that movie before you become an actor."

He averts his eyes, surveying the garden. "I wasn't formally trained. I didn't watch many movies growing up."

He's becoming more interesting by the second. "Really?" You wouldn't know it from the way he delivers on screen.

The intensity on his face gives way to a smirk as he gently swirls his wine. "But I'm a quick learner."

"I can see that." I bite my lip, and he watches while another

blush creeps up my neck. The last twenty-four hours have epitomized surreal.

"I don't have to be told more than once."

Already, I'm strangely drawn toward this man, something more than just attraction, but I have to admit at this point, the chemistry is enough. He seems shy, but not in a way that he lacks confidence. He's curious in a way that sounds sincere. He seems eager to learn about whatever knowledge he's devoid of, and that's a turn on for me.

There's a good chance, given enough time, I could fall for him.

And it's probably not a good idea.

I can practically hear my mother's upcoming rants as I drink him in fully.

But I've never been fond of playing it safe. I find life boring on the safe side. I give myself permission to give into the attraction if that's my decision. The intimacy of the setting and the intensity of his unwavering stare both have me restless with want. He's waiting, and I practically have to rip my eyes from him to keep my mind from racing further.

"Okay, so we have three bottles today, not nearly enough but it's a start." I kneel before him, my lavender sundress pooling at my knees as he lays on his side next to me, propped on his elbow with his wine in hand.

"This," I say, swirling my glass, "is Caymus which is bottled in Napa Valley, it's a cabernet which is the most popular red wine." I pop open the container with mixed cheese and grab a slice of Swiss. "Take a nibble of the cheese and then take a sip and tell me what you taste."

He does it, and I can see his derision for it the minute it hits his tongue.

He swallows it down. "I tended bar for ten minutes, and I know what cabernet is, I just can't believe people voluntarily drink this shit."

"Blasphemy," I scorn. "Do you drink beer?"

"Yes," he answers, staring at the wine like it's a red-headed stepchild.

"Well, wine is an acquired taste, much like beer."

"Understood, but this...tastes like I'm drinking a tire. No thanks." He passes me the glass, and I sip it. "Mmm. Goodyear." We both laugh at the stupid joke, and he pops a pear into his mouth. I playfully slap his hand.

"Not yet, I'm doing a presentation," I say, covering my pears with the plastic lid.

He puts his palms up. "Sorry."

"I went to a lot of effort to put this together," I chide.

He bows his head with a smirk. "And I'm grateful, I assure you."

Rolling my eyes, I can't help my smile. "Are you going to take this seriously?"

"I will, I am," he clears his throat. "Promise."

"Okay," I say, sipping the last of the spilled grapes and corking the bottle.

"This might be more to your liking."

I pour a touch of my new selection into his glass. "This is a rosé from the Allegretto Vineyard, that's in Paso Robles. The vineyard is only three hours from here and happens to be one of my favorite places in the world. Rosé wines are made when red grape skins are left in contact with the wine for a brief time, allowing a little color to be imparted but not as much as for red wine. This particular brand is a little less dry, and I think that's what you're having trouble with. It's got hints of melon and berry." I look up to see I'm being watched. Needles of adrenaline prick my skin as I begin to succumb to the draw and realize we're both gravitating toward the other with each second that passes.

I go on nervously pouring him a taste, and he takes it eyeing my offering before his attention shifts back to me. As nervous as I am to have his audience, it's equally enthralling. "You know there's a reason wine has been used in celebrations for thousands of years. It's magical in a way." I glance over to see him studying my lips. "Something drawn from earth, plucked at its peak and aged for just the right moment. It's symbolic."

I'm helpless to his gaze and get lost in his depths as I try to find my words. I fail, my whole body heated. Instead, I pluck a pear from the container with an appetizer fork and press it against his lips. "Take a bite of this," I say, and he takes a healthy nibble never taking his eyes off of me. "Now, sip."

He concedes.

I raise a brow. "Well?"

"It's good."

"Good," I repeat in his tone, slightly disheartened. "Okay, well I have one other—"

"Seriously, Mila?" He cuts me off with a chuckle before he moves to sit. My heart sputters in my chest as he reaches for my face, frames it with warm hands and draws me toward him. "How long are you going to ignore this?"

"Wha…" I'm visibly shaking with evidence that I'm not oblivious to what he's talking about. And here we are again, in the same pregnant pause we've been at a dozen or more times since we met. Without thinking, I catch the rogue drop of wine that sits on his bottom lip with my tongue and hear a low groan. I close my eyes and let it melt. "Exactly," leaves his throat just before he captures my lips and his flavor coats my tongue. Going lax, I sink into his kiss, our tongues sliding against each other. He commands my mouth, tilting my head with steady hands, so I open for him and he deepens our kiss to a level I wasn't expecting. I whimper, gripping his hands on the side of my face as he plunges, carefully flicking his tongue in all corners, seeking, and finding me willing before we sync into perfect rhythm. He kisses me until we're both panting, chests heaving with want. When he finally

pulls away, he leaves his hands where they are, his fingers gently strok-
ing my cheeks. It's the kind of kiss that can get you in trouble because
you don't pause, you go straight to the source again for whatever it
will give you. And we do, we lean in again to connect, all rational
thought flying out the window.

He's good at it. Too good. And my only thought is more. I'm float-
ing high with him, the intoxicating thrusts of his tongue dizzying me
to the point of recklessness. When he closes the kiss, he keeps his hold
on me, his lips lingering so close I feel all the breath of his words.

"I'm pretty sure I've never tasted anything that good," he
whispers.

I shake my head in his hands. "You still hate the wine."

"I'm a changed man," he assures me, pressing his lips again softly
to mine before he lets me go. "I don't need a taste of anything else."

"That's quite a compliment, even if it's complete bullshit," I
muse, still electrified with what just happened. I'm proud of myself
for being able to keep it together.

"Mila," he whispers gruffly as wetness gathers at my core. I'm
soaked, and it only took a kiss. "Tell me you don't feel this."

"Oh, I feel it, Mr. Hollywood, but you need to slow down, or
you're going to give me the wrong idea."

He lifts a shoulder, his eyes alight with something I can't make
out. "Think whatever you want. I know what I think."

"What's that?"

"I think this became a date," he whispers, lifting his thumb and
tracing my lower lip.

"It was always a date."

"Right about that," he says, leaning in again to capture my lower
lip. Clit pulsing, I press myself against him, taking his kiss and thread-
ing my fingers into his thick hair. We taste and tease for endless min-
utes, our tongues growing urgent as he slides his hands down my body
and pulls me closer to him. We're making out like teenagers, glued to

each other in an exploration of hands and meshing tongues. When the ache between my thighs grows unbearable, I pull away and sit across from him on the edge of the blanket putting some much-needed space between us. I'm already in over my head with Lucas Walker.

"You don't want to be over there," he states matter-of-factly. He's absolutely right. Instead of denying anything, I decide to be forthcoming.

"If this is just going to be sex, I have no problem with it, but it would be a good idea to know, now."

"Why?"

"Where can this go?"

"Anywhere we decide it can go," he says easily, reaching for me and I shy away from his touch. His next order is practically a growl. "Get back over here."

"No."

He grins, his eyes playful. "I'm just as weirded out as you are."

"Doesn't seem like it." I straighten my dress, tossing my hair back.

He takes a sip of his wine before staring into his glass, his voice lower when he speaks. "Like I said, I'm a changed man."

"Oh, you think it happens, just like that?" I snap my fingers.

He waits for my attention which I can't help but give. His presence commands it. And his words hit well. "Didn't it?"

I cover my smile with my hand, shaking my head. "You're crazy."

"I don't disagree. And you're radiant, Mila." He covers his heart with his hand, and I melt a little more.

I look over at him through my lashes. "See how good wine is doing for you? Just a few sips and you've upped your game."

That earns me an eye roll. "Sure you don't want to come back over here?" That allure is the reason millions of women flock to the theater, for just a chance to drink him in, and why this is all too consuming. I realize because of it, I'll probably never have a decent date again. They'll all fail in comparison. I'm teetering on the edge of indecision.

It was either a catastrophic mistake to accept his date or easily the best decision I've ever made. I hate the power he holds, and I refuse to hand it all over.

"I'm good where I am, thanks."

I want to be over there, sucking his tongue, rubbing against his cock. I can see the outline of it in his jeans. He's hard as stone and looks well endowed, which has me further reeling.

There are a few things in my life I take seriously, one of them is wine, the other is the presence of a beautiful cock and both typically bring me immense pleasure. I don't shy away from sex when the man doesn't have the ability to hurt me. This doesn't seem the case with Lucas Walker. I'm a little under his spell and more than curious as to how this will play out. He's treating me like a lady, and that's rare. I want more of his royal treatment.

"Did you break up with Laura Lee last night?"

His gaze drifts to the grass at the edge of our shared blanket and he plucks a little, studying it between his fingers. Long dark lashes skim over his prominent cheekbones before he lifts his eyes to mine. "No, that ended over a month ago. The statement last night made it public official."

"Not the commitment type?"

Damn Mila, subtle much?

He captures his top lip with his teeth to try to hide his grin at my candor.

"Just forget I asked that."

He plucks more grass. "I'm of a different mind-set than I was ten years ago. Women have come in and out of my life for different reasons. One of them was my greatest teacher, others have helped me in lifesaving ways, so I have great love and respect for them."

"So definitely not a one-woman man," I say, processing that.

"Actually, aside from a few fun nights way back when, that's exactly the case for me."

"Did you…release that statement for me to see?"

"Partially, yes."

"Why?"

"In case you were looking for a reason to get out of our date. And because she deserves that respect before I'm seen in public with anyone else."

He's a gentleman.

I sink a little further under. He plans on being seen with me. It's something. I've never needed so much reassurance from anyone I was on a first date with, but these circumstances are different. People can say they would act differently in this situation all they want. Before Lucas showed up at my door, I'm sure I would be another guilty party who'd dole out advice to someone in my position to treat him like he's just another person. But he's not, at least not yet. He's a movie star and a wet dream to many, to me. And having him in the flesh, having his lips on mine isn't something I can just ignore. The whole situation is very fairy tale, and that's putting it mildly. And the knowledge that he's just as attracted is a whole other level.

I hadn't let myself web search further than the alert because I knew I would embarrass myself asking questions unearthed due to browsing. If I wanted to really know Lucas, I wasn't going to find out who he was through his Wikipedia page. Still, the whole thing was too surreal to process in just a day.

"More rosé?"

"Sure," he says, resigned to the limits I've set, before relaxing back into position and extending his glass.

We drank the bottle of rosé and left just after sunset. It was sublime, easily the best first date of my life. He couldn't stop touching me, and I couldn't stop letting him. By the time we were standing on my porch to bid each other goodnight, I still had no idea if the man had taken a fancy to wine, but I was thoroughly seduced. As he crowded me at my door with relentless lips, I forced myself back. The idea of his profession, of what he was capable of and that any part of our date was contrived gnawed at me as I stood a willing victim to his charms. Only time would tell.

I'd read somewhere that Leo DiCaprio looked through a Victoria's Secret catalog to pick out his next conquest and the idea disgusted me. Though that story may be total bullshit, if any man in Hollywood had the power to do something so objectifying as point to the woman he wanted, and have his invitation accepted, it was Lucas Walker. He could have practically any woman he wanted, and I wanted that woman to be me. And though before our date, I thought I had healthy confidence, we didn't make much sense. That idea alone had me closing my door with a sigh and insecurity rearing its ugly head in a way I wasn't comfortable with. I could've invited him in, fucked him and made him a memory. I could have lured him into my bed with a decision that for one night, in the city of stars, I shared my body with one of the brightest. But I didn't. Instead, I let myself hope to fall without any sort of net. Where that drop of insecurity could eventually turn into a sea of doubt that I could drown in. I rose to the challenge of falling for Lucas Walker praying he'd prove to be worth it.

Besides, I wasn't the only one smitten. After that night, there was no way Lucas would ever let me consider him a memory. *Ever.* I just didn't know it yet.

CHAPTER 14

MILA
Present

SPOTTING A COMFORTABLE LOUNGER ON THE BRICK DECK OF the inn, I settle in as morning light begins to blanket the vast canvas in front of me. It's then that some semblance of peace wafts over me. Cocooned in the dream-like setting, I bat away the guilt of unplugging. I'd turned off my phone when I'd arrived here, not out of spite, but because of temptation. For so long I've counted on my marriage as my grounding, my foundation. It's what's expected when you accept the invitation to share your life with someone. But it's a single question that gnaws at me now. Without Lucas, without the life we built together, who would I be?

I swore myself independent when we met. I'd never looked for my happiness in someone else. My dreams were my mission to accomplish. Somehow, in the years Lucas and I have shared together, our relationship, and his career had become a crutch for me, and that was what I feared most when we got together. With faith, I made the decision to step away and travel with Lucas, to be his partner, and that had drastically backfired. Even though I had already taken measures to kick-start my career back into motion, the thought of going at life again without the man who had molded and shaped me for the last six years to rely on him, to trust him, has me paralyzed. He'd worked so hard to earn that trust, asked for that reliance, and I gave it to him wholeheartedly.

Where are we supposed to draw the line? How do you trust, rely on, love, and build all the while keeping your sense of self? These are answers I need to figure out before I can face him. Lucas was always resilient when it came to us and any obstacle that revealed itself along the way. Our chemistry was addicting, his refusal to let it be only that was what drew me in further. Nothing about our courting was typical, and Lucas did most of the grunt work. He was invested in us from the beginning and proved as much after our first date when I got my first glimpse of *real* Hollywood.

He hadn't called or texted in the days following our 'non' date, and I'd been trying my best not to obsess over it. I'd been in two long-term relationships in my life and had never considered permanency with either guy, at least it hadn't been at the forefront of my mind. My mother instilled in me that it was more important to grow in my skin before I commit myself to anyone else. It's sound advice, it keeps me subjective...and mostly single. The truth is I've been holding out. My relationship with my ex, Daniel, had been easy, too easy. We had a lot in common. On paper, we would have been perfect had we lasted, but in the end and after years of my life with him, I realized he was a snapshot, not part of the bigger picture. We grew comfortable, and I got bored. I vowed I would never waste my time on anyone else I could do without. Playing it safe in love kills optimism for something more. I'd wasted half my twenties with men who it would never have occurred to me to love in the forever sense. And I wasn't about to re-peat that same mistake. Maybe I'd been too busy growing into myself to concentrate on what love meant to me, but I was awake now, and I didn't want to close my eyes anymore to the desires of my heart, which had laid dormant far too long. I wanted something intense, something more exciting, consuming. Getting swept up in an affair with Hollywood royalty wouldn't be the worst thing for my flavorless love life, and from our last date it was obvious Lucas was a robust salt.

Every night for the past four days I've gone to bed with my fingers between my legs, exhausting myself with want. Even if I never heard from him again, it was better to picture his face in my fantasies than any other. Growing up in LA, it's become second nature to spot screen stars and not give it a second thought. But it's completely different to be on the receiving end of their attention, their affection. To find yourself at the center of their universe. It's addicting to get intimate with someone so seemingly untouchable, an adrenaline spike like no other. But it isn't so much Lucas's status as it is the way he looks at me, and the heady touch of his lips, the breath I lose when he pulls away and our eyes connect. It's intoxicating, so much so I can't play indifferent to it, not that he lets me. It may be foolish to want more, but I can't fault myself for it. Lucas Walker is my new wet dream, and I just want to linger in it a little longer. Finally accepting that our date is going to remain a permanent daydream, I resign myself to be grateful for the experience. As soon as I make that decision my phone rings, his deep voice covering me in a thin veil of expectation. As much as I like him, I will not be an afterthought.

"Mila, how are you, beauty?"

Curious as to why you haven't called me in four days.

Instead of being petty, my reply is guarded but polite. "Just about to take a shower and uncork a bottle."

"Save that cork. I'm sending a car for you."

"Oh? Another private lesson?"

"Such a smartass. I want to see you. I'm leaving tomorrow, and I could use some advice."

"On what?"

He pauses a few seconds.

"Lucas, are you there?"

"Yes, I'm here, sorry. I'll ask for it when you get here."

"This is a conditional solicitation for advice?"

There's a barrage of noise in the background, and I hear his muffled voice as if he's put his phone to his chest.

Annoyed with only half his attention and his lack of manners—in more ways than one—my irritation leaks when I speak. "Do you need to call me back?"

"No, no. And yes, you have to be present. So will you come?" Though distracted, the hopeful lift.in his voice brings me back to our blanket and the shy, vulnerable side of him I find so attractive.

"Why?"

"Why what?"

"Why do you want to see me?"

"You want a reason?"

"Yes, I do."

"Fine, I'll take the bait because…I can't stop thinking about you."

I smile at myself in the bathroom mirror. It's a start.

"What exactly is it that you can't stop thinking about?"

I can sense his grin over the line. "I can make you blush, Mila. It's a beautiful sight. I bet you're doing it now thinking along the same lines as I am. I bet you can feel that warmth creeping up your neck as I speak."

Studying my reflection, I note the rapid rise and fall of my chest and the light pink hue burning my cheeks. The silver-tongued bastard has seduced me in seconds by phone.

"I won't be so easily swayed."

"Oh, don't I know it." The melodic rumble of his laugh sounds over the line. "What if I promise to put in the work?"

I hold my tongue making him wait for it.

"You there?"

"Give me half an hour for the car?"

Satisfaction coats his reply. "My driver, Paul, is already there. Come out when you're ready."

I head to my living room, peeking through my blinds as a blacked-out sedan comes into view. This scenario leaves me a little unimpressed. "So very Hollywood, Mr. Walker."

"Couldn't be helped."

Walking back into my bathroom, I hit the speaker and start to undress.

"And what if I had plans tonight?"

"You just told me you didn't."

"What if I did?"

"Well, then I would hope you would break them. I know it's a little presumptuous, but you're coming, so it's settled."

"I can change my mind."

"Don't. And Mila?"

The sound of my name on his lips coats my insides.

"Yes?" *It's there, the anticipation, the adrenaline spike.*

"I've missed you."

He sounds so sincere that I'm stunned silent. My heart starts beating in a beautiful rhythm as I kick my panties aside. It's a good thing I'm speechless because his silence tells me he's ended the call.

"Could've fooled me, Hollywood," *I mutter drawing the shower curtain.*

"I heard that," *he says with a chuckle.* "See you soon." *And then he does hang up.*

Palming my face, I can't help but free the growing smile underneath.

Nearly an hour later, I'm chauffeured into the studio parking lot, thankful I'm not overdressed. Clad in dark jeans, black ankle boots, and an off-the-shoulder shirt, it's just casual enough. My dark hair is down in waves that end just past my shoulders. I've smoked out my eyes to match their color and thoroughly glossed my lips. I never thought to ask where I was going. Excitement spikes when I take in the darkened lot, though it's hardly deserted. Someone is bustling around every corner. In a way, it's what I expected. A series of buildings that hold executive offices and stages scattered along the lot. We glide past streets full of production warehouses when the car comes to a stop to one of the same. A building marked Stage 7. A woman who seems to be around my age and is all smiles waits for me at the curb. As I take the driver's hand in a guided exit from the car, she's sputtering off niceties when she greets me. She's dressed casually in short shorts, a collared tee, and has her dark blonde hair tightly braided, a walkie-talkie in one hand and a clipboard in the other. "Hi, Mila. I'm Nova, Lucas's assistant."

"Hi," *I parrot back shouldering my purse and thanking the driver, Paul, who'd spoken only two sentences since he'd picked me up. Surveying the lot, I look back to Nova.* "I'm weirded out," *I tell her honestly.*

"I can imagine. I was too the first time. Unfortunately, it's rather depressing when you actually see the process. I think it ruins the magic. He's doing you an injustice by bringing you here. It's a lot of lights, sound, and position, and that's on a good day."

I eye the building behind her and the ones connected. "And on a bad day?"

"Wardrobe malfunction, pyrotechnic disasters, a clusterfuck of attitude, too much noise, and a pathetic spread from Craft service."

I smile, and she smiles back. We're going to get along just fine.

"Still, it's pretty epic to watch it all come together. Come on, I know he's been waiting for you. He hasn't shut up about you all day." *She looks back at me in the hope I perceive her comment as supportive, and it does. I like her.*

"That's good to hear, thanks."

As we fall in step, she gives me the side-eye. "He doesn't bring women on set, so you must be doing something right."

"We've only been on one date," I confess, out of character.

"Must have been some date."

I grin. "It was."

"I don't have to say this because I'm getting paid either way, but just so you know, he's a good one. I've worked for two other actors since I started, and Lucas is like a fish out of water here. Which is a good thing."

"What do you mean?"

"I mean, he's too new to be demeaning or demanding, and he's too good to turn into that kind of an asshole."

"Good to know."

"We'll have to be really quiet," she says, approaching the door. "I just got here. Your boy likes to run me ragged, but I think they're in the middle of filming a scene. Lucas should have a break coming up."

"Okay." It occurred to me then that on our date we hadn't even talked about movies much at all, not to mention I didn't ask him what he was working on. Truth be told, I was a little intimidated to bring it up. I didn't know what was acceptable to ask from a date's point of view and where the line would cross into fandom. 'I've missed you,' is what has me following Nova inside.

"He didn't tell me he was working on anything."

"We had a few preproduction issues and just started a few days ago."

Shrouded in darkness, we see the crowd further back in the warehouse surrounded by blinding lights. Perched high above them is an empty crane made for camera equipment.

"What's it about?" I whisper, detecting the change in the air as we head toward the brightly lit part of the studio.

"Spy movie called Cairo. Lots of action and so not my bag."

"Mine either."

Nova rounds a cluster of men looking on at the commotion in the warehouse. It takes a few seconds for my eyes to adjust to my *surroundings, but when they do, I want to gouge them out. In the middle of the warehouse, on top of a brightly lit bed, Lucas is fucking the hell out of Marie Toll, an up-and-coming actress who I just so happen to think is one of the prettiest and most talented.*

Is this some kind of sick joke?

Lucas is practically naked as he swivels his hips, gripping her hair while the whole set watches on, rapt. There are people everywhere, and I glance between them to gauge their reactions as I shrink where I stand. Nova seems just as shocked at the scene as I am. She flips through her clipboard furiously as if she can somehow stop what I'm seeing and then leans over to me on a whisper. "I'm so sorry. They weren't supposed to film this today." I can feel her eyes on me as my face flames. I know Lucas is not having sex, I know it's acting, I know that. But when he leans down and takes her mouth so completely, unexpected jealousy surfaces and courses through me. I can't look away. And when he lifts her leg underneath the knee to drive in harder, my panties flood. I want it just like that. I want him the way she has him. With complete attention. Rough and wild. I want to be the woman beneath him.

What in the hell is wrong with you, Mila?

Acting, he's just acting.

He's so perfect fully naked, his rock-hard ass pumping furiously, his jeans around his ankles atop muddied construction boots. It's as if they were so hot for each other, that they couldn't take the time to undress. He's grinding into her as I watch on, anger and lust battling inside. Lucas draws her perfect nipple into his mouth as she tilts her head back, a true-to-life moan escaping her lips. The scene is off the charts hot, and yet, I'm furious and hornier than I've ever been in my entire life. I'm fully aware of the boom operator holding the mic above them, of the camera capturing their every move, but it's not what I'm transfixed on. It seems to last forever, and I, along with everyone else on set, am entranced until Lucas stills, collapsing on top of her. She smiles, murmuring into his neck. "That's one way to start a conversation." Someone next to the camera yells, "Cut." And I'm snapped back into reality. Lucas pulls away, and I see a small pillow emerge from between them. Nova looks on at me horrified as I do my best to keep a level expression.

"I thought this was a spy movie," I grit through my teeth.

"It is. This is the only sex scene."

"So glad I could make it for this."

Nova bursts into laughter and palms my shoulder. "She is so not his type. I'll be back."

Once dressed, Lucas sits on the edge of the bed and begins talking to Marie conversationally, while a man, who I assume is the director, walks over to them. After a few words and nods are exchanged, they both leave the set, and Lucas spots Nova, who gives him a jerk of her head in my direction. I can visibly see his curse as he scans the crowd until his eyes find mine. He doesn't smile, and I don't either. Lucas studies me briefly and then hangs his head.

He didn't want me to see this.

That makes two of us.

Nova walks back to join me where I stand. "Oh, he likes you."

My heated reply is instant. "Great. If this is like, let's hope he doesn't fall in love."

She laughs, and I do too, but begrudgingly.

I wait on the sidelines for Lucas, praying that I don't have to witness another take. When someone yells for a break, Lucas approaches slowly before moving in to kiss me. "You look beautiful."

"Thank you." I turn my head dodging his lips, and his eyes reflect his agitation when he pulls back to study me. We get a few curious looks from those surrounding us. Noticing the attention, he curses and grabs my hand.

"Nova, we'll be in my trailer. I want forty-five minutes without interruption."

She eyes him warily. "Got it."

"Lucas, maybe this is a bad idea," I say, glancing back over my shoulder at Nova, who shoos me off with the wave of her hand. I've been blindsided, but my jealousy and confusion outweigh any residual nerves. I feel like I'm being dragged by his tight grip on my hand until he strokes the top of my wrist with his thumb. Somehow with that act, I'm strangely betrayed.

I'm hostile and have zero right to be jealous. I hardly know him. There's no way to unsee the way he kissed her, the way he looked at her. It was familiar, and it hurt that the look he gave wasn't distinctly mine, wasn't exclusive to me. Conflicted is an understatement.

"Dammit to hell," he grumbles, leading me out of the warehouse and into the lit parking lot. It takes us a few minutes to make the silent but intense walk to his trailer, and he leads me in, slamming the door behind me. It's spacious and simple but has every modern convenience.

Lucas jerks open the fridge grabbing a bottle of water and downing half of it before he pulls out a bottle of wine. I can see from the label it's the one we didn't get to on our date, but not the same bottle, that one I have at home. He bought this one from memory.

"How pissed are you right now?" he asks, twisting the corkscrew in.

"I'm fine."

He looks up to see I'm lying. "Your face is flushed."

Along with my hostility, I'm aroused to the point of madness. I'm angry, but I'm also soaked and ready to pounce on him where he stands. That's if I don't slap him first.

It's the oddest situation I've ever been in. I'm no saint, but this predicament questions my morals in a way I'm unfamiliar with.

My silence has him cursing again as he uncorks the bottle and pours me a glass. It's then when he's got it extended toward me that I see true remorse in his jade eyes. "I'm so fucking sorry. We weren't supposed to be filming that scene today."

"Nova told me." I take the wine, and I do a huge disservice to it by guzzling half. "I'm okay. This is your job. If we're going to…" I pause, and he draws out the bob of his head in reassurance, "date."

I swallow the rest of the glass and hold it out to him. He pours freely.

"Date, I have to get used to it, right?"

"That's what you're supposed to say, but we both know you're lying," he says with a sigh. He put on a shirt after the scene finished, but I can't stop picturing the cuts of his body, and he looks so insanely gorgeous without clothes. If I'm objective enough, and woman enough, I could admit that it turned me on, but I'm having a hard time admitting it to myself.

"Mila, even if this were your job, I wouldn't want to see another man's hands on your body or tongue in your mouth. Fucking ever."

"We barely know each other." But the sentence rings hollow. There's something between us, and it's grown even with the lack of contact. I could chalk it up to expectations and imagination, which it very well could be, but it doesn't feel like that either. It's not the truth.

He runs a hand through his 'just fucked' hair. "I promise you, it's the most uncomfortable part of filming. There's nothing natural about it."

I try to stay objective because it could be my saving grace.

"You were rather convincing."

Shit. That sounded bitter and to top it off, I openly eye his crotch and am thankful he's not hard. He catches my gaze and runs an impatient hand down his face.

"You're disgusted, right?"

"No," I whisper, downing the second helping of wine and place the glass on the counter. "It's your job."

"So you've said," he counters dryly. "Twice. Why do I get the feeling that doesn't matter?"

"*Fine, it stung a little.*" I flush at the memory of it. "*That doesn't mean I have a say.*"

"*What if you do?*"

I shrug. "*Even then, you didn't purposefully do it to hurt me.*"

"*I wouldn't.*" He surveys my body, my nipples betray me hardening beneath my thin T-shirt as I picture his grind, the way he gripped her body, her slack jaw.

He bites his full bottom lip and both of his brows lift. "*Convincing, huh?*"

"*The wine…*" I trail off in a shit excuse.

The corners of his mouth lift as he takes a menacing step toward me.

"*You're turned on.*" He surveys me and catches the shiver I'm unable to disguise.

Body flushing, I close my eyes and nod.

"*But you won't kiss me?*" That has him more distraught than I am. He shakes his head in frustration. "*I'll be honest. I've never been in this position.*"

"*That makes two of us.*"

"*I don't like it.*" He takes another aggressive step toward me, and I shy away from his touch.

"*Lucas, you just had another woman's nipple in your mouth, so, no, I don't want to kiss you just yet. I mean, I do, but should I?*"

The timbre of his voice skates over my heated skin. "*Four days I've been thinking about your lips, about touching you,*" he whispers as his eyes trail slowly down my body. "*I wanted to call, but we've been clocking seventeen-hour days since filming started and they blurred. I should have texted.*"

I shrug. "*It's fine.*"

"*Stop lying, where the hell is that refreshing honesty I love so much?*" His eyes blaze another path over me and static sparks off between us.

I'm molten, the wine batting away any moral dilemma. I can't stop replaying his movements, the sight of his bare ass. I'm sick with need, and I make a decision to toss delicate and demure over my shoulder because my body is screaming for relief.

Maybe I'm not cut out for this, and we probably won't last anyway.

Seize the moment, Mila. It's been eight months!

Resigned, I move toward him placing my hands on his chest. He tenses beneath my palms as I make my proposition. "I won't kiss you," *I whisper thickly,* "but I will take the only part of you that hasn't touched her."

Sliding my hand down his chest and past the cut edges of his stomach, I cup his cock and find he's already hard, for me.

He pauses, his eyes flaring. He's stunned. Good, because I'm equally as shocked that I said it.

He watches as I slowly unfasten the buttons of his jeans and take him heavy in my hand. His cock jerks in my palm. Glancing down, I encase him, my fingers unable to touch due to his sizable girth before I hear his breath escape in a hiss. Pumping him once, my eyes flit back to his in challenge. "Tonight, this belongs to only me."

We're at the tipping point, and when he licks his lips, my only thought is...Checkmate. He moves in to claim me, and I shake my head.

"No touching."

"You aren't serious."

"Oh, I am," *I assure him with a lusty edge to my voice.* "You touch, we stop."

His eyes hood. "Fuck, Mila."

His reaction to my touch spurs me on as I shamelessly stroke him.

"I don't have a condom," *he says, pushing his jeans down before he begins to toe off his boots.* "But you can trust I'm good. I take this seriously."

"We're going to have to trust each other," I whisper as I push him to sit at the breakfast bench in front of a small table. He leans back, as I pull off my T-shirt and unhook my bra.

His thick cock is pointing north and beads at the tip as I discard my bra and hear a groan coming from his lips while I unveil myself. Taking my time, I strip bare. Naked and unashamed, whether it be from wine or want, I'm in this. His eyes take in my every curve, and his knuckles whiten with the grip he has on the padding at the edge of the seat.

"You're so fucking perfect," he says, gripping himself in his hand and pumping slowly as he sucks in his full lower lip.

"Hands off, Lucas," I order. He groans and releases himself.

Fully naked, I straddle his thighs and take him in my hand between us, resuming my tease. Teeth gnashing, he closes his eyes, and when he opens them, I see an evergreen forest full of fire. Sliding my thumb over his thick tip, I play with the growing wetness covering the head of him, loving the feel of the silky skin. I hold his gaze and soak it in. In my fantasies I'd never staked my claim on him, it was just the opposite. My appreciation for the unpredictable grows in abundance because I love this story already no matter the length of it, and it had only just begun. He moves to touch me, and I shake my head. "I was helpless watching you touch her, now it's your turn."

"Mila," he grits out in warning while balling his hands into fists at his sides. "I need to touch you."

"No." I lift myself to hover above him and then slowly sink onto his stone cock, taking him in greedily, inch by inch while watching his lids lower further as lust-filled eyes penetrate mine. I've never been so in control, and at the same time, I feel like I'm on the verge of losing it any second, my body buzzing at his intrusion as I attempt to take him into me. There is no sound other than the humming motor of the fridge and our mingled, fast breaths. I'm too small for his size. Lucas grunts at the stretch, gently thrusting his hips and bites his lip so hard, it leaves a mark when he lets it go. Chest heaving, his eyes stay fixed on my sex as chorded muscles flex in his neck. When I'm unable to sink further, he goes to speak, and I silence him by sliding my tongue across his bottom lip. Lifting from him, I soak my palm with my tongue and wrap it around him, and he jerks his hips.

"Jesus Christ."

Back on his thighs, I spread myself out resting my feet on the cushions next to him, and he watches as I ready myself, gathering my wetness and sliding it around my opening. Every part of this is filthy, and I revel in it.

"Mila," he protests, his body taut and on the verge and I shake my head. Again, coating my palm with saliva I pump him vigorously before I lift to sink onto him. We both moan when I'm finally able to take him to the root.

"Fuck," he grinds out hoarsely as he jerks inside of me and I begin to move. "I'm not going to last," he threatens, his heart thundering against my palm. I tug off his shirt, and he helps me, tossing it aside like the nuisance it is. He's my new playground, solid muscle covered in sculpted beauty and I let my fingers roam the defined contours of his chest while his hands remain idle. I ride him agonizingly slow, and it's exquisite. The connection surpasses my daydreams. The air in the trailer is heavy with the weight of us. He takes it all in, his cock stretching me, my arousal seeping between. Control wavering, I swivel my hips, and his eyes flare, the intensity pushing us both to the edge of sanity.

He sinks into my rhythm, his hands lingering at my sides, waiting for permission, nostrils flaring.

"Fuck, Mila, please let me touch you!" He's practically shouting, and I again shake my head, as I keep a steady pace before I reach between us massaging my clit. I'm flying and crashing all at once. Sweat beads above his top lip and I lean in, so our heavy breaths mingle.

"Fuck this," he shakes his head as he begins to pump from below me and we both call out to the other as he thrusts up getting impossibly deep. Resolve breaks on both sides as he grips the back of my neck, hot mouth claiming mine before he fucks me with his tongue. After a thorough kiss, we separate and he leans back, watching me avidly as we work together, our movements and needs the same. Open-mouthed, we stare at each other, jaws slack in awe while we explode in movement. Leaning forward, he stills, reaching behind me and clearing the table of everything on it. I hear the loud crash of the script, his laptop, and the bottle of wine as I'm spread out before him. He attacks, hovering close, sucking my tongue while he furiously pumps into me thrusting so hard, I'm gasping his name. I'm getting exactly what I asked for.

I reach between my thighs and he bats my hand away.

"I can't come this way," I tell him. He pulls his brows together and stares down at me before pulling out. I lift to my elbows in confusion as he strokes my thighs with open palms.

"You can't come what way?"

He bites his lower lip, a mischievous glint in his eyes before flattening me to the table with his palm and pushing his fingers inside.

With those two digits, he rubs me until sensation overwhelms me. "Right there, huh?" His lips curve up. "I think I can take it from here."

I let out a low moan in reply as he works me, palming my breasts and stroking my nipples. I'm on the verge when he lowers his head sucking my clit while working magic with his fingers. Thighs shaking, I begin to quake. "Oh, God." He sucks eagerly following the urgency in my voice, his fingers quickening along with my body. In a blind second, his cock replaces his fingers, and he drags the ridge along my G-spot, pinpointing where I need him.

"Come on, beauty," he grunts. His thumb picking up the slack of his tongue. Within a few thrusts, I come violently, grasping onto him

like a woman possessed. He drives in hard, eyes blazing, skin on fire as he ravages me.

With a few hard thrusts, he comes with a long groan. I have no time to recover because his kiss intensifies as he pushes me further back, lifting my legs at his hips and grinding at a slow, languid pace until he's fully hard again. I've never been fucked from round one into the next, but nothing about Lucas is ordinary. In this round he worships me, whispering filthy things as he drinks me in with thirsty eyes. The position is uncomfortable; my back aches on the unforgiving and cheap table, my throat burns from lack of air, and we're both a sweaty mess, but it feels too good to stop any of it. My need to dominate the situation has already given way to growing addiction. I'm hooked. He's got everything but my heart, and I know I have to be greedy with that. Maybe it's because he's a God of men, or maybe it's because he's that guy, the one I'm supposed to be this drawn to. Either way, he's claiming me, and I welcome every minute of it.

"Damn…Perfect. Fucking. Fit." he whispers heatedly, bending over at the edge of the table, hitting me with crazed fervor. I'm on the verge of having another orgasm when he slips a hand between us. His delicious ass peeks over the edge of my line of sight as I let myself get carried away.

"Kiss me, Lucas," I murmur, reaching for him just as he descends for the same connection, the slow thrust of his tongue in my mouth matching his strokes until we both let go.

He collapses on top of me, his words muffled in my neck.

"What in the hell was that?"

We both break into an odd fit of laughter. I have no words for what just went down between us. A jealousy fuck on date two can't be a good sign, but I refuse to think that way. *Being intimate with him felt too damn good. It was too soon for any of it. But it happened, and I can't bring myself to regret it, yet.*

He pulls away from my neck, a heart-stealing grin on his lips. "Did we just have our first fight?"

"That wasn't fighting," I say. "I don't know what that was."

He studies me skeptically beneath him, sweat sliding down his forehead. "Sure, you don't know what that was?"

I shrug.

"So that wasn't you marking your territory?"

"I'm not a dog, Hollywood."

He bites his lower lip. "Can't just admit it, huh? Nothing comes easy with you, does it?"

"I would say that was pretty easy."

"That's not what I meant. You're a ballbuster, and you know it. And please don't mention anything about your mother while my cock is still inside you."

He kisses my shoulders, my collarbone, my chin, cheeks, nose, and lips. I'm so incredibly high, I can't imagine the crash. He rests his weight on his forearms next to my head as he continues to kiss me.

"You can't be comfortable," I mumble against his lips.

"This, beauty," he whispers softly, "this is bliss." After another thorough kiss, he pulls away. Taking his discarded T-shirt, he cleans between my legs, the act so intimate, I redden a little with embarrassment. He does this so carefully, I can't help but to close my eyes and push his hands away.

"Oh no you fucking don't, not after that show," he says, gently spreading my legs and pushing his fingers inside before running them through my folds. His mussed-up hair and nail-marked shoulders a sure sign of my own disheveled state. I'm finally crashing down with realization as he presses a kiss on the top of my mound and grins up at me. "I don't think I'll ever get over how perfect that felt." The view is spectacular from where I lay as he touches me so gently, the pads of

his fingers spurring me on even after I'm well spent. "You're filthy," he says matter-of-fact, "gotta say I wasn't expecting that. And here I thought you'd never see me again."

"I wasn't planning on it."

His brows draw as he frowns down at me. "Really? Because of what you saw in there?"

"No...I mean, kind of. I don't know that I fit with you."

"So, this was going to be it? Is this what you think you're worth to me?"

"Of course not, give me a little credit. But we hardly live comparable lives."

His eyes darken as he looks me over. "We were going to have to give in to this attraction at some point."

"True, but—"

"You think you can't have something real with me?" He frowns down at me, a pissed off edge to his tone before he lifts me by the arms to sit bare-assed on his table. "I didn't plan on sleeping with you tonight, Mila, and you know it."

I'm finding it hard to regret anything with the way he's doting on me. It's nothing short of the bliss he spoke of. I feel beautiful. I've just been thoroughly fucked in the trailer of a movie set, and somehow, I feel like a queen, his queen. I have no idea how he managed that. I'm pretty sure it's his hands, the way they explore, adore, worship. Reality can go fuck itself, I want to live in my daydream.

Ashamed at my previous train of thought, I nod. "You're right."

He's still aggravated, it's in the set of his jaw. He tucks himself back into his jeans and places his hands on either side of the table, leaning down to get eye level with me.

"So, is this it? I kiss you goodnight, and have Paul take you home. Is that what you want?"

Tucking my lip underneath my teeth, I shake my head and look up at him.

"Why don't you allow me to show you what you're worth to me?"

It's the second time I've been blindsided. I agree readily because it's what I want. "Okay."

I give him a shy smile before he cups the back of my head and takes my lips in a kiss telling me he means it. When he pulls away, I make idiotic small talk because all I want to do is beg him for more of what he just gave me. I've never had sex quite like that.

"Now onto that advice," he says, smoothing warm hands down my naked arms before picking up my panties. He slips my feet into them and then pulls me to stand, sliding them in place before he grabs my bra. One side of his mouth lifts. "Maybe I should leave you naked, so I can get my way."

"That's not the way this works," I say, reaching for my bra before he yanks me flush to him.

"Don't test me," he says, rubbing his fresh erection against me.

"Wow," I mouth. "Don't tease me."

"Oh, like you just played fair?"

"Touché."

"So," he says, slipping my bra on and fastening it without issue, "there is this extremely beautiful, intelligent, woman I'm crazy about and want to get to know better, but I have this work obligation coming up, and I was wondering if I should ask her to wait for me?"

"How long will you be gone?"

"Seven weeks. We're doing most of the principal photography in Cairo."

"Hmm…That's a lot to ask from someone you've only been on two dates with."

"Yeah," he agrees, stroking my nipples through my bra with deft thumbs. I sink into his touch.

It's his hands, definitely his hands.

"But I have this feeling she wants to wait for me."

"You do?"

"I have to play this just right though. This isn't just any woman."

"No?"

"No," he grins, gesturing for me to lift my arms before he slides on my T-shirt.

"And what if she doesn't agree to wait?"

"She could be the one to break my heart."

I roll my eyes. "Let's not get dramatic."

"Hazard of the job," he says before he leans in taking my lips. His kisses are deep and leisurely, the best kind.

He captures my lip between his teeth. "Don't ever try to deny me your kiss again."

"Now we're giving orders?"

His expression changes as does his tone, both filled with authority. "I like you, Mila. A lot." He places my hand on his chest and covers it with his own. "And if you don't like me the same, you damned sure shouldn't have slept with me."

I shrug doing a horrible job of playing coy. "Meh, you're okay. You could use a shower."

His expression doesn't change. "So what do you say?"

"I'll think about it." It's a pretty lie. Even if it only turns out to be the best sexual chemistry in history, it's worth waiting for.

As soon as we're dressed, he pulls me into his lap and gives me a kiss that lasts until the knock sounds at the door.

Later that night I lay in bed, my head racing with should haves. I left shortly after they called him back to the set. I didn't want any part of watching him touch another woman. Acting or not, I'm just not the type. Maybe if I got to a point where I was more comfortable and secure in whatever we have brewing, but we were too new. And that's *if I didn't ruin it by letting my blazing libido take over. Tossing in my bed, I kick off the sheets and sit up, completely restless when I swipe my phone, and it lights up with the time. 4:45 am. It's then I see a text Lucas sent hours ago.*

Lucas: Don't you dare regret it.

I decide not to reply. I didn't want him thinking I was up doing precisely that. After another twenty minutes of staring into space, I throw my covers off and head toward my kitchen, flinching when I hear pounding at my front door. Peeking through the hole, I jerk back when I see Lucas peering through it.

Without thinking, I open it to see him leaning in on the frame, his eyes blazing a trail from my bare feet up to my panties and cami.

He looks so incredible, his hair damp, in well-fitting dark jeans, a long-sleeved zipped hoodie, and sand-colored boots, his breaths coming fast as if he's just run miles to get to my door. Everything inside clenches in memory of his touch.

"That's not how I wanted this to start," he states as if we were still in mid-conversation. "I'll never regret it, but..." His eyes zero in on the silk triangle between my thighs, "Jesus, this is how you typically answer the door?"

Opening the door wider to give him a better view, I cock my hip. "You were saying?"

Without hesitation, he scoops me in his arms and kicks the door closed behind him. "After."

"After?"

"After I do the hundred things that I want to do to you before I can complete that sentence."

Claiming my mouth, he sweeps me away in his hungry kiss. Thoroughly seduced, he allows little space between us once he's taken his fill, his warm breath tickling my lips when he speaks, "I leave at six tonight, not nearly enough time."

We grin at each other as he slowly walks me into the living room.

Eyes intent on mine, he carries me easily. "Mila, you've got me going crazy here," *he whispers,* "what are you thinking?"

"This is going fast."

"True," *he agrees, before softly pressing another kiss to my lips,* "but I plan on taking it slow this morning. Where is your bedroom?"

The feel of his lips and tongue assault my senses as I lay listless in a dream-like state. We'd been caught up in a mix of sexing, sleeping, and eating since he showed up at my door. Keeping my eyes closed, I thread my fingers in his dark mane as he presses kiss after kiss to my stomach. Smiling, I open my eyes to see him staring at me from where he's perched above me. His arms bulk with the strain of his weight and I feather my fingers over the mouth-watering curves.

"My car will be here soon." *His expression is grave.* "Fuck," *he grumbles.* "I don't want to leave." *Biting his lower lip, he looks down at me thoughtfully.* "Come with me."

My eyes widen. "Come with you to Egypt?"

"Yeah, pack a bag and come with me," *he says with baffling ease.*

"Uh, no, I can't come to Egypt." *He kneels on the bed, and I sit up, pulling the sheet over my exposed breasts. He lowers it with a scowl.*

"Why not? Because of work?"

"Yes, well no, I don't have anything until next week."

"Great, come with me today, right now."

"I can't go to Egypt today."

He draws his brows. "You have a passport, right? You said you were in France."

"Yes, I have a passport, but…"

He tugs my legs so I'm trapped beneath him and then cages me in his hold. "Then come with me to Egypt. Just for a week."

"You're crazy."

"We've chartered a plane and have plenty of extra seats. You can sit in the one next to me, beauty. We can get to know each other better."

"In Egypt," I deadpan.

He chuckles. "Yes, Cairo."

"You realize how crazy this sounds, right?"

He looks upward as if he's mulling it over and blows out a heavy breath. "It's a perk, right? I mean, I can see how it might seem a little nuts, trust me. But if it's not about losing your job, and you have a passport, what's the hesitation?"

"Because it's just...a lot."

"It seems excessive, yes." He gives a sharp nod. "But the alternative is shit. I leave you here, we don't see each other for two months. Maybe this loses its appeal for you. I'm not willing to take that risk. Not with you."

"You aren't making this easy."

He lifts a sharp brow. "Says the kettle."

"Lucas, this has been wonderful, really..." I trail off because I'm considering it, and he must sense it because I can see a smile budding on his perfect lips. "I meant what I said this morning."

"You didn't really say anything."

He plants his head on my chest. "Yeah, well, I wasn't planning on you answering your door naked."

"I wasn't naked."

"Stop stalling. Come with me, let's not leave it alone, not yet. Let's explore this thing."

It was exactly what I'd asked for—risky, consuming, a whirlwind, and still, I was terrified to embrace it. But there's a fine line between being responsible and being predictable. So I leap.

"Okay."

"I brought you some tea," the woman who had introduced herself as Audrey when I checked into the inn approaches, setting it down on the table. "You've been out here for hours."

I sit up in the lounge chair and thank her. "With a view like this, I don't think many can blame me."

"You didn't touch your breakfast," she presses, concern lining her features. She's an older woman with white-tipped hair and kind eyes. Dressed casually in jeans and a sweater, she has a 'no bullshit' air about her that puts me at ease. "I'll be happy to warm something up for you."

"I'm not very hungry."

She nods and then turns to leave before pausing and looking back at me with maternal regard. "You know, I don't often say this to guests; in fact, I never do, but if you want to talk, I'd be happy to listen."

"Thank you so much, but I just came to clear my head." I look out at the endless rows of vines lined perfectly over the rolling hills. "It's so beautiful here."

"Thank you, my husband and I have spent our lifetime building this place."

This piques my interest. "How long have you been married?"

"Thirty-six years this spring." She gives me a knowing grin. "I'm guessing a few more years than you've been alive."

I nod, mustering a weak smile. "A few."

"Well, it's taken a lot of hard work for us to get here," she says, looking out at the sun-kissed rows of budding vines. "Maintenance, oh God, the maintenance, the cost. We've had some failed years so bad we didn't think we would see another."

I'm positive she's not talking about her vineyard now, and I can't help my reply. "Was it worth it?"

"That's the golden question and deserves a straight to the point answer. Some days, I can't imagine doing it another way. Others, I wish I had."

I sip my tea in silent encouragement for her to continue. She takes the lounge chair next to me.

"Every person decides their own path, I guess; but ultimately, it's a decision to stay on the one you've chosen, and no one in the world can tell you what is best for you—better than you."

"I agree with that." I sit up further, pulling a blanket at the end of the chair over my skin to batter the sunset chill. "What do you do on the days you wish you had chosen differently?" We exchange a look when she hears the slight crack in my question.

"Well," she says, soaking in the view before turning back to me, "I embrace those days because it's all a cycle, and in the end, I know the other days are coming. You know, love grows right alongside resentment and neither are more powerful than the other. We're the ones who balance that scale."

Nodding, I sip my tea in attempt to hide my threatening tears.

"There is no secret, just a decision you have to make every *single* day and my decision has always been love. I can tell you this, if I would have gone the other way, I would have missed today." She stands. "And today was *good.*"

Unable to hold them, the tears slip from my eyes, and I bat them away. "Sorry, I've been off the grid emotionally lately." Embarrassed, I sink where I sit.

"Mila, I'm not going to play dumb to your celebrity. I've been watching the two of you for years, and I think you're both lovely. But at no point in time when I watched did I think you were perfect because no marriage is. You are safe here, I promise."

Unable to speak around the lump in my throat, I nod, eyes cast down.

"Hey, you," she says pointedly. I look up to where she stands. "I've been there. I've been exactly where you are, and hopefully that tells you something."

"It does," I say with a nod. "Thank you."

"I'll just be inside if you need anything."

"There's probably no one who understands Method acting better academically than I do, or actually uses it more in his work. But it's funny—nobody really sees that. It's perception versus reality, I suppose."
—Jack Nicholson

CHAPTER 15

LUCAS
Three and a half months ago

Clasping my watch, I look over to where Mila sleeps naked on her stomach. Her subtle curves and sun-kissed skin have my cock swelling, and, I'm hard in seconds just from studying her parted lips. I finish dressing and kneel by the bed, pushing her silky dark hair away from her forehead. There was a time when I was unsure if I was enough for her, and even when I put the ring on her finger, I still wasn't convinced. I married her anyway because I worshipped her for the woman she is, and because she'd convinced me thoroughly to believe in the love that reflected in her eyes. She was the easiest addiction I'd ever allowed myself to have, and now that I've let myself become accustomed to the fix, I couldn't imagine living a second without her. Last night I was unfair to her in a way she didn't deserve. She'd come through for both of us by helping Amanda pack Blake's house, and I'd left her alone to deal with the ache it caused. She came home needing me, and I gave her nothing but my back while I strummed my guitar.

I'm such a fucking prick.

Guilt gnaws at me as she slowly opens her eyes and frowns when she sees I'm dressed. "Where are you going?"

"To the shooting range. I'm meeting with a weapons specialist. Come with me."

"Really?" Her enthusiasm breaks my heart. I've done a shit job of meeting her needs, but I still can't bring myself to get it together. I'm no longer comfortable in my skin. I don't know how to relay that to her without worrying her further. I've never been at odds with my own mind before, and I'm out of my element. There's more guilt and denial swimming between my ears than I could ever live comfortably with. I need answers.

"Give me ten minutes?"

I nod, and she bounds off the bed. I smack her bare ass and take satisfaction in the slight jiggle. I'm seconds from taking her, but I have plans for today. "Hurry up. I need my partner."

"I'm all over it, baby," she says, swaying her hips seductively.

"Keep that up, and *I'll* be all over it, baby."

"Wouldn't be the worst thing to happen," she spouts sarcastically.

"Later." It's a promise and her eyes light up in understanding.

She grins at me over her shoulder and disappears into the bathroom. I glance around our bedroom. Mila did a beautiful job decorating our beach house. It's too much house for two but feels like a real home because of her mix of soft plush furniture and her warm color choices. She'd insisted on doing it herself which was great because I was too cheap to hire a decorator. She'd taken her time pulling pieces from the various places we visited while I filmed getting it just right for us. Everywhere I look there's a reminder of us, of where we've been and how far we've come. She loved the beach house just as much because collectively it was both our first home and investment in us. I'd gone with my gut my whole life, and it had never once led me wrong. The minute I set foot in this house with my bride, I knew.

Shoving my hands in my pockets, I stare out the window at the view I'd never tire from. When I got to LA, I'd never seen the ocean, to me it was the ultimate sign of freedom. The stopping point of running because it was the farthest. I loved the symbolism of living so far from the world I came from.

"No man, no," Blake says, pacing our stained carpet. "You're sputtering through the lines like they don't mean shit to you.

Frustrated, I run a hand down my face. We've been at it for hours. We're set to start filming in a week, and I have yet to get a handle on my role. He takes a long pull on his beer, eyeing me before he speaks.

"Have you ever heard of Method?"

"Don't think so." I sink into the couch feeling out of my element. Reading my expression, he cups the back of his neck and nods before flipping through the open script on our table and pointing to a few of my lines.

"Okay, bro, Maddie did a pretty good job teaching you some of the fundamentals, but you need to start thinking outside of the box. You aren't playing one of her tough guy roles. You're playing a soft-spoken introvert who turns into the tough guy, right?"

"Right."

"You have the asshole part nailed." He gives me a sly grin, and I give him the finger.

"You've got to dig a little deeper and show the change happening during this scene. This confrontation is bringing it out of him. So here," he points out, "you're about to get your ass kicked, and you're laughing maniacally as he pushes you up against the wall. He's shaking the fucking monster front and center. Get up," he says, nodding toward the wall. "Let's say this here," he scrutinizes the carpet, "shit-stain is the marker."

I follow him over and eye the stain, "my bad, I think it's Yooh—"
Before I can get it out, he slams me against the wall, hard.

I wrack my brain and can't remember what the fuck maniacal means. I'm instantly furious. Blake reads my confusion.

"You go from fear to laughing like you're a little bit crazy, and the hits don't hurt. Like you asked for it, like you wanted it to happen."

I nod. "Got it."

"Now, think back to a time where you just didn't give a shit what happened. Dig and think of something that hit you hard, something painful and use it." As he speaks, he continually slams me against the wall, before rattling off the lines. "Fucking pussy."

I shove at his hands. "Give me a second, man."

He shoves me again. "Camera's rolling, and you're wasting film."

My back jars when he pushes me again and anger spikes as he taunts me.

"Go back, trailer trash," he says, shoving me harder. Eyes blazing, he smirks and slams me into the wall again. "Momma was embarrassing, wasn't she? Did she have a mullet, Joe Dirt?"

In a blink, I'm back in front of middle school swearing to my mother that I didn't take her cigarette money while she repeatedly swats me on the back of my head. Kids in every grade line the sidewalk and stare either gawking or laughing. It's the first time I admit to myself that I hate her and detect the shift in the withdrawal of my heart.

Once she's berated me, she screeches off in our rust-colored minivan leaving me to walk the four miles back to the trailer. Everyone is staring, jaws slack. And with every step I take toward home I get more and more pissed off. Blake shoves me again, and I let that kid take over as I spout off my lines.

"Scene," Blake says, breaking me out of my stupor. "Not bad, even with the improv." There's a glint of respect in his eyes. "Where did you go?"

"Somewhere I didn't want to be," I mutter before I realize my lip is bleeding.

"Draw, identify, and live it. Get it?"

I did, and I was fascinated. "What's that called again?"

"Drawing from experience, that's part of the Lee Strasberg Method. But there are others, and there's this whole debate about what it is and isn't."

I follow him to the kitchen, and he cracks our last two beers handing one to me.

"Strasberg, who's that?"

Blake takes a sip of his beer the bottle still pressed to his mouth while he shakes his head. "Stop worrying about your training. There are plenty of untrained actors out there, and from what I can tell, you're a natural. Morton Weary doesn't just work with anyone."

Morton Weary is the type of director that makes stars out of unknowns and has cast Blake and I both in Misfits, *our first movie.*

"He sees something in you, and I've seen what you can do."

"Just tell me," *I prod. During our scene I felt some sort of universal click inside me. Maybe it's because somehow, I can use the filth I grew up in to fuel me, but I want to know.*

"Look we're broke now, and neither of us can afford a coach, so go to the library, get on the web and look up Method acting." *Grabbing a pen from our counter, he pulls a bill from our unpaid stack, flips the envelope, scribbling on it while he speaks.* "You've got the godfather Stanislavski, Lee Strasberg's Method, Meisner, Chekhov, and then there's those that go to the extreme; like Brando, DeNiro, Bale, the list is endless."

"What do they do?"

He hands me the envelope. "They go way beyond classroom technique and spend months prepping, making sacrifices some think idiotic. That's why there's a debate. They live, breathe, eat, and shit their characters while they prep and during filming."

"Really?"

"Yep," *he drains his beer.* "They rarely ever break character. DeNiro is a beast. For Taxi Driver, he worked shifts as a cabbie."

"To play a sociopath?"

"I'm guessing he did it so he looked comfortable behind the wheel, and grasped the mannerisms involved while driving a fare so they became first nature. You know, it's a senses thing. It's about relaxation, *but not in the way you think of it. It's allowing your body and mind to relax enough to become a sort of vessel. How can it look natural on film if you've never done it? And how can you relate to a bloodthirsty psycho if you've never been one?"*

"I get it. Maddie had mentioned something about that, about the senses. She used to do an object exercise with me so I could memorize sensations of holding things, and then do the scene without it in hand."

"Right. Method has a lot of exercises you can use to figure out who you are, get into the mind-set, help concentration, build your character, and bring truth to them by using some truths of your own and a little imagination. It's a process, but it works for a lot of A-listers."

"A lot of them do this?"

"Look it up. There are a ton of articles. A good percentage of Oscar winners use it."

"How many?"

"More than half. But I'm telling you right now it takes dedication."

"That, I've got," I say, handing over my beer and sliding my wallet into my jeans.

He raises a brow as I grab my keys. "Where are you going?"

I swipe my script off the floor. "Library."

Pausing, I turn back to him with my hand on the door. "Have you ever used it?"

He starts working on my beer and takes a long pull. "Never had a reason to, every part I've played so far is a loose cannon with mommy issues." He flashes me a sly grin. "I've got that down pat."

"What are you thinking about, handsome?" Mila asks, walking through our bedroom with nothing but a towel on her head. She grins at me with a bit of the devil in her eyes. My attraction to her hasn't diminished in the years I've known her. If anything, it's grown, it's as if we became wired when we got together.

"I'm thinking if you keep prancing around here naked that I'm going to do my worst."

"Like that's a threat." She rolls her eyes before disappearing into her closet, and I can hear her thumbing through a rack. "Aren't you sick of me, yet?"

"Never. That will never happen," I say with confidence. "I've got way too much love for you, beauty."

She pokes her head out of the closet. "God, can you imagine dating again?"

"I was just thinking about that."

"About dating again?" she asks testily.

"No, about how glad I am I don't have to, because I have you."

"Good, you were seconds away from losing a testicle."

"Just a testicle?"

"When you came to your senses and back to me, you would need your make up tool," she eyes my crotch without apology, "a testicle won't hurt us."

"Ah."

She continues her search through her racks. "Bleh. I don't think I would do this again. I don't think I would ever get married a second time. I mean I love you, I love us. But the work. Geesh."

"You aren't exactly campaigning for a good anniversary present this year, sweetheart."

She pokes her head out at my tone and laughs at my frown. "I'm just talking about the routine. It's exhausting. Getting past the representative down to the heart of the person, and then dealing with the real person. No, thank you."

"Wow," I say. "You're batting fucking zero right now. I'm glad I'm not lacking in confidence today, baby."

"Like you need more. For you, it would be easy. You snap your fingers, and an array of vaginas apply for the job."

That comment has me shaking my head with a laugh.

"You laugh, but you know damn well that's the case. But me, I'd have to retrain someone else."

I raise a brow. "Retrain?"

She hops out of the closet pulling on her jeans with a wrinkled nose. "Oh, please. You just started replacing the toilet paper."

"That's training, huh?"

"Part of it. But we still have a way to go."

She doesn't realize I'm in front of her as she pulls a T-shirt over her face. Blinded by the material, I sweep her up in my arms and hear her yelp as I toss her on the bed.

"You ass," she giggles, a sound I haven't heard in a while. She slides her arms through the light material of her shirt regaining her balance on the bed and looks up at me through her lashes. Taking a second, I admire the pale freckles that dot her nose and the beautiful smile underneath. I live for that smile.

"No makeup today, we're in a hurry." And I like her better without it.

"I wasn't planning on it, *boss*."

She kneels on the bed and looks at me pointedly. "You know, you were a circus animal, and look at you now," she says, puffing some breath on her nails and polishing them just above her breast. "Living evidence of a job well-done. You could *almost* pass for a gentleman."

"Sorry to disappoint you, my beloved."

"Never said that." She steps off the bed and waves her hand dismissively. "Now put some of that training to use and make our bed, slob."

I'm already pulling the six pillows she insisted we needed that no one ever sees off the floors.

"Don't forget the pillows," she bellows from the bathroom.

"Yes, dear."

She pokes her head out. "We could always hire someone."

We have a lady come once a month to deep clean. I refuse to have anyone in my house in case I decide to get my wife naked on a whim. I do enough acting outside of the house. I don't want either of us holding back for any reason for fear the staff will hear. And we can do our own damned dishes. Mila agrees with my logic a hundred percent and is just poking the bear because she loves pissing me off. It's a pastime of hers to do it just enough to get me agitated while luring me into ravaging her. And I let her. Every. Single. Time.

"Lines out, you cheap bastard," she says, critiquing the way I set the pillows up before dodging the one I toss it at her.

We run lines the whole way to the shooting range.

"That's hard work, I'm not afraid of hard work," I snap. "Bring him to me."

Mila reads as one of Rayo's soldiers. "It's not that simple."

"Make it simple."

She pauses, turning the page. "Wow. This next scene is brutal."

"Yeah," I agree.

She flips another page. "Just in the script notes I can tell Wes is obsessed. It's overwritten."

"That's what I love about it," I say as we pull up to the lot.

"I'm digging this," she says with a sigh. Normally by now, she would have read the script twice. Guilty eyes meet mine.

"I'll start and finish tonight. I promise. I've been holding a grudge," she admits. "But that's over." She's finally showing her support, and it's all I can ask for at this point. After parking the SUV, I reach over the console and grip her face, pulling her to me and kissing her soundly on the mouth. "Thank you."

"I'm behind you, Lucas. Always. I promise."

"I'm sorry about last night."

"You should be. You broke our wine date to play rock star."

"I am."

She opens her mouth to speak, and I pinch her lips. Her eyes narrow.

"I know I'm not dealing with this the way you think I should. And I'm glad you're behind me in this. I'm grateful. And I love you more than any husband has ever loved a wife. I mean that. But today I just want you and me, nothing else."

She pulls her lips away from my grasp. "I'm worried." Empathy begins to well in her eyes, and I shake my head.

"Just you and me today, Mila, I mean it."

With an exaggerated sigh, she opens her door. "Stubborn ass man." Her rambling fades as she rounds the hood. And I can't help but to laugh when I hear the grumbling mix of French and English catching words like 'blood pressure' and 'wrinkles.' She's playfully helping me bat away the seriousness of the situation because it's what I need. She opens my door growling at me, "Fine, come on, let's go shoot some shit."

There's my Dame.

CHAPTER 16

LUCAS

"**O**KAY, BEAUTY, NOW SQUEEZE THE TRIGGER AND BE READY for the kickback."

She fires the gun, and Jake and I both laugh when we hear her scream.

She makes a quick turn and our balls shrink as we verbally squeak with protest, due to the loaded cannon in her hand. Her dark gray eyes widen with her attempt to play dumb, and she's anything but. I've told her time and time again she could be an amazing actress, and she replies that it's my job, not hers. We'd just spent the better part of two hours firing off a small list of guns Wes specified for the movie. It's important for me to look like holding a gun is second nature. I'd done a war movie, but those guns were much different, had a different feel, weight, shape. These are the things I'd learned over the years that can take a character to the next level. Jake had brought a few others that he thought I would enjoy including a .38 Special, which my wife was currently aiming at the target.

After another shot and scream, she shakes her head. "Nope. Too much gun for me."

Jake laughs, and I catch him eyeing her appreciatively. If he weren't in his mid-fifties, I would take offense, but he is more amused than anything. My wife is a handful.

"I think we're good," Jake says, turning to me. "Keep them here, they'll lock them up for me. I'm coming back tomorrow. Roth is coming in."

"Matt Roth?" my wife asks, looking over at me expectantly. I may have intentionally left that part out.

"Thanks a lot," I tell Jake, who reads the situation. "Now she'll be on set every day."

"Seriously?" she asks, placing small fists on her curvy hips. "Matt Roth is in it?"

"Yep," I deadpan. She thinks it's hysterical.

"Mila, nice to meet you. Keep him in line."

"Will do. Nice to meet you too," she says, packing up his guns.

Once we're alone, she turns to me. "Who plays your wife?"

"Adriana Long."

I only see a slight reaction in the subtle twitch of her lips, which confirms she's a born actress. But Mila never acts, and it's her tone that gives her away. "She's attractive," she says dryly, picking the Colt we'd been using and firing twice at the target. "If you like that dark-haired, long-legged, bombshell kind of thing." She shakes her head in aggravation and looks back at me with a cloudy glare. "Dammit Lucas, really? Adriana Long? She was a fucking supermodel. Whatever." She clicks a new magazine into place and fires off several rounds nailing the target just below the navel. When she's done, she looks back at me and cocks a brow.

"We should go," I say with a chuckle.

"Why? Because I'm getting good?"

"Yes," I say, carefully taking her gun and discarding it before pulling her to me. "And I'll be sending my representative to the set."

I feel her smile against my cheek. "Good thing."

We grab dinner at a local place we both love and take it to go. I want her alone in my favorite place—home. We dine out on the patio, and the conversation is easy. I tell her of my plans, and we both take notes of the ideas we have for research.

I've told her a majority of the plot and how Rayo deteriorates slowly in brain and body from the heroin, fucking up a lifetime of work that ultimately leads to his demise.

She sees the glint in my eyes as I pour her more wine and sip my beer. "You can do this. You were born to do this. I have so much faith in you."

"Thanks, Dame," I say, sitting back in my seat.

"I'm so proud of you. I know I tell you from time to time but to witness all you've done, it's such an incredible gift."

"Oh, now you're trying for that anniversary gift?"

She gives me a wink. "Yes. I wonder what it is this year." She pulls her phone off the table and starts to Google.

"Last year was easy and readily available." I bite my lip around the word, *"wood."*

She rolls her eyes and studies her phone. "It's iron or candy for six years. But honey, next year is copper, all you'll have to do is pull one of those pennies you've been pinching out of your ass." She bats her eyes at me as I burst into laughter.

"I'm not that cheap."

"We did a timeshare honeymoon!"

"It was not! I got the place on loan from a friend," I defend.

"And it was his timeshare."

"It was beautiful."

"It was," she says with a grin. "It was perfect. I would not change a damn thing."

"Me neither." The ocean crashes beneath us as I try to come up with the right words, but she watches me closely while I shift in my seat.

"Shit," she says softly. "Shit, this is it? Isn't it?"

I nod.

"Okay," she sighs, turning to face the darkening sky. She's so incredibly beautiful that I just stare at her features in wait. "I knew today was too good to be true."

"I have to focus, baby."

A different silence, one filled with tension passes before she speaks. "This is so weird," she says before taking a sip of her wine. "Saying goodbye to a man you're still living with."

"I don't get to clock out."

"I know."

"It's too hard for me," I plead with her. "I can't be a cold-blooded killer one minute and a doting husband the next. I have to start isolating a little. We're going to shoot some in El Paso, I think, so you'll get a break, but Wes guaranteed a lot will be shot locally. So, I'll be home for at least half of it."

"Okay."

"Dame—"

She cuts me off and her venom burns. "You know, you've spent a lot of time telling me how it's okay for you to feel how you want to. Let me fucking feel the way I want about this. I don't want my husband to have to sit behind closed doors digging into his brain for things that bother him. I don't want to miss you when you're sleeping right next to me. I don't want to spend three months as a fucking outsider looking into your life, unaware of what's going on in your head. I agreed to it, and I'll keep my end of the bargain, but I don't have to like going through it. So just give me a second." She turns her head away from me, one arm crossed protectively over her body while the other holds her wine glass.

"Okay," I say, rising from my seat and walking into the house, sliding the patio door closed behind me. I want to beg for her forgiveness but now isn't the time. I need her on board, I need her to stick to our plan, but I need her more than anything to make peace with it. After changing into my gym clothes, I peek out on the balcony to see her reading the script. The salty breeze catches her hair pulling it away from her face, and I can see she's focused, so I take the stairs down to wait for her.

"I'm sorry, I keep going back on my promises," I hear her say as she pads into the gym where I'm pounding at the bag. I'll have to drop at least twenty to look like a younger Nikki, and up my workouts.

"I broke my promise too," I say, slowing my pace. "We're supposed to be in Spain in the La Rioja region tasting wine."

She smiles. "I love that you remember my wine ramblings."

"We're a team," I say, stilling the bag to focus on her.

"It's fantastic, Lucas. Bold, captivating, and a bit horrific. This is your part."

"Fuck, I love you," I say, hanging my head. "Thank you, baby."

She keeps her tone upbeat. "We'll get to Spain. Besides, Rayo is a Spanish surname. Looks like you're bringing a little Spanish to me."

I scoop her into my arms. "Yeah, well, variety is the spice of life."

"Lucky me," she says as she looks down at our position. "This is familiar," she says, wrapping her hands around my neck and pressing her forehead to mine. "Do you remember scooping me up like this on my porch?"

"Of course."

"Well, you forget a lot," she scorns.

"I haven't forgotten that," I assure her, stealing a kiss before

I carry her up the stairs. "Now, who wants some more of last year's anniversary present?"

"Lucas," Mila whispers as she trails the pads of her fingers down my back. "You awake?"

"Yes. What's up, baby?"

In response, she slowly traces the first line of an X and draws out the word, "Criiiissss."

"No, you don't." I jerk against the mattress to dodge her fingers. "You know that creeps me out."

She giggles, pulling me closer before again, drawing a finger diagonally across my back, "cross," and then punctuates her next three words with dots down the middle, "ap-ple sauce."

"Cut it out, woman," I say as she traps me with her leg. "Behave."

"Fine."

When she bumps her closed fist against my head to recite the rest of the absurd nursery rhyme/medieval massage, I charge. She yelps when I pin her easily beneath me and grin down at her. "You are such a weirdo. Where did you learn that anyway?"

"From a friend, I think, a sleepover," she says, smiling up at me, breathless. "I don't understand why that drives you nuts."

"But you do it to continually torture me anyway."

She lifts a shoulder while still in my hold. "Of course."

"Apparently, I didn't do a good enough job of wearing you out," I mutter before bending to suck on her neck.

"You did fine," she says, gripping my hair and lifting her chin to allow more access.

"Fine," I repeat in a monotone voice, lifting my head and

narrowing my eyes. "What the hell, wife? If I had recorded your insults today, it would be grounds for divorce."

"You would miss me," she sasses.

"But at least I wouldn't have to deal with the verbal abuse."

"You married this mouth and me."

"Don't remind me."

"Lucas!" she scolds just before I kiss her the way she likes it. When I pull away, her face is solemn and her eyes fill with apprehension.

"You get both of us, forever."

I nod. "Can't live without either."

"Where you go, I go…right?"

I slowly shake my head.

"You can't come here, Dame." I push the hair away from her face as she swallows and nods. "I love you."

"Remember the rules," I remind her, before I lean in and take her lips.

ACT II

"The actor becomes an emotional athlete. The process is painful—my personal life suffers."
—Al Pacino

CHAPTER 17

LUCAS
Three months ago

THE NEXT MORNING, GABRIELA CALLS OUT TO ME FROM THE sidewalk. "Lucas, how are you?"

I wave at her with a forced smile as she enters the restaurant where I sit at a table on the other side of an open partition. I had no choice but to meet her at the place of her choosing because she'd told Nova she had a hectic schedule. It's bullshit, and we both know it. She doesn't want a private meeting due to fear of getting ambushed in hostile territory. She's testing the waters. It's a smart move on her part because she knows I can't publicly react to whatever she's willing to reveal. I have to play it just right to get answers. She walks up, and I stand to greet her. "Gabriela, it's been a long time."

She kisses me on the cheek, her perfume filling my nostrils and I force myself not to cringe at the pungent smell. It's always been hard for me to gauge Gabriela as a person. She's guarded, but direct, and that's what worries me. You don't want to have any skeletal stories with her as your narrator. She's worn a blatant chip on her shoulder due to the way her career nose-dived after we filmed our second movie, *Dissident*, the follow-up to *Misfits*. Blake and I got more offers, she didn't. Her audience has substantially faded, and ears no longer perk up at the mention of her name unless she drags other names in, like Blake's. I can't help but think her vague interviews are a ploy for short-lived attention. This type of shit is the reason I keep my circle tight.

"How have you been, Lucas?" she asks, taking the seat across from me.

"Good, getting back to work."

"Anything I'd know about?"

"Doing a flick with Wes."

She lifts a tattooed eyebrow. *"Silver Ghost?"*

I nod.

"Wow, congrats."

"Thank you."

"You deserve it." She grabs the water I ordered before she arrived and sips it. It's then I see the cracks beneath the makeup. Half of her is injected collagen and scalpel at this point. Mere years ago, she looked fantastic, but she's refusing to age gracefully. From my side of things women really don't win that battle by spending thousands in procedures. I can't deny aging actresses have it rough, I feel for them, but it seems as if it's a trend now to look like a blow-up doll. She speaks up under my scrutiny. "I have a meeting in an hour, so I can't stay long."

"I won't keep you."

"When do you start filming?"

"Soon."

"You'll be great," she assures me.

"Hope so," I say.

"Any idea what angle you're going to take?"

"I'm working on it."

"Ah," she says with a grin, "look at us, all grown up." Her eyes shine with sincerity. "It seems like yesterday we were getting stoned between takes and trailer hopping." She gives me a wink, and I hide my shudder. In those days sexual favors were a regular occurrence, but I brush off the ill feeling because I know I've never fucked her. My dick was a liability back then, but I'm thankful I had more sense than to sleep with her.

"We've both come a long way," I say, avoiding the implication in her voice and scanning the menu knowing I'm not going to eat.

"How is Mila?"

"Perfect," I answer without hesitation.

"Lucas," she laughs, "you don't have to worry. Our secrets are safe."

I raise a skeptical brow. "Are they?"

She swallows and darts her eyes away as the waitress approaches. We both order egg-whites and fruit and I sip on carrot juice while she sips on black coffee.

I can sense the nervous energy radiating from her, so I play on it, intensifying the silence with an expectant gaze.

"I loved Blake," she says softly, staring through the open space next to us. "I fell in love with him when we filmed." Her eyes glaze over as she speaks, submerged in a different time. "He was so…tempting? No, that's not the right word. But whatever it was, it was alluring. I guess bad boys always are."

I remain silent, giving her the segue. She wants to talk, that much is obvious. She looks over at me.

"We were kind of a thing."

That I didn't know. But I didn't see Blake much during the filming of the second movie. It was when he was using the most, and after bailing him out of jail when we wrapped, I moved out and got my own place. We could both afford it. What I couldn't afford was his lifestyle, it was wearing on me.

"You know dating an actor is insanity," she says. "I can see why you married out. But the payoff with Blake, the fun we had." She shakes her head in fond memory. "You know he filled my head with plans for us, I had actual stars in my eyes. It was perfect, until it wasn't. You know how he was."

I nod in silent agreement.

"I can't believe he's gone." She looks up to me with tear-filled eyes. "And he loved you. It was so obvious with the way he talked about you. He was so protective…if anyone said anything negative, he got crazy aggressive," she says, pulling the flimsy napkin from the wrapped silverware to catch a tear underneath her eye.

Ache begins to throb in my chest, and I resist the urge to rub it.

"Okay, so we all loved each other, right?" I ask, playing on her words.

"I thought so, yes."

I clasp my hands together on the table. "Then why are you bringing his name into this?"

Silence. She takes another sip of coffee, and fearful eyes meet mine over the cup. She's cracking a lot faster than I'd anticipated, and I need to strike.

"Gabriela, when is the last time you talked to Blake?"

She hangs her head and more tears fall. It takes every bit of strength I have not to lash out, and I know then my assumptions about her were right. She knows.

"The night he died?"

I barely catch the dip of her chin.

"I'm not angry," I coax gently, doing my best to keep from jerking her out of her seat. "I just need to know what happened."

She glances over her shoulder as more tears streak down her cheeks. "It's nice out. I'm craving a cigarette, how about you?"

I grit out my response. "I don't smoke."

She nods her head toward the door slightly widening her eyes, and I take the hint. "Then keep me company?"

"Fine." We signal to our waitress that we're stepping out and then I follow her out the door into the alley.

MILA

I drive toward the Bistro noting the subtle changes in the landscape. I've spent so much time on location with Lucas often opting not to step out of the sanctuary of our home once he wraps. In a way, I feel like I'm no longer a citizen of my own city. In LA, there are some landmarks that will never change while construction rises and falls in a blur around them. Kind of like a fast-forward reel around a still image. Time marches on, and trends come and go, but the rich history of who is and who was forever remains the theme.

Though this sea of stars has many shapes, Lucas's is the one I'm most fond of, though it's getting more unrecognizable as the days pass. He's changed his walk and is talking more with his hands, his movements more calculated than relaxed, his jaw set while his eyes dance with obscurity. His eating habits have also shifted, and he's dropped a good amount of weight, his much slimmer build giving way to a more youthful appearance. He looks fresh out of boot camp but with longer hair. These things don't alarm me, and I'm positive there are other less subtle things I haven't caught onto yet.

With me, he keeps conversations short and only gets irritated at any mention of Blake. Instead of dwelling on it, I help him research and leave sticky notes on his desk of characteristics I've unveiled from a respectable source about the mobster. Rayo loved pistachios, and they were sometimes found at a few of his crime scenes, but it was never enough to convict him, especially in the sixties and the seventies when he carried out his own killing. Lucas thanked me for that little tidbit with a quickie and the next day, I was picking up shells all over the house.

We are a team.

Though at times my resentment grows for his station in life, not every movie star who's made it is promised a long and prosperous career. A lot of extended success relies on behavior, ability, and relevance and there may come a time where Lucas isn't relevant anymore. This is his window, and he has to take it. Some actors disappear overnight, fading away into the background to make room for more, while others, like Blake, implode publicly and remind us all they are complex humans who get overlooked by the movement.

It's been almost a month since we buried Blake and Lucas is set to start shooting in a few days. For the last few weeks since our night on the balcony, he's been holed up in his office doing extensive research or keeping appointments with wardrobe. Nova drops by every day or so to run lines with him which hurts me because I've been replaced for the job. Maybe he's giving me the freedom because I'm going back to work, and I can't dwell on that.

We have rules for a reason.

It's what I signed up for when I married Lucas. What I didn't expect was when it came to the most compelling roles, how far he would take his absences and how much of himself he would let his characters absorb. The process for any actor who lives for their passion is taxing, but the creative isn't the only one who has to suffer through it.

I read somewhere that before Angelina Jolie filmed *Gia*, she told her then-husband that she wouldn't be talking to him during filming because she was now a gay, dying supermodel. Nothing is off the table, nor is it a ploy for attention. Half the time, the public has no idea what these artists go through to prep and execute a character. For Method actors, what looks effortless on screen takes far longer to put together.

When I got involved with Lucas, and he explained the

process, I'd done my homework and found out plenty of actors used these insane tactics and went beyond just the basic principles.

Adrien Brody shed thirty pounds, declared himself homeless, left his girlfriend and possessions and fled the country so he could identify with a Holocaust survivor for *The Pianist*.

Heath Ledger was rumored to have isolated in a motel room for weeks to deprive himself of sleep catapulting him into a state of perpetual madness to play the Joker in *The Dark Knight*.

Christian Bale has done things that borderline lunacy and yet all of his performances have been brilliant. The list goes on and on.

Even though I was aware of this when I took my vows, it doesn't make the progression any less grueling. Once immersed, Lucas never breaks character, *ever*, for any reason.

Pulling up to the small restaurant overlooking the Pacific, I scour the bistro and park. Striding toward the restaurant I smile when I see Yanni opening the door for me.

Every light step I take confirms my decision to get back to work. Lucas has his passion, and I have mine, and we both get to indulge until he comes back to me in pieces, in need of the refuge he'll seek and that I'll offer without hesitation. And once the layers he's so carefully cloaking himself in are peeled away, I'll have him back. We'll talk. We'll work through his grief. Three months, give or take a week, and I'll get my husband back.

That's showbiz.

"Remember the rules, Dame."

Taking a deep breath, I let go and trust.

Two hours later, we've narrowed down six selections for the menu, and I've just had one of the best meals of my life. Yanni kisses me goodbye on both cheeks with enthusiastic thanks, and I'm validated for all the work and research I've done to prep for our meeting. He doesn't just want my suggestions; he wants me to be a more integral part of the opening and present the tasting for the investors coming in a month.

Happily, I accept the job, far too excited to pass up the opportunity. And the paycheck is enough to have me daydreaming again about the possibility of trying my own label. Though a cheap millionaire, Lucas has offered many times to buy me a spot in wine country and make my dream a reality, but the truth is, I want to be self-made.

The drive home is much more relaxed.

When I arrive, I find Lucas on the balcony of our bedroom, his script in his lap, slowly flipping a coin between the slots of his fingers. He'd left early this morning for a meeting, and I was surprised to see him home at this hour so close to filming. The door is open, the breeze lifting our sheer white curtains and filling the room with salty air. He's staring out at the sea, so I don't feel like I'm interrupting. Tossing my purse on the bed, I kick my heels off stretching my toes in the plush carpet and begin to undress.

"Babe, I'm back. God, it was wonderful, I'm so excited. Yanni loved my ideas, and the place is perfect. I think this is going to be good for me! I'm stuffed, but I don't mind cooking for you if you're hungry."

He stands abruptly and turns to look at me, still flipping the coin through skilled knuckles. Audibly I gasp when I see his eyes are bloodshot, blotchy stains on his tan cheeks. The look in his eyes terrifies me.

"Lucas?" Taking a tentative step forward, he sharply shakes

his head once as he studies me.

"Lucas, what's wrong?" My voice is filled with fear. Shoulders rigid, his whole body draws tight as if he's about to explode. I move to go to him, and he takes the few steps to the door before sliding it closed and shutting me out. Open-mouthed, I stand in my bra and panties sinking with unease.

We face off like that for endless seconds, before he averts his gaze, resuming his seat and picking up his script.

Rule number one, don't take the process personally.

Nothing about this situation seems like process, and I fight myself to keep from opening the door and demanding answers. Something is horribly wrong. I've never seen such devastation on his face, never seen him so distraught.

I have to believe he's finally broken down about Blake, which is probably the right explanation and maybe what he needs, but the look on my husband's face will haunt me for the rest of my life.

CHAPTER 18

LUCAS

GABRIELA'S CONFESSION STABS ME CONTINUALLY AS I PACE MY trailer. In that alley, I was brought to my knees by her revelation. Blake was guilty, but not in a way I could have ever fathomed. I'd demanded her silence, accused her of being the reason his life was over because of her inability to keep him out of it. In that respect, she was guilty, and I'd been quick to point a finger at her in anger. She'd all but begged for my forgiveness as I ripped myself away from her clutches, threatening her with every fiber of my being to keep his name out of the press. She'd tearfully agreed, I assumed due to guilt and the threats I was spewing before she left me to bleed out. Once I managed to make it to my SUV, my racing thoughts lined up as if her confession pulled the handle on a slot machine.

"Yo, Blake," I say, knocking on his bedroom door before peeking inside. He's sitting on the edge of the bed with his face in his hands. His answering silence has me pushing past the door and studying him in the center of his bedroom.

"Whatever it is, I'm not up for it." He sighs and pulls open his bedside drawer grabbing a prescription bottle. I step forward and take it from him.

"What the hell is this? This isn't prescribed to you."

He snatches the bottle from my hand. "Chill out, man. It's just something to help me with aches and pains."

"Yeah, what's aching?"

Shrewd eyes scrutinize me. "I've got it handled."

I study his gray complexion. We're supposed to start filming our next movie in a few days, and he's nowhere near ready for it.

"What in the hell is going on with you, man? You've been out all hours of the night, and we haven't run lines. I can't carry you through this."

"Then don't," he snaps. "I'm not asking you for shit."

"I didn't mean it like that."

"Look," he says, lighting a cigarette and blowing a puff of smoke in the dense air between us. "I get you're worried, but I'll be there. This isn't my first rodeo."

"No, it's your second. A stint on a TV show and one movie credit doesn't make you an expert."

He shakes his head and stares at me incredulously. "Yeah, and reading a few fucking books doesn't make you an actor."

I resist the urge to tug him up by his collar. We've been roommates for almost five years, and I've never seen him so self-destructive. More and more he's numbing himself, and I can't think of one good reason why. We've upgraded our West Hollywood bungalow with every imaginable comfort. For the first time since we became roommates, we're able to pay rent without issue. The offers are coming in, and the champagne and women keep flowing.

"Are you looking for a reason to fuck it up? We're onto something here. Coke last night, Percocet this morning, what's next? Mainlining heroin?"

"How about whatever the fuck I feel like?" he snaps with the pinched cigarette between his lips while pulling up his jeans. He's lost weight, and they hang low on his hips. He points the burning cherry in my direction along with an accusing finger. "Don't tough love me, man, you're so out of your depth."

"Then why don't you clue me in, because from where I'm standing, you don't have a reason for this bullshit."

"You're such a good guy," he snaps sarcastically, "a real Boy

Scout. *You think they're going to appreciate all that work you do when they aren't looking? They won't. Get ready to be disappointed."* Disposing of his cigarette in an empty beer bottle, he grabs a waiting T-shirt off his bed and pulls it on.

"You're a real asshole, you know that?"

"Matter of fact, I do," he says carelessly. "I'm glad you finally figured it out, but you're a day late. There comes a point in life where you just have to acknowledge who you are. It's not such a bad gig. It's pretty fucking liberating actually, and it's time to embrace it, and it's been...fun." He widens his eyes, his lips curling up. "Fuck this life and the next one, I don't want to be the good guy in either one of them."

I shake my head and glare down at him. "You're strung out, and you need to sleep. You're going to blow this ride, Blake. This is what we've been working for."

"You think they know?" he asks absently, his pupils a pinpoint when he finally looks at me.

"Know what?" His speech is slurring and has worsened since our conversation started.

"They know, they can always pick us out." Confused, I watch as he swipes some cash off his bedside table and shoves it in his pocket.

"Dude, you're wasted, you don't need to go anywhere."

He laughs sarcastically. "What should I do instead? You want me to carry your books to the library for you? Haven't I helped enough?"

"Of course, you know I'm grateful—"

He cuts me off with a swipe of his hand through the air. "Then how about we consider that help my one good deed. Everyone needs a point of redemption, right? 'Sides you know the saying; no good deed goes unpunished. Find another mentor, man, don't make me yours."

"Don't flatter yourself. This is steady work. You know what this means for the both of us."

His eyes flash with disappointment before they dull. "This is about the movie." He glances at the carpet before his lips upturn, and *he slaps my face playfully. "But isn't it always? Don't worry your pretty little head, I won't fuck up your movie." Grabbing the pills, he pushes past me. "Sky is the limit, Luc, you're going to be a big, big star!" he shouts sarcastically before he slams the front door behind him.*

I didn't lay eyes on him again until the day we started filming. The director didn't say shit about the way he looked, no one did because it fit his character perfectly. Blake disappeared the minute filming stopped for the day, and I didn't see him again until it was his turn to shoot. He was brilliant in that movie, and it earned him his first lead in the next. Out of the blue, a few weeks after filming wrapped, Blake came back to the bungalow acting more himself than I'd seen in months. I assumed he'd put himself in that place for the movie. I couldn't have been more wrong.

Shaking, I run a hand down my face.

I wasn't listening, too afraid he would screw up our chances of making it while never understanding the implication of his words. I'd been too obsessed he might cost me becoming that movie star I dreamed of being.

As it turns out, being that movie star, cost me Blake.

Choking, I cough as heated tears slide away clearing my vision in more ways than one. I stare at a picture of us on my cell phone that Mila snapped years ago in Mexico.

"I'm so fucking sorry, man," I whisper into the void. "Tell me what to do."

"Lucas," Nova's voice sounds along with a sharp knock outside my trailer. "They're ready for you on set."

CHAPTER 19

MILA
Present

MY CELL PHONE ALARM GOES OFF BESIDE ME IN THE COMFORTABLE bed of the inn, and I scrape myself from the mattress checking the time. I'm due to meet Audrey downstairs for breakfast in ten minutes.

Lucas: I love you.

Pain rocks me as his latest text pops up on screen and I turn off my phone.

Love, is that enough for me? Not today. Maybe not tomorrow either. With every breath I manage and every beat of my heart, it's clear I'm still in love with my husband, but that doesn't make anything okay. It was so easy to fall for him. So ridiculously easy. Our third date began with a trip to Cairo, but even if it took place in the shittiest section of the universe, I still would have started to fall for him. It was Lucas that I was drawn to; his energy, his smile, his tenderness, his patience. Letting the water pour down my body, I shampoo my hair, recalling the week we became something more than the girl next door dating a movie star.

Our time in Egypt is a testament to living the dream, every day more surreal. We've only dined out once, barely managing a glimpse of the city. It's about all Lucas's shooting schedule will allow. It's been enough for me. Shooting takes place mostly on closed off streets or remote parts of the desert. On set we spend the long wait time in between takes together; talking, eating, laughing, and when granted enough privacy, tearing into each other like animals.

Lucas has introduced me to most of the movie crew by first name. I love that he takes the time to get to know them, that he could tell me little details about everyone he works with. It is his third movie playing lead, and I can see the excitement in his expression and the depth of his dedication. I've never realized just how much work goes into every film. Being on set is a lot different than I thought it would be. It's been a week of firsts. There's an unbelievable amount of waiting involved in setting up a scene and pinpointing the right light. Before every take, Lucas makes sure to isolate himself with the script to try to get into character. Those who aren't scrambling around trying to fight the sun for the shot sometimes come and chat with me about the process. I'm an eager student, more interested than I thought I would be to know the ins and outs of production. The hours are grueling, but he never complains. Several of the scenes have zero script and are heavily choreographed fighting sequences. Most of the time, it's all I can do to keep my hands off him, especially when he approaches me on a break, sweat covering his gladiator-like build. He takes his job seriously and gets along well with the director who is merciless in the number of takes he makes him go through. I'd watched them all closely, appreciating the experience. It's eye-opening, to say the least.

Some nights he's so exhausted when we get back to the hotel room, he can only manage a shower and a few sentences before he passes out.

Last night, after a shower he had asked me for a massage. I obliged, diligently rubbing him for a few minutes and trying to savor what time we had left but had worked myself up all day to be on the receiving end of his attention. It's easy to get riled up after watching while he showcases the limits of his body and talent for endless hours. Though selfish, I think better of putting him to sleep and can't help *my wicked idea to keep him awake, if only for a little longer. He grunts when I straddle his back, putting most of my weight on his firm bare ass. He's a bit of a nudist when we're behind closed doors, and that gets no complaints from me.*

Admiring his lean athletic frame, his tan skin, and the naturally drawn muscle of his biceps due to the way he's situated, I allow myself a few seconds of appreciation before I strike.

Lazily I draw an X on his back while trying to stifle my laugh.

"I need all your fingers," he groans, "not just one."

"Don't worry, you'll love this. Crissss, cross, ap-ple-sauce."

He lifts his head and turns to address me over his shoulder. "What in the hell is criss cross applesauce?"

"It's a Swedish technique, trust me," I say, pressing my lips together to hide my grin. "You'll love it."

He shakes his head, red-rimmed eyes closing before he plants his head in the pillow. "If you say so."

I start from the beginning as if the interruption ruined my process, but when I tap the back of his head with the side of my closed fist and belt out the rest, he goes stiff beneath me. "Crack an egg on your head!" I slide my fingers in an ooze-like motion down his back, "feel the yolk gushing down."

"What the fuck, Mila?" He groans into his pillow too tired to move.

I'm already laughing when I smack my fist against his back.

"Stab a knife, in your back, feel the blood gushing down." I walk my fingers up his toned muscle and spout the rest in a sing-song voice. "Spiders crawling up your back, spiders crawling down."

"Worst masseuse ever," he grunts. "Are you being serious right now?"

I'm barely able to get out the rest through my snorts. "S-S-Snakes slithering up your back, snakes slithering down. Criss cross app-le-sauce."

"Swedish, woman? What kind of fucking torture was that?"

"You didn't like it?" I say, bursting into laughter as he lifts to pin me beneath him, eyes narrowed. I shrug in his hold unable to hide my smile. "Maybe you shouldn't ask me for massages."

He shakes his head with a knowing grin. "That's a man's tactic. Do a shitty job so they don't ask you to do it again. And Mila, baby, don't ever do that again." He leans in further with a flash of teeth. "You little weirdo."

"None of the other men in my life have had a problem with it," I smart. His eyes glaze over with something that looks a lot like jealousy.

"Good thing I'm the only one left."

"Are you?"

He nods as the air between us charges with something indescribable. "I'll be the last man standing. I assure you."

"Ah, and how will thee persuade me?"

"Oh, trust me," he says, sliding his hand down my body and pulling up my silk negligee before slipping thick fingers inside my panties, "I'm gonna get the girl. Even if she's shit at giving a massage."

"Think so?" I say breathlessly, already pulled in the undertow.

"I know so."

"Do your worst, Hollywood," I murmur just as he presses inside me and takes all the words away. He spends the next hour torturing me with delayed gratification before we collapse in a heap, limbs tangled, whispering softly before we drift to sleep.

On my last night in Cairo, once filming has wrapped for the day, Lucas rushes us back to the hotel to freshen up. Just as I tie my sandals, he enters the room with a black insulated bag.

"What's in there?" I ask, gathering my hair into a loose bun on top of my head.

"You'll have to wait and see." He takes my hand. "Ready?"

"Yes, I just need to grab my purse."

"You don't need it," he says before tugging my hand and whisking me into the back of a waiting SUV. Once we're in, the driver takes off without a word.

"What's going on? Where are we going?"

He strokes my wrist with his thumb putting me at ease but doesn't answer.

"Can you at least tell me if I'm dressed okay?" I didn't get a chance to pack well with our time crunch. He leans in and kisses me silent, and I let him. Within the hour we're stopped, the darkness outside making it impossible to see where we are through the thick tint of the windows.

Lucas gets out with the bag and leans in on the frame of the door.

"Hold on a second."

"Okay."

He shuts it, and the driver joins him. They exchange words at the back of the car where the trunk is lifted briefly and then closed. Lucas opens my door with a thick comforter in hand, one that matches the type at our hotel, and ushers me out the SUV. When I see what waits outside, my jaw drops. He's standing in front of the pyramids shadowed by the full moon. "Oh, my God. Lucas, oh my GOD!" Lucas seems satisfied with my reaction, a dazzling smile lighting up his face. "It's pretty incredible, right?"

"I can't believe this."

"How about we taste some wine here?"

I'm already nodding. "Yes, please."

We are parked directly in front of the Sphinx, and I see the towering Giza pyramid ahead, the smaller of the two pyramids to the left of it. The driver speaks briefly with a few waiting guards, and then we're led to an easy access entrance before we're set free to explore for ourselves. The view is indescribable. It's like walking through a screen saver. We stroll along the rough terrain for a few minutes until we're lined up with the marvels that point heaven's way.

"This is incredible." I look at him thoroughly impressed. *"You bring me to one of the Seven Wonders of the World? You've outdone yourself already, Hollywood,"* I say jokingly. *"It's all downhill from here."*

"We got lucky with that moon, or else we wouldn't have been able to see shit."

"You planned this?"

He grins at me. *"Always have a plan, but this one was tricky."* He spreads the comforter, which looks ridiculous on the sand, situates the cooler and then himself on it before he pulls me down into his lap. Snugly between his legs, he rests his chin on my shoulder, and I rest my hands on his thighs.

"Are you having fun?" he asks softly.

"God, yes, this has been so incredible. Thank you."

"Don't thank me," he whispers, *"too impersonal. And I fucking hate that you're leaving tomorrow."*

"Me too."

"So stay," he urges, pulling me tighter into him.

"You know I can't. This is your life, not mine."

We sit for a few quiet moments equally in awe of our surroundings. The smooth rumble of his voice sounds from behind me, but it feels so far away.

"I never thought I would see this," he says softly. *"Never. This is not something I ever thought I'd experience in my lifetime."*

"Me neither."

The air around us is as ancient as the free-standing structures, and the silence is surprisingly peaceful.

Lucas speaks up on a whisper. *"They're smaller than I thought they would be."*

"Does that ruin it for you?"

"No," he says. *"It just goes to show what builds in the mind and surfaces in reality can be so different."*

Unsure if we're still talking about pyramids, I glance his way *and see him mystified which stuns me silent. Lucas isn't at all what I expected. He's not accustomed to the life he's leading, he doesn't demand anything from anyone. He's full of hope and just as in awe of this new world as I am. He's humble, appreciative, highly affectionate, giving, and there's not much more I need to know.*

A few minutes later, I'm still admiring the view when Lucas gently shifts me from his lap and starts fishing around in the cooler. As he unpacks, he unveils a small feast and a little lamp which illuminates our blanket.

"Wow, you really did think of everything."

He takes a forkful of a dish with the provided silverware and brings it up to my mouth.

"The chef said these are the things we have to try while we're here. He said this one you'll love or hate."

"That must be Molokhia." *He lowers the fork he just offered to me and reads the scribbled label on top of the container.* "How in the hell did you know that?"

I shrug. "I picked it up somewhere."

"Just picked it up," *he says, his voice full of sarcasm as he lifts the fork and I take a bite.*

"This is one of the last places on my bucket list," *I say around a mouthful,* "I studied up on Egypt years ago. But I'll have to have another bite to decide about the food."

He grins, forking another bite. "Of course you will."

He gives me another mouthful before taking one of his own.

"Did you know Egyptians invented the three hundred sixty-five-day calendar?"

He shakes his head slowly as he feeds me another forkful.

"We have them to thank for the year mark, the measurement of life. They invented time. Such fascinating and intelligent people."

"Yeah," *he mumbles, closing the container putting it back in the bag.*

"I think I love it," I say, "the Molokhia. Oh," I exclaim grabbing the next container, "I bet this is Shawarma." I read the label. "Yep, it is. This is like Egypt's version of a Gyro. These are supposed to be fantastic."

Lucas eyes me as he uncorks a bottle.

"And did you know wine was scarce here until the last twenty years?"

"Nope, didn't know that either," he says with a sigh. "Why is that?"

"Look around, not exactly the best place to grow vines."

"Right," he mutters, pouring me a glass.

"They brought some experts in to help the quality. I'm so excited to try it."

He looks a little miffed as he hands it to me. "Then maybe you should try it."

I sit up straighter and frown. "Did I say something wrong?"

His eyes dart away. I can see his aggravated expression clearly when he lies and responds with a, "No."

"Hey," I say leaning in. "What have I said?"

"Nothing, beauty," he lifts his chin toward my glass. "Taste it."

I take a sip and give him wide eyes. "Pretty good."

His eyes glide over the shadowed peaks while more sarcasm laces his words. "And is that your expert opinion?"

"All right, dammit, that was uncalled for," I snap. "Tell me, superstar, did you bring me out here and give me the world just to shit on it?"

His eyes snap to mine. He reads my face and curses under his breath. "No, shit, no. I'm sorry."

"Then come out with it already. What happened in the last five minutes that made me the enemy?"

"You haven't done anything."

"Could've fooled me. Maybe we should head back to the hotel."

He lets out a sigh and sits back on the blanket. In the next second,

I'm back in his lap, and his head is again buried in the crook of my neck. He presses a gentle kiss to my shoulder before murmuring a low, "Sorry."

"Forgiven," I reply shifting in his lap to straddle him. "Now tell me why you're acting like an ass."

"Just...tired."

"We can go back," I offer running my fingers through the hair at the back of his neck. "You can get some decent sleep tonight."

"No, I'm good here."

"You sure?"

He nods.

Chest rattling with indecision, I move to give him space just as he cups my neck and brings me closer, so our foreheads touch.

"Mila," he rasps out just before capturing my lips to assault me with a soul-stealing kiss. His tongue delves into every corner of my mouth before setting a languid pace. Breath stolen, I moan into his eager mouth as he erases the existence of time, the idea of space, and the need to measure either. There is nothing but us, our connection, our creation. Stunned when he pulls away my breath stutters against his lips and I realize we're both shaking with the loss of gravity.

Pushing the hair away from my face with gentle hands, he searches my eyes and finds satisfaction somewhere inside them. "I'm going to tell you something, and I want you to believe me."

"I'll try."

"There is nowhere and no one else I'd rather be with than you. I promise you. This isn't the end of us."

"If you say so, Hollywood."

"Just got to have a little faith, Dame."

"Dame?"

"My Dame," he whispers before crushing his mouth to mine.

The first week I get back we've spoken every day, making plans for after the movie wraps. Some days he can only talk for mere minutes, but I greedily take them. Other days I miss his call due to the seven-hour time difference. Even with my phone set to blast, I sleep through a few. It's like an out of control first crush all over again.

"Mila, I've been dreaming about you," he says when I manage to catch a call.

"Have you?"

"Yes. I miss you." He says it so effortlessly it scares me, but I allow it because it feels amazing too. The kind of amazing that has me daydreaming about possibilities.

"It's so hot here. I don't remember it being this hot when you were here."

"It was."

"Maybe you made it more bearable. I just had a camel slap me upside the head with half a bucket of spit. I threw up for twenty minutes."

Uncontrollable laughter pours out of me as he goes on.

"I should warn you now, I have a horrible, and I mean horrible, track record with animals."

"All animals?"

"Yes, goldfish included. Blake says it's because they can sense evil. But I think that applies to kids."

"It applies to both kids and animals."

"Of course, you'd know that," he smarts. "Kids are okay, but I'm afraid it's a hard no on pets."

"Are we having kids already?"

"Whatever we want it to be," he murmurs.

"Right. Cart before the camel, Lucas."

"Hey, I'm not proposing."

"Good, I'm not accepting."

"Marry me." I can hear his smile over the line.

"Hell, no."

"Smart lady. Wait until I start earning the real paychecks."

"I'd take your paycheck over mine any day, Walker."

His reply is instant. "Do you need money?"

"Jesus, did you really just ask me that? No, of course not."

There's a long pause over the line. "I didn't...I didn't mean it the way it came out, not to insult you. Not at all." Not for one second do I think he meant it that way. "I just want you to be okay. That's all."

"I'm fine. But honestly, Lucas, I could never take a dime from you. That's not how I'm built."

"Okay, I just want you to be good."

"I'm more than good."

"Happy?"

"Yes."

"God, lady, as mean as you are, you move me."

I can't even pretend not to be caught up in the sincerity in his voice. "The feeling is mutual, I assure you."

Another pause.

"I really feel good about this," he whispers.

"Me too."

"Shit's the same on set, so tell me what's going on with you."

"Just working hard. Trying to reel in some clients."

"You'll get there."

"Thanks for the vote of confidence, but have you drunk any wine lately?"

His answering silence has me laughing.

"Oh my God, do I really want to give my heart to a guy who hates my passion?" I say it with a laugh but get silence in response.

Shit. Shit. Shit.

I pull the phone away from my ear and see we're still connected. "Lucas, are you there?"

"Yeah, I'm here, Dame."

"The more you call me that, the more I like it."

"Well, it's all yours. They're calling me to set, baby." My heart explodes with his sentiment. "I'll call you soon."

"Okay...and Lucas?"

"Yes?"

"I really do miss you."

"It's weird, isn't it? Two weeks ago, we had no idea what we were missing."

And then he's gone. Right after we hang up, I get a knock on my door. I answer to see an older man looking at me while he slides on dirt-covered gloves.

"You must be Mila."

"Yes?" I reply cautiously.

"I'm Denny."

"Hi, Denny."

"I'm sorry to bother you, but I just wanted to get an idea from you of where you want them."

"Where I want what?"

Denny draws on my confusion. "Ah, this must be a surprise. Well, that makes things difficult." He shakes his head. "Leave it to Lucas."

"I'm sorry, but I'm totally lost here."

"Lucas sent me."

"O-kay," I say, still not catching on.

"It's probably best if you come out and look."

I follow him outside and see a large utility truck parked to the right of my porch. A few guys are sitting in wait on the back of the bed. It's only when I round the hood and see what's in it, that my jaw goes slack.

Denny looks at me with a rueful grin as do the guys. "Thought this might help you figure it out."

"All of these are for me?"

Dozens of rose bushes are lined up in the bed, in various shades of red, pink, orange, the majority of them lavender, which is my favorite color and the color of the dress I wore on our first date. Lucas misses nothing.

Denny shakes his head and looks over to me with a drawn brow. "Guess sending roses was a little too traditional?"

"No," I whisper as emotion swells in my chest and my eyes water, choking a little on my reply, "too temporary."

CHAPTER 20

MILA

SEVEN WEEKS OF WAIT HAVE TURNED INTO TEN. THEN TEN BECOMES twelve. And it has been days since I've heard from him. Four to be exact. Filming has gone over; over time, over budget and suddenly they are having issues with shooting permits a week before the film wraps. So basically, Lucas is being held hostage in Cairo until they can sort it all out. The first eight weeks he'd been diligent about calling me at least once a day, but as of late, it has dwindled. Understanding is wearing thin when we have modern technology. A text would do, any text.

Sitting in the middle of my newly planted rose garden on the cliffside of the house, I sip on a bottle of red and try my best not to be offended by his silence. The movie has taken a shit turn as far as production, and he is probably trying to help sort things out. Not to mention the fact he has to be exhausted. It's the next sip of my wine that has me switching positions.

"Or he's decided having a maybe girlfriend half a world away isn't worth the trouble," I mutter to the rose bushes he gave me to remember him by. Maybe the situation has lost its charm for him, and he is too much of a coward to make good on his promises. Either way, I am fading on breadcrumbs which has now left me at a dead end.

"Fuck this," I say, heading into my house picturing him seducing some on-set Egyptian goddess with the same smile he gave me.

"I LIVE FOR NO MAN!" I declare as I stomp toward my door, empty wine bottle in hand. I've been nothing short of patient, and I don't deserve silence. I shoot off a text just before I hit the door and head into my house.

It was fun. Take care of yourself.

Just to be a spiteful shit, I add.

Thank you.

He doesn't like being thanked, says it's too impersonal.

Thank you so much, Hollywood!

It's then my wine buzz kicks into overdrive. After a scalding shower, I wipe the condensation from my mirror and drunkenly scold myself.

"You stupid woman, he's a movie star. He doesn't want to play house with you." *Ripping through my closet, I attempt to find something that may give me a little pride back. Picking the most form-fitting dress I own and fuck-me heels, I throw my shoulders back resigned to move on quickly. It's the only way.* "Make it painless. Rip off the band-aid," *I spur myself on, denying the dart of my eyes to check my phone to see if he responded over the last hour and a half I spent getting ready. Lips trembling, I paint my face carefully.* "Who marries a movie star? Like what in the hell were you thinking?"

I crumble as I remember the way he lingered after kissing me. I loved that. "Dammit! I knew it!" *I say, gripping the edge of the sink and glaring at myself.* "You will never, ever tell your mother about this."

I need friends. I make it a point to get out more, starting right now. I have no one to call. No one to tell me what to do when a movie star ghosts you.

"Shit, he did. He ghosted me." *I check my phone one last time and decide to let in the ache. I've purposefully prolonged leaving the house for three hours in case I was overreacting and to marginally sober up.*

Certain he's seen my *fuck off* texts, I power down my phone and head toward the door determined to gain some gravity back. Dating a movie star has fucked with my head.

Opening my front door, I stop short when I see a breathless Nova coming toward me full speed with a phone to her ear. Taken aback by the expression on her face, I meet her halfway on the porch. Fear paralyzes me when I realize I might have been thinking along the wrong lines. A thousand scenarios cross my mind as I began to sink with dread.

"Thank God you're home," she says, stopping a few feet away from me.

I go to speak when she lifts her finger. "Yeah, I've got her. She looks pretty smoking," Nova says with a smile which has some of the fear lifting.

"Is that Lucas? He's okay?" I ask hoarsely. I'm a basket case of emotion, the last few hours alone with my mind, wine, and pride have proved to be a lethal combination. I'm on the verge of tears as Nova eyes me and sees the battle scars which make up my expression.

"She's decked out. What? Oh, sure."

She lifts her phone and takes a photo.

"Hey!" I bark.

"On its way. She looks pretty pissed off, boss. Yeah, well everyone needs time off. Okay, chill out. Here she is."

She holds out her cell phone to me. "Told you he likes you."

Taking it, I raise it to my ear. "Hello?"

"Fuck, baby, I'm so sorry. I lost my phone on set, and I didn't have your number! I've been going out of my fucking mind trying to get in touch with Nova. I forgot she took a few vacation days."

As the truth sinks in, I realize I'm certifiable.

My voice is barely a whisper. "You lost it?"

"Yeah. Someone tried to reach you at your house yesterday, but you weren't home."

"*Oh,*" I say, utterly perplexed. *Nova eyes me as I try to mask a relieved tear that falls.*

"*Where were you going?*"

Thrown by his question, I realize I have no idea. "*What?*"

"*Nova said you were dressed to kill. Where were you going?*"

"*I was…*" *I trail off knowing the truth is ridiculous. What was I supposed to say? That I was trying to gain some semblance of life after being wooed and dumped by Lucas Walker? That I had talked myself into trying to forget him?*

"*I thought…*" *I walk off to give myself some privacy from Nova's prying eyes,* "*well, I thought maybe—*"

"*Never mind, the picture just came through.*" *His disappointment bleeds through the line.* "*You look beautiful.*" *His tone turns to ice.* "*Who for?*"

"*Sorry?*" *I ask as the blood drains from my face.*

"*Who are you dressed like that for?*"

"*For?*" *I'm stuttering out, terrified at what he must think and the fact that I might have ruined it by thinking the same way.*

"*For me,*" *I say truthfully.* "*I wanted to feel better because I thought—*"

"*You thought wrong,*" *he cuts me off sharply.* "*Don't even think about doing what you were about to do.*" *His voice lacks warmth, ringing through detached which only makes it worse.*

It's then I let some of my weakness show. "*I suck at this. I don't know what I was doing.*"

"*You aren't meeting anyone?*"

"*No,*" *I sigh,* "*I was trying to talk myself into it.*"

He lets out a long breath.

"*I know it seems like a lot to ask, and it is. But I want us to happen. And if you do too, we can't second-guess each other like this.*"

Hating how much I've already let myself care, I nod in agreement.

"Mila. You there?"

"Yes, yes, Lucas, yes. I just…I didn't hear from you and I started thinking—"

"Too much. Too fucking much. You can't do that. I miss you, still. Don't forget a second of what we have. I sure as hell haven't."

That was the problem. I couldn't forget any of it, drunk, sober, or sedated wearing a second-skin dress or a robe and rollers. "I better not regret this."

"I'm gonna get the girl," he says in an aggravated whisper, "even if she's trying to give me a fucking heart attack."

I sniff through my laugh and nod because exhaustion and a headache have set in.

"Mila," he whispers.

"Yeah?"

"I hate Egypt without you."

CHAPTER 21

MILA

MY PHONE RANG EXACTLY THREE DAYS AFTER LUCAS'S CALL, AND *I* answer eagerly, with renewed faith.

"Hi," I say, sipping a new red. "How did it go today?"

"I'm exhausted. What are you doing?"

"Cooking dinner."

"What's on the menu?"

"Chicken Marsala? It's my specialty. Do you like pasta?"

"Love it. Sounds amazing."

"I'll cook it for you when you get home."

"And then?"

"And then what? You want the whole night laid out?"

"Why not?"

Grinning I pour more wine. "Okay, well if we're doing a date my way, we'll take dessert out into my rose garden."

"Okay."

"And then, I'll give you a massage."

"Please God, no," he rasps out.

"Shut up, Walker. And then we'll sleep."

"That's it?" he prods. "Sounds pretty anti-climactic."

"Oh, yeah, that massage is actually a blow job. Another specialty."

"Mila," he growls.

"Hey, I tried to keep it PG."

"Don't hold back." His voice is thick, and I'm sure we're about to initiate another phone session.

"Okay," I say, taking another sip of wine and lowering the

temperature of my sauce. "I'm buzzed, so this could get detailed."

"Let's get detailed."

I hear the crunch of rocks in my drive and look to see incoming headlights out of my kitchen window. "Crap, I think my mom just pulled up."

"Ignore her and talk dirty to me."

"Lucas," I scold with a laugh. "I have to go."

"Okay, but make sure you keep those details close."

"Promise. Get some sleep, you must be exhausted."

It's then that I see his Land Rover come into view and hear the playful lift to his voice. "Jet-lagged for sure."

"Lucas!" I scream, dropping the phone and throwing open my front door. I'm already sprinting toward him as he hops out of his SUV and opens for me just as I crash into him. Inhaling him, I hold him tight to me, and he keeps me there. "Oh, God, you just made the drive worth it. Double vision is a bitch, for a minute there I thought I was going to steer right off a fucking cliff."

I'm kissing every inch of his face as he speaks, his chin, his nose, his jaw before I pull back to catch his megawatt smile.

"Why didn't you tell me?"

"Isn't this better?" he says, reading the elation in my expression that I'm doing nothing to hide.

"Everything is better."

"Give me those fucking lips." His kiss is both foreign and familiar and in minutes we're back into a rhythm, tongues dancing furiously as he carries me into the house.

"Wait!" I say when he gets me halfway down the hall. "Go back to the kitchen."

He frowns. "Not exactly comfortable."

"I have to turn off the sauce." Still in his tight grip, he carries me to the kitchen and sets me down in front of the stove. I'm stirring the sauce and killing the burners when he moves my hair to the side to *nibble at the skin of my neck. "Are you hungry?"*

"Starving, but that's priority number two." He turns me to face him and takes my lips with surety and possession. "I need inside you right now."

An orgasm later, we're eating lukewarm pasta in our underwear while I'm tracing his every feature with my eyes as he sucks the sauce-coated noodles into his mouth. Resting against my headboard while he dines, I'm finally able to drink him in. His tan is much darker, and he's weary-eyed, but the rest of him looks incredible.

"I can't believe you're here."

"I can't believe how good this is," he says, taking the half-full bowl of pasta I'd set on my nightstand and digging in. "You said this was Chicken Marsala?"

"Yes. And I made fudge cake. My comfort foods."

His eyes lift to mine. "Comfort food, huh?"

"Yes, I've been a little lonely. I mean, of course. Work and home, just very routine, well it didn't seem routine…" I trail off because I've said too much.

"And you were going to throw us away," he says, his tone laced with contempt.

"I don't know what I was about to do, but I was hurt, okay?"

"Not okay," he says, shoving in more noodles and cleaning up the sauce on his jaw with his hand. "What hurts is that you would think the worst about me."

"You don't know what I was thinking."

He sets the bowl down and brings ice green eyes to mine. "Let me see if I can take a guess. You were thinking, movie star, he's probably found someone to fuck on set."

Guilty, my eyes drop.

"Let's analyze this and then table it because I've been trying pretty damn hard from the onset to make myself clear. I want to build something with you. And I can't do it alone. I'm not a movie star, I'm

an actor. And I love my job, but it's my job. I want the same things as everyone else, a place to call home, reciprocal love. I'm not at the place of party and pussy anymore."

"Geesh, okay," I say, gathering our dishes. "We haven't been dating that long."

"Three months," he says pointedly, grabbing my wrist. "Longer, really. All of that time apart counts. Those phone calls count. It's a part of it. This time apart was a test we passed, no thanks to you."

"I wasn't going to—"

"You were a woman who thought she'd been scorned which made you unpredictable. You have no idea what you would have done."

I sit at the edge of the bed next to his muscled thigh and look over to where he rests against my headboard. "This is hard, Lucas."

"Just as hard for me," he says unwavering. "All relationships are hard. Right?"

"Right."

"Just try to have a little more faith in me, in us, and trust." He leans over and sucks my nipple into his mouth tugging the taut skin softly with his teeth. And then his hands, his perfect hands are on my skin, and I'm underneath him. Hovering above me as I lay panting, he doesn't move just stares down at me expectantly.

"Okay. I'm sorry. You're right."

"Good, because I propose you agree to a few more things," he murmurs before turning me into a puddle of agreement beneath him.

"Hit 'em, knock 'em over—with an attitude, with a word, with a look."—Marlon Brando

CHAPTER 22

LUCAS
Two and half months ago

"H EY, *BOSS*," NOVA CALLS OUT TO ME WHERE I SIT IN A director's chair on set. "We're about forty in of forty-five." I nod in acknowledgment, and she leaves me to prep. Satisfied with what I've rehearsed, I let my eyes drift from the script to the clouds above trying to blink away the fatigue. I refuse to let it slow me down. Body aching from lack of sleep, I stretch my neck and arms as exhaustion threatens to set in. Batting away my needs, I think of Maddie, of the way she worked me constantly to rid me of all selfish thoughts while she prepped me. Though she mercilessly drilled into me that the emotions of my characters mattered most, Maddie had her own points of weakness. In all our years together, I can only think of one time that she begrudgingly revealed them to me.

I take the cracked cement steps to her trailer and knock twice before I open the door.

"Maddie," I call softly before I close it behind me. Sunlight streams through the window past the sheet in the empty living room. I never take my shoes off at home, but I do at Maddie's because she keeps her carpets clean. Sliding them off, I call her name again.

"Go home, boy," she orders from her bedroom. "We aren't running lines today."

Too excited to mind her, I run to her bedroom. "I brought you something."

"*Lucas,*" *she scolds when I reach the threshold and see her lifting to sit in her robe. She doesn't have any makeup on, and there's an empty bottle next to her nightstand.*

"*You aren't supposed to drink, it will dry out your skin.*"

"*Do as I say, not as I do,*" *she says, gathering tissues and tossing them in the seashell covered wastebasket next to her.* "*I'm tired, boy, run on home. We can run lines tomorrow.*"

"*It's okay, I just,*" *I approach the bed and hold out the drawing.* "*I made you something.*"

She straightens up further, and her eyes focus on the paper I have in hand. She takes it from me and studies it until her eyes start to spill.

"*I didn't want to make you cry,*" *I say, backing away.*

"*You drew this?*" *she asks, her voice chalky.* "*It's pretty good.*"

"*They told us to draw stars,*" *I say, thinking myself clever.* "*So, I drew us. My teacher got mad, but I don't care.*"

Maddie begins to cry again, and I cautiously approach the bed. "*If you feel bad, I can get you some medicine. I think we have some at home.*"

She shakes her head, sniffing and pulls a used tissue to her face to wipe her tears away. "*I'm not that kind of sick.*"

"*What's wrong?*"

She waves me away. "*I heard from my old agent today, just a little sting of rejection. It will pass.*"

"*You weren't right for the part,*" *I declare because that's what she taught me.* "*Or the part wasn't right for you.*"

"*There are no parts left for me, Lucas,*" *she sighs.*

"*It's just not your time, you have to keep your head up. I'll get you some juice.*" *I race to the kitchen and grab her favorite glass from the sink, rinse it out and fill it up with carrot juice. Back in the bedroom, I thrust it at her, spilling a little on her comforter and wincing when she sees it.*

She cracks a smile and shakes her head. "*I've created a monster.*"

"You know it, Dame," I say, chucking her chin.

Laughter erupts from her as she sets the juice down and motions for me to come closer. "You know better than to toss that word around."

"Yes, ma'am."

"Come closer, Lucas. Let me look at you."

Swallowing, I take a step forward as she scrutinizes me. "Wow, look at you. You're getting so big. Hopefully, you grow into that nose."

"I'm eleven tomorrow."

She waves a dismissive hand. "And then you're sixteen and then you're fifty-six. Do yourself a favor and remember that."

Unsure of what she means, I just nod. "Okay."

"Hit them hard, or they'll forget about you before the tape runs out," she says on a shaky voice just as another tear falls. Climbing up into the bed next to her, I throw my arm around her like my favorite character Terrance does in The Sky's Limit.

"I won't forget about you, Maddie. I promise."

Pushing from my chair, I roll the script in my hand and walk toward my mark.

This one is for you, Maddie.

CHAPTER 23

MILA

HUMMING TO THE RADIO, I DRIVE DOWN THE STRETCH OF ROAD leading to our beach house, hopes for the night floating around my head, a bag of supplies in my back seat. It's only when I'm close to home that I see endless rows of cars parked on either side of the street. "What in the hell?" I mumble after clicking my signal to see our driveway full. I manage to find a spot several houses down. Giving myself a little pep talk, I carry the bags that originally felt light in weight that now weigh heavy in my arms as I'm forced to haul them to the house. The sun beats down on my shoulders and music blares from all corners of our home as I approach. Opening our front door, I feel a thud and peek my head around. A man I've never seen greets me. "I think you might have the wrong house, miss. This is Lucas Walker's place."

"Is it?" I snap, balancing the bags on my leg and holding up my wedding ring. "Does this gain me entry?"

"That's Walker's wife, you idiot," another guy says, stepping toward me with a grin. "Sorry about him."

"And you are?"

"Lance, I'm one of the crew."

"Ah," I say as I attempt to shove through the warm bodies blocking the doorway, the bags getting heavier by the second. The smell of weed wafts into the living room from the kitchen terrace as I set the grocery bags down. A blonde in a bikini top and barely-there shorts raises my favorite wine glass and a bottle I'd been saving for a special occasion. "Would you like a glass? It's really good."

"Don't mind if I do," I say, snatching the bottle from her hand and hearing "bitch" muttered behind me. Taking the bag I'd waited weeks to pick up down the hall and into our bedroom, I toss it into our closet as I try to talk myself down from murder one to assault and battery. At least Lucas had made our bedroom off limits, and I was relieved to see there wasn't a soul in sight. Standing in my closet, I fume as I tip the wine back.

What in the hell, Lucas?

"Just a party. Maybe he has a plan. Don't freak. Be the cool wife. Don't kill him. Don't kill him." The longer I swig, the easier it is to try to relax. That is until I hear a loud roar come from the living room and glass shatter.

"Come on, really?" Sipping more wine, I count to a thousand before stepping out of our bedroom. Lucas loves this house and is typically highly protective of it rarely ever inviting anyone over, especially when he's working.

Rule two. Go with it and trust.

Swallowing more wine straight from the bottle, I look around the top floor for any sign of Lucas and come up empty. The music stops suddenly and is replaced by the unmistakable sound of an organ, drums, and a guitar. Don Henley's "Dirty Laundry" blares from every speaker.

It's then I hear the unmistakable voice of one of my favorite people in the world. "Stop your whining, if I'm going to tolerate this frat party, *I'm the deejay.* That's right, bow down, bow down to the King!"

Unable to stop my grin, I land at the stairs of the gym and see Stella on my elliptical with a bottle of tequila in hand.

"Crowne," Reid corrects from the porch. "That's bow down to the Crowne. That's what you meant to say right, wife?"

Stella's eyes bulge a little before she nods. "Of course."

"Thought so," Reid says, chuckling. He watches her with amusement while she picks up her pace on the machine. "Put that tequila down, babe. I'm not carrying you out of here."

"You *so will* carry me out of here, and you'll love it," she sasses back. "Besides it's Cinco De Mayo."

That's when Rye steps in. "Uh, Stella, aren't you the one who says every day you aren't from Mexico?"

She pauses her exercise and takes a sip from her bottle. "It's complicated." They both crack up, and I can see Lucas standing behind them on the porch. Reid and Rye spot me first with a wave I return, and Lucas sounds from behind them.

"There's the lady of the house." Lucas smiles at me, and it's genuine, and I'm utterly confused. Narrowing my eyes, I move to go to him when Stella spots me and stops me in my tracks.

"Mila, thank God. If I had to be here one more hour surrounded by this cock fest, I was gonna puke." Delaying the inevitable fight with my husband, I walk over to where she's working the machine. Stella is a force of nature, half Latina and stunning in appearance with dark hair, natural beauty and never-ending opinions that lengthen her smaller stature. She's a fireball to put it mildly and one of the few women I respect.

I met Stella on the set of *Drive*, where Lucas played the lead guitarist, Rye. Though Stella is a music journalist, she decided to write a memoir of her journey with the band and her relationship with her husband shortly after her wedding. When she submitted the script, it ended up in a bidding war between two major studios. With the ball in her court, she'd made it a stipulation to oversee both casting and production along with her husband's band, The Dead Sergeants, who wrote some of the music for the soundtrack. The Dead Sergeants were globally known, and the movie made a killing at the box office. Rye had personally charged himself to train Lucas on the guitar, and he'd done a fantastic job, but Stella was the one to suggest Lucas for the role.

It's all I can do to keep from laughing as she waves me over to her.

"What in the hell are you doing?"

"Cardio and a buzz, it's the same as dancing. Looks like I'm not the only one with a bottle in hand."

"True," I say with a grin. It's damn near impossible to be pissed around Stella. She's my only consolation for what the day has turned into.

She steps off the elliptical, and we toast, drink, and then hug.

"What are you doing here?"

She narrows her eyes at me. "If you would have called me back yesterday, you would know."

"Sorry," I say. "I've been busy."

"Busy looking hot! You look good, girl," she says with a wink. "Maybe I should switch to wine."

"Not a bad idea," Reid's voice carries from the porch.

She raises her hand in his direction. "Hush, man, or no drunken sex for you and you know damn well I'm getting good at it."

I lift a brow at Reid, and his gaze is fixed on his wife as he slowly shakes his head.

"Keep it up," he warns before turning his back and continuing his conversation. Reid looks every bit the rock star he is and if I wasn't living the dream with one of my own, I would be jealous of their connection. Though I have to admit today, I'm feeling a small stab of it.

Stella keeps her eyes on me.

"Is he still looking at me?" she asks.

"No."

"I'm trying to be more assertive with his alpha before we procreate. Momming is no joke. I will not barter on certain issues."

"Looks like it's working," I say.

"Really?" she asks, hopeful.

"Absolutely not," I reply with a laugh.

She joins me. "Yeah, I didn't think so either."

"So, what brings you from Seattle?"

She takes the bottle from my hand and sips my wine. "Why music, of course. The boys have a concert tomorrow and we wanted to see you guys. I couldn't get a hold of you, but Reid managed to get Lucas."

"Funny," I snort. "I haven't managed to get Lucas today."

She stops my wine bottle halfway to her mouth. "I thought this party was odd. I didn't think Lucas got down like this."

"Lucas doesn't."

"Ah, yeah, he's a gangster now, right? I have to admit, I'm excited to see him bring it like that."

We both glance over at Lucas who looks gorgeous in jeans and a T-shirt. He's talking so casually and looks lighter on his feet today, like there's less weight on his shoulders. It's enough to curb my anger for the moment.

"So, I'm guessing this little impromptu party wasn't your idea?"

"Nope," I say, grabbing the bottle.

"Shit, woman, I'm sorry. If I were you, I would be dismembering people. How are you keeping calm?"

"Because fuck it," I say simply. "Go with the flow. At least for another couple of months."

"Your tortured artist strikes again, huh?"

"Looks to be that way."

"You know, Reid goes off the grid sometimes when he writes music. He doesn't talk for days, gets heavy and locks himself in the studio, doesn't eat. I'm not a fan of that shit, but in a way, I guess I understand it. Music takes me there sometimes. But I don't necessarily think you have to bleed to get the job done."

"It's the way he was taught," I say with a shrug.

"Yeah, well, what works, right?"

"Right," I nod.

"Come on, lady, we won't let this get you down. We'll go get drunk and then swim naked just to piss them off."

"I fucking dare you," Reid sounds from the porch. Lucas is standing right next to him, staring me down with an expression I can't read. I'm too upset to care.

"How long have you two been listening to our conversation?" Stella demands.

"For as long as you've been yelling it, Grenade," Reid answers with a smirk.

"My bad," she yells my way. Lucas's eyes are still on me as I raise my sundress over my head baring myself in a bra and panties.

"Clean up my kitchen, Walker," I snap, grabbing Stella's hand and making my way toward the door to brush past Lucas.

"See," Stella says, turning back to Reid when we get halfway across the deck, "she gets to swim naked."

"She's not naked," Reid mutters dryly.

"Fine, I'll keep my underwear on."

"Bra too," he snaps.

"Fine," she says, laughing as we make our way to the surf. We plant our asses on the sand and stare out at the ocean.

"It's so beautiful here," Stella says. "Maybe we should get

a place here too."

"You can just stay here. You know that. Anytime."

"No offense, babe," she says, discarding her T-shirt, "but if you can't tolerate a house party, we really aren't your style."

"I can."

Stella turns to face me her gaze inquisitive.

"You okay?"

"Trying to be."

"I was sorry to hear about Blake. I wish I would have gotten a chance to know him better. Is Lucas handling it okay?"

I nod over my shoulder toward the party. "I wish I knew."

She nudges my shoulder. "It's just a movie. He'll be back to his charming self in no time."

"It's not the party or the movie."

"Then what's wrong?"

I can't hide the hurt in my voice when I reply. "Today's our sixth wedding anniversary."

She immediately uncaps the tequila bottle and starts pouring some in the sand in front of us.

"What are you doing?"

"Pouring some out for my homie, Lucas. May he rest in peace."

Hours later I wake up confused when rough hands grip my hips and pull me toward the edge of our bed. Caught off guard and still mildly buzzed, I look up to see Lucas briefly before I'm flipped on my stomach and lifted on all fours. Any protest on the edge of my tongue comes out as a moan as his teeth sink into my neck. My panties are yanked down to my knees before rough fingers plunge into my sex and find me ready. Moaning,

I push back into them and hear how slick I am before I'm left empty. Wet fingers circle my neck, and I'm gripped from behind before I hear the hiss of his zipper. Anticipation pulses in my clit as my breath picks up. Seconds later, it's stolen when he buries himself in one unforgiving thrust...before he unleashes hell. He fucks me like a savage, taking his pleasure with no thought for mine. Skin slapping skin, he keeps me stationary, his hand tightening around my neck as he builds an animalistic pace.

No words are spoken, no kisses are exchanged. It doesn't matter, my body recognizes his and my need outweighs all moral thought. Relentless, he drives in, again and again, his stamina jarring as I try my best to balance on shaky arms. I take my own pleasure sliding my hand between my legs and bringing myself to orgasm just before he thrusts one last time and stills, filling me with a grunt. Collapsing on the bed, I turn in time to see him in the half-light of the bathroom before he closes the door. I use his discarded T-shirt to clean myself before curling back into bed with upturned lips. I'd either pushed a button earlier and pissed off my husband when I stripped in front of his friends, or I'd just been fucked by Nikki Rayo. Either way, I loved every minute of it. I'd taken pleasure out of his punishment and was already thirsty for more. Maybe it's wrong to tempt the devil he's creating, but it's the only hand I have.

"Okay, Nikki, let's play."

"There are four questions of value in life…What is sacred? Of what is the spirit made? What is worth living for, and what is worth dying for? The answer to each is the same. Only love."
— Johnny Depp in *Don Juan DeMarco*
Lord Byron

CHAPTER 24

MILA
Present

Hugging Audrey tightly, I thank her for saving me the past three days. I'd accepted her invitation for food the night she offered, and we got to talking. Once she learned I was a sommelier, my reality break took a different turn. She'd kept me busy from sunup to sundown each day and taught me everything she knew about growing vines. We laughed like girlfriends and worked ourselves ragged enough to the point I went to sleep at night without much issue.

"I can't thank you enough."

"Just promise to come back and see me."

"Oh, I will, don't you worry."

"Then that's thanks enough."

We share a smile as I open the door to the SUV and slide in. Sighing, I grip the wheel as she stands with her palm on the frame. "Now back to real life."

"Make it a good one."

"Right," I say with an uneasy nod. "I can do that."

"Yes, you can."

"In a way, I feel reborn."

"But the ache is still there, huh?"

"Yes."

"Growing pains," she assures, "good for all of us. Have a safe trip home."

"Home," I repeat. "Just have to figure out where that is."

"You know where it is, Mila."

Tears threaten, but I tamp them down. "I'm glad you have so much faith in me."

"Just a decision," she says confidently.

I nod, and she shuts the door with a wave. After a few back-road turns navigating out of the winery, I'm on my way. An hour into my drive, I find the strength to turn on the radio. I'm relieved when I scan the channels and don't hear any mention of Lucas. The sun beams heavily into the SUV, and the drive is peaceful. Stopping for gas, I keep my head low and fill up at the pump. I don't get spotted often but, I have an understanding of sorts with a few paparazzi. They know if I'm in the mood, I'll chat a little and smile for pictures, but if I'm not, they usually give me my breathing room. I'm relatively safe this far from LA, but with Lucas making so many headlines, it's anyone's guess, and I'm sure at this point, they're looking for me. My only saving grace is that none of them know about the cottage which is still titled to my parents and they'd have to dig deep to find it. Feeling stronger than I have in months, I finish gassing up, and slide into the driver's seat. It's only when I turn the ignition, and the song starts to play that I'm transported back.

Your well-hung man: The car will pick you up in thirty minutes.

I burst into laughter when I read his handle. The man is a bit intrusive when it comes to my personal property, but it never really bothers me. I gave him my password after four months of dating because he'd earned that trust and I didn't have anything to hide. He never demanded it, but I know somehow, he wanted that trust. He's been asking for it in small doses since we met and as of late, it's become second nature.

Okay.

Your well-hung man: Dress casual, but don't do your hair and makeup. I've got an appt for you.

Okay. Can't wait to see you.

Your well-hung man: Missed you, baby.

He'd been doing a lot of pre and postproduction work on his movies, and we'd barely had a day to ourselves the last few weeks. His next project is set to start in a month, and we are stealing every bit of time we can. I've been getting more and more jobs, and I know it has everything to do with him, though he fiercely denies it.

Racing to the shower after a day of pruning our rose bushes, I spend fifteen minutes getting the dirt out from beneath my fingernails before I survey my appearance in the mirror. I'm a little scratched up by the thorns, but I've gotten a good bit of sun. Sticking to his rules of no makeup, I take careful care to moisturize. It all feels so Pretty Woman. I hope there will be wardrobe too as I slip on a thin black long-sleeve top with a wide neck that I can easily slip off, dark jeans, and boots.

Satisfied with my appearance, I spritz on some clean-smelling perfume and gloss my lips just as the doorbell rings.

Grabbing my purse, I make it to the door on the second knock.

An older man with a British accent greets me.

"Good evening, Madam," he says cheerfully.

"Hello, there," I say, locking the door behind me. "Is Paul off tonight?"

"Yes, he's on vacation. I'm filling in."

"Can't imagine that grumpy ass sipping fruity drinks anywhere," I grumble behind him as he walks toward the limo and opens the door.

Paul is both Lucas's bodyguard and driver but has a zero-personality side effect. Once inside, I shoot off a text.

Heads up, Hollywood! I'll have you know I've just been kidnapped by a handsome older man with a very sexy accent.

Your well-hung man: Good. See you soon, beauty.

Will you give me a hint?

Your well-hung man: Nope.

How about a favor for favor exchange? I'll throw in some incentive. Your cock, my tongue.

Your well-hung man: Behave.

Fine. X

    A few minutes into the drive I decide to make polite conversation to disburse some of my nervous energy.
    "Have you been a driver long?"
    "No, just picked it up, actually. I'm retired and got bored."
    "Well, you'll love working for Lucas," I say, watching our route for any clue.
    "Will I?"
    "Yes."
    "Why's that?"
    "He's a good man."
    "Have you known him long?"
    "Not very, we've only been dating a few months."
    He eyes me in the rearview, turning left into the hills instead of

right toward the main road. "Do you act?"

"Me," *I nearly snort.* "God no, I would be horrible at it."

"Must be hard to date someone so scrutinized by the public."

"It's been wonderful," *I say softly.* "We haven't outed ourselves just yet, he, we…" *Just thinking about him makes me a grinning fool. I'm falling hard, and it's wonderful and terrifying, and I've had to stop myself a few times from letting the words spill.* "He's making it easy."

"You're happy then?"

"Very," *I bob my head.* "When you meet him, you'll know why."

"I look forward to it. Is he a good actor then?"

"You haven't seen his movies?"

"No, I'm afraid my wife and I watch a lot of old classics if we watch the telly at all."

"Oh, well, do yourself a favor and watch Takedown, it's my favorite."

"Will do."

"It's nice to have someone to talk to, his other driver is a bit of a mute. What's your name?"

"Sean."

"Lovely to meet you, Sean."

"Pleasure."

A few minutes later, we pull up to a well-lit ranch style home nestled in the hills and confusion sets in. "Oh, Lucas, what are you up to?"

Butterflies emerge and begin to circle in my chest as Sean offers his hand to escort me out of the limo.

"I hope to see you again."

"Me too," *I say, studying the house. Does he expect me to just knock on the door?*

"Problem, Miss?" *Sean asks, his hand still outstretched before I take it.* "I'm just kind of unsure what I'm doing here."

I'm still trying to figure out where I am and gain my footing out-side the limo when Sean's thumb slides across my wrist before he lets go. All the air leaves me as I turn my head and meet Sean's eyes, his light green eyes.

"What the fuc—Oh, my God, Lucas?!"

"Hey there, Dame," he says, his wrinkled mouth pulling up into *a satisfied smile.*

My jaw drops as I try to grasp what just happened.

Pleased with himself, he slides his hands in his slacks. "So, Takedown, huh? That's your favorite? Good to know."

I'm too stunned to say anything as I study his face. Tentatively, I reach out a hand and run it along his jaw, snatching it back when I touch the latex. "It looks so real."

He quirks his thick, bushy gray brows and chuckles. "That's kind of the point."

"I can't even be mad right now. That was…" *I narrow my eyes.* "You were fishing big time."

His grin grows. "Maybe."

Still reeling with the aftershock, I shake my head. "You got me good."

"Seems like it," *he says, milking my gushing to 'Sean.'*

"You're an ass. If you want to know how I feel about you, just ask."

"This was a lot more fun."

"You want to tell me the point of this grand scheme?"

"After."

"After what?"

"Enough with the questions." *He tugs at my hand closing the car door behind me.* "Come on."

"You're infuriating."

"An infuriatingly good man," *he says, tossing my words back at me with a smirk.*

"That too."

He pauses on the bottom step at the base of the porch and looks down at me. The air shifts as awareness pricks my spine and my pulse spikes. As different as he looks, I would know those eyes anywhere and they soften as they scour my face with curiosity.

"You are… a very good man," I confess readily.

He pulls me tightly to him, bending at my level to wrap me fully and we linger in the embrace before he whispers, "I'm your man, Dame."

Somehow, I know in that moment, we are official. No more words need to be spoken, and they aren't as he guides me into the house.

An hour and a half later, Bert and Noni, an Oscar-winning team of professional makeup artists, turn me in my chair to face my reflection and I shriek out in surprise before bursting into laughter. Lucas walks up behind me looking satisfied. He studies me closely while chuckling. "Wow."

Leaning toward the mirror, I study my aged face and the newly attached wrinkled skin hanging a half inch from my throat. Extensions of light gray are woven expertly into my dark hair. The difference is realistic and somewhat disheartening.

"Remind me to moisturize later," I tell Lucas as I study the middle-aged me.

"You're still so beautiful," he murmurs, planting a kiss on my cheek.

Noni smiles at my reflection. "I agree." Bert walks up with a bag of supplies to help safely get the adhesive off later. Lucas thanks him and I hug them both with my own gratitude as we make our way onto the porch where I spot Paul waiting next to the limo.

"Your movement is too agile to be convincing," Lucas notes as I bound out of the house.

"Is it?"

He nods, and I still can't get over the change in both our faces.

"So, does this mean I get to act tonight?"

"Yes, Miss," he says with his British tongue.

"Okay, well then teach me, Obie Wan."

"Try to move like you just woke up from a deep sleep, like you're stiff with sore muscles and you can't quite get the kinks out."

"Like this?" I say, walking across the porch with stilted movement.

"Better," he says with a smile.

"How about this?" I say, holding onto the railing of the steps with both hands and taking one at a time.

The rumble of his chuckle sounds behind me. "Maybe if you're ninety."

"Fine," I huff.

"Just slow down a little, you'll be good." He joins me on the steps and we slowly descend while I try and mimic his movement.

"So, where are we going?"

"Still a surprise."

"Come on, this is making me nervous."

"I promise you'll be fine." He links our fingers. "Trust me?"

"Yes."

When we get to the limo, Paul pulls something from his pocket and hands it to Lucas. "Thanks, man."

I glance over to see it's his phone.

"What?!" Shocked, I look up to see a smirk on Paul's face and feel my cheeks heat. I didn't think to ask how he had texted me back, and I'd propositioned him with sexual favors.

Reading my shock, Lucas looks down at the phone and swipes it to read our conversation before a laugh bursts out of him.

"Thanks for keeping it PG," Lucas says, nudging his shoulder.

"No problem," Paul mutters low, unable to hide his smile.

"I hate you both," I declare, sliding into the limo, my face on fire.

Lucas slides in next to me, and I immediately start slapping at his chest. "You dick!"

His laughter rumbles throughout the limo as he tries to dodge my playful fists.

"Sorry, I had to make sure you didn't catch on. I didn't expect sexual propositions."

"You prepped him well enough to call me beauty?"

"It worked," he says, pulling me against his chest.

"You thought of everything," I say, thoroughly impressed.

"Always have a plan," he says, lifting his finger to his temple.

"Well, don't expect your cock and my tongue tonight."

His chest bounces against my back. "Not my fault you're a pervert."

"Yeah, well you're a little old for me."

"Not anymore."

"That's right." I pat my face in wonder. "I forgot I look like I eat prunes for breakfast." It hits me then just how hard it might be for him to feel like himself in a different skin, portraying someone else.

"I think I understand how complex your job is now."

"Do you?"

"Yeah, I think I get it. I mean you transform with or without makeup, but I can't seem to be anyone but me right now, if that makes sense."

His arms tighten around me. "It does."

"This is…" I laugh nervously, "this is fantastic, whatever you have planned, I think you should know I'm having an awesome time already."

He turns me to face him, the warmth in his eyes stunning me silent before he cups my face and his lips descend, his thick brows tickling my forehead.

It's a strange sensation, and I have to fight a smile when his lips prompt me for more. We try to dive to connect but break apart when *a laugh bursts out of me and I'm met with his old man frown.*

"Sorry, that was a little weird."

"Yeah, this is definitely only for tonight," he says, slightly aggravated.

"But oh, what a night it is already," I say with a smile. He turns my hand over in his lap running his fingers from my palm to my wrist. His tender touch prompts my question. "You still think you can get the girl, Hollywood?"

"I'll never stop trying," he replies before we manage another kiss, one that goes far deeper.

We're dropped a few blocks from our stop and get nothing but disappointed looks from expectant faces waiting to see who's emerging from the limo. It's all I can do to keep from laughing when Lucas grips my hand. "Wow. They have no clue."

He picks up the pace with me in tow.

"Hey, we're supposed to be old."

"We need to make up a little time."

"Want to let me in on the secret now?"

"We're almost there," he assures me. "Just follow my lead."

We start to approach the theater, and Lucas slows his walk to a leisurely pace, so I follow suit.

"We're going to the movies?"

He stays silent and squeezes my hand. I zip it. Within seconds of entering the ticket line, we're approached by a man with a clipboard.

"Hey, there folks, how are we doing tonight?"

Lucas responds in his new native tongue.

"Good evening. We're well, thank you."

"I'm sorry to interrupt you folks, but I was wondering if you'd be interested in a special screening we have tonight."

Lucas plays his part. *"What movie?"*

"Not at liberty to say, but it's coming out in the next year, and I think you and your wife may enjoy it. Once you sign this release, I'll be able to give you more details."

Lucas turns to me brows raised as if it all depends on my answer and I take my cue and nod.

"Great," the guy says, handing us a waiver to fill out when we step out of line. *"Just take this to the man over there when you're done, and he'll get you where you need to be.*

I stand idly by as Lucas fills out the form.

"Gladys? Really?"

"Shut up, Dame," he says in a whistle through his teeth.

"Sorry. But your name better damn well be as...wait," I say in a heated whisper reading as he writes, *"you get to be Sean McConnery?"*

He chuckles as he walks us over to the usher and hands him the papers. "Welcome, Mr. and Mrs. McConnery."

A few minutes later we're guided into the theater and placed closer to the front due to my 'hearing' problem.

"Funny," I say, jabbing him in the ribs once we're seated. *"Not only do I get the worst of southern names but you make me hard of hearing as well."*

"You apparently are since you can't seem to follow direction and keep your mouth shut," he says, giving me the side-eye.

"Geesh, sorry, I'm just...excited."

"I know, baby," he says, kissing the back of my hand.

"So, will you tell me now?"

"It's our movie, Dame."

"What?" I say, sitting up in my seat turning to look at him. *"Cairo? You're kidding."*

"Shhh," he says. *"It's a test screen."*

"I figured that much, but surely the movie can't be ready?"

"It's not totally, you'll see."

"*This is so exciting!*"

He leans over and smashes his mouth to mine to shut me up, and my laughter bubbles between us. He pulls away, shaking his head.

"*Okay, I'm using my inside voice. So, this is how it works, they pull regular people off the street?*"

He nods. "*It's the best way to get a genuine reaction.*"

"*How did you know they would pick us?*"

"*We're the top of the food chain demographic wise. People our age don't go to movies that often. They want our input too.*"

"*That's smart. And you do this with every movie?*"

"*No, rarely ever. But I don't come to watch the movie,*" *he juts his chin toward the people seated.* "*I come to watch them.*"

"*Alone?*"

"*Not anymore,*" *he says, squeezing my hand.* "*As long as I bring a muzzle.*"

"*Har, har.*" *He's joking, but I can sense the slightly new strain in his posture.* "*Has it ever been bad?*"

"*Yes.*" *He looks over at me, and I see a small hint of distress in his eyes.* "*Could be bad tonight,*" *he shrugs,* "*but it wouldn't be my first disaster.*"

It takes guts to do this, to surround yourself by the public, to be judged for something you spent endless hours giving your everything to and he seems mostly okay with it. It's admirable. I open my mouth to tell him just that when a man with a mic walks to the middle of the front row to address the theater.

We amble out of the theater, Lucas taking long strides and practically dragging me with him.

"*Did you see their faces! That was amazing!*" *My heart pounds in time with my steps as he keeps us walking.*

"Lucas, you're jerking my arm out of the socket," I say as he keeps his stride. "That part where you imitated Bruce Willis with Yippee Ki Yay, was hilarious." My man is possessed by movement, and nothing I say seems to be reaching him. I barely managed to fill out the form with my feedback before he yanked me out of the theater.

"Hey," I order after another agonizing minute of silence. "Stop."

"We're almost to the limo," he says in a tone I can't decipher. Paul pops out of the driver's side just in time to get the door open before we climb inside. Lucas covers his face with his hands. I sit there, breath heaving, watching him have what looks like a panic attack. After seconds of indecision, he finally brings his eyes to meet mine.

"They were clapping, Lucas, that movie was amazing, and I don't even like action."

His grin lights up his face, and it's then I see it. He's happy.

Throwing myself in his arms, we embrace as he buries his head in my neck. "You scared me," I muffle into his neck as he holds me tightly to him. "Why did you run off like that?"

"Adrenaline," he answers on an exhale. "I had to get rid of some of it."

"So," I pull away. "You believe me?"

"You're biased, but I want to believe them."

I don't take offense. "Then believe them."

He grips me tighter as relief washes over him, the adrenaline leaving when he sags against me. He cares about his work, he truly cares about the work he's doing, and my respect grows.

"Let's get you a drink."

He pulls away, nodding, eyes full of light. "Night's not over, beauty."

"More surprises?"

A thousand-watt smile is part of my answer. "Let's not waste this anonymity."

Lucas escorts us toward the door entrance of *The Sayers Club* after texting Nova in the limo. *The doorman is obviously expecting us as he gives us a thorough once-over and grunts out an,* "Epic."

"Ready, Gladys?" *Lucas keeps his gaze forward to avoid my scowl. My neck is itching after our sprint to the car.*

Once inside, we're ushered by one of the bouncers through the crowd and seated at one of many cherry leather couches, ours close to an empty stage.

"Oh, think they'll have music?" *I ask as we take a seat. A waitress is already standing in wait for our order.*

"Hope so. We'll need to be as close as we can get with your hearing problem," *Lucas says, placing an order for a shot and a beer. I do the same and meet his confused eyes.*

"No wine tonight?"

"Gladys doesn't drink wine. She's a beer girl."

He gives me an amused grin, and the waitress takes off with our order. After a few minutes of visual crowd surfing, Lucas pulls me into his lap, and we get a few odd looks. Visually, we're the oldest people in the club, and I can't help myself when I press the button on my cell phone to check the time. "Oh, honey, it's ten fifty-five. You haven't taken your pill," *I lean in and waggle my eyebrows,* "you know the blue one."

He rubs his erection against my ass, and I mock a gasp.

"Oh, my, it's a miracle."

"I'll show you a miracle."

"This isn't appropriate, you know. We're not setting a good example for these kids."

"No, this is the perfect example to set," *he says, running his fingers under the back of my shirt and strumming them along my skin in a seductive caress.*

Drinks delivered we hold up our shots, and I propose the toast. "To you. Congrats."

"No, not to me. Sorry, I made one of our dates about a movie."

I lower my shot. "What? No. That's...no. This is amazing. You think I don't want to be a part of it?"

He shrugs. "It's a movie, Mila. I'm not exactly changing lives."

"I disagree entirely. If anything, you're creating an escape for a few hours, that's something. And music, movies, books, they all have the power to change a lot, or at the very least, leave a lasting impression."

"I'm not trying to downplay it...I just don't want it to touch us too much, not yet."

"Well, the only thing touching me right now is you, you dirty, old bastard."

"Cute," he says, slowing his fingers.

I lift my shot, and he does the same. "Let's make it simple then, to Gladys and Sean."

"Gladys and Sean." We toss them back, the burn of the liquid coating my throat. We drink two more before sipping our beers, and I'm feeling dizzy from the buzz and the workings of his hands. When his fingers dip lower, I begin to pant.

"Please stop that unless you plan on doing something about it. And even then, I don't know if I can handle the visual just yet. I'll need like twenty, thirty years."

He chuckles and leans into my good ear. "Trust me, Dame, the minute I push inside you tonight, you're going to know exactly who's fucking you."

I give him a coy smile. "Not that you aren't a handsome older man, but..." I trail my fingers along his neck, and I'm cut off by a chorus of applause when the club goes dark. Emerging from a small black curtain, a group of guys take the stage.

"Oh, awesome," I say, sure Lucas can't hear me. It takes me a *second to realize we're surrounded by a ton of warm bodies.*

I lean over and see Lucas jump when I raise my voice to make sure he hears me. I laugh through my question. "When did it get so crowded?"

"When we were locked in our bubble, baby," he whispers warmly. He pulls me up to stand on the edge of the couch so I have a clear view of the stage past the people lining up.

"I wonder if they're local," I yell down at him and he shrugs.

Seconds later, I hear the familiar opening guitar riff of "Mr. Jones" and the club goes apeshit just as the spotlights hit.

"Oh my God, it's the Counting Crows!" I scream like the sixty-year-old southerner I am. I glance down at Lucas whose laugh I can't hear but can clearly see.

"Did you know this?" He lifts his finger to his temple. The man with a plan.

"Of course, you did," I say, rolling my eyes giving him my best smile. "God, I love—"

Of all the times he could have missed my words, he didn't. Even surrounded by a screaming hundred, he caught every syllable. I move in for quick recovery. "This is awesome, thank you," I say, leaning down to kiss him and grabbing my beer from his hand. He lets me off the hook and we jam out as they play a list of classics. Whisked off the couch after a few songs, I'm on the floor with the rest of the mob and Lucas stands behind me in his protective hold. It's unnecessary, but I bask in it anyway.

When we're drenched in sweat and heavily buzzed, a man takes the piano, and Adam Duritz grabs the mic from the stand. "Thank you, thank you. We're going to slow it down a little." Lucas tightens his hold when the man at the piano plays the opening chords of "Colorblind." Instantly I have a lump in my throat.

Lucas bends in just as I lean back to whisper, "This is my favorite."

"Mine too," he says softly as we sway, half drunk and dizzy with affection. The song, the words, hit me and send me reeling as he pulls me tighter to him, seemingly just as affected. I'm madly in love with this man and have been for months, and I'm losing the battle in holding it in any longer. He makes me insanely happy, he makes life exciting, his presence is all-consuming, his kiss a whirlwind and he says he's mine. I was wrong to assume we didn't fit, but it was him who made me see how perfectly we do.

Overcome with what I feel, tears surface and slide down my cheeks. It didn't sneak up on me, I've known for a while how I felt, but the fear of having something so perfect does. This, this feeling is what I've been holding out for, it's mine, and he gave it to me, we built it together. It's one of the best and most terrifying moments of my life. Cursing my hormones, I'm busted when one of his fingers lifts a tear from my cheek, and he turns me to face him. Unable to hold it any longer, the tears multiply rapidly but his concerned eyes warm when he sees the smile I'm wearing beneath.

"I shouldn't do shots without eating dinner first," I proclaim with a laugh. Patient eyes gaze down at me as he waits for me to speak truthfully because he knows me, he knows I will.

"Okay, Hollywood," I admit tearfully, "you got the girl. Now what?"

"Now everything," he promises before his lips crush mine.

"One of the things about acting is it allows you to live other people's lives without having to pay the price."
—Robert De Niro

CHAPTER 25

LUCAS
Two Months Ago

INT: Nikki sits in a dim room on a metal counter gripping his calf, teeth clenching as he sorts through surgical tools.

> ALEJANDRO
> Wait for the doctor. He should be here soon.

> NIKKI
> I don't wait. He's late.

> ALEJANDRO
> It's too deep. You can't get that bullet out on your own.

> NIKKI
> Give me some of that Chiba.

Alejandro leans in with a spoonful, and Nikki sniffs it back with vigor

Nikki grips the scalpel

> NIKKI
> In five minutes, this will have been a dream.

                        ALEJANDRO
Patience,   brother.   You   could   get   an
infection.

                          NIKKI
No, that's only if I lay down with your
fat wife.

                        ALEJANDRO
She's not fat, she has the build of her
father.

                          NIKKI
Even worse.

"Lucas," a knock sounds on my trailer door and Nova comes walking in with a package in hand. "Sorry to interrupt, but this just came for you. The courier said it was urgent and I spent twenty minutes arguing with him because he insisted he give it to you directly."

Nodding, I keep my eyes on the script, flipping the metal through my fingers.

"Need anything?"

I know she's eyeing my lunch which I haven't touched.

When I don't answer, she shows her concern the only way she knows how...by bitching.

"You need to eat, Lucas."

When I keep my head down, I hear her grumble and the door slams a few seconds later.

Getting back to the script, I spend a few more minutes with the words, letting the architect take over—sort, pull, compose, and draw before laying it all out flat like a blueprint in front of me. Glancing over at the package, I assume is a script, I dismiss it until my vision blurs. Curiosity wins and I finally rip it open. Inside is a script, but for a movie I've already made. An envelope falls out with a note scribbled on the front.

It's all up to you.

G

Ripping it open, I tilt it, so the contents fall in my hand. Thumbing the flash drive, I flip it into my palm, turning it over, the weight of it making my stomach roll.

And then my laptop is open, and the screen rotates briefly when I pull up the media source and click play. And I'm there, in the room, familiar voices sounding. Resuming the flip of the coin I turn the volume up and quicken my fingers, sweat sliding down my back in rivulets. I watch on, second by second, speeding the workings of my knuckles, collecting all the air I can as I'm gutted from one end of me to the other. I can't look away, I can't erase what I've seen. My chest begins to cave, but only briefly before it expands to the point of exploding.

Thirst like I've never known dries my throat, traveling down my insides and chokes me like a suffocating blanket.

It's when the screen goes black that I see red.

Flames of outrage lick me from all sides. And then I'm ablaze, engulfed in disbelief and fury. Glass shatters as my heart rattles in my chest begging for relief, my mind reeling as I try to rip all thoughts away. Wood splinters around my knuckles as I fuel the fire, dousing myself in kerosene to escape the searing inside.

But there's no extinguishing this hatred.

There's no extinguishing this truth.

Rage overtakes me.

And I let it, ripping the life around me apart to match the rubble left inside. I rage until I'm gratified with the wreckage and can't see through the blur of destruction. I rage until I'm burning so white-hot that I can see nothing else. I rage and let it wreak its havoc because anything feels better than this reality. I rage until I go numb. I rage until I suffocate.

CHAPTER 26

MILA
Present

Lucas: When, when will you talk to me?

Lucas: Tell me where you are.

Lucas: I didn't do this to hurt you.

Lucas: Please just tell me you're okay.

I hadn't texted him since I left for the winery. It was wrong, immature to make him worry like that, but I needed space and he refused to give it. He was a hypocrite that way, and it only fueled my anger.

As time went on, his texts got more aggressive which meant he was drinking.

Lucas: Thanks, wife. Really. You never trusted me, did you?

Lucas: I guess you want to start over now? The problem is WE ARE NOT FUCKING FINISHED. I won't let you go.

Lucas: Jesus Christ, Mila, don't do this.

Lucas: I have the right to fucking know where you are!

Mila: I'm home. Don't come.

Lucas: Home? Our home?

If he's not there, where is he? I can't bring myself to ask.

Mila: The cottage

Lucas: I'll give you space. I swear to God I will, but please don't ever do that again. I'm begging you.

Aching to fire back with a "how does it feel?" I refrain from a reply. Anger is still winning. That's my decision today. I know I need to open up the lines of communication but everything I want to say is petty, pointless, and more aggression than progression.

Running a shower, I decide to extend a temporary olive branch.

Mila: I won't do it again. That's the only promise I'm making.

Lucas: I love you.

Toweling off, I lick the tears from my lips. Once dressed, I run my sleeve under my nose and crawl into bed, exhausted. My fingers linger over my cell pad briefly before I decide not to respond. Love isn't the issue. It never was. We've had it in abundance, along with a healthy dose of trust. He'd rearranged our universe to revolve around the other, and once we did, we were both sealed in our fate, destined to be the moon and obeying tide. I glowed in his affection while he swept me away with one electrifying wave after another. The week after Lucas and I went to the movies, we came out as a couple at my first Hollywood gala, which just so happened to be a star-studded union party.

Sitting in the back of the limo, I smooth down my dress for the hundredth time. I bought a Valentino I could not afford and spent the day working my hair into something resembling a half up-do I saw on YouTube. I'm nervous, and of course, he senses it as he takes my hand and pulls it to his lips.

"Stop staring," I snap, and he chuckles.

"If you didn't want me to stare, you shouldn't have worn that. It's sexy as fuck, and you look stunning."

"Sorry," I say, swallowing. "I get snappy when I'm nervous."

"Don't be nervous."

"Is there a stocked bar somewhere in here?" I open the cupboard next to me and frown when I come up empty and turn on him. "Shouldn't limos have a stocked bar?"

"Not this one, sorry. I'll get you some champagne as soon as we get there."

"Okay," I nod. "I swear to God, this is nothing like the movies. You people are all liars."

I see him in my peripheral trying to stifle his grin.

"It's not funny, don't be a dick!" I lift my chin and glare in his direction which only has his smile growing wider. I'm a hot mess. It's not that I can't handle it, it's just that I've always been on the sidelines, not front and center. Not to mention as soon as the world knows, my mother will too. That thought alone is enough to have me breaking out in hives. I'm blindsiding her with this because I wussed out of having the conversation. I can already see the mushroom cloud forming in the distance when the news hits her. But it's my decision, my life, and I had to give myself time to form my own opinion before she has any say with hers. Steadying my breaths, I force myself

to chill, deciding my behavior is unwarranted. Somewhat calm, I straighten my shoulders and lift my eyes to his.

"There's my Dame." He grins. "I was wondering when you would show up."

"Just nerves. I've never been around so many celebrities at once."

"Just remember that some of them used to work at Burger King and you'll be good."

"You're kidding?"

"Nope," he says, popping the P. "I worked in a gay bar with Blake. He'll be here. You'll get to meet him."

"Really?" I ask with a grin. "Always wanted to meet your other half."

"Don't count yourself lucky," he retorts with a humorous warning.

But I do count myself lucky when I gaze on at my man who looks gorgeous in another fitted tux. The tie is silver tonight and makes his glittering eyes pop. I bite my lip imagining ripping it off him later. It's then I see brief unease cross his features.

"You don't look so at peace yourself."

"That's because I'm making a decision."

"What kind of decision?" I ask as his depths roam molten over my dress and then flick back to mine.

Jesus, he's perfect.

"Do you trust me?"

"I did a minute ago, but now that you asked, no. What are you up to, Hollywood?"

His mouth lifts. "God, I love your honesty."

"I have plenty to go around."

"I can't wait to rid you of that dress," he says, sliding his palm down over the silk covering my thigh.

"Stop stalling. What decision did you just make?" Fear creeps up as mischievous eyes dance around in his beautiful head. "Remember on our first date when you said you didn't give a shit about other people's perception?"

"Vaguely, you had your tongue in my mouth most of the night."

"And you loved it," he coos.

"Not the point, Walker. What's going on?"

He gives me an indecipherable grin.

"Lucas," I prod, hackles rising. "I'm nervous enough." The limo comes to a stop, and I see the flash of the bulbs go off outside the idling car. I'm briefly distracted by them until warm hands cradle my face and I meet the eyes of a king. "I think now would be an appropriate time to tell you I'm in love with you." He gently strokes my cheeks with his thumbs. "I love you, Dame."

Between one breath and the next, the door opens, and Lucas emerges from the limo before I get a chance to respond. Shrieking ensues once he's spotted and he turns back and offers me his hand. He must like what reaction he sees because his eyes sparkle down on me and it only takes a second to realize my smile is just as wide as his. And then we're on the carpet posing as paparazzi calls out to Lucas asking who I am and screaming directions at us to shift position for better shots.

Heart thundering at his confession, I gaze at him, and he returns it with the same loving look. He loves me, and he's given me this time to let it sink in all the while it's being captured by hundreds of cameras. It still feels so intimate, like it's only ours. He never lets go of my hand, smiling back at me through several shots. Though the lights are blinding, all I see is him. I want so much to reciprocate his words, but he knows and gives me a wink to show as much. I'm fully lit inside.

He's in love with me. I have that, I have his love, and I never want to be without this feeling again. Somehow, I'm still existing in this daydream. In this place where I have this immaculate love that seemed to appear out of nowhere and now reigns permanently in my soul. He slides his thumb over my wrist to let me know it's not a dream. It's *our reality, together. I barely have a minute to enjoy the peace it brings before I'm ushered inside.*

The party itself is exactly what I expect. The ceiling consists of a gold and white silk tent, and drips with softly lit chandeliers. Lush tropical plants and solid white flower arrangements are placed strategically throughout the space to give it a more intimate vibe. There's a well-lit dance floor on the far side of the room next to several open doors that lead out to small, half-moon shaped balconies. Waiters are bustling around wielding tray after tray of champagne to the scattered stars filling the room. But it's one star in particular that commands my attention when he leans down to me with a heated whisper, "I can feel you surrounding me already. I want inside you so bad right now." It's all I can do to keep my mouth shut. "I'll be right back."

Alarmed, I turn to him. "Where are you going?" He doesn't answer but keeps our hands clasped as we enter the party. Everywhere I look there's a face I recognize, and I'm overwhelmed by the stimuli.

Champagne passing at every turn, suddenly I have one in hand, and I'm sipping it. Dizzy with the events of the last ten minutes, I follow Lucas blindly as he searches the room and comes to a sudden stop when he spots someone in the crowd. Defying gravity, I'm floating on air just before I crash down when his voice sounds beside me.

"Well, well, well. Isn't this fucking sweet!?" Every head within twenty feet turns in our direction as Lucas shouts our arrival. "Look at you all, nothing but a bunch of fucking puppets dressed for the ball!"

Jesus Christ!

My whole face purples as I try and fail not to burst out in nervous laughter.

Stunned, I keep up with his long strides as he saunters toward his target in full swagger introducing me to his ex-girlfriend, Laura Lee. Grappling with what just happened, we exchange pleasantries as I shrink a little standing next to her flawlessness. I'm fumbling with words trying to figure out why he would make such a show in front of her. Had he planned this? Was I some sort of means to get back at her? *Furious, I try to rip my hand away, and Lucas keeps a tight grip as his eyes trail down her form, his expression openly hostile as she compliments my dress. She's in the midst of making more polite conversation which I'm thankful for when he interrupts her.*

"You really shouldn't have gotten that nose job." *A gasp escapes my lips and a few others behind me as well. I immediately start stuttering in both scorn for Lucas and apology to Laura. Ignoring me, Lucas smirks down at her, and her face pinches briefly in annoyance before she cracks a grin.* "Dear God, Lucas, what did you take?"

"Nothing," *he says flatly.* "But looking at you now, I'm so glad you were a fucking phase."

The corners of her mouth lift higher. "What are you up to, Walker?"

"Better things," *he replies, pulling me tighter to him as I glare at the side of his face. I want to sink into the carpet beneath us, but I don't have any time to plot any sort of escape because in seconds I'm being dragged past her and some heavy hitters who all try and fail to get his attention. He's just snubbed Sean Penn when he approaches a man I don't recognize, whose eyes are trained on the both of us.* "Lucas, what the hell are you doing?" *I hiss as he jerks me front and center.*

"Hey, Dobs, I want you to meet my new girl. She was raised on a grape farm and believes bottles are magical. Isn't it cool?" *He widens his eyes as he says it.* "A little naïve but she's pretty nice to look at, right?"

I glare at him openly as he shakes the man's hand. Every good feeling I had minutes earlier washed away by the fact that I'm seeing red.

"I'm Mila," *I interject before Lucas has a chance to do it.*

"Nice to meet you, Mila. Is this—"

Lucas rudely interrupts. "This your party, Dobs? Food is shit, wouldn't you agree?"

The man smirks.

Lucas claps him roughly on the back. "*You should call me, but if you're this cheap, I'm not sure you can pay my bill. Though I've seen your wife, not bad, maybe you can have her work some overtime.*"

"*Lucas,*" *I hiss.* Trust him. Trust him.

"*Maybe you'll hear from me,*" *Dobs says with an amused grin.* "*Try not to strangle the waitstaff, Walker.*"

"*I'll do my best,*" *he says snidely.* "*But I think we both know you picked them off Skid Row and called it charity for the cheap labor.*"

He's a man possessed as he cuts the conversation short and abruptly walks away with me in tow. When he's gripped by the shoulder by one of his Cairo *co-stars, I seize the opportunity, nodding my hello before breaking away. Face on fire, I stalk to the closest exit, one of several small terraces. Fuming, I pace on the veranda while a man puts out a cigarette after reading my expression and leaves me to smolder alone. It's barely a minute later when Lucas joins me. I can see his grin before I fully face him. I'm burning hot, my face flaming as I down my champagne and try not to throw the glass at him.*

"*Well done, you just alienated half of Hollywood,*" *I snap.* "*I'll be leaving you here to you know…*" *I jut my chin toward the balcony,* "*you can go on and take a flying leap because you just committed career suicide. Hope it was worth it.*"

He smirks down at his champagne. "*Pretty sure it was.*"

"*What the hell is wrong with you? You know what? I don't want to know. The land of grapes? I'm pretty sure I hate you. Take me home this instant!*"

"*I may have a lot to learn about squishing grapes, but you sure do have a lot to learn about performance.*"

"*Oh, that, 'I'll be right back?' I got it about halfway through. I'm not impressed. What in the hell was the point of that?!*"

"*There's a part coming up that I want to read for and Dobs didn't think I was a good fit.*"

"All that was to show you could play an obnoxious asshole? Are you serious?"

"Desperate times," he winks.

"And you think those people will forgive you?"

"They already have. Every person I spoke to knows."

"Knows what?"

"How seriously I take this."

"Apparently I'm the last to know," I say, pacing in front of him. I'm sputtering, angrier than I've ever been and he's watching me without apology.

His low admission cuts through my racing thoughts. "This is how it will be if we go further, Mila."

"I'm humiliated and irrational right now, this isn't a good time to discuss this."

He observes me carefully. "It's the perfect time."

A couple joins us on the terrace, and Lucas stops them, asking them to give us a moment before shutting one of the doors. They eye me over his shoulder and smile before disappearing back into the party.

"I won't be typecast, Mila. I was trying to make a point. It was just a gag."

"On me."

"I warned you."

"What if I don't like it?"

"This is what I do, and if we go further, it's going to affect you too."

I jerk my thumb over my shoulder. "And that's the way you decide to introduce me?"

"It's the only way," he says, with something like an apology in his eyes. "I want this, us, to work. It's a large part of who I am. It won't always be that intense, but sometimes it will be, and for extended periods of time, months, and I need you to be okay with that."

"You just hurt me back there!" I whisper-yell, "embarrassed me. Used private things about me and twisted them for your fucking amusement."

"It shouldn't hurt you if you know what I'm doing."

"How can you say that? How do I know that wasn't what you're really thinking?"

"Maybe I'm jealous of the way you grew up."

That gives me pause. "Are you?"

He takes a drink of champagne and slides a hand in his slacks. "Maybe, a little."

I shake my head. "I'm sorry for that. I really am, but in there, the way you demeaned my dreams, that hurt."

"I draw from life. It's a regular practice. Comedians do it too."

"You're not a comedian," I huffed.

"I could be tomorrow," he whispers, cornering me where I stand on the balcony. "You'll get better at ignoring it."

Shaking my head, I think about Laura's reaction.

"You were cruel to her."

"To Laura?" He shrugs. "She's a dear friend, we love each other. She understands."

"Not a great thing to hear since you've fucked her."

"We did for a while, until we got bored. There's nothing left there."

"So, this is Hollywood? I can see why my mother kept me away."

"As much as it rips me to say it, there are plenty of guys out there that can give you something more along the lines of normal."

I gawk at him. "You just told me you loved me, now you're giving me an out?"

"Yes," he whispers softly. "Because you need to know what you're dealing with. Because if you decide you're in," he crowds me further, his breath hitting my lips, "I'm keeping you in. I can't picture a future without you, Mila. I don't want to. But it's going to take a shitload of work to keep us solid. We have to be in this together. And I mean in it. We can make some rules, but this is my life."

"This is insane."

"This is show biz. The schedule is hell, I haven't stopped working since I was twenty, if I'm honest, eight. I rarely think about much more than my next project. I get utterly absorbed, I lose myself completely at times, and when I do, half the time I can't tell you what day it is and not much else matters but the role I'm playing. But the good is there for you to see and I hope you do because I do love you. You're the perfect distraction from this madness, you're what I look forward to, and I want this, you, so much."

This is so not how I saw this party going. "I don't know what to think."

He lets out a long breath. "Loving me back will take a huge amount of patience."

"I already love you back," I snap with a wobbling chin, "and you dropped a bomb on it."

True remorse shines in his eyes. "I'm sorry, Dame. You're the only woman I've ever known or wanted that can hold me down."

"And this is what you love?"

"Yes." He sighs. "There's this pride, satisfaction I get at certain times knowing I helped create something, knowing when I did it, I gave it everything I had. This profession brought me to life, Mila, and it saved me too. It's just as much now who I am as what I do."

"Because of Maddie?"

He nods. He's told me bits and pieces, but when he does, I sense he leaves a lot out.

"So, this is the part you tell me the rest of the perks, right?"

His expression turns grave. "If by perks you mean insanely lavish vacations on fifty-foot yachts, open doors everywhere we go, and big toys with big tags? Sure, that can be a part of it, but it's not really what I'm into. I rarely enjoy my downtime. When I'm home, I'm picking through scripts in an attempt to create more tunnel vision. I'm ambitious, cheap, and moody at times, especially when the role is tough. I get lost in my head and often. But I will love you, Mila and I'll show you just how much."

"Sounds toxic. I'm not a babysitter."

"For you, I'll grow up."

Lips still trembling, I sink into his gaze and I know I'm already screwed. For the moment, I love him just as much as I loathe him.

"I need to think about this." It's all I've got. I'm too afraid to hold the ink at the moment and sign on the dotted line. My life will change with Lucas, and drastically. Inside I already have, I've made the room, I've dreamed of a possible future. I want him, but he himself is warning me away.

He reads my indecision, and I see the hurt it draws. "If you really want to go, I'll take you home."

"No, stay," I manage. "I'll stay too."

He looks surprised and equally defeated pressing his brows together. "Mila—"

I didn't realize a tear had slipped out. He leans in and takes it away with his lips before closing his eyes with a sigh. "That fucking hurt worse than anything I've ever felt. I'm sorry."

"But you can't promise you won't do it again?"

He slowly shakes his head.

"So, what you're telling me is I'm in love with both Jekyll and Hyde?"

He gradually nods.

"Is that all? Any kids running around I don't know about?"

"I think this is enough, don't you?"

A voice sounds up from behind us.

"He tried to get me pregnant once, then again, he could have been aiming for the toilet." Lucas turns with a grin and Blake comes into view. His short curly blond hair is swept up in a faux-hawk, and his solid black tux looks poured on him. He grins at me, his eyes trailing from mine down the length of my gown.

"Ah, Lucas, you weren't lying, she's a knockout."

My cheeks heat slightly as Blake jabs him with his elbow. "Nice job in there, asshole, I think you just got yourself banned from the union."

"Risk and reward," Lucas says confidently.

Blake rolls his eyes still smiling at me. "This guy won't do anything interesting on a school night, but give him a Hollywood party, and he goes all Evel Knievel." He winks and extends his arm toward me. "Would the lady care to dance?"

"Absolutely—"

"Absolutely not," Lucas snaps with a jealous edge that I feel to my toes.

"Does this mean we aren't friends anymore?" Blake says in an exaggerated southern drawl. "If I thought you weren't my friend anymore, Lucas, I just don't think I could bear it."

I'm giggling like a school girl, and Lucas exhales, tossing his head back. "Fine. Mind yourself, Iceman."

"Understood," Blake retorts with the same drawl, tilting his head and extending his arm further as he leans in. "Let's go make him crazy jealous."

"Let's," I take his arm and hear Lucas mumble, "fucker," as we pass.

"I'll have her back before the clock strikes midnight, pumpkin. Be sure to tip your waitress."

Lucas sounds up behind us. "You've got five minutes."

"Oh, me, oh, my, the boy is hopeless, good job, Cinderella." He lets go of my hand briefly before taking two glasses of champagne off one of the passed trays.

"Bottoms up, darlin'. I could sure use a drink after what I just heard."

Smiling, I tip my glass. "Don't tell me you're jealous."

"Nope. I met my lady love, married her. Poor woman," he says with a grin. "But I am quite shocked at the conversation I walked into."

"You mean eavesdropped on," I say as he takes our glasses away and discards them before leading me to the dance floor.

Once we're dancing, he wastes no time.

"So, things are getting serious. I wonder what pet name the press is coming up with for you two right now. Something catchy, though I'm not sure what they can do with Lucas and Mila." He cocks his head as if puzzled while guiding me through Sting's "My One and Only Love".

I stay mute.

"What? No comment, you can trust me. I know a little about a lot."

He winks, and I can't help myself, I sigh inside a little. Blake West is gorgeous, and I've been a fan of his for years.

"Things were getting too serious out there, thanks for the dance."

"Not over yet," he says, guiding us forward and back on perfectly timed feet.

"I'm glad we finally got to meet. I've heard a lot about you."

He tilts his head playfully. "Have you?"

"I have," I say, matching his infectious grin.

"Well, it's all true, all of it. I deny nothing."

"That's not smart," I laugh.

He looks down at me, his eyes softening. "So, you're the one my brother's decided on."

"I think so."

"And have you decided on him?"

I shrug in his arms. "I'm screwed. The man got me to fall in love with him before telling me he was the villain."

He chuckles and spins me effortlessly out of his arms before pulling me back to him. "Don't worry, beautiful, that role's taken."

"By you, I presume?"

He smirks. "My brother represented me well. You know," he says, maneuvering us expertly across the floor, "he's always taken this job too seriously."

"You don't take it seriously?"

"Not as much as I used to, not anymore."

"Why is that?"

He pauses our dance as if lost in thought and then resumes it. "You ever heard the story of the ant and the grasshopper? You know, the ant works hard every day warning the grasshopper not to sing and play, because if he sings and plays all summer, by winter, he'll surely starve."

He doesn't give me time to answer before he dips me low bringing his lips a centimeter from the divot at my throat. His eyes dart past my profile, and a victory smile lights up his face. I follow his line of sight to see Lucas's glare from feet away and can't help the draw of my conspiratorial smile when I turn back to face Blake.

"Oh, you are terrible," I say, openly laughing.

"Everybody has to pay the devil his due."

He slowly pulls us back to stand and resumes our dance and conversation as if his head isn't being lasered off by violent green eyes.

"Where were we? Right, the ant and the grasshopper." He guides us into another song with no care for Lucas's ticking clock. "Well, the way I see it, we are taught to work like ants, not to think like grasshoppers."

I nod.

He looks down at me with prodding brown eyes. "But eventually that ant has to wipe his brow and wonder if that singing grasshopper had the fuller life." He twirls me again and brings me back to him.

"And you think Lucas is an ant?"

"Yes," he answers easily, "and so are you. But it's the best way to be, I promise you."

"So, who's going to save you come winter, grasshopper?"

"That's easy," he says, turning us both to face a gorgeous red-head I recognize as his wife, who is now dancing with Lucas. Blake leans in so we're cheek to cheek. "I married an ant."

———————————

The ride back to my house is mostly silent. The heaviness of what he revealed to me thick between us as we both come down from the party. I sense Lucas's gaze on me as I stare out the onyx window.

"Fuck this." In seconds, I'm in his lap. "I didn't do it to scare you away."

"Well, you did a shit job of that. Couldn't you have just said it? Warned me a little more with a, 'Hey, I'm a bit of a sociopath' for a living, and I'm about to demonstrate."

"That's what you think of me?" His voice has an icy edge, and I take the cue and slide off his lap.

"You used me, made fun of me to try to benefit your career. It's not something I'm willing to forget because you look incredible in a tux."

He slowly exhales. "Mila, it wasn't personal. It's what came to me."

He lifts his cell. "I just got an email. Dobs wants a meeting."

"Well then, I guess congrats are in order."

"Fuck," he mutters just as we pull up to my house. "This is exactly what I want to avoid in the future. I don't want us at odds when it's time to work."

"Does it matter to you that this could hurt me?"

"Of course, it does."

"Then don't hurt me."

"It's not that simple."

"So, what, if you're a comedian tomorrow and I hate your

jokes or your character, I have to live with them for as long as you film?"

"Basically, yes. I don't leave my work at the office."

"You didn't act that way on the set of Cairo.*"*

"Different part. Different circumstances. It changes constantly."

"You expect a lot of me."

"Yes, I do, and you'll get the best of me too." The authority of his next statement cuts me in half. *"This is it, Mila. This is the life of an actor, and this is the reason I rarely date, and when I do, I date other actors. It's also the reason I can't promise you much beyond loving you the best way I know how."*

"Sounds like an ultimatum."

"It's the truth. I figured you'd appreciate that."

"So, all this time we've been together... was I the one auditioning?"

"No," he pinches the bridge of his nose, *"Mila, no, I've been trying to ease you into the idea. You already know the schedule is hell, this is the rest of it."*

"I feel manipulated."

"That was not my intention. Not at all. I'm sorry."

Silence lingers as gravity hurdles me back to Earth and the car comes to a stop.

"Good night, Lucas."

"Goddammit!" He slams his fist into the roof and brings furious eyes to mine. *"You really going to do this? Really?"*

"I don't know what you want from me."

"You know exactly what the hell I want from you," his tone grows unbearably cold, *"I've made it crystal clear."*

When I don't respond, he clasps his hands in front of his mouth and exhales closing his eyes. *"Okay. You're gonna have to be the one that walks away from this, because it won't be me."*

"Lucas, I—"

"It's okay," he says softly, shaking his head in disappointment before he averts his gaze.

Paul opens the door, and I take his hand, exiting the limo.

I'm at my door when the first of the tears fall and I press my head against it. "Fuck." I don't want to be without him, no matter how crazy his lifestyle is, no matter how scared I am. He's just confessed his love and offered me a place with him. I'd always claimed safe was boring, and the first time I'm faced with something more, an unconventional way of living, especially with the man I'm madly in love with, I shy away. I let fear overrule my own convictions. I want him, and he wants me. And right then it seems so simple. I turn to try and catch sight of the limo and see Lucas standing at the edge of my porch watching me intently.

Elated, I take a step forward. "That was ballsy."

"I told him to circle around and come back." He slowly approaches before wiping the tears from my face with gentle thumbs. "At least now I know."

I sniff. "Know what?"

"That you really do love me too."

"I told you that."

"Actions speak louder, right? I'm not wrong about you."

"It's just a lot to absorb."

Cupping my face, he presses a gentle kiss to my lips and traces my jaw with his thumbs. "Do you know why I call you Dame?"

"It's an old generalized term for a woman in show biz, kind of a Humphrey Bogart type term, right, like kid or broad?"

He nods, his fingers gliding along my back to the small of it where he strokes me softly. "That's true, but it's also the female equivalent of a knight." He lifts one side of his mouth. "You told me yourself, you're no princess." He presses a kiss to my temple.

"I'm not."

"No, you aren't, although you are very much a pain in the ass."

I playfully slap his chest. "But you're tough and pure of heart, you say what you mean, and it's the sexiest thing about you," he grins as he palms my ass, "well, one of the sexiest."

"So, you think I'm a knight, huh?"

"You're my knight. You saved me the minute you walked up to me in that black dress looking more beautiful than anything I've ever seen."

"I've never relied on anyone, Mila. Not for anything, not ever, because this life hasn't given me much to count on. I can appreciate what a gift you are. I think you're a reward for my patience. I've never had anyone there for me, not like this. I feel a sort of peace I've never had before." Tears trail down my cheeks. "You changed my luck, Dame. And for the first time in my life, I feel like if I ever need rescuing, I'll have somebody there to help save me."

Any brick or mortar I have left surrounding my heart disintegrates with his confession. He gives me all his trust, and I take it, and in return, I give him mine. Because he is worth it. "I will, Lucas. If you ever need saving, I'll be there. I promise."

He presses his forehead to mine. "I'm counting on it."

"The less someone knows about me, the better, because my intention is to play a variety of characters."
—Joaquin Phoenix

CHAPTER 27

MILA
One Month Ago

"**M**ILA," MY MOTHER SAYS MY NAME OVER THE LINE LIKE it's a final warning rather than a greeting.

"Hey, Mom."

"What do I have to do to get a call back from my daughter?"

"How about not putting me on the defensive within two seconds of speaking? That's a start."

"I'm irritated."

"Yes, I can tell from the fire you're breathing."

"Such disrespect."

"Sorry, Mom, I'm tired."

"Yes, well, I was wanting to take you to an exhibit, but it's passed."

"I'm sorry, truly." And I am. I've been neglecting time with my parents in the last few years to travel with Lucas, but it was always for good reason. This time I have left with them is precious, I realize that now more than ever and I'm determined not to waste it.

"I've been meaning to take you up on your dinner invite, but why don't you come over instead, I'll cook."

We speak for a few minutes and make the arrangements. I can tell she's still a little miffed when I end the call but am relieved when it's over. I'll have to answer to her at some point, but it doesn't have to be today. I made sure to invite her at a time I know Lucas will be on set. With the way he's been acting,

I want to avoid a meeting of the two like the plague. Pulling into the driveway after a long day at the bistro, I close my eyes and recount the first time they came face-to-face.

"Stop worrying, Dame, I've got this," Lucas says confidently.

"I'm fine," I reply with a squeak, my nerves giving me away. His laughter fills the Land Rover while a warm hand squeezes my thigh with reassurance. He looks glorious in loose-fitting dark jeans, a T-shirt, and a blazer. His hair is brushed back in thick waves making him look the part of a posh sophisticate. We've been dating for seven months, and it's been utter bliss. At the moment we're on our way toward another milestone, meet the parents, well my parents. He's filmed another movie since we began dating, but the role was a minor, no stress part with an all-star cast. Lucas had only been on set for three weeks before he got home and we'd more than made up for lost time. We'd gone to a few more outings as a couple and so far, so good. I've been diligent about not paying attention to the tabloids or reading on-line comments from his fans about the status of his new relationship. Ignorance is indeed bliss as far as I'm concerned.

Life is good. He practically lives at my house at this point. When he isn't filming, he admitted he mostly lived in a hotel, so most of our time together is spent at my cottage. Currently, he has two of his own drawers at my house which means we are on the cusp of more com-mitment. Everything inside me tells me he is my forever man and our exchanged words have started to deepen to an extent. Inside, I feel a glow I'd never known was possible.

Lucas is my best friend and remains the most spectacular of lov-ers. He is still guarded about some parts of his life and doesn't want to talk much about the past, but I've always known eventually he will come clean to me. We are in the best place we could be, so at my moth-er's insistence and with a brief window in his schedule, we agree to finally take her invite for dinner. My mother and I have been on a rare out of sorts since the party, but I refuse to let her influence my relationship. It's her own brand of dramatic flair that has me worried about this meet.

When we pull up to the house, I can see the surprise on Lucas's face.

"You lied." Disappointment covers his features when he turns to me in front of the two-story house.

"I didn't lie. I told you they obtained their wealth later in life. It's just a house. I've never lived in it."

"I've never asked what your father does."

"He was a psychiatrist and a college professor, retired now."

His smile is nonexistent at this point.

"I...I didn't think to tell you, well, because he's retired."

Unease seeps from him and I place my hand on his stone jaw turning him to face me. "He is the kindest man you will ever meet, and he will love you like I do."

His eyes soften, but the light in them is weak.

"Come on, Hollywood, come have some French meatloaf."

He nods as if my shitty pep talk worked and grips my hand as I lead him toward the house.

Within the first thirty seconds of opening the door, I'm almost positive my mother has seared off more of his confidence with her lava gaze and ice-cold greeting. It's clear to both of us she's holding a grudge due to our secret relationship.

We're in the seventh circle of hell now in her sitting room waiting for my father to get home and completely at her mercy. It's taking every bit of strength I have not to glare at her and poke the bear.

Lucas studies old pictures of me situated over the mantle and on the side tables as my mother brags about my past accomplishments like I'm a prize pig.

"She was an amazing pianist. I don't know why she quit."

"It got boring," I say simply as the sides of Lucas's mouth lift up. "Just like horse riding and everything else you wanted me to love."

"*Thank God for that,*" Lucas adds. "*No horse riding.*"

We share a laugh, and my mother lifts a brow.

"*What's wrong with horse riding, Mr. Walker?*"

"*Lucas,*" *he corrects for the second time.* "*I'm just not a fan of animals. Well, actually I think it's the other way around.*"

"*Why is that?*"

"*Just, well, the first time I pet a dog it bit me, I have the scar to prove it. And then I went to the zoo with my class when I was ten, and a monkey threw...waste at me.*"

She shrugs. "*That's common.*"

"*I thought so too until it kept happening. The first time I swam in the ocean, I got welcomed by a school of jellyfish.*"

"*Ouch,*" *I say.* "*You never told me that. Those little faded scars on your back?*"

He nods.

"*Well, you can't know everything about the man,*" *my mother pipes in,* "*you've only been sleeping with him for ten minutes.*"

"*Mom,*" *I scold, before narrowing my eyes. She shrugs sitting as pretty as she pleases with her teacup in hand.*

I can't resist. I poke the bear. "*Actually, mother dearest, ten minutes isn't accurate. Lucas is far more generous,*" *I suck my bottom lip through my teeth,* "*the last round went well over an hour and a half.*"

Lucas mutters an "*oh shit,'* *as she chokes on a sip of tea.*

"*Hello all,*" *my father interjects as he comes into the room, his warmth casting off her dark cloud. Relief washes over me as I hug him tightly in greeting.*

"*Hey, Dad,*" *I turn to see Lucas standing, and don't miss my mother's eyes rolling down his form. I decide then it's going to be a dine and dash. I can't subject him to this. Once we're seated at the table, I swear I hear the bell ring, and it isn't the dinner bell.*

"*So, where are you from, Mr. Walker?*"

"Maïwenn, please call me Lucas and I was raised in West Virginia."

I lean in, letting her have this round even though I know it's wrong.

"And your parents?"

"They're still there, I think."

"Oh?"

Lucas pats his mouth with the napkin. "I cut all ties when I got to California."

She sips her wine. "I see."

"Seriously, Mom? This line of questioning is a page straight from the script out of every meet the parent's movie conversation ever had."

"Then he'll be able to easily follow," she turns and flashes Lucas a sickening smile.

I white knuckle my fork.

"So, Mila tells me you worked for the press?" Lucas asks, taking the reins. I lean in and whisper to him so only he can hear me. "I love you. Great battle tactic, kill, kill, kill." The corners of his mouth lift and he grabs my hand under the table. I'm pretty sure his palm is sweating.

"Yes, I worked with the press. But I got out when I realized the type of circus I was supporting."

My father clears his throat with a sharply whispered, "Maïwenn," before he picks more pistachios from his loaf.

"Are you in the union?" my mother asks as casually as a fire alarm.

"Yes," Lucas grins proudly. "I got my card when I was nineteen."

"What job got you that paycheck?"

"Mom, money talk is rude. You taught me that."

"It's interesting, Mila, and a different line of questioning. That should please you."

"A commercial," Lucas *referees easily passing me the salad bowl with a wink.*

"Oh, would I have seen it?"

"It was an awareness commercial."

"Oh, for what?"

"Mom, your food is getting cold."

"Herpes," Lucas *says, clearing his throat and I can't help the nervous laugh that escapes me.*

"I see," *my mother says dryly.*

"Cut it out, Mom, we haven't taken five bites."

This time my father inadvertently asks the million-dollar question. "So, Lucas, where did you go to school?"

Lucas *gives him a scene-stealing grin.* "Ever heard of Hard Knocks?"

My dad laughs, and my mother scowls.

It's then I find some small ray of hope.

"Come on, Mom, loosen that bun, you're looking a little stressed."

I'm trying to make light of the situation, but I can still feel the tension brewing.

"Well, you've done well for yourself, considering," *she says, eyeing him like he's a disease.*

I drop my fork.

"Considering," *I grit out,* "Considering what? He's made more on his last movie than you have your whole life."

My mother turns to me as if we're behind closed doors. "Looks fade, Mila, what are you going to talk about in twenty years? This is ridiculous. You must have low self-esteem."

"Maïwenn!" *My father says, finally showing up to the battle.*

But it's already too late. She doesn't stop there, she goes straight for the jugular turning to her husband as if we're being ridiculous. "She's highly educated in art and graduated summa cum laude with a double major, and he has a degree in herpes." *She turns back* to me with shrewd eyes. "You honestly expect me to give you my blessing?"

"I don't give a damn about your blessing, I'm twenty-seven years old!"

I'm partially lying. Of course, I want her to like him and thought her acceptance would be a little hard-earned, but this I was not prepared for. I have no idea what has gotten into her that brought her to this point, to go to these lengths, but I refuse to subject Lucas to another minute.

Before I get a chance to say a word Lucas pushes away from the table. "I'm full. Thank you for dinner. I have an early morning."

"Please," I whisper, grabbing his hand. "She'll apologize. She will." I glare at my mother. "Why, why, why would you do this?"

"Because this man is not your match, Mila, and he knows it." Their eyes meet in a silent standoff over the table. As the seconds pass, I can see a wordless understanding relay between them. My mother speaks up never taking her eyes off his. "He'll be the one marrying up, Mila, not you and he knows it. He's got you fooled now, but later it will be impossible."

I stand, throwing my napkin down as the gauntlet. "I'll never forgive you. Lucas, let's go."

My parents are arguing before we close the door. Heat radiates off him as we make our way toward his SUV. I'm mortified. "I'm so sorry," I say as tears fall down my cheeks. "I'm so sorry, Lucas. Please," I cry, and he looks over at me, shaking his head.

"Hey, don't worry about it, I can take it. I've had years to learn how to deal with rejection."

His words gut me as we round his truck. "Please don't take her words for truth. She just doesn't know you."

We both slam our doors, and he wastes no time turning the ignition and speeding off. A few quiet minutes pass and I apologize again.

"She's really not as bad as that, Lucas. I don't know what in the hell she was thinking."

"It's fine," he says softly, his eyes losing focus, the drive becoming an afterthought. He's checking out on me, and I won't allow it.

"Please, don't let it get to you. She's an awful bitch. I had no idea she would go for your jugular like that."

"She's right."

"What?" Turning in my seat, I see his jaw has set again, and it terrifies me.

"She's right. Mila, I don't know much about anything."

"Are you kidding me? You're brilliant. You were teaching me about String Theory just this morning."

"Yeah, because I researched it for a movie."

"Yeah, and last week it was the history of the NRA and the Irish Mob."

"All for movies," he repeats as if I'm not getting it.

"So," I say in both reply and question. *"What does that matter?"*

"I read on a tenth-grade level. I'm not...I'm not a lot of things. She's right."

"Lucas, you don't really think that."

He speeds up. My parents are only a forty-minute drive from my house, but it feels like a small and silent eternity when we finally pull up in front of my cottage. Lucas sits idle while I study his face. *"Come in,"* I say, opening my door, but I know it's in vain. Inside my chest, just around the lodged bullet delivered by my own mother, tiny pieces of me are starting to fracture in a web-like pattern around it. He's got his hand on the top of the wheel, his eyes bleary when he speaks.

"You know, I spent the night after our first date looking up what your degree meant. I had no fucking clue."

"Most people don't."

"But some do." He glances at me. *"Isn't that the type for you?"*

"Come on, Lucas, she spoke out of her ass. She's a horrible woman, and I'll never talk to her again after this."

He shakes his head. "Not true, you two talk often."

"I love you," I insist. "Right now, I don't love her." But he's not hearing me.

A sad smile lifts the corner of his mouth. "I stayed up until four in the morning watching The Graduate, so I would know about it the next time you brought it up, but you never did."

My heart sinks as he turns to me with a resignation that starts to tear me apart. Another crack, and then another, the web expanding across the whole of me threatening to shatter like glass.

More confession spills from his lips as I sit stunned. "That night at the pyramids, when I got upset, it wasn't because I was tired." He swallows audibly. "It was because I'd been trying to impress you and instead, you fucking schooled me."

"It's just stuff I learned in geography and other stuff I picked up."

"Your mother is right, you'd be marrying down. And I do know it, I've always known it."

"Jesus, Lucas, who said anything about marriage?"

"I just did," he snaps without missing a beat, before scrutinizing my reaction. "Was that never a thought for you? Fuck, am I completely wrong about this, about us?"

"No, Lucas, God, no, I just, I didn't think…"

"Think what?" he asks testily. "That I'm capable of marriage?"

"Stop. I'm not her, stop putting words in my mouth."

"You look at me the way she does sometimes, like I'm an idiot."

"Yeah, well, I hope you're getting that look from me right now because you're acting like one!"

He goes on as if he's stuck in his own headspace instead of our conversation. "Maybe I fooled myself. Maybe we both did."

"Stop," I say. "Stop it. Stop right now. This is ridiculous. We're happy."

"But for how long? What will we talk about in twenty years?"

My head shakes repeatedly as I speak. "What is wrong with you? She's the ignorant one, she has no idea who we are."

"I'm not good enough! I'm not! I'm not on your level. I don't know what the hell you're talking about sometimes and it kills me! I don't know half the definitions of the words in your vocabulary!"

He's never yelled at me and instant tears spring to my eyes. "I had no idea," I confess, chin wobbling.

"Of course you didn't, I'm a fucking actor, Mila! I can lie my way through walls. Why would your own boyfriend tell you he's an illiterate fuck? He wouldn't, he would just wait for your mother to figure it out for you." He glances down at the console between us. "Maybe, it's not so farfetched, maybe I'm really not the man for you."

Another crack, this one so deep I have to fight for breath.

"Lucas, look at me, this is insane!"

His voice is shaking as he grips the steering wheel. "I just think you truly deserve better."

"Please, don't hurt me. Please, Lucas. Don't break my heart, don't break your own. We love each other, I don't give a shit about your lack of education."

"But I do."

"This is really happening? You're letting me go because you're afraid you aren't intelligent enough for me?"

He bites his lip, his voice low when he manages to speak. "I think about it constantly."

"So what? I have to live with the scrutiny of the public, forever, just to be with you, you think that's not something I think about? But I do it because I love you!" When he gives me silence for an answer, I bat away the sick feeling washing over me, summoning the rest of my fight.

"Lucas," I whisper, lifting my hand to his jaw. He jerks away from my touch, gripping my wrist and setting it between us.

"I just don't want you to regret me." His eyes finally drift to mine *resolute, and that's when the glass bursts.*

Unimaginably shattered, I visibly crumble in front of him as he stares at me. I'm out of words, all of them falling away due to the jagged edges rustling inside my chest. Anger trumps hurt in those seconds and I embrace it.

"You're a coward. And this, this right here, is the stupidest thing you've ever done." I sob, and he flinches the minute it fills the cabin of his Land Rover. Jumping out, I begin to shake uncontrollably at the anger coursing through me and the pain racing to catch up, not far behind. Lit up in his headlights, I slam my purse on his hood, livid, and meet his eyes through the glass. He watches me intently, and I can see his remorse, but my mind is also made up. "I regret you already, Hollywood!" I spout, not from the heart, but from the silver tongue my mother graced me with. "Don't give me a second thought."

If he's this clueless about my love for him, maybe he's right, he's a stupid fucking man. Stomping toward my porch, I let out a mewled cry just before I slam the door behind me, locking it and tossing my purse in the hall. I don't even make it a step in before I slink down to the hardwood floor. For endless minutes I sit there, counting our days and nights together, crying my eyes out, unable to breathe, think, move.

All of the time he spent convincing me that we were real, wasted.

But I'd been so sure this time. I'd let him sweep me into the whirlwind, but never let my feet leave the ground until I was certain. And now it was far too late. My heart had memorized his, matched his rhythm and synced, declaring itself loyal.

It will never be the same.

I will never be the same.

Never again.

"There's a point in time in your life where you think was I happy, or was I just not aware?"—Philip Seymour Hoffman

CHAPTER 28

LUCAS
One Month Ago

STAGNANT AIR RECYCLES IN THE TRAILER AS I LIGHT A CIGARETTE to accompany my drink, taking a long sip of the stout liquid while I watch the old reel on my laptop screen. Maddie tosses a withering look at her opponent before spewing venomous lines. I take my cue, repeating them back to her with a bitter chuckle as I toss back the rest of my drink and pour another. She turns her head, the purse of her lips showing her annoyance, it's one of her tells. And for a few seconds, I'm back in front of her.

"You think you know me? You don't know a damned thing about me. Take your assumptions and go back to your husband." Maddie slaps me, and I move forward and grip her chin with rough fingers. "You need to leave, Mary, right now, before I throw you out of here."

"I'm sorry," she whimpers as a tear falls down her cracked face. "I love you, Terrance."

I wiggle her chin in between my fingers before I let go. "You don't know anything about it, doll."

Maddie straightens into her natural posture breaking the scene. "That was good, but next time you need to show more disdain with the last line. She's been jerking your chain long enough."

"What is disdain?"

"Another word for disgust. Go to the mirror," she instructs. I do as I'm told and stand in front of the floor-length mirror. She watches behind me. "This isn't a good habit to start because if you practice it *this way and the director wants it another way, it can cause conflict, but we'll do it today. Now, show me anger."*

I flare my nostrils like she taught me and press my brows together. "Good. Now tell me about something that makes you cringe."

"I hate hot dogs. Mom boils them." And we eat them at home practically every day.

"Good, that's good. Now make a face to show me how bad you hate the sight of them. The smell of them as they boil."

This time my nostrils flare, but my mouth waters at the thought and I look a little more of a mix of sick and angry.

She lifts a painted-on brow, and I can tell she's pleased.

She repeats the line. "I love you, Terrance."

I push the words through my teeth. "You don't know anything about it, doll."

"And that's disdain." She claps her hands with glee, and I grin. "Only thirteen-years-old and you can play any lead any writer dreams up. You've got it, kid. I'd say our work is done."

"Done?" I panic because running lines with Maddie for the last five years is all I've had to look forward to. I've been coming to her house every day since I was eight years old playing the part of Donald Ross, Troy Wilbur, Arnold Scott, and Terrance Cooper. These men are a part of me. I know their mannerisms, how they move, how they walk, and breathe. They are, despite being mostly bad men, my best friends and the fathers that raised me. Without them, I wouldn't know who to be. It's how I survive, as these men, as Maddie's partner. It's all I have.

None of the kids in the trailer park are my age, and I don't have any friends at school who live close by.

Maddie reads my mind and pats my shoulder. "Don't worry, there's always room for improvement. Did you sign up for drama this year like I told you to?"

"Yes," I say sourly because I know what's coming. A lot of shit from the kids I already despise.

"Don't worry. You'll find your tribe there."

"My tribe? In drama?" I roll my eyes. "Bunch of fags."

She slaps the back of my head. "Your parents are ignorant, so I'm going to let that slide just this once. Fag is no longer in your vocabulary. Do you understand me?"

My thirteen-year-old brain is pissed at the burn on the back of my neck, but Maddie's been good to me, always keeping a stock of burritos so I'm never hungry and I never much liked the word anyway. I nod, and her eyes soften, a tell that I've done something good. Maddie believes in tells over words and that you can always know the difference in what people feel and say by their signals. She said most men are too damned dumb for their own good and sometimes 'I hate you' means 'I love you,' that I've just got to pay close attention to tells because those are the truth. She says you can end up living years with a stranger if you can't figure out what their eyes and hands say. I love watching the kids at my school for their tells. It's a hobby of mine. I always know when Derick Jones is about to pounce me because his lip curls and he tightens his fists right before he strikes. It's always with his right fist. Soft eyes are how I know Jessie Soto wants to talk to me, but she loses her nerve every time I get close. I wish she would talk to me. She hasn't said a word to me since second grade when the lice got so big, they trailed down my forehead like a bunch of ants, and the teacher screamed before kicking me out of class.

Maddie was the one to buy me the special shampoo and combed my head because my momma wouldn't listen. It was one of the most embarrassing days of my life. No one spoke to me much after that. But they came up with enough nicknames to make sure I would never say a word to them. Maddie says my station in life will only be made greater through trials like this. I didn't see how. She said I didn't need to know anything yet.

"Quit daydreaming and go get us some carrot juice," she orders, pulling the fedora off my head and gathering the other props we've used.

I walk over to her fridge and grab the glasses out of the dish drainer when a knock sounds on Maddie's hollow door. I worry about her sometimes at night. She doesn't have a lot of valuables, but she's old and alone, so I sometimes watch out for her through my bedroom blinds until I fall asleep. Her husband died of a heart attack which Maddie only tells me about when she drinks, which isn't much. He was a manipulator of the worst kind. She said she fell for him because she couldn't ever memorize his tells. That's what drew her to him and led to her losing both her fame and fortune.

"Maddie," my mother's voice sounds, and it's then I fully understand the word disdain because her tone is full of it. "My boy needs to get back home. And he won't be coming over for a while."

Maddie shoots me a worried look over her shoulder as she holds the door tightly to her. "Can I ask why? Has he done something wrong?"

"Because he's almost thirteen and he needs to be spending time with kids his own age. Not some old lady."

Maddie takes immediate offense. My mother might as well have shot her. "But it was okay when you needed someone to watch him all these years so you could work."

My mother pauses as if she didn't expect Maddie to put up a fight. "That was different."

"You mean convenient for you, until you got fired."

"I paid you."

"Ten dollars a week," she says sourly.

"And you took it." I know that tone. My mother is about to blow, and Maddie is close. I gather my book bag and head to the door. "Anyway. He's old enough now that he doesn't need keeping."

"He still needs to be looked after. He needs guidance."

"He's coming home. That's the end of it."

Maddie glances my way, the same fear in her eyes as I'm sure she sees in mine.

"I'll be back," I mouth. She nods as her eyes trail over me like I'm her entire world, and I feel the same because she's mine. Her trailer is my escape. And this world we create gives me the break I need from my parents and their crap.

I move to stand at the door and stare down at my mother who cuts eyes the color of mine up to me in a dark blue robe that's seen better decades. She jerks her head in the direction of our trailer. "Come on."

I step outside and turn to Maddie who nods at me, forcing a smile and her signature wink. "See you soon, boy."

It's the first time my heart ever broke, and I can feel the tear between us as my eyes swell. I'd been by her side since I was eight years old and there's something so unnatural about what's happening that I immediately stop my feet and start to protest.

"No, Mom, I'm good over here. I'll be home before dinner."

"Home, now!"

Maddie chirps up from behind me. "Mind your mother, Lucas."

But I shake my head. "This is bullshit, Mom! What happened? Did Dad hurt you again?"

My mother snaps to attention, looks back at Maddie embarrassed and then leans in to me with a vicious bite. "You have no business at your age staying with that woman. You're growing." My mother leans in, brows quirked. "Is she asking you to touch her?"

My eyes widen. "What? No!"

Maddie's door slams shut before we hear the shatter of glass. I glare at her accusingly. "She heard you!"

"Good, she needs to keep her paws off my son!" she shouts past me toward Maddie's trailer.

"All we do is run lines!" I say, standing my ground. "What's wrong with that? I need all the practice I can get!"

She harrumphs. "You should be playing football or something. That's not good for you."

"What do you care what's good for me!?" I dig my feet in as she tries to pull me toward our trailer. "There's nothing to do in there!"

"You need to study and make good grades," she says, clearing the two cement steps up to push the broken button on our screen door.

"All of a sudden you're a mother?" I yell at her from where I stand. "She's more a mother to me, and you know it." I must have lost my mind, but my tirade is cut short when she looks back at me.

"What's that red mark on your face?"

"What?"

She peers closer. "Did she slap you?"

"No, Mom! We were just acting."

"She hit you?"

"No, that's your job when you drink too much, smoke all your cigarettes, and have no one else to blame."

The truth barely pauses her tirade. "She's an old weirdo. You either stay away from her or I'm calling the cops!"

And with those words, my universe crumbles.

The next day when I get home from school, there's a dictionary and a glass of carrot juice on the steps of my trailer. I look over to see Maddie staring through the window and drink the juice in a few gulps before I begin to walk toward her door using the glass as an excuse. She shakes her head as I approach and lets her curtain fall. I grab the dictionary and open it to see a note scribbled on the back of the front cover.

I don't know why this is happening, my boy, but everything in life is a test, and you have to be ready to play the part. I don't know what they're teaching you in school, but you're going to need a better vocabulary to make it in the biz. Drink your juice.

X
Maddie

Maddie died alone of pneumonia in her sleep the day after my fifteenth birthday. She was only sixty years old. She didn't have enough money or a way to get the medical attention she needed. Actually, she did have enough money to be seen, but she'd refused to waste it saving her life in order to save mine. Some may not see it that way, but when you're in the shittiest and most desperate of circumstances the way we were, you have no choice but to see it. Giving up anything when you have nothing is the biggest of sacrifices. And she did save me. What she left was just enough to get me a ticket to Hollywood and off the streets for a few weeks. It was a chance, and that's all it was, and I took it. Because I wanted out of that hell and because I wanted to make her proud.

Her hopes were all pinned on me. I'd bided my time until my parents started taking my paychecks. Luckily, I'd had my girlfriend Jessie hide some of my cash at her house. She was loaded and looked out for me. Aside from leaving her behind, I didn't hesitate when my father and I had it out over their constant harping on payday. I had no future there. None. And no amount of sitting idle would help it. Some family had moved into Maddie's trailer a few weeks after she died, and it was all I could do to watch life moving on without her. I didn't leave my parents in the trailer in West Virginia. The only parent I had died. So I took her money, kissed the girl that took my virginity, and left.

And I did it.

I did it all.

I fulfilled our every dream. But even as I should be satisfied, I'm not. I'm considered the picture of success in my community and I feel like I'm nowhere. Because I'm still the same kid worrying if the lights are going to get cut off in freezing temperatures. Still afraid they'll see the scars from my scratching when I shave my head for a role. Still the same bastard whose dad came home drunk from NASCAR and told him his mother was a whore and he'd played daddy long enough. I'd fooled them all. All of them, except my wife. Even now I see the pity in her eyes when my childhood comes up. Money, fame, it's all a fucking lie we tell ourselves, and others strive for.

"Maddie, what the fuck is all this for?" I whisper as I peer out into the parking lot from my trailer. At first, it was a means to get out of hell. To make something of myself. And then somehow it got twisted into a pile of ambition where I now find myself unrecognizable. I've got nothing left to prove, no goals to aim for.

I'm on top of my mountain. I got the money, the career, the girl. I've got everything I could possibly want, and yet nothing I genuinely need, aside from Mila. She's growing tired of my charade, and pretty soon she's going to realize I'm just a fucked-up guy who says some words on camera, who's void inside, and then where will we be?

Did Blake feel this vacant when he was on top? Or was looking up at the mountain a lot worse after hitting ground? It had to be. Then again, we'd both seemed happier in the struggle, at least in the beginning. There was so much to look forward to, so many milestones to reach. Maybe we were both happier with the idea, the lie that if we got to a certain place, that place is where we would find *it*, whatever *it* is.

I arrived alone, and there is nothing here.

I'm sure the idea of success is far better than success itself. That realization has me paralyzed where I sit. I've traveled a million miles and gone fucking nowhere.

The knock on my door jars me.

"Lucas, they're ready for you."

CHAPTER 29

MILA

T HE PHONE RINGS TWICE BEFORE SHE PICKS UP.

"Nova," I whisper, just as Lucas turns on the shower.

"Hey, Mila, how are you?"

"I'm good. I'm uh…"

Her light laugh puts me at ease. "What's up, girl?"

"I just…wanted to make sure everything was going okay on set."

Her brief pause swats me back to the edge. "He's not talking to anyone but Wes. Roth is being a dick about the number of takes Lucas wants, but Wes seems into it."

Sighing I nod though she can't see me.

"He's holing up in his trailer a lot."

"He's doing the same at home."

I uncap the bottle and count the remaining pills.

"He's nailing it so far, Wes seems pleased."

"Well, as long as Wes is pleased," I say with a bite she knows isn't meant for her.

"Is he drinking? Do you smell booze on him a lot?"

"No, not really."

"I'm sorry to bother you with this, I'm just worried. Do me a favor, if things get to be too much, call me."

"I will."

"Thank you."

"I don't need you to fucking spy on me," I hear gruffly muttered from behind me just as I swipe to end the call.

"What is this?" I ask not bothering to defend myself. He looks at the bottle of Oxy that was prescribed to him over a year ago and shrugs.

"I'm playing a heroin addict, that's heroin in pill form. I only took a few so I could understand the effect. Don't be such a prude."

"You don't do this!" I screech and immediately regret it when his face turns to stone. I press on anyway. "You don't throw weekend parties and take pills for recreation and you sure as hell don't forget our anniversary! You aren't eating, you barely sleep. You mumble through what conversations we do have. I'm worried, Lucas, you're pushing too hard!"

"That's not worrying," he snaps, the accusation in his eyes stinging me to the point I have to look away. "You have no idea what it takes. You don't have a fucking clue."

"Sure, I don't?" I snap incredulously.

"You don't. And I don't need to be policed. Your husband is not a drug addict. You need to chill out and stop being so paranoid."

This time, I glare at him. "Don't you dare talk to me like that."

"Then don't check up on me like a mother."

Cold eyes study me, and before I can think of a reasonable response, he's grabbing a duffle bag from his closet and stuffing clothes into it.

"What in the hell are you doing?"

"I'm going to sleep on the set for a while. It's just easier. I don't have time for this. Coming back and forth every day is wearing me out."

"Bullshit."

Contempt-filled eyes stare back at me. "Why is it bullshit, because it will only make it that much harder for you to keep tabs on me?"

"Because I don't want you to go!"

He throws the bag against the wall. "Then act like you want me to stay!"

Tears slip and fall down my cheeks, and he doesn't flinch. My husband hates the sight of me crying. The man in front of me could care less. He gives me room to speak, but I have nothing to say. I'm at a loss. I'm supposed to embrace this monster, and all I want is a sign that my husband is still here.

"You haven't touched me in weeks, Lucas."

"I'm working," he says dryly.

"Surely big bad Nikki Rayo occasionally needs his cock attended to?"

"By all means, *wife*," he gestures toward his crotch and my stomach rolls.

"Just go," I say, disgusted. "If you want to go, just fucking go."

Shutting the bathroom door behind me, I wash my face with cold water. Seconds later, I hear the slam of the front door.

"Mila, you're doing too much," Yanni tells me softly as we sip a bottle on the porch of the bistro the next day. "You should go rest."

"I'm happy to help."

We sit in a comfortable silence before he turns inquisitive eyes to me. I sigh in resignation before he asks.

"Lucas has taken a role he's heavily involved in. This is the only place I'm useful right now. I'm sorry if I've become bothersome."

"Not at all, you're more than welcome here."

I didn't know how to explain I was waiting on Lucas and I didn't want to. The worst part is, in the past we'd always kept the lines of communication open, that was our saving grace. He doesn't want my help, my worry. He's made it crystal clear. I'm angry and resentful he's taken that aspect away. He's breaking our rules by the day, leaving me uncertain of our future, of my place in his life. I don't want to discuss my marital problems with another outsider, so I finish my wine and leave him with a forced smile. On the drive home I realize Lucas has tossed me into the same place of uncertainty I was in after I left Egypt.

It had been nearly a week since he left to sleep on set. The longer he remains quiet, the more pissed off I become.

Speeding toward the studio, I decide I've had enough. He's going to talk to me. Instead of joining him on set, I wait for him in his trailer. The silence has stretched long enough. Resentment has reached its peak, and by the time he walks in, I'm fuming.

When the door opens, I'm struck by how different he looks. He's dressed in a blue suit, his eyes tinted brown by contacts, his demeanor ice-cold. Lifeless eyes sweep me, but he doesn't pause a single second before climbing the steps to move past me where I sit at the breakfast bench. I'm stinging with indifference as he opens the fridge eyeing the contents and overlooking me as if I'm one of his staff.

I stand. "It's time to come home."

"Is it?" His nose twitches in annoyance as if he's dealing with a petulant child. "Gee, Mom, I'm having so much fun. Can't I play just a little longer?"

His voice is unrecognizable to me, and I damn near gasp at the difference.

I'm staring at the spitting image of Nikki Rayo.

"We need to talk."

"Nah," he says, sweeping me again with cold eyes. "We don't."

"You're breaking rules."

His slow-building and menacing grin brings on a wave of nausea.

"You're making a mockery out of our marriage."

"Whatsa' matter, *sweetheart*? Still mad I'm not dicking you enough?"

"Jesus. You bastard."

He grins again and I can see by the second that coming here was a mistake. "It's been a long day, but if you're offering," he says, ripping off his jacket to reveal a vest underneath. In seconds he has me pinned to the table, his mouth close as he rubs his erection along my stomach.

"Just give me something," I plea. "We don't do it like this. I'm worried."

"Shut your mouth and lift your skirt or we're done talking."

His eyes flare with amusement as my anger bubbles over. "Fuck you."

His chuckle has the hairs rising on the back of my neck. "This what you came for?" I'm repulsed that I'm turned on by his crudeness, but I need something, some sort of connection. Resigned that this is as close as I'm going to get to my estranged husband, I give in and trust.

"You're not my type," I say, my words laced with venom. "Not even close. You're just a dumb kid playing a big man with a gun."

"You're really starting to agitate me." It's unreal—the eyes, the voice the intimidation. This man is not my husband.

"Agitate is a big word for you, isn't it?" I say, grabbing my best weapon and hurling it at him.

With a fistful of hair in his hand, he pulls painfully. "Bitch," he says, stealing all the breath from me, before slamming me against the table, not enough to hurt me but enough to try to scare me. I rip at his chest, his hands and fingers snatch away my panties before he rubs his engorged cock between my legs. Brown eyes flash down at me before he buries himself so deep, I scream out. He pumps furiously, eyes blazing as I rip at his hair and slap at his face and am rewarded with a sinister grin. I want him so badly, but I'm still reeling from the bite I asked for.

"Lucas," I plea, praying for him to slow down so I can savor these precious minutes, have some semblance of connection, but he's stripped away all the intimacy. He's not here. Nikki is, and Nikki could give a shit about Mila Walker. He's fully immersed, and he's not coming back until it's over. He jackhammers inside me savagely until he spills with a muffled groan. It only takes him seconds to gather himself and tuck his cock back into his pants. I rise, still hungry, unsated as he adjusts himself. He doesn't help me dress, he simply grabs his script off the counter and looks back at me, unaffected as I pull my skirt down. Ignoring my stare, he reads on as if nothing ever happened. Furious, I stomp toward the door when he says behind me, "Come by anytime."

Sobbing on the way home, I try to get a grip on what I'm feeling. What the hell did I expect? The man that just fucked me wasn't my husband. He hadn't hurt me, in fact, I hated that I didn't hate it, but the lack of connection is ripping me apart. After a hot shower at home, I sink into my lounge chair with a glass of wine, praying that he'll come home tonight, not to talk but just to sleep in our bed. An action of remorse is better than none at all. I miss him so much. We're growing further and further apart, and he's allowing it. That part of it I'm afraid I won't be able to forgive him for.

"Stop it," I say over and over. "Stop it. You are his life, and he is yours," I repeat, batting my tears away. Every decision Lucas has ever made when it came to us has been calculated, not in manipulation but in love. It had always been that way. But I see no logic in this, no plan. He always thought through his actions, always. He'd meant that episode in that trailer to be a warning. He wasn't there, and no amount of fight on my part was going to bring him out. I had to see this through if I wanted him back. The problem was it was getting harder and harder to want him at all.

CHAPTER 30

MILA

T HE FOLLOWING NIGHT, I'M UNLOADING MY GROCERIES WHILE I mentally prepare myself for my mother's arrival and uncork some red. I need that calm before she comes in with her version of the inquisition. It had been too long since we'd had dinner together, mostly due to avoidance on Lucas's part. It was only fair. She'd terrorized him the first time I brought him home which had instigated the most spectacular fight in our relationship.

After draining myself on the floor in front of my door. I vow to myself that I will never date men again. My dismantled heart agrees it's reasonable. Furious, I draw myself from the hardwood in a rage storming through the cottage happy to again exchange pain for re-newed anger. I go to his drawer and gather his shit before taking his shaving cream and gel from the medicine cabinet. Still hiccupping, I open my front door and hurl it out only to hear an "oomph." Looking into the dark porch, I see Lucas with his hands held up in surrender rising to his feet from the ground.

Anger pours from my every limb as I flip on the light. "Leave," I say, swallowing more tears. "Leave."

"I'm sorry."

"You should be. And I've never, ever thought of you the way you see yourself. Trust me, you are the only one who has shed light on what a dumbass you are."

"You're right, it's my issue."

"Glad that's settled," I point at his truck behind him, "leave."

"Mila, I can't. I was driving for mere minutes before I realized what a fucking idiot I truly am. I just…I'm sorry."

"Not good enough, Hollywood. You don't get to play ping-pong with my heart. No one does."

His lips curl up as if he's fighting a smile, and eventually, it wins.

"You're seriously smiling at me right now?" I'm seconds away from ripping him to shreds.

"You're so beautiful when you're mad, really mad." Something in my eyes must have shifted to crazy town because his smile drops. "Which isn't funny."

"I hate you."

"No, you don't," he says softly, his smile making a maddening appearance. "You love me. I felt it in every tear that dropped from your beautiful face. You don't want to let go any more than I do. I'm sorry."

"Not good enough." I turn to shut the door, and he catches it. "That's not all my stuff."

"How do you know, you haven't even looked at all I've tossed."

"Well, I have more."

"Fine," I say, letting go of the handle and taking a step back. "Then see to it, Romeo, and get the hell out!"

He opens the door further and leans down to whisper to me, "You don't mean that."

"Just get your stuff and go." He heads toward my kitchen, and I'm hot on his heels.

"You don't have anything in there."

"Actually, I do," he says, walking over to my coffee canister and lifting the lid.

"Seriously? You're going to take the coffee?"

"No, this," he says, pulling a box from the container and shoving it into his pocket. Jaw slack, I stand in the middle of the kitchen as more tears fall. He watches me for several seconds before brushing past me and grabbing my hand. "Come on."

"What?"

"I want to show you something."

"I'm not going anywhere with you!"

"Mila—"

I rip my hand out of his grip. "Leave and don't come back. I mean it!"

"That's it," he snaps, pinning me to the wall, his eyes hellfire and jaw set. I'm helpless in the hold he tightens on my wrists as he challenges me.

"You're going to hear me out."

"Save it. Let go."

His eyes flare. "Never."

"I'll never forgive you."

"Yes, you will."

He presses in, so I'm forced to look up at him. "I fucked up. I'm allowed to fuck up once in a while and be forgiven. That's how it works. Same goes for you. This isn't over, so fucking far from it. Take a good look, baby, I'm the one who owns your lips, your pussy, and your immaculate heart. I am the last man standing."

I don't know what comes over me, but I bite him.

I bite him.

And then we're doing something resembling kissing, I'm sucking his tongue, and he's gripping my hair. We're ripping off each other's clothes like it's our job. In a blink, I'm naked on my counter, and he's licking me furiously between my legs while I rip at his hair. Neither of us is backing down. I come on his tongue, and in the next breath, I'm on my knees sucking his cock, licking his thick head before he fucks my mouth. Then I'm pulled up by my arms, my hands flattened by his on the counter while he slams into me from behind so hard both our legs nearly give out. I come again. He stretches my ass with his fingers, pounding into me, and I come again. I ride him backward on my hard tiles, I come again. And then I'm resting on his thighs watching his thick cock go in and out of me, our foreheads bent because we can't tear our eyes away. I come again. It's the best sex of my life, and just when I think it can't get any better, he reaches for me, not in the way that hurts, in the way that heals. Our mouths collide in a kiss that finishes me for all others. It's so profound, it leaves me raw. He buries himself when he comes, wringing out his pleasure with my name on his lips. Sated, we sit in a tangled sweaty heap on the floor until he pulls away and presses a finger to his lip.

"Damn, I think I'm bleeding."

"Good."

Chuckling, he presses a kiss to my shoulder before he starts to pull our scattered clothes in from all sides of us.

"Get dressed," he orders, unraveling us to stand before he tugs on his jeans.

"Lord, man, I just came more than a porn star working overtime. Give a woman a rest." His throaty chuckle makes me smile, but my eyes are still closed. "Can it wait?"

"No," he says, pushing the soaked hair away from my face and kissing my lips.

"What time is it?"

He pulls his phone from the pocket of his jeans. "Midnight."

"Damn, how long did you listen to me cry, you sadist?!"

"Not long before I was slapped upside the head with my shaving cream, but trust me, that was more my punishment than yours." His next words are filled with remorse. "And I don't ever want to hear you cry like that again."

"Well, then don't break my fucking heart."

"Sounds like a plan."

"Yeah, well," I say, fastening my bra, "I wish that plan had been in motion before this."

"I'll make you glad it happened," he says easily.

"You're going to make me glad it happened? Going to make me

glad that I have no water left in my body?"

"Yes," he answers with a chuckle.

"Do your worst, Hollywood."

Once he's buckled me inside his truck, he leans in on the frame.

"I'm sorry, I've never been in love like this, I've never felt so help-less to someone else. I have to admit it's hard for me to let go of control."

"Can't you see you have the same power over me?"

"It's just hard for me to let go."

"Because you've been hurt?" I ask, my words stuttered as a de-layed hiccup escapes me. He winces when it happens and slides the back of his hand down my cheek. "I guess I freaked out. I didn't ever want you to know."

"Lucas, just because you aren't well-versed in art or wine, it doesn't make you not suitable. I meant what I said, you're one of the most intelligent men I know."

He leans in and kisses me, thoroughly before shutting the door. We ride in silence for a few minutes before he speaks up. "I was raised in the outskirts of a town in West Virginia, I told you some of it, but not really the truth. My father did odd jobs to pay the bills but mostly left during the day to get drunk with his buddies. My mother worked at a gas station. To my parents, I was both obligation and nuisance. My dad lived for NASCAR, and my mom lived for my dad. They fought and fucked, and neither was pretty. We lived in a trailer with thin walls and a leaky roof. I slept on the same lumpy twin mattress for sixteen years. I was the kid everyone avoided because I was poor."

"Did they hurt you?"

"My mom slapped me around a little, but it wasn't anything I still lose sleep over. She did do it once at school, and that stuck with me. Maddie, she was the one who gave me a mother's love…" he fumbles a little with his words and I can tell it pains him. "She's the one who showed me what a mother was supposed to be like, as reluctant as she was."

"I'm sorry."

"Don't be. I had Maddie. I think the universe interjects people in your life for a reason, brief or otherwise, to make up for a few shortcomings, to help make sense of things you can't figure out."

"But, Lucas, you can't just make decisions for the both of us."

"I know."

He drives in silence for a few minutes, and before I know it, we're parked at a duplex.

"Where are we?"

"My place."

I turn in my seat. "I thought you lived at a hotel when you weren't working?"

He blows out a breath. "I lied."

"What? Why?"

"You're about to see, come on."

To say the outside of the town house is meager is an understatement. He guides me through a small fence, and I can see the courtyard is well taken care of, in fact, it's beautiful. "This is lovely," I remark, looking at the lush green yard.

Lucas nods. "Denny does a good job."

"He seems like a really nice man."

"He owns the town house. I give him extra for yard work."

"I'm confused," I say, pausing on the porch as he pulls out his keys.

"I know."

"I mean this is nice, but it's...can't you afford more? You're renting?"

"Money talk is rude," he says with a wink.

I swallow. "Sorry."

"No, this is exactly why I brought you here." He unlocks the house and pushes the door letting me in ahead of him. I gasp when I see the scarce furnishings. There is no life, barely any personality.

There's a large TV and a recliner in the living room and nothing else. No pictures, nothing that makes the space personal, warm, or inviting. I turn to him completely floored. "You live here?"

He bites his upper lip and nods.

"What's upstairs?"

"Just a bed and necessities."

"That's all?"

Another nod.

"Lucas..."

He leans against the wall and shoves his hands in his pockets. "My mom had this legal notepad, and she terrorized me with it."

"A legal pad?"

"Funny how something so ordinary can become the bane of your existence." *He shakes his head.* "Anyway, on that legal pad was this list of monthly bills she had to pay and nightly she'd drink about a fifth of brandy and sit me down to tell me exactly how much money we had, and what we didn't. She would cry, and it scared the shit out of me. We lost our power once for almost a month in the dead of winter, so her fears weren't that farfetched. Maddie got it turned back on."

My eyes are already tearing up.

"My mom did this, for years and years, always instilling in me that there was never enough money. I guess it made me a little sick too." *He swallows, looking around his house.* "That Land Rover you dented tonight is leased, and I don't have to pay for it."

I wince. "I'm sorry."

He's already shaking his head. "That's not...baby, that's not why I told you that. I can afford to buy every Land Rover in the state of California and probably several states over. I've barely spent any of the money I've made off the movies. I've been living off the interest, which is plenty."

Realization has my chest constricting. "Because you're scared it's not enough?"

"Shit, I know. It's crazy. I don't expect you to fully understand, but I hope you'll try. This is scary for me. I have tens of millions in the bank, and I know how hard it is to wrap your mind around this, but I'm scared to spend a dime." He runs a hand through his hair. "Does that make me crazy?" Shaking my head with shimmering eyes, I close the space between us.

"Mila, I don't want your sympathy, I swear this isn't what this is about. This is about you understanding me, I don't know," he says, scanning his living room, "maybe you can help me let go of it, but...for me, it's still hard. I was the smelly kid, you know? I was the one that had to steal deodorant from The Family Dollar so I wouldn't fucking reek after gym. The one with the shredded clothes who took a friend's hand-me-down sneakers a size too small. I was that kid, and I was okay with that because I never wanted to have to explain myself or my parents. So I was quiet, and I dissolved into whatever color the wall was because it made life easier on me. I'm not upset about it, well not anymore. I use it on the job all the time, and I make a lot of money because I can remember how bad it was, how desperate I felt, how much I just wanted someone to take notice and just once consider me worthy."

"God, Lucas, you are, you are so worthy."

"It's okay, Dame. I know that now, to some degree I do know that. But I haven't felt the way your mother made me feel in a very long time."

"I'm so sorry."

He closes the space between us. "Baby, don't get upset. She saw it, she sniffed out the side of me I've been desperately trying to hide from you, and I have no right to ask you to be with me if you don't know everything. I don't know what I was thinking. I guess I thought I could ignore this and when we made our life together, this would be history. I know it's stupid now, it was stupid to think that."

"We don't lie to each other."

"And I'm done. I swear to you, I'm done."

"I don't ever want to meet your parents." I sniff.

"You won't ever have to. That was a whole different life," he says, shaking his head, his gaze somewhere in the past. "I'm still in aftershock of how drastically things have changed. Of the places I've been. Mila, I'm still not fully comfortable in this life. Even when I got to LA, I lived pretty desperately. Blake and I stayed hungry. The last few years have been unreal. I still don't believe my bank statements."

"No one has discovered you live here?"

He shrugs. "I don't think anyone would believe it. I have Nova rent it in her name so there's no record of me anywhere, and I just stay here, and I save." He peers down at me. "I've never considered myself lucky. Like you, I've had to work for every single thing I've ever gotten. It's been shitty in the way no one has ever been there for me, but I see the other side of it now." He swallows, his eyes so gentle as his hands cover me in a caress. "You make me want to let go, take more chances, free myself up. So," he says, pulling the box from his pocket, "I finally spent a little for a very good reason."

Burying my face in my hands, I cry openly in front of him. When I pull my palms away, he's kneeling in front of me. "I love fighting with you. I love the way you look at me. I love the way it feels when we're together. I love the silk of your skin, the velvet of your beautiful voice. I love the way you caress my forehead when you think I'm asleep. I love that you take all of the socks out of the dryer and count them. I love that you feel so fucking perfect when I push inside you, the way you moan, the way you come. I love your elf ears, the noises you make after you sip wine. The fact that you pick up pennies, no one does that anymore." We smile at each other as his eyes water, and his voice clogs with emotion. "I love that you laugh inappropriately when you're nervous. I love that you're so smart. I love that, Mila. I love that you're a natural teacher because I've already learned so much from you. I wasn't ever able to tell you that before because of foolish pride, but you know all of me now. All of me, even the parts I didn't want you to."

"I love you," he says, standing, the ring hooked on his thumb as he takes my face in his hands. "I'm so undeniably in love with you. I want this, I want you to be mine, to make that promise to me. Mine. Forever."

I'm a mess, every fiber of my being shaking with the strike of each word. He's perfect, and he has no idea. That thought keeps running through my head as his love rips through me, striking again and again where it's intended.

"I'm already yours."

His tearful smile elates me. "Oh, baby, did I fuck this up, but if you can forgive me for this, we're gold. Mila, will you marry me?"

CHAPTER 31

MILA

STIRRING THE MIXTURE IN MY BOWL, TEARS ESCAPE ME AT THE memory of Lucas's proposal when the doorbell rings. Quickly I wipe them away before opening the door for my mother who spots the evidence immediately. I can see the worry on her face when she reads mine. "I'm fine, Mom. I just got a little bit sentimental."

She lifts her shoulders defensively. "I didn't say a word."

"You don't have to," I snark behind her as she bounds through the doorway with her typical air of authority scrutinizing our spacious house before turning to me. "Is he here?"

"No, he's working. I told you it would just be us."

"Your father sends his regrets as well. He's got some nasty cold."

"You told me."

"You could call him." Guilt riddles me. It's the truth. I've been so wrapped up with Lucas and getting my footing back at work that I've been completely avoiding my parents. "I'll call him tonight." Mom follows me into the kitchen as I wash my hands and then roll up my sleeves. She looks pleased as I pour her some wine and she eyes the ingredients.

"What's this?"

"You know what it is," I say with a smile. "Yanni, my new boss taught me how to make it for you."

"What a lovely surprise. Can I help?"

"I insist you do," I say as she rounds the marble countertop and washes her hands. We spend hours drinking wine and talking about simpler times. I can see her worry as she brings up Lucas and I bat the subject away. I'm enjoying the moment, just being her daughter. She tells me a few stories I'd forgotten about when I was younger and when Lucas walks into the kitchen unexpectedly, we both have smiles on our faces. Scowling he looks between us, his expression stern as he greets my mother. "Maïwenn," he says sharply, and I see her flinch. It takes everything in me not to walk over and pummel him. "Lucas, I wasn't expecting you home."

"Funny, I remember you demanding I *come*," he says, his voice full of acid. "Smells great."

"Have some," I grate out, plating the rich meat, vegetables, and heavy cream sauce before I thrust it toward him.

Eyeing it, he looks directly at my mother with a dead stare before sauntering off. "I'll eat later. I'll be in my office." Anger boiling, I turn to my mother humiliated. "I'm so sorry."

She's paling rapidly as she watches Lucas's retreating back. "Mila, what's going on?"

"He's just…" I shake my head. "He's sad about Blake."

"And this rudeness comes from his grief?"

Lucas's voice bellows from the hall. "You can always leave if you aren't feeling welcome."

I gasp audibly, and my mother pushes past me. I curse as I follow her down the hall. "Have I offended you in some way, Lucas?"

He turns on his heel, and I can see from the way he's standing there's no going back from what he's about to say.

"Offending me? Now, why would you think that? Because you ruined your daughter's wedding by humiliating yourself, or the fact that you think you have some right or some say in her life after?"

My mother stands her ground. "Silly man, you're just the husband, I created that human. I have every right to her, as much as you."

"Should she invite you into the bedroom too so you can watch, Mom? Will that satisfy you?"

I feel slapped, and it's obvious my mother does too. "I'll forgive you for that, but no more."

"Don't bother," Lucas says, retreating down the hall before slamming his office door."

My mother turns to me, her eyes welling with tears as she pushes past me to grab her purse off the entryway table. "I didn't know he felt this way."

"I'm sorry, Mom, don't believe it. Don't...listen to him, he's not himself."

Both of us shriek as Lucas speaks from behind us, leaning against the wall with an empty lowball glass in hand, his eyes as wide as his deviant smile. "Maïwenn, you *should* believe me."

"Lucas, stop! Stop!" I scream just as my mother shuts the front door behind her. I chase her out to her car, and she turns back to me with a small tear running down her cheek. "I'm so sorry, Mila. I've felt so guilty for that day for so long. I should have apologized to you both years ago."

"Mom, he's not himself, he's immersed in this role, and he's just being...unreasonable. Please come back inside. I'll talk to him."

She starts her car. "It's best if I leave."

"I'll call you later," I offer as she pulls away.

Taking steadying breaths, I do my best to calm down. Minutes later, I'm on the verge of hyperventilating. Maybe she deserved it, but then, not six years after the fact. What Lucas did was just as cutthroat, it was the best revenge. I am just as furious with him as I was with her all those years ago. Slamming the door behind me, I make my way into the hall and see he's talking on the phone. He didn't even have the decency to wait on the argument he picked. Heading to the kitchen, I toss the carefully prepared dinner into the sink and start the dishes. Lucas emerges a few minutes later and opens the fridge taking a beer from it. "I'll take my dinner on the patio."

"Your dinner is in the fucking trash. Feed yourself and don't ever talk to my mother like that again."

He lifts a brow. "She deserved a lot worse."

"Maybe then, but not now. Your behavior was deplorable, and you two have been civil for years!"

"Because your husband has made it that way," he adds easily. "I think it's about time he stood up for himself as far as that woman is concerned."

"That woman?" I say, shaking my head. "Go back to your cave, madman," I snap testily before glancing up to look at him and what I see when I do, disgusts me. "You think this is funny?"

"You're cute when you're angry."

"Don't you dare!" I say as livid tears threaten. Grabbing my keys off the counter, I move to gather my purse when he catches my wrist and jerks me to him. Our bodies align naturally, but everything else is foreign.

"Where do you think you're going?"

"Anywhere but here, with you," I say, jerking away before fleeing out the door.

The next morning, I wake up to a red Cartier box on the pillow next to me and am instantly furious. My husband has never bought me a piece of jewelry other than my wedding ring. I walk down the hall with it in my hand never opening the box and find Lucas in the kitchen lifting a coffee cup for a drink. Coffee. The monster in the kitchen is not my husband.

He eyes me carefully not saying a word. Even Nikki Rayo has redeeming moments in the script. There's a bit of a romance mixed in with that psychopathic killer, the man in front of me is lost, utterly void of emotion. I throw the box into the trash can next to him and leave him there.

Listening to the crash of the waves, I decide to sit on our deck and wait him out. He's probably due at the studio soon, and I don't want to be anywhere near him. Avoiding his company is definitely not something I'd have ever thought myself capable of.

The sound of the door sliding open lifts me from where I dwell in a life that now seems so distant, it's piercing the deepest parts of me. Lucas's new voice sounds from behind me, kicking my heart into an aimless state.

"I finally have enough money to get you nice things, and you throw them in the trash?"

"Fuck off…Nikki," I mutter into the sea breeze.

"That's not nice." He's standing directly behind my chair, in a ploy of intimidation I'm no longer playing into.

"I don't want to know you," I say. "At all. So please, just pretend I don't exist. Can you do that? Take some direction from your wife for once? I don't want to know you."

He circles the chair and squats down in front of me, a killer smile in place. It's eerie, and it reminds me of someone, probably because he's someone else. It's a smile that insinuates that I'm the one being unreasonable, that I've imagined his behavior and I'm the crazy one. I'm not buying it, just like I'm not buying into that jewelry. He's still acting.

"I work hard for you, you could show some appreciation." He palms my thigh, and I smack it away. He clenches his fists, his eyes on me as I do anything but give him the attention he's asking for.

"I'm under so much pressure," he says testily. "You don't know what it's like. You don't know what I had to do to get roles like this."

I gawk at him. "I've been married to you through enough movies, Lucas, I know exactly what it's like. I made sure of it. You've never gone to these lengths."

"I've never had to!" His voice rises, and I cower away, not because I'm afraid of him because it's just not worth it. This conversation is pointless, and I'm no longer open to negotiation. He's made his point, I have my own to make.

"I don't think you even know who you are anymore." I'm crying again, and I hate it, but I'm fighting for the love of my life, and he's lost in some oblivion I have no map for. He's the only one with the clues. "I miss you so much."

He runs his hands along the solid white stone wall of our terrace. "You didn't like the necklace?"

"What the fuck are you even saying?" I sniff and avert my eyes. "That's not even you."

"This job is over soon," he says matter-of-fact, as he turns back to me weighing my response as if my hurt doesn't faze him. If it's Lucas finally speaking up, it's not enough.

"Yeah, well, I'm all out of faith," I say, standing. "And make sure you do a good job because that might be all you have left when you come home."

I dress, get in my car, and leave.

"All it takes is a beautiful fake smile to hide an injured soul and they will never notice how broken you really are."
—Robin Williams

LUCAS

WALKING TOWARD THE CHATEAU MARMONT WHERE BLAKE'S BEEN holed up the last six months, I stop short when I see him and Amanda just inside the entrance. He's holding her tightly to him, whispering words of comfort while she crumbles in his arms. It's painful to see. A few years ago, they were the picture of happiness. Blake still hasn't been forthright about the reasons behind their divorce, and it irks me. If I were a betting man, I would have placed my money on the two of them. They'd been a good influence on me in finding my other half to complete my own picture. I'd envied their effortless connection as I'd watched them come together. In the front row, I'd witnessed their linking as it flowered and stood at Blake's side at their wedding while they tearfully pledged themselves to each other. It was easily the most romantic wedding I'd ever attended and not because of the setting, but because their love for each other was tangible. They made me want for something more and taught me not to settle. I'd tried my first hand at a relationship with Laura. The night of their wedding, I'd made us official. Thinking back, I knew it was due to the sentiment of the day. But when it had turned out to be nothing more than convenience, we called it off. I waited for Mila, and it turned out to be the best decision of my life. Somewhere inside, I knew the choice Blake made to end his marriage wasn't about love lost.

Blake has calmed Amanda to the point he could get her into the car as the valet pulls up. I stare on as he shoves his hands in his jeans and watches her drive away. He hadn't asked me to be there, but he'd told me they'd be signing papers today and I've shown up just in time *to witness the soul-crushing end of it. Blake wipes his face repeatedly, looking the way the car had left long after it was out of sight. He spots me as I walk toward his car which the valet had already parked. Briefly, he pauses when he sees me approaching.*

"Come to get me drunk, bro? Amazing suggestion. Your blessed universe couldn't have delivered a better friend today. What's your poison? I'm thinking tequila."

"This is a mistake," *I say without apology.*

Without a response, he walks around the side of the car, and I climb in before he has a chance to protest. In the driver's seat, he sits idle collecting himself. He's on the edge of breaking, and I can feel it in the dense cabin of his Ferrari.

I speak first. "This is a mistake."

"I know," *he says.* "But I can't be married to her anymore."

"What the hell are you talking about? You don't love that woman any less than you did when you married her."

"You're right. I love her more, that's why I had to set her free. I'm not what she needs."

"Isn't that for her to decide?"

He swallows hard, his eyes glazing over. "Things got bad behind closed doors. Six months ago, I got blackout drunk and destroyed almost everything in our house."

"Did you hurt her?"

"She says I didn't." *He turns to me.* "But do you think she deserves that? You know Amanda, she couldn't hurt anyone like that. There's not a menacing bone in that woman's body. She's perfect. I can't have a hand in destroying that. And I fucking won't. I love her too much."

"So you seek counseling, and you shrink it down to manageable, you don't divorce a woman you're still in love with."

He laughs sarcastically. "There's no cure for being me. Haven't you learned that yet?"

I scoff. "Guess not, I'm still here. What makes you think she wouldn't be?"

"I don't want that woman to ever hate me."

"I don't hate you."

He glances my way. "Yeah you do, a little. You resent me for the messes I've made. It was only a matter of time before she realized she wasted her youth, her beauty, on a piece of shit incapable of being who she wanted. I'm tired, Lucas. It was more exhausting being her husband than any other job. She's the only woman I've ever had to answer to, and I couldn't hack it anymore."

"So, this martyring you think you're doing is all about the asshole?"

"It's freedom," he says, turning the ignition, "to be exactly who I am without constantly having to apologize for it."

"You honestly think you're that toxic? This isn't healthy."

"Never said it was." He pulls a cigarette from a pack on his dash and lights it up.

"So you divorced her to protect her? This is bullshit, man. She could help you."

He shakes his head impatiently and glares at me. "All right, you want the skeletons? Here they come," he says, taking a long drag of his cigarette before looking at me pointedly. "The day after I destroyed our house, I went on a coke bender and snorted lines off a whore for two days while I fucked her bareback. So, you tell me, Boy Scout. Is that a good enough reason to set her free?"

"Jesus Christ, Blake." I'm sick thinking about it.

"Thought so," he says, tearing out of the parking lot. He makes a hard right, and the rev of the engine draws heads our way. Paparazzi who were ready at the curb manage to get a few shots in. Blake is oblivious as he glances my way. "You love me with the same blind fucking eyes, Lucas. I'm never going to change, no matter how much I need to. She couldn't change me either, that's why I'm divorced," he *says, wiping at his face trying to hide the hurt that's leaking from his every pore.*

"This is destroying you, man. You just shot off your own fucking foot."

"Whiskey...I think this is a whiskey kind of day," he mutters before speeding down Sunset. It's a different dynamic now than what it was for us years ago. We used to use our looks to try to charm our way into A-list places, and now we reign over them. Despite Blake's bad boy rep, he's still invited regularly to the old hot spots to further desecrate his image in the public. The street is a wasteland now in that respect, at least for me. The irony strikes me that while my life had completely changed, Blake is still working the same circuit, hanging with the same people.

A few minutes of silence ensue before he speaks up, his voice thick with a mix of guilt and hurt before tossing his cigarette and reaching for another, but the pack falls to the floorboard. "You don't have to agree with me, bro, that's the beauty of it. But you do have to drink with me, to her freedom."

"Blake, if you need help—"

"I'm not using, and I haven't since then."

"Then why?"

His voice is gravel with his next admission. "Because it was just a phase," he says, swallowing thickly. "I'm just a phase," he adds darkly, "a phase everyone in my life eventually outgrows."

"Bullshit. Come stay with us for a couple of months. It would be good to have you around."

He shakes his head. "Your wife isn't a fan of mine. I'm good, I'm covered."

"We can—"

"It's done," he cuts me off, resigned. "Let's outgrow this conversation and catch up." He leans over and roughly runs knuckles through my hair. "It's been a while."

Rolling my eyes, I slap his hand away. "If that's what you need."
He ignores the grudge in my voice.

"Yeah, it's exactly what I need. Thanks, man."

"Anytime," I say, pulling the pack from the floorboard, fishing out a cigarette and lighting it for him. He takes it, and we exchange a look that expresses our clear difference of opinion but garners no more conversation. It's an understanding that passes between us. And as usual, I give him the last word.

Looking back, it's the one time I wish I wouldn't have. From there everything went downhill. He was in the process of making nice with his demons, letting them take over and having more fun while destroying what was left of himself. The conversations that followed—after Mila had to drag me from his hotel room that night after berating us both—had been few and far between. Our phone calls felt like an obligation on both our parts. I couldn't be where he was, and he'd tossed me collectively into a group of people he'd have to answer to. Whether it was concern or his need to be able to act out without the voice of reason or consequence, either way, he'd dealt my sentence.

I'd never once told my brother how much I needed him. Not once had I said those words, though I was sure it wouldn't have made a difference. But what if it had? What if I had slain just one of the demons he'd embraced and dwelled with? What if I'd just taken the time to introduce myself to a single one of them and made it harder for them to exist within him?

What if I had told him just once that he was more than the sum of the shitty things he'd done? That he was a gifted actor and good friend. That what I saw in him wasn't a result of blind faith, but a truth he couldn't see for himself.

"Lucas," I hear Jeremy, the assistant director, mutter as he guides me through the action Wes has in mind for the next scene. "You'll pull the gun out, and as soon as you see him roll and reach, you fire twice. Once at a distance and then again when you approach, get him point-blank, got it?"

I nod, looking around the set.

"You with me?" Jeremy asks unsure. "You want to repeat that back?" he says, with a hint to his voice that hits a raw nerve.

I tug at my collar as the heat from the lights bears down on my scalp.

"You all right?" Jeremy asks, eyeing me without a fucking ounce of genuine concern. I'm just a hired monkey.

"Aren't I always?" I snap, uncomfortable in the cheap polyester suit. "This suit is bullshit. This isn't how I dress."

He rolls his eyes. "Yes, *Nikki*, that's a wardrobe issue. Let's get through this shot, and we can have a discussion after."

"What's the fucking point if we have to re-shoot?" I snap, pulling the tie from around my neck. "Where is Wes? I need a word."

"Don't be that prick," Jeremy mutters beneath his breath.

"What the fuck did you just say?" Narrowing my eyes, I see underlying animosity rise in his.

"I said, don't start the power plays today. We're all aware you don't agree with the fucking suits. We're working on it. We have an exhausted crew trying to wrap up an eighteen-hour day. Thirty of those people haven't eaten shit since lunch, thanks to the schedule you've fucked up. I have no doubt the union is going to hear about this. Let's wrap the day and we can worry about re-shoot later."

"I think we both know this has nothing to do with me, and everything to do with the fuck-me eyes your wife keeps tossing my way on set."

His eyes flare, but he waves a dismissive hand. "Come on, man, you can't be this big of an asshole."

"I'm not, but I'm pretty sure *she* thinks you are."

He shrugs. "Look, Wes wanted you on this one. It's no secret I'm not a fan of yours, especially now. But this is his show, and I'm just trying to give him what he wants. If that means I have to be the prick, that's my job, not yours. I need you to focus."

"Focus?" I snap. "Are you fucking serious right now? You insult me then ask for a favor. Go fuck yourself. I want to speak with Wes."

"Wes is breaking, so you'll have to deal with me."

"Not happening."

"Fucking figures," he mutters. "You're a joke, you know that? All this shit you're putting us through is ridiculous. You know damn well when word gets around about what a little bitch—"

My fist lands squarely where I intend it to. The bone crunch utterly satisfying as he reels back covering his nose, his eyes wide. I don't stop there. I swing again and again until I've connected at least two more blows.

"Call me a bitch again, you piece of shit," I snap. "Please, say it again, you stupid motherfucker," I snarl, charging toward him. "Who am I? I'm the man paying the bills! That's who the fuck I am." It takes me a second to realize the cinematographer is shooting every single minute of our altercation and white-hot light erupts from me as I pull the trigger and let the lava flow. I only come to when I'm in my chair and reports are being filed. Bottle in hand, I flex my fist studying the blood on my knuckles before I wipe it on the sad excuse of a shirt.

"Get off set, Walker," Wes orders as Jeremy glares at me from behind him, holding an ice pack to his nose. "Go get some rest."

The next hour is a blur of lawyer calls, set announcements, and the production team scrambling around my trailer. Odd looks are tossed my way, and I reciprocate with a wink, taking another drink. "Ah, liberating, I get it now."

CHAPTER 33

MILA

MY PHONE BUZZES ON THE NIGHTSTAND AND I OPEN MY EYES, sitting straight up in bed. Swiping to answer, I ask the only question there is to ask while panic races through my veins. "Lucas? What's wrong?"

"Mila."

"What happened?"

His breathing is labored. The hairs on my neck rise. His voice is barely recognizable. "Lucas, please tell me what's going on."

"I don't know how I got here." Fear, it's fear I hear cracking his voice.

"I'm coming."

"Don't. You won't find who you're looking for," he says in warning.

Throwing the covers off, I dash for my closet. "Doesn't matter."

"It does. Don't come here."

That has me pausing in my closet.

"Why?"

"Because you'll be disappointed. Your love is conditional. You've never loved the bad guy."

"That's not true. I love you no matter what," I say, my voice breaking over the line. "I'm coming. Where are you now?"

"I'm nowhere," he says, his voice taking on an edge. The only sound I hear is ice clinking into a glass before the line goes dead.

I stare at the phone in my hand, blinking before I register the time. It's just before daybreak. He's not sleeping at all. He says he's not there, but I know damn well my husband is the one that reached out to me. I won't let him down, I promised I wouldn't. We're living in a land of fiction, and it's up to me to decipher the truths from the lies. He's imploding. I just hope I can save him before the lies swallow us both whole.

Getting a drink of water, I check my texts and see an incoming message from Nova a few hours prior.

Nova: Lucas just lost his shit on the AD and broke his nose. Wes is doing his best to keep him from pressing charges. It's a damn mess.

I'm on my way.

CHAPTER 34

MILA

I HAVE TO SEE HIM, TO LAY EYES ON HIM. THEY'RE SET TO WRAP IN El Paso within the week, but that doesn't stop me from booking the first available flight. They're far along in the movie. The desert scenes are close to last in the sequence but some of the most grueling. This part of the storyboard is where Nikki makes a power play for the throne, savagely killing over a dozen men and demanding loyalty from his wife in the most brutal of ways. These scenes are taxing, and I know his stamina is wilting. I need a purpose, a reason to believe all this sacrifice is worth it. It's the only thing that will reel me back in from breaking at the seams. I'm overwhelmed with the change in Lucas and completely unsure what I'm up against anymore.

Taking my seat, I buckle my belt and stare out the window cursing Blake. If he were here, he would know just how to deal with Lucas. At this point, I can't decipher if this is Lucas acting or if he's using it as an excuse to act bad.

"Mila," Nova calls out to me from the car she's standing next to at the terminal. She looks nervous, and I can see the fatigue in her as I approach with my carry-on.

"I'm so glad you came," she says, hugging me briefly before popping the trunk on the rental car.

"Thanks for picking me up," I say, tossing my bag in and

opening the passenger door. She stands at the driver's side, and I can hear the guilt in her words while the heat-infused wind whips the hair around her face.

"I should have called you sooner. I'm sorry. Something isn't right."

"I know."

Tears imminent on both our parts, we collectively get in the car and sigh. She's the first to speak. "He's nailing it. Really, I've never seen him do better. It's unreal. But instead of being proud of him, I'm almost embarrassed at this point."

Though Nova and I are friends, I've rarely ever abused that friendship to get information...until he took this role.

She looks me over. "How are you?"

"Not good," I confess honestly.

"Can I be honest with you?"

I frown. "You know you can."

"He's on time to set every day, there's no issue there but..."

"But what?"

"Okay, like normally he stays in character, and I get that, it's his way, but he's so, I don't know. He's on a rampage. I mean this guy *is* Nikki fucking Rayo."

"What is he doing?"

She bites her lip. "He's not talking to me. He's not even using me. When I talk to him, it's like he stares straight through me. He's drinking, a lot. Partying with the crew at all hours but not saying much. And when he does, he's constantly pissed off, destructive, and just outright fucking rude to me and to everyone who shows concern."

"Is he paying you?"

"Yeah, I pay all the bills, so we're safe there. But honestly, right now, I'm unsure if I even have a job."

She pulls out of the terminal and sighs. "If he won't even

work with me, what am I here for, you know? Leann is constantly calling because the fucking crew won't keep their mouth shut about what's going on. I think it's purposeful to help promote the movie. He won't even address the PR shitstorm he's causing."

"Take the night off."

"No, he'll be furious," Nova says, navigating us out of the airport.

"Or he won't notice," I say pointedly. "Nova, I'm so sorry. It's been no better at home."

"You think this is about Blake?"

"I know it is."

"I'm worried about him," she says, her eyes filling. "I think he's gone off the grid."

"Or it's just good acting," I try to remind her, more furious than I've ever been. Nova is Lucas's most valuable asset.

"What should we do?"

I shrug and let out a heavy breath. "I guess we'll know in a few weeks when filming wraps."

"It's never been this bad," she says, shuddering.

"I'm so sorry, I don't know what else to say."

"It's my job, I'm just at my wits' end with him." She glances over at me.

"Do you want to drop your stuff at the hotel? I got you a key card to his room."

"No, let's get to the set."

"Okay," she says, taking a few turns that lead us to a long stretch of road.

"I'll be honest. I don't know if I can keep working with him if this is going to be the new norm." She sniffs, wiping a tear from her face. "He's scaring the shit out of me." I take in the fading El Paso skyline and turn to face her from my seat.

"Nova, you have to trust him. He would never hurt you."

"I'm trying. I just don't know if I can at this point," she says, leaning up on her seat, searching the road to look for the turnoff. "I'm really creeped out."

"If you want to look for something else, I'll understand."

"I'm under contract with him. I'll finish it out. You said things are bad at home?"

"I don't even know how to explain it."

"Well, if it's anything like it is here, I wouldn't blame you if you kicked rocks for a while."

"What does Wes say?"

"He's being tolerant because he's too happy with the results."

"It's that good?"

"So good, incredible," she says honestly. "And, God, I wish it wasn't. I don't want to encourage this shit. This is not Lucas."

"I know," I say softly. "It's Nikki." We share a mutual look of disdain over the seat.

"You know what's sad? I've seen this before, not to this extent, but similar and I've heard the stories too. It's like once they decide to let it take over, there is no limit to what they will do. Whatever it takes to keep it authentic. But, never, would I ever have expected this from Lucas."

"That's the point."

"Without totally throwing myself under the bus just in case I still have a job, I think the whole thing is ridiculous."

"But it's the best he's ever done?"

She grips the wheel tight in frustration. "Yes."

"So what scene are they on?"

She visibly pales and glances over at me. "It's like you're cursed."

Of course.

"Listen, I know technically Lucas is your employer but if he's not listening to you anyway, I'm giving you the night off. Take it."

"You sure?"

"Positive."

Nova finds her turn, and it takes the better part of twenty minutes during sundown to get to the set. By the time we do, I gawk at the sight ahead. While the El Paso desert is the perfect backdrop to the scene, it's pitch black now aside from the set lights. Our headlights barely help the visual on the road ahead, and it's a bit creepy as we approach, nothing but the breeze drifting through the car. All we can hear is silence as we head toward the stadium-like illumination surrounded in a sea of nothingness.

"This is creepy."

"Agreed," Nova says. "I'll be happy when we get back to LA."

I turn to look behind us, and all I see is black.

"I don't know how I feel about you going back down that road alone."

She timidly lifts a shoulder, "Uh, I won't be."

"Crew?"

"Yeah."

"Oh, good for you. Who is he?"

"She."

My jaw drops. "Nova, how in the hell did I not know this? I thought you were straight."

"I was?"

I cross my arms. "Explain."

"It's my ex-boyfriend's ex-girlfriend. At first, it was out of revenge and then it wasn't. Sounds like a plot, right? I'm a terrible person." She parks the car at the edge of the motorcade and briefly palms her face. "I think I'm in love with her."

"Can't be wrong if it makes you happy," I tell her. "And be happy, Nova. Be so happy and cherish these firsts, you won't get them again."

When she remains quiet, I glance her way.

"What?"

"Okay, so he's being impossible, but you two are different. *You* can get through to him."

"It's not Lucas."

That statement is my mantra, my saving grace, my hope, and my deniability.

She reaches over and pulls me into a hug. "Well then, I hope like hell you can get through to Nikki Rayo."

―――――――――

When I reach the set, I stand behind Wes and the cinematographer as they both chat with the man who unmistakably is the AD Lucas fought with, evidenced by the swollen nose and fresh black eyes. Cringing at the amount of damage, I survey the scene and easily find Lucas sitting inside a seventies model Coupe de Ville behind Adriana—who is parked sideways in a similar car.

I know exactly what's about to go down and I brace myself for impact as Kelly, a producer who worked with Lucas on another movie, walks up to greet me.

"Hey, Mila, how are you?"

"I'm good, Kelly, how are you? It's been a while," I acknowledge her in the same friendly tone, while never taking my eyes off Lucas. He's dressed to the nines in a well-fitted suit reminiscent of the era. His dark hair is slicked back, jaw set in a firm line, and I know he's spending the last few seconds mentally prepping before go time.

"It has been a while. They're keeping your boy busy."

"As are *you*," I say, lifting my tone playfully finally glancing her way.

"Sorry about that," she offers.

"No, you're not," I fire back, and we share a smile.

"Guilty, but with the way he's nailing it, I don't foresee going over in production time."

"Good to hear."

"Beneficial to both of us, but it's always good saving money," she retorts.

"Heard about last night," I say, wincing.

She waves her hand. "Ugh, men. They say we could never rule the world due to PMS, but they forget so easily about their constant cock fights. It's fine. We got through it."

"Good, good to hear. Any talk of legal ramifications?"

"Wes is trying to work that out, but he uses that one often." As if he knows he's being talked about, the AD looks our way. "So, if he wants his steady paycheck, then he best bend a little."

"Do you know what was said?"

"Not the details but I'm sure it went something like…" She puts her hands up to mock fighting puppets.

"My ego is bigger than yours."

"My ego is shinier."

"Mine has more horsepower."

We both burst into laughter and get strange looks from a few on set.

Kelly nudges my shoulder with hers. "He's killing it. I'm calling it now…if they do a good enough job in postproduction, your husband is going to be the most in-demand actor on the planet."

It's all he's ever wanted, and I can't deny the pride that momentarily trumps the concern. "He's earned it."

"Well, I'm heading out. I have a martini and a hot bath calling. Sure, you want to stay for this?"

"No."

We share a smirk, and she shakes her head. "I don't know how you do it."

"Me neither," I say, knowing mere weeks ago I could have come up with a hundred reasons.

"Good to see you, Mila."

"See you, Kelly."

Just as she leaves me, the assistant barks through the megaphone. "Rolling."

Taking a step forward to get a clear view, I mentally run the pre-sequence in my head. It starts in the desert with Anya, Nikki's wife, being dragged out of the car by one of his soldiers. Nikki then executes each man kneeling in front of the headlights with his revolver. Once he gets to his wife's brother, she flings herself over him to protect him, pleading for his life. Nikki rips her away, pointing a gun to his head and shoots him point blank. Terrified, she runs away screaming and makes a beeline for an idling car and takes off. Nikki laughs manically, following behind her in his coupe which leads to an aimless chase around a desert she can't navigate. Anya's car screeches to a halt when she realizes she can never outrun her husband and resigns herself to confront him. It's at this point they've set up the scene, where she's accepted her fate.

The marker is snapped and "ACTION!" is called.

Anya immediately starts slamming her manicured hands on the wheel sobbing before she bounds out of the car colliding with Nikki full force, her fists pounding on his chest as she fights with her grief and the monster she married.

"You bastard! He didn't turn on you, he didn't say a word!"

Nikki smiles without an ounce of pity as she repeatedly strikes him. He allows her very little before becoming fed up and grips her by both her hair and the edge of her coat, dragging her toward his car.

Anya is still fighting as they struggle in front of Nikki's hood. "Kill me," she screams. "Kill me too, you son of a bitch. Kill me too!" He stops and looks down at her with a sick sort of reverence. "This is a good look on you."

"I'll never love you again. Not like I did. You destroyed everything. You're disgusting." She fights him, scratching at his jaw, clawing at his shirt until she sinks into him, tears streaming down her face. It's all too familiar until he licks the blood from her cheek and makes her taste it as she cries into his mouth. And with one swift move, he has her pinned to the hood, his kiss deepening as my heart and head begin the ever-present battle. Refusing to look away, I watch as their lips connect, their chemistry sizzles as she gives in completely and allows his assault.

I'm as ravaged as her and experiencing all she feels as she visibly weakens, the fight leaving her. Heartache shines in her eyes, making her declaration nothing but a lie, and in those seconds, I identify with her more than I care to admit. But in the next second, I *am* her.

"*Come here, Mrs. Walker,*" *Lucas says from only feet away from where he stands half submerged in the lagoon. Tilting my head back to wet my hair, I take in the sight of him in front of the waterfall. Droplets of water rest on his thick black lashes while others stream down the sharp angles of his nose and jaw, his onyx hair slicked back to give me an arresting view. Brilliant green eyes glitter over me in reverence and appreciation. It's unnerving just how breathtaking he is, but the ring on my finger and the look in his eyes are more than enough for me to embrace it. I'm irrevocably his, and we've been left completely alone to* our own devices. It's another perk I'm all too happy to take advantage of. We're on a honeymoon straight out of a dream, surrounded by lush tropics in the cool blue iridescent water. I swim over to where he stands and wrap my arms around his neck.

"Yes, husband?"

He doesn't utter a word, but I can feel the depth of everything he's trying to convey before he slowly leans in and takes my lips. They part naturally in a gasp as he thrusts his tongue in, filling me up to the brink of something more than love, something close to supernatural. The slow thrust of his kiss coaxes me into the most blissful of states and my whole body sighs in to him. When he pulls away, we press our foreheads together. I'm too overwhelmed with emotion, too stunned at the daydream I'm still dwelling in, and the undeniable strength of our connection.

"Still surprises me too," he murmurs, reading my thoughts. "You are my life, and I am yours." Gentle eyes roam me. "Every piece belongs to me."

Sliding my thumbs across his jaw, I nod. "And to me."

He nods, his eyes imploring. "Only you, Mila, I swear it. You'll be the only one who gets them all."

"No," I gasp through the distance between us, at the separation I feel from that moment to this one. Promises and actions collide as I lose myself in the agony of watching it unfold, his words twisting from the purest form stemmed from the deepest kind of love into an agonizing lie.

I tell myself I imagined the sight of it, that it didn't happen, until it happens again and again. I see the same thrust of his tongue into her mouth. His hands are touching her, the hands that belong to me, my hands, my lips, my mouth. All the parts that belong to me now belong to her because he's kissing her, he's *really* kissing her and what's left of my hope dismantles in ashes at my feet.

Rule number three: Every piece belongs to me.

A muffled sob escapes my lips, and I sense the stare of a man next to me but keep my eyes fixed on my deceitful husband. It took days, months, and years to build us, and with one final act, he's destroying it all. It goes by in a blink, but the image burns itself into my memory desecrating my heart and destroying what's left of my trust.

Lucas pulls away suddenly, a sinister grin in place as he sneers above her. "You don't love me anymore? Shame," he whispers a breath from her lips. "I'll take loyalty instead." Lucas flips her then, pulling up her skirt and savagely ripping her panties away.

In my head and heart, I've already departed, but I'm a hundred yards away when I hear the unmistakable, "Cut!" ring out in the distance.

Two hours later, I find myself in front of his hotel room. They wrapped shortly after a few more takes, and I've been forcing myself to try to get a grip before I confront him. At least that's what I tell myself I'm doing. Another part of me thinks I've been waiting on Adriana to show up, but if that were the case, someone on set would have told her the wife had arrived, and the party was temporarily over.

Closing my eyes, I try to stifle back the tears. We hadn't been intimate since that day in his trailer weeks ago, if you can call it that.

Is Lucas capable of doing that to me? Am I a fucking fool who let my husband hide his infidelity behind an acting job?

Fury surges through my veins as I open the door with the key card Nova gave me. I spot him on the suite couch with a half-eaten sandwich next to his script. He's flipping that fucking coin in his fingers as if my world hasn't just ended when his eyes drift up. He doesn't look at all surprised to see me.

"I told you not to come."

I step inside the room and shut the door.

"Did you know I was watching?"

Silence.

"Answer me! What are you doing?!"

He smirks, but not the smirk I love, the smirk I loathe.

"I think that's obvious," he says snidely.

"Lucas," I say, my tears blinding me, "why?"

He lets out an audible sigh. "Look, Mila—"

"Don't you dare! You fucking promised me! Those are sacred promises we made! Those mean something to me! No fucking tongue, it's in the contract. We put it specifically in the contract!"

"You need to calm down right now," he says in a tone he's never, *ever* used with me. "And if you can't do that, you need to leave."

"Leave? Are you fucking serious? No tongue! It was your rule. You're the one who made it. I watched you kiss her over and over, you bastard! Are you fucking her?"

"You're embarrassing yourself," he says, looking back down at his script. "Your husband has never been unfaithful."

I walk over and clear the table in front of him, loving the horrific crash against the wall. Angrier than I've ever been in my life, I lean down so we're face-to-face. He chuckles dryly, his gaze deadly as he challenges me with a look alone. In those seconds I hate him, and it's nothing I've ever felt for him. "Has Nikki been unfaithful?"

His eyes dull as he looks over at me. "I don't repeat myself."

"Far be it from you to stoop so low. You're purposely

sabotaging our marriage, in fact, you're disrupting all of your relationships and for what? Why? You're going too far, Lucas! Nova is about to quit, your director probably won't ever hire you again, and your wife is about to leave you!"

Not even that statement changes anything about his expression, his posture. "I want my husband back, right fucking now! Lucas now!"

Openly, I sob in front of him while he stares at me as if I've just spit on his sandwich. I'm a nuisance, a bother, someone he has to deal with.

"This is not what I signed up for," I say vehemently. The man I married would have swallowed me in his arms by now, taken my face in his hands along with my pain, and done his best to do away with it, but he isn't here. "So," I cough out incredulous, "we don't follow our rules, anymore? Okay, maybe I'll start breaking them too."

"Now you're threatening me?" he says, shaking his head slowly while clicking his tongue.

"Yeah, I am," I say crossly.

"This is classic," he scoffs. "Maybe you don't feel like you're getting enough attention," he says with a hiss as he stands and grips my hand jerking me toward him. He presses his bulging cock between us and I hate myself for wanting it, wanting him any way I can get him. He takes my lips, his kiss is violent, and I fight him, disgusted. I pull away from him, covering my mouth in horror.

He harrumphs and slowly shakes his head. "This was about a kiss, right? That one was just for you." He tilts his head. "But if you're feeling needy," he says with a sardonic hiss, "we can take care of that too."

"Go to hell."

"Tempting," he utters without missing a beat, his eyes

flaring with sick humor. "I like it warm." He turns away from me and straightens his tie while I try to calm myself to the point of reason. Anger is getting me nowhere.

Scouring the hotel room, I see very few signs of life. The bed is freshly made but it doesn't look like it's been slept in. There is a pillow on the couch he's squatting on and a blanket folded beneath it.

"Lucas," I whisper at his rigid back. "I can't keep going on like this. I need you to hear me. I'm fading. Please just give me some sign that you're here."

Without a reply, he walks over to the door and opens it before he picks up his script, dusts off the piece of sandwich that's stuck to it, and resumes his seat. "Like I told you, *not here.*"

He doesn't bother to look up as I stand there watching him sink back into the couch scanning his script. I'm not even an afterthought at this point. Making my way toward the door, I look back as he shells a pistachio before popping it into his mouth. He's listening but no words will get through, and I'm past the point of caring, the raw betrayal too fresh in my chest.

"I'm so done, I won't sit back and watch this fucking freak show anymore. You're on your own, *Nikki.*" Walking toward the door, I hear the flip of a page and look back to see he's already reading. I was screaming at a wall.

Shutting the door behind me, I look up and see several of the crew standing at the threshold of their own rooms and crowding the hall. It's obvious they all heard, and they begin to part like the Red Sea as I walk down the corridor. Not bothering to look up to see the pity in their eyes, I march toward the elevator as a wave of humiliation wipes my every conviction away.

I'm just another Hollywood wife who got jealous, a wife who lost her husband to his career and a possible on-screen romance. Truth from fiction. A month ago, I would have said none of it was true, and I wouldn't have cared who believed it. I feel the opposite of that now. I want to scream that my husband loves me, that what we have is rare, that we are the exception, that our love story is genuine, that we can't be fazed, that we are unbreakable, but it's no longer the truth.

I check into a separate room and fly out the next day.

"In Method acting, you can't have preconceived ideas. You have to live in the moment. You have to keep yourself open."

—Dennis Hopper

CHAPTER 35

MILA

HOLLYWOOD DOESN'T RESPECT THE SANCTITY OF MARRIAGE.
To me, that statement was always a cop-out. I never
really believed that to be true because while the lifestyle
is a worthy adversary to the fairy tale ending it often promotes;
ultimately, it's the people, its inhabitants, who make the life-altering decisions.

But maybe its influence is the most destructive because all
I know is that in the past few hours, everything has changed
and all due to the fact that my husband has been pulled heavily
under.

It's not the night I spent sobbing in the hotel room without
a single word from Lucas, or the plane ride home that made me
feel more alone than I've felt in years. It isn't the mundane task
of driving through traffic. It's a simple errand that's changed
my mind. That combined with the fact that I've done everything in my power since I arrived back in LA to avoid the route
back to a life I no longer believe is mine.

I stop at the light clicking my signal to turn on the road
that leads home, to the place I once considered our safe haven.
Where nothing outside the walls could touch us, the house itself a representation of what we built on faith. I have to leave
him, of that I'm sure, at least until the film wraps. The more I
pressure him to come back to me, the more damage is done to
our relationship, which at this point, is nonexistent. But when a
horn sounds behind me, I can't bring myself to turn.

"Dame! Come here!" Lucas shouts from the bedroom. Running through the cottage, I see he's still wrapped up in the sheet from our morning tussle, his laptop open. Crashing into him, I hear his grunt as I wrap myself around him. "Yes, husband?"

His voice is muffled as he tries to speak around me. "This laptop is expensive." Rolling my eyes, I move to sit. He lifts up, opening his legs to straddle me, propping the computer on my lap.

"It's beautiful. Whose is it?"

"Ours. It's your anniversary present," he says, flipping through the pictures the realtor sent. We've been holing up in my parents' cottage and know we will eventually outgrow it. Though Lucas insisted on giving my parents well over the market value and kept it titled to them, for privacy and so my mother didn't have a say. They had been thrilled with the additional income and even more thrilled that we wanted to keep it in the family because it was their only goal. We'd been looking for the last few months for something to make our own since we planned on having a family, but the cottage was our end game. Because of my love for my childhood home, Lucas vowed we would come back when our children were grown and live out the rest of our days here, old and wrinkled and just as happy. He said it made sense, and he was a believer of coming full circle. He said we'd be starting out at our finish line. I loved the idea of it.

"Look at the views," he says, his breath hitting my neck as I actively scroll.

I'm wowed. "Oh, God, we could set up a table here and eat every night."

"And this master," he says, with a healthy amount of dream in his voice.

"This is just dreaming, right?" I toss a look over my shoulder. "This is a mansion."

"No, beauty, I want this for us."

"Lucas, I can't afford to pay half that mortgage."

"Let's be realistic," he says, "I make too much money for you to contribute half."

"No, realistically, I could afford half of something less expensive."

"But this is us, Dame."

"It's so beautiful. You know if you would have married Laura Lee, she could have afforded to go halvsies."

"Halvsies?" he parrots with a soft laugh, as I try to squirm out of his hold.

"Keep looking."

"No need, we're going to look at it today, and then I'm putting in an offer."

"I don't want to fight," I say testily. "This is too expensive for me to even afford the electric bill. You married a poor wine steward."

"No fighting necessary. I'm making enough on this movie to pay for this outright. It's an investment. My one and only and I want you to say yes, because you love me, because you trust me, and because you know this is the place."

"Lucas, it's too expensive, and we agreed we wouldn't buy anything I couldn't contribute to."

"Do you want to move out of California?"

"No."

"Then you need to give a little."

"Oh, there's something else?"

"Yeah, nowhere near LA." He gives me the side-eye. "Mila, you had to squat at your parents' house to stay in a decent place. Real estate is ridiculous here, and you know it."

"Point taken, but we don't need a multi-million-dollar mansion."

"It's an investment, one I'm actually not that terrified to make."

"Guilt me why don't you, so I can't even argue with this!"

He grins. "You'll make this place a home. And we'll fill it with little brats."

"I don't like you going back on our agreements."

"I get it, baby, but when I agreed to ditch that town home, the deal was we find a place of our own, one that makes us both happy until we start having brats."

"Who says they'll be brats? And you think I'll be happy knowing I'm a kept woman?"

"They will be brats. Case in point, the look on your face. And God, that's so sexy, say 'kept woman' again," he says with a laugh as I nail him in the head with a pillow. "Say it again. No wait, say 'barefoot and pregnant.'"

"You're a pig."

"God, I'm getting hard just thinking of you naked on that kitchen island."

"Lucas, focus. Go cheaper. It's not that much of a stretch."

"This is our house, Dame. If it's anything like the pictures, it's ours."

"It would be your house. You would be the one paying for it."

"Stop it. We didn't sign a prenup for a reason."

"Yeah, and that reason is temporary insanity on your part. This is serious, Lucas. What if we don't work out?"

"Then you have this place. And I'll give you 50 percent of what the house is worth."

"How is that fair?"

"Trust me, you'll earn it," he swears, eyeing the screen. Rarely have I seen him this excited. "Dame, I want this for us. I want this space, I want you to cook dinner for me in this kitchen. I want this."

The eagerness in his voice isn't something I'm used to, and I can't help but give into his logic. We'll never be on even playing ground. He's a millionaire, and I'll be lucky to earn six figures every other year when doing well as a sommelier. There's no contest.

"Fine."

"Fine?"

"I just don't want you holding this against me. And no laughing *at my paychecks."*

He shakes his beautiful head. "You know me better than that."

I do. And I trust him with everything I have.

"And don't say we won't last again. That's some shitty talk, Mrs. Walker."

"Because all Hollywood marriages last, right?"

"Stop it," he says softly. "We will last. You have to know that deep down. We are different. We aren't like anyone else. And I'm so proud of that. So proud."

Feeling guilty, I flick my eyes to the carpet. "Sorry. You're right. That was a shitty thing to say."

"You've got entirely too much sass in that beautiful ass of yours. You know," he says, his voice dropping low as he closes his laptop and tosses off the sheet, his expression telling me to run while I have the chance. "You could have a little more faith."

Nervous laughter escapes me as he emerges naked from the bed and I give chase. Squealing through the cottage, I fake left then right, running through the house as my naked man chases me at a full sprint.

"I have faith!" I scream at the top of my lungs as he lunges for me and misses, smacking into a wall before pivoting on his feet lightning fast.

"How in the hell did you do that?" I screech as I make a run for the couch and he captures me before we both go over the lip. He lands at my back in the cushion behind me.

"I'll never get the image of you running naked out of my head," I huff in an attempt to catch my breath as he starts working my panties down my thighs, using his heel to drag them the rest of the way. Our chests are rising and falling rapidly as he whispers into my shoulder. "Sexy, huh?"

"More like disturbing," I say as he bites into my shoulder. "I mean I guess your cock looks cute bouncing around like it's homeless."

"Cute," he says with a grunt, pressing his new hard-on between my ass cheeks as a threat.

"Maybe I can knit it a little hat, so it doesn't catch a draft as much as you run around here naked. I swear I married a nudist."

"Are you complaining?"

"Maybe," I say cheekily. I would absolutely hate it if he started wearing more clothes.

He lifts my hair with his fingers and nips at the back of my neck. "Well, I love you naked," he says, lifting my T-shirt off and slowly pumping his cock through my legs, toying with me as my clit pulses.

"Please," I say, grinding my ass against him. "No more playing."

"You need to have more faith, Mila."

"Maybe," I gasp out, his length nudging me from beneath. He slides his palm from my belly to my sex, tracing the pad of his finger over my clit, back and forth, using my slickness to ready me.

He's everywhere, his hot mouth melting me into a wanton puddle beneath his magic hands. I don't realize how big I'm smiling until it fades and I moan as he drags the head of his cock through my pussy from behind. "Oh, God."

"Now we're talking."

My smile returns. "You were just waiting for that."

"It never takes long. You're always talking to either the Father or the Son when I'm the one doing all the hard work."

"Cute."

He presses into me in one swift thrust. "Is this…cute?"

"Jesus, Lucas."

"Make up your mind," he grunts, burying himself to the root and pinching my nipple.

"Fuck, yes," I murmur. He pumps into me slow, slipping his arms through mine and gripping my shoulders to use as leverage to go as deep as he can go.

"Play with your clit, baby," he urges. I slip my hands between my thighs doing his bidding. "Fuck, that turns me on so much."

"I'm going to come."

"*Hold on, Dame,*" he murmurs into my hair. *I can feel how turned on he is, his chest is drawn tight, his movements becoming less controlled.*

"*Fuck me, Lucas,*" I whisper, getting lost to him as his thrusts quicken, and we both brace ourselves before bursting into a state of moans and exhales.

Lucas holds me to him, his arm around my neck as we both come down. His whispers surround me in a warmth more inviting than the sun streaming through the windows giving us a spectacular view of the rose garden and the hills surrounding us. He rests, still inside me in the protective hold I've come to crave as much as anything else.

"*I love you, Mila Walker. You are my whole life. I've never wanted anything more than to make you happy.*"

"*You do,*" I say, twisting to give him access to my lips. "*You do.*"

Sobbing, I make a quick turn off the road and park at a shopping center. Unable to think past the pain, I dial the number and pray for an answer.

"Mila?"

"Amanda," I croak into the phone.

"Oh, no, honey, what is it? What's wrong?"

"I need to talk to you."

Our marriage won't last through another week of filming. He's gone too deep, too far removed from the life we built, and if we have any hope of a future, I can't subject myself to any more rejection. For this, he didn't want a partner.

"Lucas, he's…I don't know what he is. I need to talk to you."

"Okay, where are you?"

"You're here, in town?"

"Yeah, I came back for a casting call."

"I'm parked at the shopping center just down from the promenade. Will you meet me?"

"Sure, give me thirty minutes."

I hadn't realized how much time had passed until Amanda knocks on my window. I'd been staring off into space and jumped when she rapped on the glass. When I get out of my SUV, I hug her tightly to me, fully identifying with the loss of the past four months, for her, for Lucas, for all of us.

"I didn't fully understand before," I tell her tearfully as she hugs me close. "Now I do," I sob as she grips me tighter. "I'm so sorry. I'm so, so, sorry."

"Hey, hey, it's okay, Mila, you were a better friend than anyone else. You couldn't know. No one knows unless they have to go through it themselves."

I can hardly speak as I unload on her and she does her best to console me. "I can't handle this. I'm losing him."

"Mila, you're scaring me, what's wrong?"

"I suppose I have a highly developed capacity for self-delusion, so it's no problem for me to believe that I'm somebody else."
—Daniel Day-Lewis

CHAPTER 36

MILA

Casey and Bonnie Morning Radio Show

Casey: This just in, Bonnie, our golden couple may be in trouble.

Bonnie: Uh, oh. What's going on with Lucas now?

Casey: A source on the set of *Silver Ghost*, Walker's new movie, says Mila Walker was on location yesterday in El Paso.

Bonnie: She's always with him on location, so what went wrong?

Casey: Rumors are circulating that tensions are running high and it's getting a little bit risqué. Walker is filming opposite of Adriana Long.

Bonnie: Not another set romance?!

Casey: Could be.

Bonnie: Come on, Lucas, you know better than that. I think Mila's prettier than Adriana. She's had too much work done. So, what happened?

Casey: Apparently Mila left the set furious and the drama went down in Walker's hotel room shortly after filming wrapped for the day.

Bonnie: Oh, no, Casey, not those two. They always look so in love.

Casey: Right? Let's hope these two can get it together.

Casey: I guess we'll see, it wouldn't be the first set romance to ruin a marriage.

Bonnie: We're rooting for you, Lucas and Mila.

Pulling into our drive, I turn off the radio and bury my head in the steering wheel. That news will broadcast on every entertainment medium by the end of the night. Over the years we'd been extremely careful to avoid that type of speculation, and even with Lucas doing his absolute worst, I was the one to bring the shitstorm to us. I wonder if Lucas was trying to warn me out of the hotel so the rumor mill wouldn't start. Had I overreacted?

So, he kissed an actress and made it look convincing. That was his job. But we agreed. We agreed on nothing that intimate, so why would he go there? I'm sure he's attracted to her in some way. Maybe Wes directed it that way, but Lucas knew that was a hard limit for me. And to twist the knife further, I felt threatened because we hadn't been intimate, in what felt like forever. That made it even more inexcusable. And I was officially, at that moment, sick of his career being a reason for anyfuckingthing.

For any of our problems, for any miscommunications. I

am exhausted with worry and fretting over the decisions he's making, his actions. His actions are his own, and he can't convince me differently. And if he is attracted to her to the point that he acted on it, what does that mean for us? Furious tears trail down my cheeks as I try to again catch my breath. It's too much.

A saint wouldn't have the patience to deal with this. Career or not, he broke promises, and I deserve some answers. But I have to wait for those.

For the first time in all our years together, I'm ready to abandon our relationship.

No excuse will be good enough. He *knew*, beneath whatever layers he's constructed, he *knew* beneath the madness he's surrounding himself in. He also knew before the premiere he would have to come clean about that kiss. So why? Why do it? Maybe if we'd discussed it and I hadn't been blindsided, I would have reacted more rationally. Or perhaps he did it to end us because he knew that would be what it took.

"You're gonna have to be the one that walks away from this, because it won't be me."

Did he purposefully push me out of his life?

Halfway down our walkway, I pause when Amanda's words from our conversation at the diner strike me like lightning. "It was like whiplash. Blake was smiling one minute and screaming the next. He was never comfortable on set or off while filming. The only time he wasn't restless was when he slept, and that too was rare. I'm telling you, Mila, it's the job that drives them crazy."

"I don't know what the hell he's doing, but he's pushing too far—himself, me."

Amanda eyes the waitress who refills her coffee before taking her leave and then leans over the table. "Sometimes, I think there was a lot more going on behind the scenes than I thought."

"What do you mean?"

"He drank a lot on the set of *Buzzed*, a lot. I remember smelling it when we filmed, and no one said a word, not even his mother. It was as if they were giving him permission. It was just weird. They constantly argued between themselves—the producers, the directors. It was a hot mess. I think that's one of the reasons the show got canceled. But they never said a word about his drinking and they didn't fire him—they just let him do whatever he wanted. Mila, he was only thirteen-years-old. You don't give a thirteen-year-old that much power."

I was in and out of my thoughts as she spoke, but it was one sentence in particular that had my whole body shuddering.

"He was so nervous back then, had these crazy habits, juggling, shuffling cards, oh and this coin trick that used to drive me crazy. He was just erratic. Lashing out one day, happy the next. It was unreal. I steered clear of him during the show. We weren't close then. When we got together years later, he had chilled out some. But that's Blake. And Lucas isn't Blake."

"Oh my God," I say, as unease settles over my bones while I pull my cell from my purse and frantically scroll for Amanda's number. Filled with trepidation, I stare at our front door, thankful when she answers on the first ring.

"Hey girl, did you get home okay? I was worried tha—"

"Amanda," I say with a jittery voice. "You said Blake did a coin trick."

"Yeah," she says, her tone a question. "Why?"

"Wh—what color was the coin?"

"What?"

"The coin Blake used for his trick. What color was it?"

"Gold. I think it was some European coin. He used to flip it constantly between his fingers when he was reading his script, you know, like Val Kilmer does in that old movie *Real Genius*? Yeah, Val was one of Blake's heroes. Come to think of it, I couldn't find it when we packed."

"Oh, God." My stomach rolls. "I think I'm going to be sick."

"What? Mila, you're scaring me."

"I'm scaring myself," I whisper as I gaze at the door, fighting the threatening nausea. "Did anyone else…do you know if Lucas had a key to Blake's condo?"

"I'm not sure. Probably…why? What's going on?"

"Amanda, I can't…oh God," I slump against the side of the house all the fight leaving my body. "I'll call you back."

"Okay, love. I'll be here."

"I'll call you back," I repeat, fixated on our front door in a daze, afraid of what I might find lurking behind it. I take deep breaths to try to calm myself. Finally finding the courage to turn the knob, I step inside far too leary for what I'm about to face.

Immediately, I hear Blake's voice fill the living room which sends a chill up my spine. "You're such a fucking square, Walker."

"And you're an asshole, Iceman."

Iceman.

My stomach rolls again as I do my best to inhale the breath I can't seem to catch. Walking into the living room, I see Lucas is fully absorbed in the home movie the four of us made in Mexico years ago. We'd vacationed together in Baja on a borrowed yacht. It was one of the best trips we'd ever had. Lucas had just wrapped a film, and Blake was still in demand but was on a filming break of his own. The trip had been thrown together in a matter of days. I was filming the movie on one of

Blake's old handhelds and had just caught Amanda as her eyes rolled. You could see the shake of the shot due to my laughter as I recorded our husbands, who were drunk off their asses, busting each other's balls. Lucas looks on at the movie, rapt with glazed eyes, agony twisting his features.

How could I not see it?

Staring at his profile, I note the cracks in his posture, heavy sorrow etched in his face. He's watching a life he'll never get back.

A life he threw away.

A life he ended.

Treading lightly until I'm just a foot away, I softly speak his name. "Blake."

My suspicions are confirmed when Lucas looks up and over to me as if he's been answering to that name his whole life. I have to fight myself not to scream out in reaction with the way he so easily responds. Swallowing, I take a step forward, engaging him. "Blake, what did you have to do to get roles like this?"

He shakes his head adamantly, and it's then that I see it. Shame. Along with profound sadness, it's written all over him as I approach the couch cautiously. It's there, the unease I feel, that I've felt every time I was in Blake's presence when he was alive. "Tell me, what did you have to do to get roles like this?"

His silence speaks volumes as his eyes dim of all light, and he reverts his gaze back to the screen.

"You did…favors for them, right? You didn't want anyone to know, did you?" I say, rounding the couch. "Am I right? Is that why you did it?"

"I don't answer to you."

Covering my mouth, I bite my lips as my tears flood. "What did they do to you?"

He leaps from the couch at warp speed, his hands clenched at his sides.

"I don't answer to you!"

"Fine," I manage calmly, "If you won't tell me, then call Amanda and answer to her. She deserves to know." Ending the stand-off I could never have prepared for, I walk down the hall and into my bedroom. Grabbing my suitcase, I stuff a few things from my bathroom I can't get on the fly and turn to see him standing at the door with his arms crossed. His face is blank when he surveys my packing. He can't possibly care that his wife is leaving because I'm not *his* wife.

"This isn't smart for the image," he snaps.

"Because that's what it's all about, right?" I shrug as I toss a few sundresses in. "Not my problem."

"You think this is easy?" It's the same accusatory tone he's used for months, and I'm done with it, done catering to it. It's exhausting being Blake West's *anything*. I'm still shaking inside with the unveiling of the truth, but I reply with my own. "Easy, no. But I think you've done the perfect job complicating things on your own. You've made one selfish decision after another. These are your sins. You created them, and we are all suffering for it."

"I'm not trying to hurt you!" Lucas is somewhere in there, but it's too late. I can't take the deceit, no matter how many clues I missed.

"You're destroying your best friend and his life. Isn't it enough you ruined your own?"

"He's doing this for me, he owes me," he insists, pressing a finger to his chest.

Closing my suitcase, I look up at him and clear my eyes before zipping it up. I walk over to where he stands. "I'm sorry, but you're not the one I'm supposed to save." Pushing past him, I walk down the hall with my bag in hand, and he follows. I turn back just before I reach the door.

"You always hated me," he snaps. "I saw the way you looked at me."

"That's not true."

"Well, you won, *happy*?" A sinister grin covers his face, and I sink further into despair. He plays him so well, how could I have missed it?

I was too close. I saw what I wanted to see, my grieving husband playing a madman.

"Am I happy?" I repeat, making my way toward the front door. "No, far from it."

"Who's breaking the rules now?" I snap my eyes to his.

Rule Number One: Don't take the process personally.

Rule Number Two: Go with it and trust.

Rule Number Three: All parts belong to me.

Rule Number Four: Only in grief do we leave the other.

Does the grief that's seized me count if it's not literal? What about his, does his grief count? It may not be the exact definition of the rule we made but grief is most definitely the reason we are breaking it.

It's then with our eyes locked I see the burden of our expectations, and just how miserably we failed each other.

Briefly, I see my husband's emerging emotions running rampant in his eyes before he schools his features and the menace is back. "He's been a good husband, hasn't he?"

"Yes," I sniff, sucking up the rest of my composure. "The best."

"You can't leave him because he's protecting me!"

Maybe it should matter that it's the first time he's come close to breaking character, but it's too late.

"Why not?" I fire back, lifting my chin to fight Blake's ghost head on. "You did."

Opening the door, I glance back at him and decide to draw the only weapon I have left. "Do me a favor, when you can, let my husband know I'm pregnant." I don't bother looking for his reaction because it will break what's left of me, so I pull the door shut.

"Mila," erupts from deep within him before his palm hits the closed door between us.

CHAPTER 37

MILA

ON MY WAY UP TO THE COTTAGE IN THE HILLS, IT ALL BEGINS TO make sense. Lucas must have been the one to go through Blake's things before Amanda and I got there. He must've unearthed the truth and the reason for Blake's demons. The more I scramble for clues, the more that strikes me of what had been apparent all along. The morning after Blake had committed suicide, I rose from sleep early and found Lucas fully dressed in the living room, shrouded in the dark. He didn't speak, hardly a word that day or the day after. And since then, Lucas became more and more absent. He'd found the answers to why Blake took his life, and it had only spiraled him to put on the mask he now wore.

Lucas isn't acting as Nikki Rayo.

Blake West is playing Nikki Rayo, and it's damn near cost my husband his sanity. I'm at a loss, dumbfounded by both his audacity and his brilliance. The characteristics I recognized while Lucas was home were *all* Blake. Things I should have caught onto much faster. It wasn't Nikki who bought me that necklace, it was a manic Blake.

All of it was Blake.

"Jesus, Lucas, what were you thinking?"

But he told me. It's as simple as guilt. He said he owed Blake. He was too buried inside his grief to realize how positively crazy this idea was. Or maybe he thought utilizing Blake's villainous traits while playing Rayo would help his process.

It's genius and crazy and nothing less than what I should have expected. My husband is a risk-taker and has been since he set foot in Hollywood. He goes to great lengths to prove a point, and he's demonstrated that time and time again. I should have known, I should have seen it, but as his wife, I feel violated and manipulated.

Maybe he thought if he could convince me, he could do a better job convincing everyone else. Whatever his reasoning is, it's torn us apart. And I let it. I broke my own rule after ostracizing him for the same. We're unrecognizable because I didn't trust him. We're unrecognizable because he broke my trust.

It's. Too. Fucking. Much.

I'm thinking on the defensive, and I don't want to hate Lucas. I don't need any more reasons to be angry. Shifting my thoughts another way I try to reason with the side that harbors the guilt. We'd lived twenty minutes away from Blake. Twenty minutes. Could we have saved him? Could we have done more?

Absolutely.

Lucas needs closure for that guilt, that's apparent. He's waged war on himself because of it. How do you make it up to your best friend for the fact you weren't there for both his downfall and ultimately his demise? How do you turn his tragedy into something you can make peace with?

Lucas had colored every part of himself in the insignia of Blake West.

Mind scattered, I pull up to my cottage as the weight settles. I may have broken my own rule but I'm pregnant, and I have more than myself to think about. So far, every part of this revelation has felt like a betrayal, but I will not subject the well-being of myself or that of our child for any part in this lunacy. I'm breaking apart piece by piece trying to sift through the ashes of three lives. My husband is sacrificing himself and our marriage in some sort of effort to redeem Blake. He's gone much too far, and maybe he trusted me too much. But it isn't Lucas I'm leaving, it's Blake I'm abandoning. Or perhaps it's both.

And what a performance.

CHAPTER 38

LUCAS

"HEY, MAN, YOU WANT ANOTHER BEER?"

"Yeah," I say, sprawled on the large beach mat next to him looking across the water. It's hot but the bleached sand is deflecting it nicely, and there's just enough of a breeze where it's comfortable. "This is beautiful."

"Not bad," Blake says, taking a sip of his beer. "Peaceful." He pops the top of a Corona and hands it to me as he looks on at Mila and Amanda frolicking in the ocean. They're wearing brilliant twin smiles and occasionally looking back at us. I bite my lip at the sight of my wife's beautiful ass in her new bikini, the curve of her hips, the lines of her neck, the loose tendrils of hair that have escaped her sloppy bun. She's in her element in the sparkling surf.

"You really do love her," Blake says, eyeing me as I admire her. "Like soul-deep love."

"I do. And you're one to talk," I nod toward them, "that redhead has you by the balls."

"That she does. I didn't like her at all when we met. She had those fucking judgy eyes. I thought no way in hell would she be the type I'd get along with. And back then, on the show, I don't think she was. But meeting her the second time, she was the opposite, just so laid-back, with dancing skeletons in her own closet, and she was honest about it. Didn't give two shits who knew about them, and I love that about her. She's beautiful, and she's brave. I admire her. I truly do. I just...I just, damn, I fell hard. There's no going back."

"I'm relieved."

He smirks. *"Why, because you're done babysitting?"*

"It's not that, man. It's just so much easier when you find someone that understands you."

Blake is already nodding. "Yeah."

"I don't think I've been honest enough with Mila about my past life."

Blake's eyes train on a seagull. "What do you mean?"

"I've told her some about the conditions but not all. The circumstances of when I was young. When she asks for more, I shut her down. I save it for film. And in a way, I feel like she doesn't need to know."

"Then don't. You don't want her pity. You don't have to always put a voice to the shit that hurt you. Therapy is a fucking joke. Especially for actors, when we get enough of it every day. We get to work through our own shit. That's the beauty of it, we get to hide in plain sight."

"I've never looked at it that way."

"No, because you do it every day already." He swallows. "Just don't let the therapy spill into your real life too much. Save the rage for the stage."

"Nice," I say, tipping my head toward him as we clank bottles.

"That's a West original, you can borrow it."

"I just might."

Another minute of waves and seagulls lulls us into where we are, a piece of paradise.

I broach the subject that's been bothering me for years. "It may be a West original, but you don't follow it."

He takes a sip. "That's true."

"Why do you let yourself spill over so much?"

The breeze drifts over us, grabbing the hair away from his forehead as he stares down at his bottle. "I think the better question is: why haven't I ever heard my internal director?"

"Meaning what?"

"Meaning, mine has never once yelled cut."

Frowning, I go to speak when we're bombarded by two soaking wet beauties. I fight to reach Blake, to grab his attention, but he wrestles his wife into his lap before he looks back at me with a million-watt smile. It's one of the only times I've ever seen him smile like that, so at peace. "It's a good life," he mouths as he trails his fingers down Amanda's bare skin. My questions fall away as Mila throws a leg over me and lays her head on my chest. Seconds later, we fall asleep next to the soothing sound of waves.

I'm being dragged by my collar into the garage. The gravel digging into my skin beneath my suit.

"He's too fucked up to know what's happening."

"Orders are orders. Tonight's the night."

"Five minutes earlier, we would have got him sober."

"Fuck, he stinks."

"That's because he shit himself. Screw this, I'm taking more of a cut on this if I have to be the one to get him in the car."

"I'm not touching him."

"What a waste. This is Nikki Rayo, huh?"

"Have respect, he's the reason I got in the game."

"Then maybe you should do the honors."

"I think I will."

Seconds later, I'm tossed into the back of the Rolls.

"This isn't much of a payback, should we wait for him to snap out of it?"

"He's got so much H running through his system, he's fucking smiling. Just get it over with."

I feel the pressure at my neck until the blood pours out. Blake's smile on that beach is the last thing I see before I hear the words, "Cut. That's a wrap."

CHAPTER 39

MILA

Nova: We wrapped an hour ago.

Putting away the rest of my dishes I muster up my courage when I see Lucas's Land Rover pull up. Standing in the hall, I hear the telling jiggle of his keys and the metal click into place, but the bolt doesn't budge.

I hear an irritated, "What the hell?" before a sharp knock sounds at the door. "Mila."

I don't know whether to laugh or cry. It's just as odd of a feeling that he's finally back, as it was when he returned from Egypt, except this time I don't want to fling open the door and fly into his arms. The fact that he thinks it's as simple as him coming home has my blood boiling.

"Mila," he says again, knocking in succession.

"I had them changed." The knocking stops. "I don't want you here."

"Baby, I'm so tired, so tired. I need to lay eyes on you. I know how upset you are, but it's over. Please open the door."

"You're right, it is over, at least for the moment. You need to leave."

"I can—"

"Explain? Surely you can think of a better line than that, *actor*."

"Mila—"

"Can you explain the kiss?" I hiss.

His tone goes defensive. "Yes, as a matter of fact, I can. It had nothing to do with her."

"This should be good."

"Mila, it meant nothing."

"How original."

It takes every bit of strength I have not to open the door just to slap him. But with one look, I'd be manipulated into letting him in, and he would try to smooth things over, and I'm not having it.

"Can you please open the fucking door, so you can see my face and know I'm telling the truth?"

"That's not going to make a difference. You conditioned me well."

"Seriously?" he whispers, "that's not what I did."

"No? All those tests you put me through when we started out, all of the prep work you put into making me your perfect little Hollywood wife. You never planned any of that, man with the plan?"

"You're really going to make me do this out here?"

"You're not getting into this house, Lucas."

He releases a heavy sigh.

"Fine. That kiss was about blood, the blood Nikki licked off her cheek. Wes asked me to do it specifically and *only* for that scene. He thought it would be more perverse if Anya were made to taste her brother's blood off Nikki's tongue. I agreed with him."

Stunned at the explanation, I bristle where I stand.

"That's actually a pretty damned good reason. And it would have changed everything if you'd have given it to me when I begged you for it. It might not have ended our marriage."

More pause. "Stop it. You took everything personally. Everything. You didn't trust me or the process. I understand you're mad, but we aren't over," he says with an uplift in his tone that makes my stomach roll. "It's one scene. I was going to tell you the minute I got here. I was coming clean about everything. Mila, I'm sorry—"

"You think that this is just about the kiss? You couldn't be more wrong, and the fact that you are still trying to hide behind your character is disgusting. You broke EVERY rule, you left me nothing to believe in. Don't you dare tell me that was acting!"

"That's what I was doing!"

"That wasn't acting, Lucas! You went too far, you're still there. You don't get to hide behind your job anymore. Every word coming out of your mouth is a lie, and I'm not listening to another. You need to leave. Right now!"

"You don't mean that."

"Yes, I do. And you know I do."

"Dame—"

"Go to your wrap party, Hollywood."

Irritation coats his voice. "I'm not going to a fucking party. I came to see my wife!"

"Fine, go see Amanda," I snap.

Silence.

"Nothing to say? Lucas? Nikki? *Blake?*"

"You don't understand, that…that just happened."

"I don't have to understand, I don't want to understand. Save your explanations. I left you, I don't want to be your wife. Not now. Maybe not ever again."

His palm slaps the door. "Don't you say that to me!"

"You took the meaning out of the ring!" I scream, letting my anger overtake me. "You broke my trust." I pound back at him. "You think this is me locking you out? You've got it all wrong! This isn't me, don't blame me! I don't want to have anything to do with this, with you. Not now. I'm too angry. Leave, Lucas!"

All of the energy drains from me as I relay the sentence, he himself dealt us. "There is no kiss and make it better. And you're not going to act your way out of this. Just go."

"Open up, Mila, I'm not going to fight through a door."

"I wish I had the strength left to fight you, Lucas, but I don't." And with that, I walk away.

Ten minutes later, I hear his Land Rover start up. The next day he comes back drunk. And the day after, and the day after that, and every night after until Paul is forced to drag him away from my door.

CHAPTER 40

MILA
Present

THREE WEEKS AFTER I LEAVE LUCAS, I GET ANOTHER RAP ON MY door, but I know with certainty it's not my husband. He's been silent the past week, aside from a daily 'I love you' text. Other than that, he's been giving me the space I asked for.

"You don't know what I had to do."

Blake was a victim of the casting couch, that much is obvious. And he was right in one respect, I don't need to know the details. Those were the secrets he died to hide.

A part of me hopes Lucas does come clean to Amanda, but it's not my call. And maybe that's some of what Lucas is still working through. But until he's transparent with me, until he shows me his battle, we have nowhere to go. Even after six years of marriage, it baffles me how much he hides, how unaware I am of what goes on inside that brilliant mind of his.

Opening my door, I see my mother standing there and hang my head as she pushes past me and steps inside.

"How did you know I was here?"

"Because when you didn't bother to text me back, I called your husband insisting he let me speak with you and do you know what he did?"

I shrug.

"He told me you didn't live there anymore and hung up on me!"

Laughter bubbles out of me as her eyes narrow. "Sorry, Mom. No one is safe lately."

"Do you mind telling me what the hell is going on? You haven't returned my calls since he chased me out of your house." She follows me into the living room, looking around before scrutinizing me.

"You moved back in?"

"Yes."

"Why?"

"As it turns out we don't have a perfect marriage. Satisfied?"

"Absolutely not and you look terrible."

"It's been a hard couple of weeks."

She waves her hand in the air. "You'll get through it."

"Says the woman who just admittedly fled from my house due to his wrath. So easy for you to say twice removed," I snap. "You have no idea what I've been through," I palm my hips, "and before you start with the 'I told you so' about marrying an actor, don't. Or you can leave."

"Don't talk to me like that," she says evenly. "I raised you better."

"I'm not myself lately, not many of us are."

"I can see that," she says, tossing her purse on the couch. "I'm going to make us some tea, and you're going to talk to me."

"You wouldn't understand."

"Do you think the only reason I didn't want you marrying an actor was because I worked for the press? Silly girl." She walks toward the kitchen, leaving me temporarily stunned before I follow her.

"Oh, I don't believe this. Who? Who did you date?"

She pauses. I read her right.

"Oh my God," I say, covering my mouth. "You have got to be fucking kidding me!"

She pushes up her sleeves before flipping the water on and filling up the kettle. Once she has the bags waiting in the cups, she turns to me and rests her back to the counter.

"Mom!?" I snap impatiently as she stares at me.

"It's not important who."

"The hell it's not, stop stalling."

"Mel Gibson and you're his love child."

My jaw drops. "What?"

"Kidding."

"You're ridiculous," I scold, before we both burst into laughter, mine reluctant.

"His name was Eric Byrne. Irish. Very, *very* good-looking, a tiger in the sack. He was all the rage for about ten minutes in the eighties, and I was madly in love with him. Well, I thought I was. This was before I met your father."

"You are such a hypocrite," I say, pointing the finger. "All this time, you made it seem like actors were the worst people when you had *sex* in the Kool-Aid!"

"I just didn't want you falling in love in a way that could torment you. And look at you." She raises a brow. "It's not fun."

"Point taken. Still, Lucas is not Eric Byrne. The way you treated him was unforgivable."

She hangs her head. "I know. And for the record, that was the worst fight your father and I have ever had. He didn't speak to me for almost a month."

"Good. Tell me what happened with the actor."

"He swept me off my feet. But those sayings about an Irish temper? Well, let's just say I can testify to them."

"He hurt you?"

"No, but he might as well have. He was a bastard best left to bed his co-stars and not put silly notions in my head. Maybe we should sit, Mila, you're so pale."

"I'm pregnant," I say, depriving her of what should have been a happy moment. She bursts into tears, and I walk over to her and hug her tightly. "I'm sorry, Mom, I'm sorry. I'm just so miserable right now. I miss Lucas so much. I'm so pissed at him. I should have faked a happy phone call or something."

"I ruined your wedding," she sniffs, "it's only fair."

"You didn't ruin it, Mom. Everyone thought you were making a spectacle because you were happy. I still laugh about it and the way Lucas squirmed."

"I'm sorry for that."

"It's inexcusable, but I understand why you were scared. We'd only been dating nine months. I was scared myself."

When we pulled away, she smiled. "I hope it's a boy. We could use a boy."

"I'll see what I can do." I pour the water into the teacups to let them steep.

"Your turn," she says, nodding in my direction. "Tell me what happened."

For the first time in years, I spare no detail. I don't see the point in hiding anything from her. I will probably regret it later, but for the moment, I trust my instinct to spill. It takes the better part of an hour for me to explain the last three months and the more I do, the angrier I get.

"Wow," my mother says with wide eyes when I finish.

"I know."

"I'm impressed," she says with the lift of her lips. "You have to admit, it's clever."

"And insane and deceptive. I don't know why he would hide it from me."

For the first time since I started my rant, I study her while she sips her cold tea.

"It's grief, and grief is another form of insanity in itself.

You haven't really gotten to experience that yet, and I pray it comes much later for you. You two will be fine. You need to go back to him."

"I can't. I'm too angry. Trust me, I'm trying."

"Try harder."

"Haven't you heard a word I said? He's unreachable," I say, pacing. "He's acting like we should resume life as it was without acknowledging what he just put us both through. He's still acting, and unless he drops the mask, we can't get past it."

"He's not ready. He still needs his wife."

"You know, Mom, there's something I've wanted to tell you for a while now."

"By all means."

"You meddle and give unsolicited advice like you're doing everyone a damned favor. You've given my husband hell for years and warned me away from being with him. I'm finally showing you our cracks but fully expected you to gloat. What does that tell you?"

She doesn't even flinch as her eyes hold mine over the side of her teacup. "That you're angry enough at him to share with me."

"Maybe," I say. "But if you want in, don't make me regret this."

"I don't stray from being honest, Mila."

"God forbid you don't alienate someone for the sake of your precious honesty."

"Hey apple," she says in her thick French tongue. "You didn't fall far from this tree. It's one of the things Lucas loves most about you because he told me so. I know what he did to me at your house came from a place of pain, but there was some truth behind it. I ask intrusive questions because I want to know you, the both of you, and it's like since the day I met him, he's had some preconceived notion about me."

I cast my eyes down because it's the truth. I had Lucas fearing my mother long before she met him.

"And maybe you were right to warn him," she says, reading my guilt. "I didn't make it easy on him, I know that. But you're my only child, and I want what's best for you. I see my mistakes, and I'm willing to admit them. I'm even willing to apologize to your husband once he comes ready with his. I might not know the day-to-day of your life with him, but I watch you two. The whole world is watching, and I along with them. I read his interviews and the way he speaks so highly of you. I see the way he looks at you and vice versa. That man loves you better than any other man could, movie star or not."

I sob into my palms, shaking my head. "Of course, you would give me your blessing when we're falling apart."

"No, my love, this is not the end for you two. Stop mourning what isn't over. You can't see past his behavior, and he's done some appalling things, perhaps a few unforgivable. But this is just a crossroads, and you'll have a lot more of them in your marriage."

"I don't know, Mom, I don't know. God, I was so sure we were unbreakable."

"No one is. You think I don't know what it's like to be that absorbed? I've lived it. You two are each other's universe. It's the same with your father and me. You have no idea how many battles we've overcome just to stay together. But this battle, this isn't about the two of you. He's doing this for Blake and for himself. It has nothing to do with you. And you're taking it personally."

"I don't know how else to take it!" Our child chooses that moment to make me purge my breakfast. Running to the toilet, I barely make it when I unleash hell into the porcelain. She wets a washrag and hands it to me. I wipe my face of the evidence before I brush my teeth. My mother stands in the doorway, arms crossed while she confronts my reflection.

"This isn't about your relationship. Not at the moment. This is about his bigger picture. You're a large part of it, but right now this isn't about marriage, this is about his friendship and his guilt, and you're just going to have to deal with it."

"Great," I snap sarcastically. "You seem to know a lot, Mom. You have a time line for this because I have a baby coming?"

"As long as it takes. Look, Lucas has been working nonstop for a very long time. He might've lost touch with himself. It often happens when creatives burn out. He's reached stardom, he's probably afraid right now that he's got nowhere to go but down."

"He's never told me that." But that isn't totally true. I just figured he had outgrown his fears the further he got in his career because he never spoke of them again. If there's merit to what she's saying, I couldn't be more wrong. Swallowing my pride, I table my anger and look over at her. "I'm listening."

"Mila, I love you. I'm talking to you from a place of love, I don't need to be right, I need you to know that. But you need to get over yourself a little. As tightly knit as you two are, sometimes our deepest fears don't get voiced to the ones we're closest to, especially when we're the most afraid. While I don't doubt you two rely on each other, maybe his problem stems from more than just Blake's death. Listen to me, dear daughter. He needs you now. It's crucial that you are there for him. A few bad years in a marriage is a reason to leave, a few bad months in a *good* marriage is a reason to *stay*. Seems to me he's got a bit more than a death to deal with going on."

"What do you mean?"

"Maybe the question isn't why is he acting as Blake, but why doesn't he want to be Lucas? From what I'm gathering, Blake's death has taken a toll in more ways than one and landed him right smack in the middle of an existential crisis."

I roll my eyes. "You've been married to a psychiatrist too long."

"What if I'm right? Do you have any idea how many patients your father treats for this very thing?"

"We were happy."

"Yes, as a couple but you and I both know there's more to life than that. Lucas isn't just your husband or an actor. He's probably finally looking up and realizing where he is in the map of his life, and he might not like it. Seems like he's lost touch with himself through this career he's starved for."

"He's never told me that."

"Because he probably wasn't in that frame of mind before Blake's death. Death changes people, Mila. It can make you question everything. He's probably terrified."

"Afraid of what?"

"Of where he is."

"Why?"

"We get told our whole lives that these things A, B, and C are what we need to make ourselves happy but obtaining them and seeing them for what they are can be utterly terrifying. One of the things your father told me is that most parents have no idea how to deal with overachieving children when they reach this point because the parents themselves cannot relate. They're still working toward their own goals, and some never get to the place Lucas is. That's the crux of the crisis."

It makes so much sense, it's scary. And I hate the fact that my mother may have more insight than I do on my own husband.

If anything, the past three months have shown me I'm not the expert I thought I was and that hurt breaks the rest of my heart.

"What do I do?"

"You can't do anything but wait, show your support, be there for him."

"I'm so pissed off, Mom. So fucking angry he locked me out and didn't share any of it with me. He broke promises."

She harrumphs. "Show me a perfect man, and I'll prove you a liar."

"Dammit. Why did I have to marry an actor!"

"You married a man. A human man. You study the beauty and rarely notice the cracks, it's easy to with a man as captivating as Lucas. He'll point them out to you when he's ready. And you could be the next one to weigh life out. And when that happens, you'll need him."

"I can't forget this, Mom. I can't forget how he shut me out."

"But can you love him the same?"

"I love him more than I ever have."

"That's marriage. On the other side of this is a different future for Lucas and I'm happy for him. Some go through never questioning any part of their existence. I've never thought much of Lucas as far as being your equal, but he may just start giving you a run for your money. He's showing you that what you've known isn't all that he is. It's kind of exciting."

"And what if what he figures out doesn't include me?"

"You grow together or apart, and both of you decide at any point in time."

"That's terrifying."

"No Mila, that's life."

CHAPTER 41

MILA

SLIPPING ON MY SHORT WHITE GLOVES, I CHECK MY appearance one last time. Thankful for the predictable LA weather, I use large sunglasses to cover up evidence of my lack of sleep. My lips are painted hot pink, but that's the only hint of color I add to my ensemble. My dress is a vintage Hepburn that I'd picked out six months ago. Inside the fabric, I'm numb.

Lucas is still calling and texting but hasn't been at my door in weeks. Some part of me recognizes that we may very well be over. My stomach rolls and I place my palm over it. "Hey, baby, Mommy could really use some help not throwing up today."

Before I know what's happening, I'm in tears at the edge of my bed, holding my abdomen. I can't feel anything yet, but I feel everything. The knock on my door kicks me out of another pity party, and I answer it to see Paul.

"Hi," I say, closing the door and locking it behind me.

"Good morning," he says, leading the way to the car.

I pause at the steps, staring into the limousine, and Paul glances back at me reading my hesitation. "He's not in there."

It would have been the perfect time for him to trap me, but he didn't. "Okay, let's go."

Once inside the limo, I clasp my hands in my lap and try my best not to ask the questions burning on my tongue, but I do.

"How is he?"

Paul's chocolate-brown eyes meet mine in the rearview, his expression grave. I nod.

"Is he still drinking?"

"Mila—"

"Fuck your NDA, Paul, answer the question. I know you care about him."

"Yes, sometimes, he's drinking. But he makes me drive him. He doesn't leave the house much since the accident."

"What accident?"

He shakes his head.

"Paul!"

"He crashed into a median a week ago, his Land Rover was the only thing that suffered."

"Was he drunk?"

"I don't know. It was early."

"What are you doing, Lucas?" I whisper under my breath.

"It's a bender," Paul says simply. "Been there myself for the same reason."

"With all your charm, I can't see how any woman could ever leave you."

He glares at me in the rearview, and I glare back before we both burst into laughter. When it subsides, I glance up to see something resembling a smile.

"So, Paul smiles. Maybe you don't hate me."

"Of course not," he says, "I've been around enough to know that I don't need to be friends with any of my clients. It's hazardous."

"I get it." I do. I can't imagine the things he's bore witness to over the years.

He bites the edge of his lip.

"What?"

His eyes zero in on my reflection. "Up until a few weeks ago, you two were the most boring of all my clients."

"Huh," I reply, staring out the window knowing his statement is a compliment.

When Paul opens the door, I hear the telling click of the cameras and school my features. Nova greets me and leads me down the sidewalk alongside two other bodyguards.

"You look beautiful," she says, giving me a quick hug. "How are you doing?"

"Thank you, I'm good. You?"

"Today is a good day."

"Indeed."

"Glad he's back," she whispers, eyeing me as we walk.

I nod but gather that she can see the lie on my face and if she can see, then everyone watching can too.

One hour, Mila. You can do this.

Determined to bury my emotions, I flash her my best smile. "How's the love life?"

Her answering grin is radiant, and I feel a small stab of jealousy at the way it isn't forced. I used to be that girl, carefree and confidently in love.

"It's awesome."

"So happy for you, I mean that." We pass a barricade where the public and paps are held at bay and are led over to a tent on the side of a small stage with a podium. Taking my seat next to Nova, I'm greeted by a few of Lucas's old co-stars who are seated behind us. Nerves threaten and my stomach rolls as I fight a wave of nausea.

I've spent days trying to decide if I would show up and

concluded on every single one to be here for him, to keep that promise, no matter what our future may bring. Lucas's back is turned to me, he's talking animatedly to the presenter.

"What a great turnout."

Fans are lined up on all sides of the closed-off tent. "Sure is."

"Did he know you were coming?" Nova asks.

"No."

As if he senses me, Lucas turns, and I'm forced to downplay the jolt that hits when our eyes connect. His eyes close briefly, and his throat bobs as ramped up emotion flits over his features.

I made the right decision.

Unable to handle the tension, I give him a wink and mouth, "Hey, Hollywood." Relief-filled eyes shimmer down on me with so much warmth, my chest constricts and my throat burns.

He's wearing a fitted navy pea coat—that fails miserably in concealing his biceps—matching slacks, a white button-down, and a gray vest and tie. His hair is freshly cut and styled back. He looks every bit the movie star he denies he is.

Nova reads my mind. "He looks good. *Really* good."

"Yes, he does, the *bastard*," I say, shaking my head with a smile. Eyes still intent on me, I swear he reads my lips, and his lift at the corners with a smirk.

"Paul said he got into an accident."

"Must have scared him straight, because he's been sober every day I've seen him this week."

I let out a relieved breath. "Thank God."

"He may be beautiful, but I gotta say, after dealing with that man for the last three months, I'm happy to be batting for the other team." We share a laugh. Looking around, I find my eyes trailing back to his as he studies me, his soul-filled depths trying to convey so much, but I can't read into it. Today isn't about us. It's about the career of a passionate actor.

The mob goes silent as the president of the Hollywood Chamber of Commerce steps up to the podium.

"Hello, Hollywood." The crowd cheers in greeting. "Today, we gather in celebration of the career of one of our most diverse and talented leading men. With such films under his belt as *Misfits*, *Erosion*, *Cairo*, and *Drive*, he has landed a reputation as one of the most respected and well-known actors of his generation. The Hollywood Chamber of Commerce is proud to honor with the twenty-six hundredth star on the Hollywood Walk of Fame, Lucas Walker!"

Tears surface, but these are different. They're tears of pride. Lucas stands humbly beside the podium, his gaze mostly averted as praise is bestowed on him from all sides. It's then I realize what a gift it's been to know him so intimately, to have witnessed his talent firsthand. To have loved him through the bad days and been present on the good.

Audrey's words hit me harder than ever as I look up to meet my husband's waiting gaze.

It's a choice. Every. Single. Day. You make a choice.

I might not have been present for all of his career, but we share years of the same memories. In a blink, I'm back in front of those pyramids, crashing into his arms outside his SUV, slapping his chest in the limo, yelling at him for leaving the toilet paper roll empty, rolling underneath him in bed as he pins me down and tickles me with his hair. We're playing in the ocean on our own strip of beach and making love by the fire after. I'm laughing as I catch him spitting out the wine at dinner that took me all day to cook, and in the next thought, he's yelling at me for buying an expensive washing machine right before I cover him in detergent. It's still my favorite fight, along with the hour-long make-up shower after.

Today I choose him, I choose those memories—over hurt, over mistakes, over miscommunications, over all of it. I don't want it anywhere near this moment. Because in a way I share it with him. Those moments have happened, but this one is just as significant, even if it's one of our last. I choose him, so I don't miss this day.

After the thought settles into me, I'm able to enjoy the ceremony. A few of his old co-stars come up and speak about what it's like to work with him, about what an amazing man he is. I laugh through stories I've heard and some that I haven't. Lucas stands idly by, humility leaking from him in the aversion of his eyes as he stares down at the carpet listening to all the kind words spoken. His lips upturning here and there and a laugh escaping him when it's appropriate.

And then it's his turn. He's introduced one last time and takes the podium. "Thank you. Thank you so much." He pauses and glances out into the street a million miles away. "It seems like just yesterday I was walking down this boulevard with a friend dreaming up big things." His eyes go murky, but he recovers and smiles at the crowd. "It's been a crazy road to get here, one I'm certain is less traveled but sprang from circumstance as most of life's gifts do." He looks directly at me when he says it, and then he's speaking again. "When I was eight years old, I met a woman by the name of Madelyn Rosera Darling."

Lucas speaks of Maddie fondly for a few minutes telling anecdotes that have us laughing and emotions swelling. He's an amazing storyteller, that's his gift, and it's why we're here. Pride pours out of me as I listen to him speak, his speech brief. "So, thank you for this honor, and I accept this along with thanks to the women in my life. Thanks to Maddie; my mother, my teacher, my best friend. Thanks to my beautiful wife, my Dame, Mila." He smiles over at me. "Thanks to the team of incredible women, who keep me," he says, nodding toward each of them, "Leann, Shannon, and Nova." I grip Nova's hand and see she's tearing up. "Basically, all the ladies in my life that try every day to keep from committing their first homicide." The crowd laughs, and Lucas gives a devilish grin I recognize now as Blake's.

"I'm honored, thank you." He steps back and is led down to the red carpet with the co-stars who spoke before his star is unveiled. When he looks down, I see it then, the crack in his armor, he's thinking about Blake, and he didn't mention him at all in his speech. Melancholy washes over his features, and in a flash, it's gone. His smile is back, and he's posing for pictures.

Once it's my turn, he tugs at my hand pulling me to him, and we embrace for long seconds. I inhale his clean cologne, revel in his hold. "I'm so proud of you," I whisper. Pulling away, I melt in his gaze. The world may be watching but the gentle kiss I return when he presses his lips to mine is genuine. He searches my eyes, and I admit the truth. "I couldn't miss it."

He crushes me again into his arms and whispers in my ear, holding me tightly to him. "Thank you so much for coming. Mila, I—"

"Not today, none of that today," I whisper softly, pulling away with what I hope looks like proud tears shimmering in my eyes. "I'm so sorry he's not here."

Blake was originally supposed to be one of those who spoke at his unveiling. Our collective hearts aching, I urge him to have his moment. "Go on, give them a few more minutes, then you're home free."

"Dame," he whispers roughly, his eyes shining with un-mistakable reverence, "you represent your title well."

"And you're *still* a good man, Lucas. An *infuriatingly* good man."

I push up on my toes and kiss his jaw like I did the night we met. "I'll see you, Hollywood." I walk away before my legs have a chance to give out.

CHAPTER 42

LUCAS

"TURNER AND MCNEIL, PLEASE HOLD. TURNER AND McNeil, please hold."

As the minutes tick by, I can't help but look around the posh office and grin. She's made a name for herself.

"Mr. Walker," the receptionist addresses me, her cheeks heating when I approach her desk, "she'll s-see you now. Last office on the right."

"Thank you." I stride toward her office and knock before opening the door.

She stands, a bright smile lighting her face.

"As I live and breathe, Lucas Walker. Have you finally fucking come back to take me to prom?"

A laugh escapes me as Jessie comes toward me and we pause briefly before we hug. "Damn," she muffles into my shirt, "you couldn't have worked out like this when we were together?"

Chuckling, I pull back and take her in.

"How are you, Jessie Soto?"

"I," she drawls out, "am kicking *ass*."

"Looks like it," I say with a grin.

"We're the only two people in the graduating class who did shit for ourselves."

"I didn't graduate," I remind her.

"Yeah, well, you're still a hero in those parts. You didn't do so bad," she says. "I mean I saw *The Willing*."

I cringe. "You're the only one."

"Really, Lucas, what in the hell possessed you to make that piece of shit? It was the worst."

She rounds her desk, and I take a seat opposite her. "Food was enough incentive back then to take any job." I exaggeratedly roll my eyes. "Everyone's a critic."

"At least it was ahead of its time with the zombie apocalypse."

"What about you, ballbuster, you never told me you moved to LA? I don't remember getting a phone call."

"Well, that's because I just so happened to fall in love with the biggest piece of shit to attend Harvard. I got two souvenirs," she nods toward the picture at the edge of her desk, "and seventy-five percent of everything else."

"You mean half, right?"

"No," she grins deviously. "I mean seventy-five percent, that's why I'm the best divorce lawyer in this state."

I pick the picture up and study it. "Cute."

"No, they aren't," she says with a laugh. "They're in that weird, awkward stage where they're losing teeth and making dumb ass fart jokes. But they were beautiful babies, so I have faith they'll be decent-looking adults."

I'm grinning from ear to ear. "It's no wonder you were my first love."

"*I* was your first *everything*."

"Sorry about that."

"Don't pity me, not many women can claim they stole a movie star's virginity."

I raise a brow. "And how many people have you told?"

She rolls her eyes. "None."

"And that's exactly why I'm here. I trust you."

"Flattery will get you everywhere," she says, giving me a

wink. "But I have the feeling you aren't here to reminisce or pick up where we left off. Unless…oh, hell, Lucas are you getting a divorce?"

Letting out all the breath in my body, I look over at her. She reads my expression perfectly. "Oh, this isn't good."

"I need your help."

It takes me an eternity on the 405 to get home, and as the early hours blur into afternoon, I find myself alone on our balcony. Scripts sit in piles next to my chair, and I can't bring myself to open a single one. The ocean pours onto the shore, and I study the waves that no longer seem tranquil to me. What I once considered a sign of freedom now feels like a border. Sweat trickles down my back at the idea that this is the extent of the life I have left, trapped behind a wall of ocean, my only task to bury myself in someone else's words.

I love you.

I send the text daily now. It's all I have. It's the truth. I've done everything I can to get her to talk to me. We've never gone this long without the other, for any reason. Six years of marriage is slipping through my hands, and she still refuses to give me permission to bridge the gap. I'm losing her, daily, every minute that ticks by is agony.

I deserve it, but the burn doesn't give a shit. It's eating me alive. I let it hurt and refuse to drink it away anymore. I have a son or daughter coming that needs a focused father. The problem is, I've lost all mine.

And maybe for Mila, there's no coming back.

I twist the band on my finger, my only reassurance that we still exist. If she won't let me try to heal us, I'm stunted. I can't move forward without her, and I can't go back.

But I can get the fuck out of LA.

My chair collides with the glass before I slide open the door and head into my closet. I grab a duffle and begin to fill it with all my shit. I can't exist in this house anymore without her. I rip my clothes off the racks one by one and shove them into the bag. Tearing through the room with the sack in hand, I head to the bathroom ripping everything that belongs to me off the shelves. I make the decision that I'm never coming back to this house. Not without the life I had when I moved into it. Heading back into the closet, I pull shoes off the shelves filling another bag. In my haste, I knock down a Nike box. The contents come pouring out and hit my chin. Pissed off, I kick the box and see a tablet pop out with a card attached. Bending down I scan the note scribbled in Mila's handwriting.

In case you forgot.

X

I fire the tablet up, and my breath catches in my throat.

Hundreds of pictures fill the screen in scattering pixels before coming together to form the words **Happy 6th Anniversary, Hollywood!**

Slumping down against the shoe rack my heart cracks when I hear the first song start to play, and a picture fades in, a candid of us on our wedding day leaving the reception. She's laughing, her head thrown back just after I've scooped her up to get her into the limo, lavender roses hanging from the hand she has draped over my shoulder. It's the perfect picture of us, and I've never seen it.

How much have I missed?

That's when I realize they are mostly all candid shots, trickles in time where we merely existed as ourselves even while in the public eye. It's the best fucking movie I've ever seen in my life.

Grunting at the ache, I rub the middle of my chest to try to subdue it. And then…it starts. And it's us, our life in music and pictures. Some I don't remember taking, parties I don't remember attending. It's then I know she's the true storyteller, our memory keeper. Tracing her picture with my finger, recognition sets in and I rip at my hair.

"I'm so sorry."

And that's when I see us. A choked gasp leaves my throat as razor-like pain rips through my chest. We're both clad in our black tuxes and lavender vests, wine country blurred in the background. Blake's standing tall, a huge shit-eating grin on his face, his arm slung around me. I'm turned into him, hysterically laughing into his shoulder, my fingers gathered at my watering eyes.

"You really did it, huh?" he says, approaching me as my bride is whisked away for pictures. *"No turning back now."*

I grin, catching my bride's eyes as she tosses a look over her shoulder. "I got the girl."

He hooks my neck, pulling me into him and runs his knuckles through my hair. "Congrats, bro."

"Stop it, you dick," I half-heartedly gripe. "Mila will be pissed if you fuck up my hair for the pictures."

He releases me and rolls his eyes. "Already catering to the wife. Life as you know it is over. Before long, you'll be carrying a dad bag, changing shitty diapers on the plane, and saying things like "yes, dear." Gone are the days of careless living."

"If I recall correctly, your ring finger is occupied, and I don't see you carrying a dad bag."

Studying me, he pulls a cigarette from his pocket, pinches it with his lips and lights it before releasing a slow exhale. *"I'm not terrorizing the population with my offspring."*

"Lucky us."

"Hey, you two," one of the photographers says, approaching us and crinkling her nose at Blake's cigarette. *"Put that out. Let's get one of you two with your jackets buttoned."*

Blake and I do her bidding and button up to pose.

"This shit here is why I eloped," Blake snarks.

"Yes, I know, I was there. Suck it up, asshole, I'm only doing this once."

"I'll have you know I've been on my best behavior these last two days in bumfucked wine country," he chides, *following the directions being spouted at us.*

"Yeah, well, you haven't given your toast yet, so the jury is still out," I remind him.

He scoffs. "I intend to say the most honorable things. I'm going to make your toast look pathetic."

"There wasn't a dry eye in the house when I gave mine, you included."

"Exactly."

"So, you're going to use your speech to compare swords with me?"

"Absolutely. May the 'best' man win."

The photographer chooses that moment to speak up. "Blake, if you don't mind, switch places with Lucas on the incline, he's got you by a few inches."

And that's when we both lose it, and the shutter is pressed.

Leaden legs lead me down the path I swore I'd never take. Each step becoming more sluggish as I keep my gaze down. Once there, I close my eyes, turning my head in one last attempt to avoid the truth but the effort is futile. When I finally focus on his headstone, it's all I can do to keep standing.

He's gone. He's really gone.

Birds sing nearby, and it's not a pleasant noise, nor is it white. It's a sign life keeps moving on without him.

Breaths burn like acid going in.

I have no words, none he can hear. He took that away from me, and from everyone else that loved him. We don't have a say. We don't get a goodbye. He robbed us of all of it with the way he left.

"Jesus, Blake," I grunt out as I grapple with the permanency of his absence. No matter how many times I spoke it aloud, how many times I tried to acknowledge it and let the reality sink in, it never caught, until now.

He's gone. My best friend is dead.

He's part of half of the life I've lived. He's a contributor to who I've become. He's imprinted in me.

There's no more denying it. There's no more avoiding it.

He's gone.

Fuck this life and the next one, I don't want to be the good guy in either one of them.

Blake wasn't the best role model, and he didn't always give sage advice, but he was there for me when I had no one and nothing. I spent a lot of our friendship trying to understand him. No matter how much of an enigma he was, the role he played in my life could have never belonged to anyone else.

"You were a good guy, you just didn't believe it."

Hanging my head, I give in to the wave and let it crush me.

Choking on a fiery exhale I kneel down, pulling the coin from my pocket, I palm my forehead as the ground shakes beneath my feet. "If you asked me...I would have been there. I would have done anything... Damn you," I rasp out, cracking wide. "I know you did what you did to protect us from the truth. I'll never understand it. But now it's my turn. I won't let you down." I try to compose myself and fail as I bury the last piece of him where he lays, pressing the coin firmly into the dirt beneath his name. "I love you, rest now, brother. I hope you found peace."

"I think everybody should get rich and famous and do everything they ever dreamed of so they can see that it's not the answer."—Jim Carrey

CHAPTER 43

MILA

"**H**EY LADY, WHAT ARE YOU UP TO?" AMANDA'S VOICE sounds over the line.

"I'm in the midst of developing Madame Bovary syndrome."

"What's that?"

"Ah, it's an old cautionary tale about a Parisian housewife who gets bored and spends all her husband's money replacing love with possessions."

"Ah, retail therapy."

"Exactly, but this time I have a good reason. I have a Martian about to take up residence, he or she will need things."

"I still can't believe you're pregnant."

"The daily vomiting declares it so. Are you doing okay?"

"Getting better. I got a job down here close to my mom. I just want to wait things out a little longer."

"If that's what you need, I'm glad, but are you really okay?"

"No, but I will be one day. And I wait for it every single day."

"I'm here for you. I hope you know that."

"Same goes for you."

"Let's not lose touch again, okay? No matter what."

"Deal."

Ending the call, I change clothes and make my way to the rose garden. It's a new routine I've found solace in since returning from the winery. It keeps me invested in something, keeps my mind focused on my goals. Waiting has always been the hardest part. No matter what role Lucas took on, it's always been the anticipation of when we could resume our life together that was the hardest. He usually sleeps for a few days, and we take small steps to carry on whatever becomes our new normal. On my knees in the thick of the bushes, I'm unsure of what this normal will bring.

Have we grown apart? Has he changed his mind? Have I?

We're in pieces because he took this burden on for the love of his brother and expected me to understand.

And it took time, but now I do understand, to an extent. It doesn't mean I don't deserve answers instead of excuses. It doesn't mean I can't be furious he refused to let me in on his plans. After the day he got his star on the Walk of Fame, I decided I would wait for him to come to me. He needs a sort of clarity I've been unable to give him, and it's the perspective my mom gave me that keeps me idle. We have a hell of a lot to fight for, but I can't do it alone. Though his apologies are sincere, and I know he means them, this isn't a simple fix. This hurt runs soul deep.

My husband loves me, but he broke my heart in a way I can't just bounce back from.

These last four months have been a blip on the radar in the map of our relationship, that much is true. That's what Lucas counted on, my memories of our past, the trust I swore I had in him, the unbreakable bond we built, but expectations like that are unrealistic and lead to failure. Humans are gloriously flawed, and some types of love are never truly unconditional. A lot of my mistake was expecting our love to stay perfect, because a lot of the time, it was. It's wanting our love even after we've seen the imperfections that makes or breaks us.

Pulling my earbuds out, I grip my pruning shears and snap

off a half dozen roses for my bedside vase. The simplistic act of gardening has given me momentary peace. I find it ironic that the garden represents our relationship in a way. For the moment, I'm stuck being the lone laborer to something we started. After a few minutes of removing the thorns, I stow away my tools and round the house, coming to a dead stop when I see Lucas standing in front of his Land Rover…crying. He doesn't see me, so I stand back and watch him. He's staring at my front door, biting his lips, his face twisted in anguish. His Adam's apple repeatedly bobs while he bats tears from his face with impatient fingers.

It's the first time I've ever seen him cry. And his suffering is so palpable that I'm frozen where I stand, witnessing his painful indecision to stay or go. He shakes his head and then looks at the ground before peering back up at the door with fear. He's breaking, visibly breaking in front of me and it's draining what's left of my anger. I grapple with it, keeping what I have left close because I'll never respect myself again if I go to him without fighting for what I'm worth, for what our child is worth, for what this family is worth, being *first*.

Stunned by the agony etched on his face, the pain pouring from him, I have to shake myself to propel forward. A groan escapes his lips as he cries openly in front of his truck and the sound cuts me in half, pausing my steps. Gripping his hair, his features twist as another harsh cry escapes him. My heart shatters at my feet when I see the depth of the emotion he's been hiding.

The second I take a step from the side of his house, his eyes drift over to mine, a breath rushes out of him, and his tears fall more rapidly. His hesitance breaks my heart as he searches my eyes for some sign of acceptance. But he doesn't clear his face again. For the first time since Blake died, he lets me see he's broken.

And that's when I know we're going to be okay.

He's overcome as he stares at me, his eyes trailing to my stomach as he swallows air in an attempt to stifle his cries.

I extend the flowers in his direction for his inspection. "These are so beautiful, don't you think?"

Twin tears streak his cheeks, and he slowly nods, his jade eyes piercing.

"They are all in bloom." I tilt my head and gesture for him to follow me. "Come see." He runs a hand along his face and pushes off the hood of the car, following me to the side of the house.

Looking back at him for his reaction, I don't miss it when he sees just how magnificent the landscape is with the flowers having grown slightly wild. "It's magical, right? We've been missing out on this."

His voice is hoarse when he finally speaks. "Beautiful."

"I've been working hard out here."

His raspy voice sounds from right behind me. "I took for granted that they would always be taken care of the way they needed."

I don't miss his double entendre, but I'm doing my best not to throw myself into his arms, which I know are waiting. Audrey was right, my love grew right along with my resentment.

I look back at him over my shoulder, trying not to crumble at the helpless expression on his face. "Do you want something to drink?"

"Stop, don't be kind to me. I don't deserve it."

"Am I kind?" I ask softly. "I hope I am."

"Mila," his voice breaks as he bites his upper lip, tears sliding down his jaw. "I don't know how to make this up to you."

"You will," I say through my own trembling lips. We

stand there in silence which gnaws at me. "I can't give you the words. You have to talk to me."

He stares at the gravel between us before lifting his eyes to mine. "I don't know how to say I'm sorry."

"You just did."

"I have no right to ask you to come home."

"Sure, you do. I'm your wife."

"Come home."

"I can't yet. I need more words, Lucas."

His demeanor sinks and is a bleak contrast to the sunshine that highlights his frame. "Dame," he whispers. "I don't deserve you at all."

"Well, that's dramatic."

He coughs out a tight laugh and clears his throat. "Yeah, well, I'm done with that."

"Done?"

"I'm done acting, I don't want to do it anymore. That was my last movie."

"Now *that's* dramatic," I say, alarmed. No matter how many times he's come back exhausted, he's never once mentioned quitting. Mom was right. I knew it, but he'd just confirmed it. It wasn't just the loss of Blake. His death was what triggered it. What happened was a culmination of everything my mother had put a voice to. I owe her because if it weren't for her, I'd still be lost. But as of now, I refuse to let Lucas get away with minimal statements. He owes me more than 'I'm sorry, come home.'

"Can you forgive—"

"I already have," I say softly. Face crumbling, he takes a step toward me, and I shake my head, dying for the touch of his hands, and his apologetic kiss, but the physical contact will have to wait. I need to know where we stand.

"I don't have it all figured out, but I'm done acting."

"Why?"

He shrugs. "It's served its purpose."

"That's a big decision you made, and without me. You seem to be doing a lot of that." Lifting the roses to my nose, I inhale their fresh scent and meet his eyes over the bouquet. "Sometimes I feel like maybe I never knew you, not the way I'm supposed to."

Shoving his hands in his jeans, he nods, his eyes cast down. "That's my fault. The boy I was…was raised to be a movie star. That's all I've known since I was eight years old, Mila. It's the only thing in my life I knew I was supposed to do, and it was the craziest damn road to be put on as a means of survival because it's the quickest way to fail. But that was my skill set. I still can't believe I pulled it off," he says, rolling his eyes upward. "The whole idea was insane in itself."

"But you did it."

"Yeah, I did. And you were the only thing I was drawn to just as strongly. I had the same green light inside when I saw you. I can't explain it any better than that. And you're right, I don't have a script for this. And for the first time in my life, I don't want one."

Fearful eyes meet mine and then spill over.

"Baby, I'm lost, and I don't know how I got here," he croaks, "I don't know…I don't know what the point of this is anymore. I don't know why I'm doing it or if it even matters."

Nodding, I let the tears flow down my cheeks while he rubs his forehead with his palm.

"I'm just…lost." He looks over to me with red-rimmed eyes. "This doesn't feel real to me." His lips part exhaling a rough gasp. "Do you know what the definition of hell is? Because I do. It's getting the life you wanted only to fuck it up because you didn't know how to embrace it and be happy."

"Lucas, you don't have to quit, you can take a break."

"No." He shakes his head firmly. "No, this ambition isn't helping me anymore, it's killing me, Mila." He points at his chest. "It's like a sickness now, and I don't want to give it any more power over me. I convinced myself as long as I was this product of success, all that other stuff didn't matter, but it hurts, it hurts so bad." He exhales a long breath. "I've been hiding from that kid in these scripts forever. And I thought this was the best way to do it but when the credits roll, I'm still here and none of this, none of it makes sense. I don't want to keep existing like this."

"Don't regret it, Lucas."

"How can I not? Look at us? Look at what happened... to Blake." He cups the back of his head with both hands and squeezes his eyes shut, his forearms covering his face. It takes him several seconds to speak.

"I met with the woman throwing Blake's name around the tabloids, and I lost it, Mila. I lost it. I couldn't believe what I was hearing, he—"

"Lucas," I whisper, and his eyes shoot up to mine. "I've gathered my own conclusions about what went down, and I think I'm right?"

He nods.

"With respect to Blake, I know he died trying to keep his secrets, and I want to honor that. I love him enough to respect that. I know it goes against the honesty I've been fighting for as far as you're concerned, and you did what you had to do. I know that. And if you want to talk about it for you—"

He shakes his head.

"Are you going to tell Amanda?"

"Maybe, probably later, but yes, I think she deserves to know."

"Good. As hard as it will be for her to hear, she probably should."

Chests laden with heartache, we get lost in our own thoughts.

"Mila," he swallows audibly, his eyes drinking me in. "Are you okay?" They drift lower. "Is our baby okay?"

"We're both perfect. It's early. I'm only six weeks along now."

"You think the universe answered that one for me?" he asks with a shy smile. I can see his wheels turning, and I clue him in.

"I hope not."

He draws his brows. "Why?"

"We conceived that day in your trailer," I say around the knot in my throat and see when the truth of it registers. "That's one of the reasons I've been so angry."

"Jesus," he says, palming his forehead. "I'll never forgive myself."

"You have to," I say, drawing his attention. "You have to, Lucas. You have to just like I have to. It's a decision."

He slowly nods. "When did you find out?"

"The morning of the day I told you."

"I ruined that too."

"That was *my* decision. I set you up to ruin that. You were so far gone."

"I'm sorry."

"I know. I am too."

His features twist with longing. "Are you ever going to let me touch you?"

"I'm kind of waiting to see what your plans are."

"Plans?" he rasps out in a thick voice, eyes watering. "I'm fresh out."

"I've made some of my own."

"You have?" His Adam's apple bobs. "Okay."

"I'm going to be a sommelier. I'm going to grow my own vines and make wine."

He pushes out a relieved breath. "I love your plan."

"I'm also going to take advice from a grasshopper and take life a little less seriously before summer runs out."

"It's good advice."

"I loved that grasshopper," I say as his face falls, "I really did."

"I know," he speaks up, his voice overcome with emotion. "God, look at you." The admiration in his eyes steals my breath. "You're so fucking beautiful, you're all I've ever wanted. You and that baby you carry, that's what I want, to have a family. With you I have all of it. You hold all of my hope, Mila. All of it. I can't lose you—"

"You haven't," I say, dropping the flowers and crashing into him. He audibly exhales and his arms wrap tightly around me. We lock together, overwhelmed and crying.

After endless seconds, he pulls away, kissing me thoroughly, the thrust of his tongue lulling us into a peaceful reprieve from all the ache. The salty kiss sparks a healing, a beginning and we both sigh into it with collective relief. When we pull away, I bury my face in his chest, and we exchange whispers.

"Let's get on this plan."

I nod into his chest. "Okay, but you're going to have to call and apologize to my mother."

"I already have."

"Good."

"I mean it. Let's leave today. Half my shit is in my truck."

"Fine with me."

"I'm serious, Mila. I'm done with this."

"We'll see."

"You don't think I'm done?"

"For the moment, yes, but at one point you loved it far more than you resent it now. And maybe in the future, you'll decide you love it again."

"Maybe, I don't know. It feels over."

"Well, if all else fails, in twenty years, when the baby is grown, we'll come back under the radar as Gladys and Sean McConnery, and you can make a comeback. Let's bounce that off into the universe and see where it lands."

He palms my face with warm hands, grinning down at me. "I missed you so much, Dame, so much."

"You can't act with me, ever again, Lucas. *Ever*."

"I won't," he says, stroking my cheeks with reverent thumbs. "I love you."

"I love you, too."

He presses our foreheads together.

"So, where are we off to?"

"We'll figure it out, the three of us."

I see the flash of brilliant white before he crushes his lips to mine.

Yazoo News Alert:
Silver Ghost grosses $150 million at the box office opening weekend!

"Never underestimate the power of silence. You can use it as the best weapon, but it's also a good indicator of re-invention. Those you see as softly-spoken and meek may have already scaled your mountain. Stay humble and grow that way. That's how you live with yourself."
—Madelyn "Maddie" Rosera Darling

Casey and Bonnie Morning Radio Show

Casey: Bonnie, what in the *hell* happened to Lucas Walker?

Bonnie: Where has that boy been?

Casey: That's a good question, and I'm going to tell you.

Bonnie: Tell me, girl, I've been missing our boy.

Casey: Apparently, Hollywood Golden Boy Lucas Walker decided to clip his own wings even after receiving an Oscar nomination for his part in the controversial crime thriller *Silver Ghost*. Close friends to Walker state he's on a much-needed hiatus due to his growing family and other personal goals. Other sources say Walker suffered severe psychological issues on the set because of the suicide of his best friend Blake West and cracked further under the pressure of playing one of the world's most notorious mobsters.

Bonnie: Damn good movie. Our boy did good. Glad he's okay.

Casey: I agree. He had me scared for a minute.

Bonnie: I miss Blake West. Blake was so talented. Underrated.

Casey: I agree. He should have gotten a lot more credit. Still miss him.

Bonnie: So where did our boy run off to?

Casey: Well, according to the reports coming in, Walker and his wife, Mila, have been living in the south of France since the birth of their son, and have been spotted with their little man globe-trotting all over Europe, Spain, India, Australia, and South Africa. Apparently, they've been working with a foundation to help fund the building of new schools.

Bonnie: That's so admirable, and that little boy is so cute. He looks just like his daddy. Good for them. But when are they coming back?

Casey: It looks like not anytime soon. Recent rumors have been circulating that Walker has enrolled in a college in London.

Bonnie: He what?! He's going to college?

Casey: Looks like our boy is going all the way and has declared a double major.

Bonnie: What in the hell for? The man is a millionaire! What's he going to do...become an architect?

Casey: Some say an education is priceless.

Bonnie: Then he can have my education and give me his millions.

Casey: It seems silly to waste all that time when he

could be making us more good movies.

Bonnie: Total waste, if you ask me.

Casey: Easy, girl, let them do them. You know we see a trend with this, actors giving back after they've made it big. They must feel a sense of responsibility for what they're capable of contributing, and the influence they have and are trying to do something good with it.

Bonnie: You're right, you're right, and they're still my favorite couple. Mila is fierce.

Casey: I guess she can support them with all that money she's making off her vines.

Bonnie: For real though, that's the best wine I've ever tasted on my Pilates.

Casey: That's palate, Bon.

Bonnie: Right. So anyway, we love you, Lucas and Mila. We'll be here when you decide to come home.

Casey: That's right, guys, we wish you the best. And when you get back, we'll welcome you back with open arms—

Bonnie: And legs.

Casey: Bonnie!

Bonnie: Just kidding, Mila. But if you ever decide to share, message a girl and good luck you two.

Casey: And rest in peace, Blake.

Bonnie: We love you, Blake.

Casey: Such a damn shame. Speaking of Blake West, remember his show *Buzzed*?

Bonnie: I loved that show. Didn't they cancel that after one season?

Casey: Yep. Anyway, check this out. Two of the producers most known for their work on *Buzzed* have just been charged with sexual harassment and assault. Aaron Thompson and Steven Tungsten went on to produce a few movies. Several of which our boys starred in.

Bonnie: Those poor women. I hope they get justice.

Casey: Me too. One source says that one of the accusers has come forward with concrete evidence that there were incidents that took place on set after taping, but the cameras weren't off. To respect the privacy of the victims, the judge has ordered the hearings to remain closed.

Bonnie: That's video evidence. Talk about caught in the act. Daaaaamn. But isn't there a statute of limitations on that?

Casey: The tape puts them right at the edge of the mark. The trial is set for next week. Guess like it's time to take out more Tinseltown trash and someone's about to pay the piper.

Bonnie: Glad our boys weren't anywhere near that mess.

Casey: Not our boys.

EPILOGUE

MILA

I CRADLE RONIN TO MY CHEST AS HE AUDIBLY SIGHS IN EXHAUSTION before passing out, his full lips making little sucking movements while his father's green eyes watched me until they finally drifted closed. I stare at his little foot, his tiny toes curling in protest when I lift it to press my lips against his heel. I can't get enough of him, he's my new addiction and every part of him is perfect. We're comfortable in our new plush bed buried in a dozen pillows, but my attention is pulled away when I see his father on the screen while Greg Kinnear reads off the nominees for Best Actor. The camera pans to Lucas's face as he gives a smile and a little nod after the film clip and the following applause.

"And the Oscar goes to..." Greg slowly opens the envelope and is clapping as he announces, "Lucas Walker for *Silver Ghost*." The crowd rises to their feet instantly, his peers shouting out their enthusiastic congrats as he stands and hugs Amanda tightly to him while she cries into his jacket. She nods once as he whispers to her before reaching over to shake Wes's hand. Pulling his tuxedo jacket closed, he buttons it before ascending the stage. He's dashing, he's a movie star, if only for a little longer.

In all my years as his wife, I've never been more in awe of him, and it's not just because he won, it's because of what it took him to get there—what he sacrificed, the demons he slayed—not only Blake's but his own. While I could never entirely forget the hell he'd turned our union into, every move was calculated, every risk he took was to protect his best friend, to resurrect him, to give them both peace, and to free himself from the shackles of expectations he'd locked himself into.

We didn't heal overnight. Between doing and saying, it took me more time to fully forgive him and trust was a little more hard-earned. At the end of it all, it became simplistic. Lucas's journey truly wasn't about me or our marriage. His journey was about a friendship that formed long before I came into the picture, a friendship I will never fully understand. A friendship that ended so abruptly it left my husband reeling, lost and unable to heal without going through the type of grieving that forever changed him. And change he did. Looking gorgeous, Lucas saunters up the steps, taking his award and his congrats before turning to the podium and staring at the Oscar long and hard before he sets it down.

"First, thank you, Wes, for trusting me. I know I didn't make it easy on you, although you did get more than you bargained for. Two for the price of one."

Wes nods toward Lucas in silent recognition. Wes knew. Maybe not entirely, but he was fully aware Lucas would bring his grief on set. Wes expected it, which is what made it work. He'd used Lucas's pain just as much as Lucas had used it for the role. Morally it was fucked up, but it's what worked. And all I see in Wes's eyes as the camera pans in on the row full of the cast is his respect. It's as clear as day. Shannon has been calling nonstop since the film released begging Lucas to consider more offers, but Lucas refuses to bother looking. He's stayed firm in his decision to quit. He has other plans. Studying him now, dressed to the nines, his hair much longer now, he looks in to the crowd with a solemn face as he speaks out for the first time about his fallen brother.

"It's no big secret Blake West was a brother to me, and if it weren't for him, I literally wouldn't be standing here. He left us, left me, in a way I could have never prepared for and will never be able to rectify. But I'm here tonight too because he was a large part of who I am today. Good or bad, he taught me a lot more than anyone ever could about this life, a life he deserved to live to the fullest." Swallowing, Lucas pulls out a folded piece of paper from the inside pocket of his jacket. It's worn, brown, and folded in fourths. My chest begins to ache because I can clearly see the emotion building in his face as he studies the words.

"Blake wrote this when we were living as rejects together in a box-sized bungalow in West Hollywood. I think it's only fitting that his 'what if' speech be my own." The camera pans in on Amanda, who Lucas took to the Oscars, while I'm stuck in our new temporary home overseas and for good reason. I'm going to have another baby. And this one was conceived in an entirely different way. Through trust and love.

More in love than I thought imaginable. I stare at the chance I took all those years ago, along with the decision I make every day and watch on in admiration of what he's achieved.

Lucas laughs through watery eyes and glances at the audience with a rueful grin. "Sorry, Blake, but I have to," he says conspiratorially before he holds a hand to the side of his mouth letting the audience in on the joke. "There's a script note first, it says, 'After a lengthy and mind-blowing standing ovation.'" The audience laughs as a picture of Blake slowly appears behind Lucas. I audibly gasp at the image, the sight of Blake as strong as his presence is in that room because Lucas brought him there. He won't let them forget. Hot tears stream down my cheeks as I study the photo. It's a candid of Blake smiling like he just ate the canary. The image is a reminder of what we lost, what we all lost. It's then that I realize that as much grief as he's given us all, I still have love for the person he was. Lucas's voice brings me back to the moment, but it's Blake's words that strike the hardest.

"This gig was hard. I lost myself in it." Lucas audibly swallows as his eyes fully glaze over and he pauses. "I trusted people, and I got burned." I can see the visible shake inside Lucas. He's doing everything he can to keep it together, but there is no acting through this, the loss is apparent, and he's trying to close the door. He looks out into the crowd. "But I got a trophy for it, and it's only worth something in this minute, this minute right here is what it's all for. The recognition that I might have done something worthwhile, that I was a part of a bigger picture, that my work means something and as an artist, I guess that's all you hope for, just a moment. This moment." The audience goes eerily silent. "That's all I get, a minute maybe more to sum up my journey before that music starts, and I'm forced to make my exit, so I'll make it quick."

Lucas hesitates as emotions get the best of him and he squeezes his eyes shut.

"Come on, baby," I whisper at the screen as I cradle our son to me and inhale the scent of his dark hair.

Lucas presses his lips together, his voice coming out hoarse when he speaks. "I don't know if it's worth the cost." Lucas falters briefly, and I can hear an audible sob in the crowd that I know belongs to Amanda. Lucas gathers himself and lifts his chin. "You know this life can take a toll, perception can be our nemesis, and the message we send is the most significant part of what we do. I can only hope I played well and hope you remember me as part of your bigger picture because legacy…that's the hardest gig of all."

"I want to thank my brother, Lucas, for trying to rescue me from myself. I know how hard you try." Lucas falters again, and the crowd applauds for him as he finally breaks on stage for the world to see. It lasts for endless seconds as they give Lucas the breathing room he needs, the room he deserves, and the encouragement to continue. When the clapping dies down, he focuses on Amanda. "And for the woman who decided to love me in spite of the bastard I am, I hope this helps you understand your sacrifice, and if it doesn't, I'm sorry, and I hope I showed you that you were always worth more."

The camera cuts to Amanda as she sobs in her hands.

Lucas folds the paper and stuffs it into his pocket. "Blake, thank you, brother, for allowing me to be a part of your legacy," he says, raising the statue toward the room. A single tear streaks down his cheek as he addresses the camera, the applause erupting to a deafening level. "And for my legacy, my baby boy, Ronin Blake Walker. For my daughter, who I can't wait to meet, and for my beautiful wife, Mila," he says, looking straight at me, "I'm coming home, Dame. This time for good."

Everyone rises to their feet, the camera cuts to several actors shedding tears before the show fades to commercial.

If this were a scene from a movie script, he would be walking through the door at this moment so I can throw my arms around him. But that's not what happens. He has a slew of press to take care of, the sale of our house to close on, another award to accept before he lets his star dim to make room for others. His flights home get delayed due to weather. He calls me twice to tell me he loves me, but he is too busy to talk, tying up more loose ends so we can continue the new path we've chosen. Life isn't anything like the movies, and as it turns out, I don't want it to be. After a hundred and forty minutes or so the story ends, and Lucas and I have a lot more story to live out. We have grand plans for this life we've made together that have nothing to do with a typical Hollywood ending.

Two weeks after the Oscars, my husband walks through our front door looking more worn than I'd ever seen him. With a weary smile, he approaches quietly and takes his sleeping son in his arms, cradling him before taking my lips in a promising kiss, his tongue thrusting slowly, deeply to show the extent of how much he missed me. Dazed when he pulls away, I get lost in his soul-filled depths, and whisper two words I've been dying to utter since we began the new leg of our journey together. "Welcome home."

THE END
(That's a wrap)

This book touched on several sensitive issues I can only hope I handled with the utmost care. While Method is a work of fiction, the varying depressions discussed in the pages are very real. A staggering amount of people suffer from mental illness and continue to struggle daily for stability. If you are hurting, or if someone close to you needs help, please consider reaching out, the effort could be lifesaving or life-changing.

National Suicide Prevention Lifeline
Call 1-800-273-8255

National Sexual Assault Hotline
Call 1-800-656-4673

ABOUT THE AUTHOR

A Texas native, Kate Stewart lives in North Carolina with her husband, Nick, and her naughty beagle, Sadie. She pens messy, sexy, angst-filled contemporary romance as well as romantic comedy and erotic suspense because it's what she loves as a reader. Kate is a lover of all things '80s and '90s, especially John Hughes films and rap. She dabbles a little in photography, can knit a simple stitch scarf for necessity, and on occasion, does very well at whisky.

Other titles available now by Kate

Room 212
Never Me
Loving the White Liar
The Fall
The Mind
The Heart
The Brave Line
Drive
The Real
Someone Else's Ocean
Heartbreak Warfare

ROMANTIC COMEDY
Anything but Minor
Major Love
Sweeping the Series
Balls in Play Box Set: Anything but Minor, Major Love, Sweeping the Series, The Golden Sombrero

EROTIC SUSPENSE
Sexual Awakenings
Excess
Predator and Prey
Lust & Lies Box Set

Let's stay in touch!

Facebook
www.facebook.com/authorkatestewart

Newsletter
www.katestewartwrites.com/contact-me.html

Twitter
twitter.com/authorklstewart

Instagram
www.instagram.com/authorkatestewart/?hl=en

Book Group
www.facebook.com/groups/793483714004942

Spotify
open.spotify.com/user/authorkatestewart

Sign up for the newsletter now and get a free
eBook from Kate's Library!

Newsletter signup
www.katestewartwrites.com/contact-me.html

THANK YOU

Thank you to everyone who took a chance on Method and any other of my titles. This job is a dream come true, and I'm forever grateful to every one of you for making it a daily reality. A thousand thank yous for every reader suggestion, every comment, every review, every tag, and every shout out. I may not always win you over, but I promise I'll always try.

Thank you to my group, my ASSKICKERS, my loves, my soulmates, my cheerleaders, my deejays, my daily bread. There is no way I would have made it to twenty books without your encouragement and support. You are in my heart, always.

Thank you to my amazing sisters, Angela and Kristan for being there as sounding boards, part-time psychologists, and comedians. You two are such a joy to know. I love where we've been and how far we've come and love both of you more than you'll ever know.

Thank you to my parents, Bob and Alta, for being my voice of reason, for lashing the whip with love when I need it, and for being altogether outstanding parents. I'm a lucky kid, so very, very lucky. Alta, you are both matriarch and glue. I thank God all the time that He put you in my life. You're an incredible stepmother and friend. Thank you for always being there no matter the weather.

Thank you to my brothers, Stephen and Tommy, for being my six foot plus team of support, for the gift of your hilarious sarcasm always coated in love. You two have grown into amazing men and I'm so proud to call you my brothers. And just so you know, for me, that pic I wrote a scene around epitomizes brotherly love.

Bex-as time flies and blurs, we stick together and I'm so happy with what we've accomplished. There is no me without you. You continue, time and again, to be a huge support without asking for much in return but friendship. I hope I am that friend. Thank you for continuing to put up with me, for being that friend to me, and for being the best assistant on the planet. You have my heart, lady.

Christy-Thank you for shaping my world with all your love and support. Hounding you into a friendship was one of the best decisions I've ever made. My love for you is bottomless.

Autumn-I'll always be grateful you're the one who said yes, without reservation, without judgment. As our friendship grows, I continue to think of that day and conversation as nothing short of a miracle. I love you, truly love you. Thank you so much.

Thank you, Christine, for being both sounding board and dear friend. Your enthusiasm is infectious and appreciated so much. You've never let me down and you know what that means to me. I love you dearly. Thank you for the fairy dust.

Thank you, Amy Queau of Q designs, for indulging me once again and piecing together the picture from my imagination and yours to make it a reality. You are so incredibly talented and I'm so thankful you share your gift with us all.

Thank you, Stacey Ryan Blake, for being my trusty go-to girl, for honoring my requests and going above and beyond to make my books beautiful, and for having a sense of humor while doing it. Working with you is a joy and I love our friendship.

A huge thank you to my betas: Anne Christine, Christy Baldwin, Kathy Sheffler, Maïwenn Blogs, Malene Dich, Maria Consigli Black, Marissa D'Onofrio, Rhonda Bobbitt Love, Jessie Soto and Stacy Hahn who continue to take a chance on whatever I manage to drum up and take great care with the job and trust I instill in all of you. You ladies are fabulous. I love you.

To my proof-tastic team: Joy Kriebel-Sadowski, Bethany Castaneda and Grey Ditto thank you for your diligence, support and your sense of humor because without it, your task would be impossible. I love you, ladies.

Donna Cooksley-Sanderson—You hear it every day from me, but I will never be able to convey just how much I love you. You continue to surprise me by being one of the most steadfast, honest, lovable, honorable, and selfless friends I've ever had. So, I'll jot it down again in writing just in case you forget. I love you. You are a blessing to me. I love your family as my own. Thank you isn't enough.

A huge thank you to my friends: MJ Fields, Jessica Florence, Ella Fields, Ella Fox, Amy Jackson, Leigh Shen, Kennedy Ryan, Mia Sheridan, Emma Scott, Pam Godwin, Katy Regnery, Carey Heywood, Tia Louise, Ilsa Madden-Mills, and Heather Orgeron for all your help and input. There is no way I could have ever finished this book without your encouragement. And to all my author friends who continue to encourage me, challenge me and make this gig more bearable. I'm one lucky gal to know you and to call you friends.

Audrey Regnery—Thank you for that hug in the kitchen, you'll never know what that meant to me. Katy, thank you for hugging me just as tight, you are truly one in a million.

Mia Sheridan—thanks for helping me flip the pieces to make them fit. I owe you one and can't wait to deliver. You give amazing hugs.

Thank you to the ladies of DHI for being real, honest, and the bad-asses you are. You enrich my life with your wisdom, strength, and judge-free love.

Thank you to my besties—scattered in all directions of the map—for being simply amazing at your job. Erica, 143ek and always. Amanda, your laughter is music for me. Ally, you make me a happier human just by existing. Irene, how lucky are we to have met as little girls? After nearly three decades of friendship, there's no way to sum it up, but I'm so thankful for it all.

Last but first, thank you to my husband, Nick, for continuing to put me first, for keeping my heart safe, and for loving me without limit. Today and tomorrow, I choose you. I love you. I pray for the same decision from both of us every day and always.

·